# Unresolved Conflicts

## Brenda Adcock

*Quest Books*
*by Regal Crest*

ISBN 978-1-61929-374-8


First Printing 2018

9 8 7 6 5 4 3 2 1



Original cover design by AcornGraphics



Published by:

Regal Crest Enterprises



Find us on the World Wide Web at
http://www.regalcrest.biz



Published in the United States of America

# Acknowledgments

As I do for every story I write, I have to thank my publisher, Cathy Bryerose. She has stuck by me no matter what and I will always treasure her friendship. I trust her and my editor, Patty Schramm, for always doing their best to bring my stories to publication. Patty and I don't always agree, but it's usually on minor points.

I would like to thank my friend, Devi Powers, who beta read this story and answered numerous questions I struggled with about the intricacies of family dynamics. Every family has secrets and when they least expect it, those secrets erupt into discord between family members that have festered over the years. What lies behind those secrets fascinates me, but I needed a little guidance to ferret out how professionals deal with the issue.

In a personal confession, I have to admit that I never intended this story to take ten years to get on paper. It is the sequel to *Redress of Grievances* and I originally intended to create a series based around my main characters. However, although I was proud of *Redress*, it was not very well received because it dealt with sensitive issues, such as child abuse, spousal abuse, and rape. I never dreamed reality would create such a negative response. That was never my intention. I was simply attempting to write about reality in an entertaining way. Knowing I had offended my readers in such a way forced me away from creating a sequel. Years later, a new group of readers accepted *Redress*, many asking me to write a sequel. Now I have, but I don't think it is quite as edgy or as offensive as *Redress*. I never want to offend my readers and hope I never do again. It hurts me to know I may have. It negatively affects how I write and what I write about even though perhaps it shouldn't. At the same time, I am nothing without my readers and appreciate the love and support they have given me over the years. It's one of life's sweet pleasures.

Certainly, no acknowledgment would be complete without mentioning the love and support of my wife, Cheryl. I lean on her every day and she has been a strong and steady part of my life for the past twenty-one years. Somehow, she makes it seem like twenty-one days and makes me laugh every, single day.

# Dedication

For Cheryl for making every day a memorable one and making me laugh because you're so damn cute!

# Chapter One

JESS RAINES WASN'T sure how many times the phone had rung unnoticed before the sound penetrated her sleep. Her eyes still closed, she felt around the nightstand before finally dragging the cordless handset beneath the bedcovers.

"Do you know what time it is?" she croaked hoarsely, trying to awaken her vocal cords. She pulled the cover down slightly and glanced at the glowing dial on her digital clock. Seven-thirty. On a Sunday morning following a night of indescribable passion.

"Harriett?" a woman's voice boomed in Jess's ear, the unexpected assault on her senses causing her to wince.

"Just a minute," Jess mumbled, fighting to untangle herself from the covers as she rolled over, dragging the handset with her and shaking her head in an attempt at semi-consciousness. Harriett was still sound asleep, peacefully nestled beneath the quilts, with only a mass of disheveled light brown hair peeking out. Jess could feel the heat of her lover's naked body as she scooted closer.

"It's for you, darlin'," Jess said, pushing the cover down slightly to place the handset over Harriett's ear after putting it on speaker, while dropping a soft kiss on her shoulder.

"Harriett Markham," Harriett mumbled.

"You sound like shit, girl!" the woman laughed loudly.

Harriett took the phone from Jess and rolled onto her back, throwing her forearm over her eyes. Jess plopped back down on her pillow, but the thought of Harriett's naked body beneath the bedcovers brought back the passion of the night before and wouldn't allow her eyes to close again. Harriett coughed slightly to clear her voice. "Who is this?"

"Ah, how soon they forget their first lover," the woman said in a low, husky voice.

Harriett sat straight up in bed, her free hand sweeping tousled hair back over her head. Jess couldn't suppress a groan at the sight of soft, full, supple breasts as the covers slid down to Harriett's waist and she ached, remembering the feel of them filling her mouth.

"KC?"

"None other," the woman laughed. "Listen, Harriett, I'm sorry to wake you up so damn early. I tried calling you last night, but no one answered."

"I...uh...was out late last night."

"You mean you disconnected the phone so you wouldn't be disturbed while you were sweatin' up the old sheets," KC chuckled.

"Something like that." Harriett blushed as she drew her knees up slightly under the covers and glanced at Jess. "How are you, KC?"

"Fact is I've been better. I have a little legal situation that requires the assistance of an attorney."

"What kind of situation?"

Jess knew there would be no more sleep as soon as she heard Harriett's question and rolled out of bed. She slipped into her terry cloth robe and stopped at the foot of the bed where Harriett could see her and pantomimed drinking. Harriett smiled and nodded as Jess left the bedroom.

"I've been arrested and you're the only damn lawyer I know."

"Arrested for what?"

"Actually, it's a boatload of bullshit, but it seems the local constabulary thinks I killed someone. Right now, I'm coolin' my heels in the Jones County Jail."

"Have you spoken to an attorney there?"

"They sent over some court appointed moron from Abilene I wouldn't trust to defend Mother Teresa on a jay-walkin' charge yesterday. I already told him I'd be hirin' my own attorney."

"Have you been arraigned yet?"

"The lawyer said it would probably be sometime Monday. You know they don't do squat around here on the weekend. Might miss drinkin' and fuckin' on Saturday before goin' to church to repent on Sunday. Hallelujah!"

Jess came back into the room and set a steaming cup on the nightstand next to Harriett. Mouthing a 'thank you,' Harriett wrote in the air with an imaginary pen. Jess sipped coffee as she gathered up a pen and paper. She returned to the bed and leaned back.

"Um, I don't want to get too much information over the phone, KC. Give me a chance to get up there and we'll talk then."

"When do you think I can get out of here?"

"I can try for bail at the arraignment, but the judge may not grant it. It's a serious charge."

"No shit! But I swear to God I didn't do it, Harriett. I might have a temper, but..."

"Don't say anything else, KC," Harriett ordered. "The phones there may be monitored and you don't want to have to explain anything you say now later on."

"Okay. Gotcha. But you're probably givin' them too much credit. So, you'll come up here then?"

"I'll try to be there some time this afternoon or early tomorrow."

"Okay. And Harriett..."

"What?"

"You gonna bring that sexy voice who answered the phone with you?"

Harriett laughed. "You'll have to consider her your fantasy woman for now," she said as she smiled across the bed at Jess and ran a hand down her arm. "But she's better than your best fantasy."

"You're killin' me, woman." KC laughed before hanging up.

Harriett leaned across Jess and set the phone into its charger. Snuggling down, she rested her head against Jess's shoulder and slipped her hand under her robe and across her waist. "Do you have any idea how much I love lying naked next to you?" she murmured softly.

"What an enticing remark," Jess said, running a hand over the exposed skin beneath her fingers.

"How do you feel?"

"In general or at the moment?"

"I thought you might still be tired after a long, but satisfying, night," Harriett said as she slowly ran a finger down Jess's chest and abdomen.

"It was my pleasure, baby." Jess kissed the top of Harriett's head. "I'm guessing we're going out of town today."

"An old friend is in a little trouble," Harriett sighed. "I have to go to Anson."

"Okay," Jess said.

"I'll call Mom in a little while to let her know she's going to have house guests for a couple of days until I find out what's going on."

"Should I be jealous of this KC person?"

Harriett shrugged. "We went to high school together, but I haven't seen her more than once or twice since then."

"You must have made quite an impression for her to think about you when she got in trouble with the law more than twenty-five years later," Jess said.

Harriett pushed herself up on the bed facing Jess. "God, you just made me feel ancient."

"I only meant it's been a long time."

Harriett pulled a slender leg up toward her chest and wrapped her arms around it. "I'll confess that KC and I had a...a moment when we were in high school, but it was really only teenage groping. Nothing serious."

"I see," Jessie said with a frown.

"I was seventeen for God's sake, living in a small West Texas oil and ranching town."

Jessie smirked. "I grew up in a small town just a few miles up the road from your small town, remember?"

"I've known KC my whole life. Her father was a foreman on one of the oil fields near town. She threw a pass at me in our senior year and I caught it."

"Was she your first love?" Jessie teased.

"No, she was the first female I was intimate with, but we definitely weren't in love. We drove to Abilene and checked into some little motel. Tacky place," Harriett said with a shiver. "We graduated and went our separate ways," Harriett shrugged.

Harriett glanced at the clock on the nightstand and took a deep breath. "As much as I would love nothing more than to spend the rest of the day in bed with you, I should call Nick and let him know I'll probably be out of the office for a few days."

As Harriett began scooting across the bed, Jess pulled her back into a deep, lingering kiss. "Just a rain check," Jess said as their lips parted.

"And you can bet your cute ass I'll be collecting later," Harriett breathed, stroking Jess's cheek. "Thanks for being so patient with me."

"You're worth it, darlin'."

"You know, now that you're officially my investigator you really should go with me."

"I'm supposed to run a few background checks for Nick on Monday," Jess said as she took Harriett's hand and kissed it.

"It's probably selfish, but I want you with me all the time. I want to know that I can turn around and see you watching me." Harriett lightly ran a fingertip over Jess's lips. "I love the way I feel when you look at me."

"How do you feel?" Jess asked with a slow grin.

"Hungry. Ravenous," Harriett said in a low voice as she walked her fingers across Jess's chest teasingly.

"Are you trying to sweet talk me, counselor?" Jess asked with a laugh.

Harriett grinned, wiggling her eyebrows. "Is it working?"

"Every damn time," Jess answered with a grin, pulling her closer and dropping a kiss on her lips.

# Chapter Two

ANSON, TEXAS WAS a little more than two hundred miles north of Austin as the crow flew. Although Harriett had grown up there, she had only returned for an occasional visit over the last twenty-eight years. With a population of just over twenty-five hundred souls, crime had always been confined to petty theft and underage drinking on the weekends. Murder wasn't a common occurrence, just something that happened in bigger cities like Abilene, twenty miles to the south.

Harriett glanced out the side window of her truck and then back at Jess. Six months. Had it really been only six months since Jess appeared, rain-soaked, at the door of Harriett's cabin on the lake? They spent that night talking, re-establishing their connection to one another.

Jess asked Harriett to share her home, but the real estate market in Austin had become unpredictable recently and Harriett declined. She hoped to sell the townhouse in the future when the market improved. Other than an occasional skeevy feeling that Renee, Jess's former lover, was somehow watching when they were intimate, being with Jess was comfortable. Harriett felt safe and truly loved without having to keep it a secret for perhaps the first time in her life. She hoped returning to Anson wouldn't force her to live secretly again.

"So, tell me about this new client," Jess said as she swung Harriett's truck onto the ramp leading to Highway 183 north out of Austin. "How serious a *moment* did you two have?"

"How serious can you get when you're a kid in a small town? It all seems so improbable and surreal looking back on it. I was insecure about my sexuality back then. But KC always knew who she was. I felt guilty afterward because I had to lie to Mom and Dad about it, but we graduated a couple of months later and left town."

"Where did she go?"

"She had a basketball scholarship at some school in Louisiana and I went to Austin."

Jessie looked across the truck at Harriett. "What does KC stand for?"

"Kerrie Carnes, but she's never been called anything except KC. Why?"

"I remember her."

"Did you ever play against her?" Harriett asked, remembering the basketball trophies in Jess's home office.

"No, but I know she was very good. What's she doing back in Anson?"

"I heard she was injured in her last year of college. As hard as this might be to believe, she's teaching and coaching basketball in Anson now. I think it's a family thing. Mom told me KC's mother, Ruth, has Alzheimer's and since her father was already dead, KC came back to take care of her mother. I think she's in a nursing home somewhere, probably in Abilene."

"That's too bad. There was a time when she could have written her own ticket."

"She'll probably leave after her mother passes away."

Although the sun was shining brightly, a crisp winter wind cut through her body like a knife as Harriett got out of the truck nearly four hours later. She pulled her parka collar up on her neck while Jess unloaded their suitcases from the jump seat of the truck. The front door of the house opened and Irene Markham, a sturdy woman in her late-sixties, stepped onto the porch, wrapping her arms around her body as protection against the wind.

Harriett hugged her mother briefly and held the door open for Jess. Once inside, the house was warm and cozy, a fire burning in the fireplace, and the whole house smelled of something sweet and delicious. Jess set the suitcases down and unzipped her jacket.

"Mom. This is my partner, Jessie Raines," Harriett said. "Jess, my mother, Irene Markham."

"Ma'am," Jess said, extending her hand. "Thanks for putting us up on such short notice."

"No one here but me anyway rambling around in this big old house," Irene said as she took Jess's hand. "Can I get you girls something hot to drink?"

"Sounds good to me," Jess said. "I forgot how the wind can cut through you up here. Where should I put these bags to get them out of the way?"

Turning to Harriett, Irene said, "Y'all can stay in your old room, sweetheart. I put clean sheets on the bed this morning after you called."

Harriett led Jess upstairs. "Nice house," Jess said.

"Lots of good memories, too. I don't think Mom has changed anything in my room since I left high school," Harriett said.

Harriett's room, in fact, hadn't changed much. There were still mementos from high school and college on a corkboard over the desk near the window. Jess lifted the suitcases onto the bed and looked around the room. Lace doilies covered the nightstands and chest of drawers. Soft yellow chintz curtains hung on the windows.

"It's very...feminine," Jess smiled. "But I can see you in here."

"We can unpack later, hon," Harriett said. "I should get down to the county jail soon."

"Hang on," Jess said as she grabbed Harriett's hand. "I have to investigate some of these knicky-knacky things. I want to know all the little secrets about your past."

"It's mostly junk from a million years ago, Jess," Harriett laughed.

Jess gazed at old ticket stubs and pictures pinned to the corkboard.

"Is this you?" she asked, pointing at one of the pictures.

"I'm afraid so," Harriett said as she stood behind Jess, peering over her shoulder and wrapping her arms around Jess's waist.

"You really *were* a fucking cheerleader?"

"I'll have you know I was an excellent fucking cheerleader."

Turning to look at Harriett, Jess smiled and wiggled her eyebrows as her eyes drifted down Harriett's body. "I would have been inspired watching you shake your...uh...pom-poms. Did you date the captain of the football team, too?"

Harriett blushed furiously. "Once. But the boy was an octopus."

Jess leaned forward and kissed Harriett softly, "I hope I'm an improvement."

"Absolutely. You know what a woman wants. Especially this one," Harriett said as she hugged Jess. "Now it's coffee time."

Irene had steaming cups waiting on the kitchen table.

"Something smells really good," Jess said as she sat down.

"I hope pot roast is all right. I need to go to the grocery store later. I hadn't stocked up for company."

"I'm sure anything you cook will be great, Mrs. Markham," Jess said, looking over the top of her coffee cup. "How come you never taught Harriett to cook anything except minute rice and boxed macaroni and cheese?"

Harriett wadded up a napkin and tossed it at Jess.

"I tried, dear," Irene laughed. "But Harriett was always more interested in academics than the domestic sciences."

Harriett glanced at the kitchen clock. "We'll be going down to the jail in a little bit. What have you heard about all this, Mom?"

"Probably no more than you already know," Irene shrugged. "I was shocked when KC called for your phone number. I haven't seen her in months. She doesn't live here, you know. She bought a house down in Abilene so she could be closer in case something happened to Ruth."

"How is Ruth?"

"As good as anyone with Alzheimer's, I guess. A few of us from the church went to see her a couple of months ago. She didn't really remember any of us. I guess that might have been the last time I saw KC, too. She dropped by while we were there. I felt real sorry for her."

"Why's that?" Harriett asked.

"Well, how can I put this nicely? Ruth wasn't very nice to KC and I won't repeat what she called her. It was almost like we weren't there. When we were leaving, KC followed us out and apologized for Ruth. I felt terrible for her."

"I've heard that sometimes people with Alzheimer's can get pretty nasty," Jess said.

"I don't know how KC can stand to visit her and listen to it. The nurse told me that KC drops in at least twice a week and Ruth is ugly to her almost every time."

"I'm surprised KC visits her at all," Harriett said. "She's never been well known for her anger management."

"Well, Ruth doesn't have anyone else," Irene said. "As far as I know even the women's church group has stopped going to see her."


WHILE HARRIETT WENT back upstairs to get her briefcase, Jess wandered into the living room to finish her coffee. Her eyes were drawn to four large portraits hanging above the fireplace. She smiled as she studied the picture of a much younger Harriett.

"We were all so young and innocent back then," Harriett said softly from behind her.

"I really miss my Dad," she added, staring at the large portrait of her father, Farley, her mother standing easily behind him resting her hand comfortably on his shoulder which hung above portraits of their children. It was always the smiling eyes of her father gazing down and welcoming her home again that made

Harriett feel settled and truly at home. She missed him more than anyone would ever know.

"Who are the other two?" Jess asked.

"That's Jerry, my older brother." Harriett smiled, pointing at the formal picture of a handsome young man just at the beginning of his life. "Lacey's father."

"She looks like him," Jess said.

"She does. And that's my younger sister, Lorraine. You might meet her while we're here." Although the younger woman's features were darker, Jess could tell they were related.

"She has your smile," Jess commented before leaning over to kiss Harriett's temple.

"That's pretty much where the similarity ends," Harriett said. "Ready?"

AN HOUR LATER Harriett and Jess waited in an interrogation room at the Jones County Jail. Harriett placed a legal pad and pen on the table and leaned back in her chair, ruffling her fingers through her hair as she looked at Jess, who was leaning against the wall and looking around. "Ever notice how all these places look the same?" she asked Harriett. "Some guy must have made a fortune designing the most depressingly plain room on the planet."

Harriett laughed, "I don't think comfort was at the top of the planning list, sweetheart."

"I hated these rooms even when I was the good guy. There's just something claustrophobic about them."

"If you feel the need to leave, I'll understand."

The door opened and KC stepped into the room. Jess was surprised that she wasn't handcuffed and still dressed in street clothes. Harriett, dressed in casual slacks and work shirt, rose from her chair when the door opened. Except for the Martina style glasses and a few age lines on her face, KC hadn't changed much over the years. She still had a tall, muscular frame that apparently had either never seen fat or burned it off before it had a chance to get comfortable.

"Thanks, Gene," KC said to the jailer with a smile.

"Just let me know if y'all need anything, KC," the jailer said. "I won't be far away."

KC patted the man on the back and turned toward Harriett, smiling and scanning her from head to toe. "Damn woman! I swear you've gotten even better lookin' than the last time I laid eyes on you."

Harriett stepped toward KC and they embraced quickly. "You still feel pretty fine, too," KC said.

Stepping back and blushing slightly, Harriett turned to Jess. "KC, this is Jessie Raines, my...investigator." KC and Jess each stepped forward a step and shook hands.

"Basketball player?" KC asked as she looked at Jess's five-eleven frame.

"Once upon a time," Jess answered.

"Jess is from Stamford," Harriett said.

"Ouch!" KC exclaimed. "The enemy camp. They're a tough team this year."

"I haven't kept up since I left Stamford...a long time ago," Jess said.

"You two can discuss sports later," Harriett said as she returned to her chair. "We don't have long before your arraignment and I need to hear your story, KC."

KC pulled out the chair across from Harriett and sat down heavily.

"I didn't do it, Harriett," she started. "God knows, I'm not all choked up about the guy's death, but I wasn't the one who caused it."

"Can I gather you didn't get along very well with the deceased?" Harriett asked. "What was his name?"

"Allen DeVore," KC answered. "And, to answer your first question, no, I didn't get along with him very well. I don't know anyone who got along with the pompous ass."

"Why were you singled out from his many fans to be arrested?"

"We had a scrimmage on October thirtieth and my girls hadn't worked off all their summer home cookin' and fast food binges yet and were playin' like a bunch of slugs. I was already pretty hot at them and ridin' them hard about it. When the scrimmage was over, I was pickin' up towels and balls when DeVore came over to me and said he wanted to talk to me in his office. I told him I'd be there as soon as I put the equipment away, but he said he wanted to talk to me like immediately. He wanted everything immediately. So, I stopped and followed him to the athletic office. The door wasn't even shut before he jumped my ass about his favorite topic."

"Which was?"

"His kid, Heather. She's your basic bench warmer and not even a very good bench warmer. He's been on my back since he got here about gettin' her more playin' time. I get every girl on the court every game. True, it might only be for a few minutes, but they all play."

"What was his complaint?"

"He claimed that one of my other players made a pass at Heather."

"One of the other girls?"

"It's an all girl basketball team, Harriett," KC said, rolling her eyes.

"Go on," Harriett smiled.

"I have this player, a coach's dream. She's like having Swoopes, Leslie and Lobo all in one body," KC said. Then she laughed. "Okay, she might not be all that, but she's way beyond very good. Passes off, never misses the basket, defends anyone they throw at her. High School All-American last year and will be again this year. Got the Big Twelve schools droolin' to recruit her."

"I get the idea, KC," Harriett chuckled.

"Okay. Okay. Anyway, DeVore said this player, Ali O'Neill, made a pass at his daughter and wanted me to remove her from the team...like immediately. I told him there was no fuckin' way I was going to do that. Whatever Ali did or didn't do off the court was irrelevant to me."

"Do you believe Ali made a pass?"

"Couldn't care less. And even if she did, I doubt it was to Heather DeVore. Girl's not exactly Miss Teen America. She's afraid she'll work up a sweat and break a nail. Plus, she hasn't missed many Happy Meals lately either. That's why her performance is so bad. Can't haul that lard ass of hers up and down the court fast enough."

"Is Ali gay?"

"Can't say. We've talked a couple of times. She's pretty confused about it, but I doubt she's ever had a sexual experience of any kind in her life," KC said. "You know how kids are at that age, Harriett."

"Yeah, I know," Harriett said. "Did DeVore have any proof that the proposition took place?"

"Just his kid's say-so as far as I could tell."

"And you refused to remove the O'Neill girl from the team?"

"Damn right! When a kid plays like her, I don't care if she fucks everything that walks, crawls, or ain't been dead three days. Besides if DeVore thought there was anything to what Heather said he should have taken it to the principal, not me. He thought if Ali was removed from the team, Heather would get more playin' time. Shit! I'd put your niece in before I would Heather."

"Jamie?" Harriett asked, surprised to hear her niece's name brought into the conversation.

"Sorry, kid. Jamie works like a demon, but it's like the messages her brain is sendin' aren't always makin' the round trip to her body. She's a team player, but doesn't have much future in basketball after high school. You seen her play?"

"No, I haven't."

"Isn't it your job as her coach to work on her basic skills?" Jess asked quietly.

KC whipped her head toward where Jess was standing. "I know what my fuckin' job is as a coach."

"Well, maybe you've spent so much time grooming this Ali that you've kind of let the others slide a little," Jess shrugged.

"Basketball is a team sport, babe," KC said as she glared at Jess, "and one player, no matter how good they are, cannot carry a team. The other four I have out there consistently are good players, too."

"Just not as good as Ali?"

"No, but they can hold their own."

Harriett cleared her throat, "What did DeVore do after you refused to remove the O'Neill girl?"

"Said he was takin' me to the school board to get me fired," KC said flatly.

"That's a pretty big switch in strategy. What was he going to tell the school board?"

"That I'm a dyke and he could prove it, thereby violatin' the morals clause of my contract and terminatin' my employment," KC said as she sat up straighter in her chair.

"Have you told anyone you're gay?"

"It's never been a topic of discussion with anyone in Anson. They might think it, but I don't give two shits about what they *think*."

"How was he planning to prove it?"

"Claimed he saw me in a bar in Abilene."

"A lesbian bar?"

"Yep."

"What was he doing in a lesbian bar?"

"Lookin' for me, accordin' to him. Said someone tipped him that I went there. We had a...discussion before school started this year about Heather. He thought if he could get rid of me they would get some little marshmallow in here and Heather would become the queen of the court. Some bullshit like that I suppose."

"It would have just been his word against yours."

"He said he had someone with him. Another coach maybe, but I never saw him."

"He didn't say who it was?"

"No."

"What was your response to his threat?"

"Murder crossed my mind. You know how my temper is, Harriett," KC shrugged. "Our...discussion got a little heated and a little loud."

"And others overheard the argument?"

"That's what they tell me, but I'm not sure who."

"But when you left DeVore was still alive?"

"Abso-fuckin-lutely."

"Anything else about your argument with DeVore that you haven't told me?"

KC frowned and examined the top of the table in front of her, tracing a crack with her fingernail.

"KC? I have to know everything. Otherwise I can't defend you."

"DeVore threatened to have Diane terminated, too," KC mumbled.

"Who's Diane?"

"She's a track coach at Abilene High. We've been livin' together about four years. He claimed he saw us together at the bar in sort of an intimate moment. He said he had a picture of us together in a compromisin' situation, knew who she was, and was goin' to report it to the Abilene School Board. I really lost my cool then and bowed up to him. He shoved me and I smacked him. He went down like a box of rocks." Holding her hand out toward Harriett, she added, "I cut my knuckles, probably on a tooth or somethin', and they're still a little bruised and swollen. It's been a long time since I actually hit anyone."

"Did he strike his head when he fell?"

KC shook her head. "If he did it was on his carpeted floor."

"Did you check for a pulse?"

"I just left," KC answered with a shrug.

"What does Diane say about all this?"

"I don't want Diane dragged into this, Harriett."

"I'll have to talk to her, KC. Was she at the game?"

"Naw, she doesn't come to the games. And I don't go to her track meets. She's afraid people will talk. So, I respect her wishes.

Not everyone's comfortable with who they are."

"She should be able to tell us when you got home though."

"I didn't go straight home after the game. I was still pissed off so I called her and said I had some paperwork I needed to catch up on and would be home by midnight. Truthfully, I just drove around to calm my ass down. I figured he'd turn me in to Warner or call the cops and press an assault charge against me. Guess someone got to him before he could get around to that."

"What time did you get home?"

"About eleven forty-five or so, but Diane was already asleep. What time was the asshole killed?"

"I haven't seen the reports and lab results yet. I should know by the next time we talk. I'll do what I can for you at the arraignment tomorrow, KC," Harriett said as she snapped the cap onto her pen and ran her fingers through her hair. "I can't promise the court will grant you bail on a murder charge though."

"I can't stay in here, Harriett," KC said with an uncharacteristically soft voice. "My mom isn't well and she might need me."

"I'll do what I can. Like you said, your reputation might be enough to get you out. Have you notified the high school yet?"

"Yeah, I called Preston earlier. I already have lessons for my classes ready for about the next month or so. My only problem will be with the team."

"Don't you have an assistant?" Jess asked.

"This is Anson, sweet cheeks, not fuckin' Austin. Preston said he'd cover it, but somehow, I have visions of football coaches dancin' in my head."

"Even if you're released on bail, you probably won't be able to coach until after the trial."

"It didn't sound like a possibility when I spoke to Preston. I mean, Heather DeVore is on the team and not even I'm chicken-shit enough to expect her to deal with my returnin' right now."

KC ran her hand through her hair and looked at Jess. "You look really familiar to me. Maybe it'll come to me later."

# Chapter Three

MID-MORNING MONDAY, Harriett and Jess were seated in a small courtroom in the Jones County Courthouse waiting for KC to be arraigned. In all the years Harriett had been practicing law, she had never been in a courtroom in her hometown. After the larger courtrooms in Dallas and Austin, the room seemed to be a miniature version of the real thing. But even in small town courtrooms, the decisions and arguments carried the same weight of importance.

As Harriett chatted with Jess, a tall, distinguished looking man carrying a white Stetson and wearing a three-piece western cut business suit entered the room and made his way confidently to the front of the courtroom where he dropped his battered briefcase onto a wooden chair behind the prosecutor's table. He glanced around the room, nodding to the bailiff who was placing a water pitcher on the judge's bench. As he turned he saw Harriett and Jess and smiled. Opening his briefcase, he pulled out a legal pad and walked toward Harriett.

"Ms. Markham?" he asked, looking at Harriett and Jess.

Harriett stood and extended her hand. "I'm Harriett Markham. And this is my investigator, Jessie Raines."

"Ms. Raines," he said as he shook Jess's hand. "Davis Barnett. I'm the Jones County prosecutor and according to a message I received this morning, you'll be representing Coach Carnes today."

"That's correct," Harriett replied.

"It's a pleasure to finally meet you, Ms. Markham. I've heard some very good things about you, especially from your mama," Barnett chuckled.

"It's a pleasure to meet you, too, Mr. Barnett," Harriett responded with a smile.

"Mostly everyone around here just calls me DB," Barnett said.

Harriett could see Jess roll her eyes and attempt to suppress a smile.

"Well, DB," Harriett continued, "what is Ms. Carnes going to be officially charged with today."

Scanning the papers in his hand he said, "Looks like murder, second degree."

"I see," Harriett said. "Then you don't think it was pre-meditated?"

"I'll be honest with you...may I call you Harriett?"

"Please do."

"I'll be honest with you, Harriett, I know KC pretty well and I know what a fast temper she has. My daughter played for her. I can believe that she lost her temper and things sort of got out of hand. But I doubt she would plan such a thing."

"And perhaps her bark is worse than her bite and she isn't responsible for Mr. DeVore's death at all."

"We've got some decent evidence or you and I wouldn't be standing here discussing it right now."

"I'm sure you had enough to indict, but getting a successful conviction is another matter."

"That's true," Barnett chuckled. "Since I know KC and I know she's been having a problem with her mama and all, I'm willing to not contest a bail request. I don't think she's going anywhere."

"I appreciate that, DB. And I think you're right about KC. She's a fighter and, if she's been wrongly accused, nothing would satisfy her more than clearing her name."

"Good enough, Harriett," Barnett said with a broad smile. "Don't get me wrong though. I will prosecute this case as zealously as any other once the bell rings to start the trial. I just don't like to see the term adversarial overused. Know what I mean?"

"Absolutely," Harriett smiled back at him.

Barnett returned to the prosecution table and Harriett sat down next to Jess and glanced at the clock on the wall behind the jury box.

"Shouldn't be much longer now," she whispered.

"That's good," Jess whispered back. "Because if something doesn't happen PDQ we'll all be SOL, HM."

Harriett laughed out loud before she could stop herself.


THE ARRAIGNMENT WENT as smoothly as Barnett had said it would and KC was released on $100,000 bond. The judge, Amelia Clemons, set the trial date for the Monday after Thanksgiving, which only allowed Harriett four weeks to prepare. Judge Clemons was a white-haired woman that Harriett thought was in either her late-sixties or early seventies. She was a pleasant, soft spoken woman, who looked as if she still worked hard at keeping in shape. She wore glasses, but her eyes never seemed to miss anything.

"Your Honor, four weeks doesn't allow me enough time to prepare an adequate defense. My client is facing an extremely serious charge."

"As you know, Anson is a small town, Ms. Markham. The court here has no backlog like you might be used to in Austin. I have every confidence you will have more than enough time to get yourself prepared. I'm reluctant to push the trial into the new year. If something comes up to change my mind, I'll be willing to consider it."

Judge Clemons smiled down at the people standing in front of her. "How's your mother, Kerrie?" she asked benignly.

"Fine, thank you, Amelia," KC answered with a smile.

"Give her my best next time you see her," Judge Clemons said as she slammed her gavel down. "We're adjourned."

"Four fucking weeks!" Harriett fumed when they left the courthouse and stepped outside.

"DB's a good old boy," KC said as she squinted into the sunlight. "His kid's playin' at Baylor now. Hard worker, nice kid. But don't underestimate him, Harriett. His nickname is the Shark. He just acts small town, but he's really a big city boy from Houston. Got tired of the grind at the Harris County D.A.'s Office and moved up here about seven or eight years ago."

"Thanks for the tip, KC," Harriett said. "I could have used a warning a little earlier about the judge though. She's taking the speedy trial thing a little too seriously."

"Yeah, I should have warned you about her. She's a tough old broad."

"Surely there's another judge who can hear your case," Harriett said.

KC laughed. "You don't want another judge. I trust her to keep everything under control."

"Then I gather you know her pretty well."

"Since I was a kid. She and Mom hung around together. I always thought she had a thing for Mom, but it was unrequited as far as I know," KC said with a shrug. "She'll be fair, but won't play any favorites."

"Then I guess we're stuck with her."

"It's like scopin' out the other team before you play them," KC said. "Just a different game."

"Do you need a ride home?" Harriett asked.

"Diane's supposed to be pickin' me up," KC said looking up

and down Commercial Street. "Must be runnin' late."

About fifteen minutes later, a dark copper brown Eddie Bauer Edition Ford Explorer wheeled into a parking space across the street from the courthouse.

"That's her," KC said as she started down the courthouse steps, followed by Harriett and Jess.

By the time they all crossed the street, a woman in her late thirties, wearing aviator sunglasses, an SMU baseball cap, and a brown distressed leather bomber jacket, was standing next to the vehicle. A mild wind blew the ends of her long blonde hair around her face and she swept it back with her right hand. She hugged KC briefly.

"Harriett, this is Diane Saunders. Honey, this is my high school friend, Harriett Markham, and her investigator, Jessie Raines."

Diane shook hands with both women and pulled her collar up against the cold wind.

"Sorry I'm late, Kerrie," Diane said. "The idiot who was supposed to cover for me got caught up somewhere."

"No problem," KC shrugged. "We were just catchin' up on old times." Turning to Harriett, she said, "Y'all want to follow us home and go over whatever we need to? Hell, I'll even spring for dinner."

"Thanks for the dinner offer," Harriett said, "but Mom has probably been slaving over the stove all morning. But there are a few things we need to discuss."

"Well, just follow us then. We live this side of Abilene so you shouldn't get lost."

Half an hour later Jess pulled into the drive of a long, split level ranch-style house in north Abilene. The yard was immaculately trimmed and low hedges lined the sidewalk to the covered entryway. A wrought iron gate opened into a small atrium walkway filled with ferns and other exotic plants. KC unlocked the front beveled glass door and held it open.

"I'll put some coffee on," Diane said quietly as she pulled off her bomber jacket and hung it on an antique hall tree inside the front door.

"Thanks, darlin'," KC said. Turning back to Harriett and Jess she said, "Take your jackets off and make yourselves comfortable."

"This is a lovely house, KC," Harriett remarked as she looked around the front room.

"Mostly Diane's doin'," KC shrugged. "I'm afraid interior

decoratin' isn't my thing and I don't know any gay guys well enough to ask them to decorate for me. Come on back to the den. That's really my space."

KC led them across a formal living area and into another room near the rear of the house. As soon as they entered, Harriett could see the difference.

"You're right, KC," Harriett smiled, "this does seem to fit you a little better."

"Make yourselves at home, ladies, while I go give Diane a hand," KC said as she excused herself.

Harriett and Jess took a self-guided tour of KC's domain. The walls were covered with pictures of KC as a player and autographed pictures of numerous sportswomen, past and present. Team pictures of the 1992 Lady Techsters, the last team from Louisiana Tech to compete for an NCAA national championship tournament, and the 1992 Women's Olympic basketball team, draped with the bronze medal the team won, were hung prominently on the wall. It was clear from the citations and pictures that Kerrie Carnes had been on the fast track to coaching big-time women's collegiate basketball before she had been forced to leave it behind. Trophies and plaques stood on built-in floor-to-ceiling bookshelves. Jess noticed a stack of DVDs on the floor near an elaborate video console and television. The DVDs were labeled with the names of various teams and players.

"Scouting tapes," Jess said as she squatted down to read the labels. "Looks like high school basketball is just as serious now as it was back when I played."

"Look at these pictures," Harriett said. "This is an incredible collection."

Jess stood up and joined her. "Some of these would be worth a tidy sum of money if she ever decided to part with them."

"That won't ever happen," KC's voice said from behind them. "Coffee's ready."

"Pretty fancy video setup you have," Jess said as she picked up a cup.

"Let's me do slo-mo and isolate individual players during a game. We can really zero in on how they move in certain situations, watch their eyes for clues. Well, you know what I mean, Jess."

"Yeah, I know what you mean."

"Would you like to see the rest of the house?" Diane asked. "We're very proud of it."

Harriett and Jess followed Diane through the remainder of the house and were duly impressed with the detailed work that had gone into each of the rooms. Jess particularly liked the Jacuzzi and weight room, while Harriett seemed more interested in the flooring of the front two rooms of the house.

"They replaced the basketball floor at my high school about three years ago and I talked the contractor into not just ripping it out. We stripped all the boards and had them put down in these rooms," Diane explained.

"It makes a beautiful floor," Harriett smiled. "Jess and I will have to keep our eyes and ears open for high school renovations from now on."

"There are always wonderful materials available in older buildings. Did you notice the fireplace?" Diane asked.

"Yes, I did," Harriett said. "It's very unusual."

"Those old bricks came from a building they were tearing down in my hometown. A wrecking ball had already been used on the building, but we were able to salvage enough to front the fireplace. As far as I've been able to tell, that building was pre-Civil War. That's why they're such an unusual color."

As they returned to the den, Diane said, "I'm sorry to be such a poor hostess, but I have to get back to my school. We have a weight training session scheduled this afternoon." She picked up the baseball cap she'd dropped earlier on a side table and adjusted it on her head.

Jess looked at the logo embroidered above the bill of the cap. "Cool hat," she said.

"Thanks. It's from my alma mater," Diane said.

"Never goes anywhere without the damn thing," KC added.

"It was a pleasure to meet you, Diane," Harriett said. "I'm sure we'll be seeing you again before this is over."

"If there's anything I can do to help, just let me know," Diane said. "I know it's driving KC crazy having to stay at home all the time like this."

KC walked Diane to the front door and then rejoined Harriett and Jess.

"Diane seems like a nice woman, KC," Harriett commented as she took her legal pad from her briefcase.

KC plopped down in an overstuffed chair. "Yeah, she's been great. Sometimes a little naive though."

"How so?" Harriett asked.

KC laughed. "Well, I know you caught that 'this is my bedroom and that is her bedroom' bullshit. I can't believe she thinks anyone believes that. But she's worried that people will talk. I'm pretty sure y'all are a couple. You got separate bedrooms?"

"No," Harriett smiled. "Everyone we care about is aware that Jess and I are a couple."

"See! That's what I mean, Harriett. Diane acts like no one knows we're gay. People know for Christ's sake! There's this guy at her school who's really closeted, you know. Thinks no one has a clue. That fuckin' queen swishes when he walks. He's practically a walkin' billboard for gay men. People ain't as clueless as Diane thinks. It's been my experience that most people don't give a shit. Oh well, enough sermonizin'. What now?"

"There are obviously some people we will need to talk to, so we should make a list. Then you can tell us everything you know about them, fact or fiction, and, hopefully, Jess will be able to follow up on any rumors or use the facts as a guide when interviewing some of those people."

"Okay," KC shrugged as she sipped her coffee. "Where do you want to start?"

"Tell me about DeVore," Harriett said. "Besides the fact you thought he was an asshole, what else do you know about him?"

"Not much, really. Let's see," KC said, leaning her elbows on her knees, "I think he arrived here about three years ago. Came from some moderately successful high school down your way, but I don't remember the name of the town. You can probably find it in his personnel records. He's married, wife's name is, uh, Peggy. Pretty decent sort as far as I could tell. They have two kids, Heather, and then a boy, in middle school, I think."

"Ever hear any rumors about him?"

"You know I don't listen to that shit, Harriett."

"Well, it's a small school. You must have heard something. Was he a good coach?"

"He hasn't been very successful since he got here, but I don't really watch football scrimmages. I've heard he had a tendency to pester his players' teachers if the kids were havin' a problem, but that's pretty standard stuff. Happens all the time. As for gossip, why don't you ask Lorri? She'd probably hear more of that than I would."

Harriett jotted down a note to herself. "Guess I'll have to pay her a visit."

"Who's Lorri?" Jess asked.

"My sister. You saw her picture yesterday," Harriett said, frowning slightly. "We haven't seen each other in a while."

Jess had never heard Harriett mention her sister and gathered they weren't on very good terms.

"What about the O'Neill girl?" Harriett asked.

"Alison O'Neill, age seventeen. But she won't know anything."

"She'll know if she made a pass at DeVore's daughter or not."

"So what? Look, she's a good kid. Got a real shot at college. I'd appreciate it if she wasn't dragged into this."

"We'll have to talk to her, KC."

"Ali comes from a barely middle-income family. If she gets a scholarship, she'll have a shot at gettin' into a decent college. She doesn't need this shit on her shoulders, too."

"Jess will be as diplomatic as humanly possible, I promise," Harriett said.

"Guess I don't have any choice. Anyone else?" KC asked as she deposited her coffee mug on her desk.

"I'd like to get a little background information about two or three of your players," Harriett said as she leaned back in an overstuffed early American chair.

KC shrugged. "Who do you need to know about?"

Harriett opened a notebook and said, "Lucero, Costa, and DeVore."

"Ah, the dynamic duo plus one," KC smiled. "Anything specific you need to know about them?"

"Just your general opinion. I can clarify anything I need to know more about later."

"Okay. Lucero is a decent player. She's been a starter in a few games. She's the plus one. Costa and DeVore are the dynamic duo. Basic bench warmers who are more concerned about who's gonna fuck them over the weekend than playin' basketball. DeVore usually warms the bench area next to Costa. The three of them have gotten pretty tight since last season. Costa and DeVore are a likely pair of friends. Same interests and all that good teenage stuff. Lucero is a new addition this year. Doesn't really fit in."

"How so?"

"Unfortunately, Lucero is a follower and too easily persuaded by the other two. I had some real hope she would develop into a good player, but she isn't willin' to put the time into it she needs to. I think Costa and DeVore are stringin' her along. But it beats the hell out of me why," KC said shaking her head.

"Are Costa and DeVore part of the in-crowd at the high school?"

"I guess so. Costa's father is a doctor and on the city council. Her mother is a partner with a real estate company in Abilene. Moved here a few years ago. You pretty much know about DeVore's father."

"And Lucero's family?"

"Lower middle class. More like O'Neill's family. In fact, I think they don't live too far apart. Lucero's parents have been supportive of the team and their daughter."

"Is Lucero friends with Ali?"

"They seemed to be close last year, but then somethin' happened over the summer. I mean they still speak and all that. Just don't hang together much anymore since Ali started hangin' out with Jamie. Then Lucero took up with Costa and DeVore. You haven't interviewed any of them yet?"

"No, I want to wait until after I read their initial statements and get a little more background information."

"Heather back at school yet?"

"According to the school, she should return by the beginning of next week."

"Well, that will be a tough time for her, I'm sure. She'll need to restore some sense of normalcy as quickly as possible."

Harriett had to smile to herself. It was obvious that KC cared for all her players, even the ones who obviously would have a reason not to like her.

"Who's the chief of police in Anson now?

"Carl Ray Thomas. Remember him?"

Harriett laughed. "I can't believe they would elect him. He was in trouble all the time."

"Well, he done seen the light, hallelujah! But he's still chasin' every skirt in town."

"He's not married?"

"Not this week. Been down the aisle about five or six times though," KC laughed.

"We should be able to get an evidence list from his office tomorrow."

"Don't wear a skirt," KC chuckled.

Forty minutes later, Jess backed out of the drive at KC's home. "So what now?" she asked as they left the Abilene city limits. "The judge only gave you four weeks to get prepared for trial."

"It's faster than I'm used to, but hopefully you'll have time to dig up everything I need. In case I haven't already said it a dozen times, thank you for agreeing to be our new investigator."

"I felt a little funny about it at first."

"Because you thought everyone would think we only hired you because you're my lover?"

"Something like that."

"Wayne actually recommended you to take his place months ago."

"Really?"

"He was impressed with how you handled yourself. I confess I was opposed to the idea at first. Not because I don't trust you, but because I was concerned about how you'd feel working for us."

"It's generally not a good idea to borrow money from your relatives or hire anyone you're personally involved with."

"I trust your instincts and even Nick thinks I'm calmer and happier with you close by."

"I'll try not to let you down, even though I do sort of feel like a kept woman," Jess admitted.

"I'm living in *your* house, so I think we're even in the kept woman department," Harriett said with a grin.

"I might have to leave you here for a couple of days, sweetie," Harriett said a few minutes later. "I need to clear up a few things at the office before I can spend much time here. I think tomorrow we should go to the high school and the police department to see what we can get. Then I'll drive to Austin Wednesday morning and be back here by Friday evening."

"Then I'll need to rent a car before you leave."

"Maybe I can convince Nick to drive yours up and he can go back with me. Remind me to call him this evening."


AT TEN THE following morning, Harriett, accompanied by Jess, stopped at the front office of Anson High School and requested a meeting with the school principal. The new high school was built after Harriett and her siblings graduated and the new building was definitely different. She watched students through the floor-to-ceiling glass windows of the main office and couldn't remember ever looking as young as the students passing by. Nothing like visiting your old high school to make you feel old, she thought with a smile.

"Miss Markham?" the receptionist asked.

"Yes," Harriett answered.

"Mr. Warner can see you now," the woman smiled.

The two women were greeted at the principal's door by Preston Warner, a sixty-ish man with a balding head and horn-rimmed glasses. Harriett remembered when he was a much younger man with hair and taught advanced biology.

He hugged Harriett and said, "It's wonderful to see you again, Harriett. Unfortunate circumstances, however. Please have a seat. How is Irene?" he asked warmly as he returned to his chair and leaned back.

"Enjoying her retirement and her grandchildren." Harriett smiled.

"Well, we sure miss her around here. Give her my regards. Now what can I do for you this morning?"

"I'll be representing Kerrie Carnes when her case goes to trial," Harriett said. Turning toward Jess, she added, "This is my investigator, Jessie Raines."

"Yes, I think she mentioned that when she called about her situation."

"I'll need to question members of your faculty and perhaps a few students, accompanied by their parents, of course. Whenever possible, I will question them away from the school. Ms. Raines will be here, mostly questioning faculty members, but I thought I should let you know."

"I appreciate that, Harriett. We have a conference room here if you, or Miss Raines, need to use it to interview faculty members."

"Who will be taking over KC's coaching duties while she's absent?" Harriett inquired.

Warner shrugged, "Right now, one of our assistant coaches is handling her duties in that regard. We have hired a long-term substitute for her science classes. Why?"

"KC is concerned about the team and how her situation might affect them."

"The girls' team has worked very hard preparing for this season and I'd hate to see them lose everything because their coach is absent."

Harriett glanced at Jess. Jess shifted uncomfortably in her chair. "I have some experience...coaching girls' basketball, sir," she said. "I'd be willing to act as a temporary coach for your team, if you'd let me. No cost to your school or district, of course."

"That's an unusual and unorthodox idea, Ms. Raines. I'll need to speak with KC and ask our superintendent to find out if

UIL rules will allow it before I can give you an answer."

"You can contact her at my mother's," Harriett said before returning to her questioning. "Now, what can you tell me about Coach DeVore?"

"On or off the record?"

"Whichever you feel comfortable with, Preston."

"When Allen first came here, he seemed like just the kind of fella we were looking for. Eager beaver, winning record at his former school, an upstanding Christian, married man. Good role model."

"Did that change?"

"Well, I don't put much stock in gossip, but I had heard some undercurrents that were not exactly what we had been led to expect."

"Such as?"

"I heard, and mind you, this is only gossip, I heard he might be...um...involved with one of our teachers. But I don't know it for a fact."

"Do you know who the teacher was?"

"No. I never heard a name. The rumor was rather vague. Idle gossip. But I did get the impression that Coach DeVore had a rather large ego based on his past coaching record."

"It's my understanding that he hadn't been very successful since he arrived in Anson."

"That's true. The best season we've had since he was hired was five and five. But there's always hope next season will be better."

"What do you know about his working relationship with Coach Carnes?"

Warner laughed. "You know KC, Harriett."

"Yes, I certainly do," Harriett smiled.

"I think she tried to avoid any contact whatsoever with Coach DeVore. He struck me as a little chauvinistic and that didn't sit real well with KC. She complained to me a couple of times that he was attempting to undermine her as a coach and trying to intimidate her players."

"Isn't his daughter on the team?"

"Yes. Heather," Warner nodded.

"Did Coach DeVore ever complain to you about how KC was handling her team?"

"As a matter of fact, he did. He accused Coach Carnes of playing favorites and not giving Heather her fair share of playing time. But coaching isn't really my area of expertise, so I told him I wouldn't try to influence who she chose to play any more than I would him."

"Have you been satisfied with KC as a teacher and a coach while she's been here?"

"I've never had any reason to be dissatisfied," Warner hedged.

"Have you heard any gossip concerning Coach Carnes?"

Warner leaned forward and rested his elbows on his desk, looking at Harriett. "How can I say this, Harriett? Any gossip I've heard concerning Kerrie Carnes is pretty much the same gossip I heard when she was a student here."

"Which was?" Harriett pressed, even though she knew it embarrassed Warner.

"That Coach Carnes was possibly...homosexual," Warner finally said after taking a deep breath.

"Is that a fact or merely a rumor, Preston?"

"As far as I know, it's never been more than a rumor and Coach Carnes has never given me any reason to think otherwise."

"Thank you for your candor. It's a possibility that rumor may play a part in her trial. I needed to make sure you were aware of it."

"Well, unfortunately, no matter how this all turns out, KC might find life difficult in Anson."

"I think she already knows that. Would it be possible for us to see where Coach DeVore was found?"

"Of course," Warner said, rising from his chair. "I'll get you a school map, but the school is essentially laid out as the former high school was when you were a student here." Extending his hand to Harriett, he added, "If there's any way I can help you further, just let me know."

"I appreciate it, Preston, and I'll be in touch."


HARRIETT AND JESS clipped yellow plastic visitor's badges to their jackets and followed the map toward the Anson High School gymnasium. As they approached the gym, they could hear the sound of basketballs reverberating off the backboards and bouncing on the hardwood floor.

"Where is DeVore's office?" Jess asked.

"The secretary said it was behind the gym."

"I'm sure whoever is in the gym now will know."

The gym doors were open and Harriett and Jess stood just inside the door. The girls' team was practicing free throws and looked bored. An equally bored-looking older man reading a newspaper was sitting halfway up the bleachers.

"Must be KC's replacement," Harriett said.

"Yeah, looks like a real motivator," Jess chuckled. "I can see why KC was concerned."

"Aunt Harriett!" a girl's voice called out.

Harriett looked at the girls, unsure who had called her name, as a pony tailed teenage girl trotted toward them. Harriett smiled when she finally recognized the girl. Hugging her tightly, she said, "Jamie! I hardly recognized you. God, but you've gotten tall."

"It's good to see you again, Aunt Harriett," the girl laughed. "I'm almost as tall as you are. Have you seen Mom yet?"

"No. We just got here. We're staying at Granny's."

"Cool! I have my license now. Maybe I can come by and see you while you're here."

"That would be great, Jamie."

"So why are you here anyway? Not that I blame you, but you *never* come to Anson."

"I've taken a case here, sweetheart. So we'll be around for a while."

Leaning closer to Harriett, Jamie said, "Are you representing Coach Carnes?"

Harriett nodded. "Yes, I am."

"She didn't do it, Aunt Harriett. There's just no way. Coach DeVore was a serious as...butthole, but Coach wouldn't have killed him."

"I don't think so either, Jamie. We need to see Coach DeVore's office. Do you know where it is?"

"Sure. Through those doors," Jamie said as she pointed toward the back of the gym. "You can't miss it. The police probably had to order more yellow tape."

Jamie looked at Jess and held her hand out. "I'm Jamie Gaither. My aunt seems to have forgotten you were standing here."

"Jessie Raines," Jess smiled.

"I'm so sorry, Jess. I haven't seen Jamie since she was in elementary school, except in pictures. Jess is my investigator, honey," Harriett said to Jamie

"Super cool!"

"What are you doing besides shooting free throws?" Jess asked with a smile.

Rolling her eyes, Jamie said, "That's been about it since

Coach Carnes has been gone." Looking over her shoulder at the man in the bleachers, she continued, "Coach Pigskin up there says 'Games are won and lost at the free throw line, ladies.'"

"Well, he's partially right," Jess laughed.

"Jamie, we've heard that some of the players overheard Coach Carnes arguing with Coach DeVore after your scrimmage on October thirtieth," Harriett said. "Do you know which girls those were by any chance?"

"Sure," Jamie answered looking over her shoulder at her teammates. "Number six is Erica Lucero and number nine is Jennifer Costa. They told the police they overheard loud voices and cussin' that sounded like an argument to them."

"Coach DeVore's daughter is on the team, too, isn't she?"

"Yeah, Heather. But she's not here today, ya know?"

"And which one is Alison O'Neill?" Jess asked.

"Number fifteen, but she's absent today for a doctor's appointment."

"We heard she's pretty good."

"Best player in the region probably. Should be a shoo-in for a scholarship somewhere."

"Do you know her very well?"

"Yeah, we're pretty tight," Jamie said, lowering her eyes and flushing slightly. "We sort of hang out together, ya know."

"Well," Harriett finally said, "you better get back to your free throws and we'd better look at the coach's office. Come by Granny's later and we'll catch up." Leaning closer, she lowered her voice slightly. "Granny made gingerbread and it's fabulous."

"Did you leave me any?"

"We did."

"Great! How's Lacey?"

"Claims college is harder than high school," Harriett said with a laugh. "Did you get to see her while she was here last summer?"

"Yeah, we went to a movie and hoisted a few milkshakes together while we tried to solve the world's problems."

After hugging Harriett again, Jamie trotted back to rejoin her team. Harriett watched her young niece who was rapidly growing into a woman. She regretted letting the rift between herself and Jamie's mother, Lorraine, keep her away from her family. What Lorri had done during the custody battle over Lacey hurt Harriett deeply. But that had been almost fifteen years earlier. Perhaps it was time to finally mend their relationship.

"Seems like a nice kid," Jess said as she and Harriett walked toward the back of the gym.

"I'm surprised she recognized me," Harriett said. "I really haven't seen her in eight or nine years except in a few pictures Mom has sent."

As soon as Harriett and Jess walked through the back door out of the gym, it was obvious where Coach DeVore's office was. Yellow police tape, warning passersby not to trespass, taped the door shut and the area around the office was cordoned off by more yellow tape.

"We won't be able to break the seal on the door until you talk to the police chief," Jess said.

Harriett nodded as she looked down the hallway from the office. "I guess the girls' locker room must be down this hallway," she said as she pointed to her left.

"Then the girls must have been coming from the locker room and passed by the office after they showered and dressed," Jess said. "KC said DeVore called her into his office after the game while she was picking up equipment."

"I don't remember a back exit from the building from here except through the gym," Harriett said.

Jess ducked under the yellow tape and walked down the hallway away from DeVore's office. Around the corner was an exit. She pushed the door open and noted that it led to the parking lot behind the gym. Anyone leaving the locker room would have to walk directly past DeVore's office to reach the parking lot. It was plausible the girls could have heard the argument between KC and DeVore. Jess retraced her steps to the girls' locker room and went inside. Off to one side was a small office. A black plastic strip next to the door identified K. Carnes as the office's occupant.

After her argument with DeVore, KC could have gone to her office and then left the building through the back door. Unless the door locked automatically, it was reasonable to assume someone else could have entered after she left and murdered DeVore. Jess pushed the door open and stepped outside, letting it slam closed behind her. When she jerked on the handle to get back in, the door was locked shut. She pounded on the metal door and waited for Harriett to re-open it. "We'll have to ask KC to retrace her steps the night of the scrimmage and find out if the door always re-locks itself," Jess said.

Harriett shrugged. "Seems like the time has arrived for us to pay a visit to Chief Thomas."

Harriett and Jessie walked back into the gym and waved at

Jamie as they passed the bored free throw shooters.


JESS CARRIED THEIR visitor's badges into the main office and waited for the student worker to retrieve their driver's licenses. She thanked the young woman and reached for the double glass doors into the main lobby. She held it open for two women loaded down with armloads of textbooks. The woman in front, a middle-aged Hispanic woman with dark hair pinned up into a French braid, smiled at her. "*Gracias,*" she said.

Jess returned the woman's smile. "*De nada, senora,*" she said.

Jess held the door for a second woman and nodded as the woman glanced at her. Although a few years older, Jess was positive she was the woman in the portrait hanging in Irene's living room next to Harriett's.

"Just put those books on the counter until Mrs. Craig can check them in," the woman said. As she spoke, the books in her arms began to shift.

"Let me take some of those for you," Jess offered.

Shifting her eyes between Jess and the teacher with her, Lorri said, "I'm fine, but thank you for offering."

"I insist, ma'am," Jess said firmly as she reached for the books and removed them from Lorri's arms.

A few minutes later, Jess joined Harriett on the front steps of the high school and returned her driver's license. "I could be mistaken, but I *think* I just met your sister," she said.

"That must have been exciting for you," Harriett said with a frown.

Jess shrugged. "No big deal. I didn't introduce myself."

# Chapter Four

"HARRIETT MARKHAM TO see Chief Thomas," Harriett said to the desk officer.

"Do you have an appointment, ma'am?" the deputy asked.

"No, I don't. Please ask Carl Ray if he can give me a minute. And please tell him that I'm representing Kerrie Carnes."

The deputy sauntered down a hallway and tapped on an office door. When he returned a minute later, Chief Carl Ray Thomas was following him. Smiling broadly, Chief Thomas walked through the swinging divider into the front desk area. Harriett smiled when she saw him approaching. Before she could speak, he grabbed her and bear hugged her.

"Whooo-ee! Damn, girl, you're lookin' some kinda fine!" Thomas boomed. He was over six feet tall and built like a barrel. Although he had put on several extra pounds since high school, Harriett could still see the handsome features that her female classmates had found so attractive.

"You're looking well, too, Carl Ray," Harriett smiled.

"Well, yeah, except for this middle age spread I've been working on lately," he said as he patted his ample belly. "Too damn much home-cookin' and not enough exercise," he laughed.

Turning to Jess, Harriett said, "Carl Ray, this is my investigator, Jessie Raines."

"A pleasure," Thomas said as he pumped Jess's hand. Turning back to Harriett, he said, "Why don't we go on back to my office? I think I have what you're lookin' for back there."

Harriett nodded and she and Jess followed Thomas through the swinging gate. Harriett smiled to herself as her mind returned to the past remembering the way he had groped her on their first and only date. The boy had been the captain of the football team, but Jess didn't need to know that.

"Take a message if anyone calls, Harold," Thomas smiled at the desk officer.

"Sure thing, Carl Ray," the deputy answered as he continued reading through a stack papers at his desk.

Thomas's office was mildly cluttered and he moved a stack of file folders from a chair to make room for Harriett and Jess to sit down before walking around his desk and dropping onto his own high back swivel chair.

"What can I do for you, Harriett?" he asked.

"I'd like to see the file you have on Kerrie Carnes," Harriett said.

"Sure thing," he said as he rifled through another stack of file folders. "You know when I first made this file, I don't think I even knew her whole name. Never called her nothin' but KC, ya know. Ah, here it is," he continued as he pulled a folder from halfway down the stack and handed it to Harriett.

Harriett and Jess glanced through the paperwork for a few minutes. There was an inventory list, autopsy report, and grand jury papers outlining the official charges.

"Could we get a copy of these papers, Carl Ray?" Harriett asked.

"Sure thing," he said as he pushed a button on his desk phone and picked up the receiver.

"Hey, Harold, I need a copy of the papers in the Carnes file. Come get it and do that for me, okay, buddy," Thomas said into the receiver.

"Won't take but a minute," he said as he hung up the phone.

"Can you tell me the sequence of events once you became involved in the case, Carl Ray?" Harriett asked as the deputy entered and took the folder from Thomas.

"Ain't that much to tell, hon," Thomas said taking a deep breath. "We got a call from the school at about eight Halloween morning. A deputy went over there and then called me at home."

"Who called it in?"

"Some janitor," Carl Ray shrugged. "Name's in the file. But he wasn't a witness to the crime. Just reported it."

"Did he touch anything in the office?" Jess asked.

"As far as I know, he only opened the door, saw the body, and called us," Carl Ray said. "We figure he probably touched the doorknob and then the receiver on the phone in the Coach's office. At least those were the only places we found his prints when we dusted the room."

"What about a weapon?" Harriett asked.

"Best we could tell, Coach DeVore got conked on the head by a trophy. We found it layin' on the floor not far from his body and there was blood and hair that matched his on a corner of the base."

"Any fingerprints?"

"Someone tried to wipe it down. We found a towel with some blood on it on a file cabinet. But whoever did that missed a partial print on the top part of the trophy. It was that partial that belonged to KC. Other than that, we couldn't lift any prints."

"So you think KC wiped the trophy off and missed a partial print," Harriett said.

"Well, that was all we found. I just gather what's there, Harriett," Carl Ray smiled. "I don't try to analyze it. That's for the forensic folks. I give them the puzzle pieces and they try to put them together to make a picture."

"We'd like to get a look at DeVore's office, if possible," Harriett added.

"No prob. I'll have a deputy meet you over at the school whenever you want."

"How about around five, after school is out," Harriett said, looking at her watch. "That way maybe there won't be any kids around. They've probably already seen enough."

"Works for me," Carl Ray said. "Is there anything else I can help you with, Harriett?"

"No," Harriett smiled as she rose from her chair, "I think that should be about it for now, Carl Ray. You've been very cooperative and I appreciate that."

"Well, I know how hot-headed KC can be," he said as he escorted Harriett and Jess to the door, "but I have a hard time believin' she could have killed DeVore. You can pick up your copies of the file at the front desk."

"Thanks again, Carl Ray," Harriett said, hugging him briefly.

"Good to see you again, hon," Carl Ray said with a smile. "Give me a call and I'll spring for dinner so we can catch up."

"I'll think about it, Carl Ray," Harriett said with a look that said no-way-in-hell as she and Jess left the office.

# Chapter Five

PEGGY DEVORE STEPPED from the back seat of the limousine provided for her family and took her son's hand. The drive from the small church in Goldthwaite, Texas had been gratefully short. Peggy and her two children shared the vehicle with Allen's parents, Irma and Herbert DeVore. Despite the fact that she was the wife of their only son, Peggy never felt welcomed in their home. They were well aware of the circumstances surrounding her marriage to Allen and blamed her for trapping their son in a marriage that was strained at best. While she waited for her in-laws to disembark, Peggy swept her hand through Brett's straight, fine hair. He looked up at her, as only a ten-year-old boy can, eyes wide, and gripped her hand a little bit harder. Now that Allen was gone, she hoped her son would find some semblance of normal childhood.

She watched her daughter, Heather, step between her grandparents and take their hands. Peggy stood a little straighter as she watched the coffin roll smoothly from the back of the hearse. Six friends of the DeVore family gripped the handles on the sides and began carrying Allen toward his final home. She smiled down at Brett, thinking how many times Allen had complained about how much he hated his small hometown. There was some justice that now he would rest in the place he hated most for eternity. She slipped her arm around Brett's shoulders and began the slow procession toward the canopy next to the gravesite. She paused at the edge of the canopy and allowed the DeVores to proceed ahead of her. Heather glanced at her mother and frowned.

"Go on with your grandparents, Heather."

"He was *your* husband," Heather hissed.

"And he was *their* only son," Peggy answered softly.

Family friends and lesser relatives moved into seats behind the immediate family. A member of the funeral home staff solemnly carried a large picture of a smiling Allen DeVore and secured it to an easel at the head of the grave. Peggy bowed her head to avoid looking at the picture. There was no arguing that Allen had been a ruggedly handsome man. Together they produced two equally handsome children, both conceived without the benefit of passion or any semblance of love.

The Pentecostal minister stepped forward and began to drone on once again about the virtues Allen DeVore had received from his parents. Peggy played with a thread she suddenly discovered on her coat and effectively tuned out the monotonous, twangy voice of the minister. Thoughts of her life with Allen seeped into her mind. She remembered accompanying a friend to a fraternity party during her senior year at Baylor University. She remembered being introduced to a handsome young man with dark chestnut hair and hazel eyes. She remembered accepting an invitation to dance following more drinks than she normally consumed. She closed her eyes tightly as she remembered the feel of hands on her body and the burning sensation as he pushed into her body.

In spite of the chilled breeze that swept across the cemetery, Peggy could feel a bead of perspiration trickle down her spine. She removed a glove from her hand and dabbed at the beads of sweat along her forehead and above her upper lip.

"Are you okay, Mom?" Brett whispered.

Peggy nodded and patted his thigh with her now cold hand. "I'm fine, honey. Thank you," she answered with a smile before returning to her reminiscences.

Allen agreed to marry Peggy once she told him she was pregnant and he was the father. Her parents wanted a lavish wedding for their oldest daughter, but she refused. She and Allen eloped and were joined as man and wife in a low-key civil ceremony witnessed by courthouse employees in Waco, Texas. A few months later they graduated from college and Allen accepted a coaching position in Leander, not far from Austin. There hadn't been a time since their marriage that Allen hadn't shown his dissatisfaction by seeking out other, more willing women to satisfy his needs.

Peggy DeVore was an attractive woman with jet black hair and stunning gray eyes that made her seem cool and aloof to many, letting very few see who she really was. She was a highly trained classical pianist who gave up her future for one drunken night of stupidity with a man who enjoyed raunchy, semi-salacious burlesque music.

Peggy considered the life she felt forced to live as punishment for her own foolish actions. She would never divorce Allen and raise her children in a single parent environment. Allen knew she didn't believe in divorce and used it against her more than once, establishing his role as the dominant half of their partnership. One of those acts of dominance resulted in Brett's conception. Allen had been ecstatic when it resulted in a son. Over the years, Peggy allowed her children to see her humiliated and belittled. Now she would have no choice but to be a single parent, keeping the fantasy of a loving father alive in their minds. Tears forced their way down her cheeks when she thought of how much she hated Allen DeVore. She felt free for the first time in nearly eighteen years and guilty for feeling that way.

# Chapter Six

HARRIETT ENTERED THE back door of her mother's house and removed her black pumps. She picked them up and walked into the kitchen. If she stayed too long at her childhood home she would need to buy another pair of house shoes to leave in the mud room. She wasn't surprised to find Irene standing over the kitchen stove.

"How did your day go?" Irene asked cheerfully.

"It was busy," Harriett answered as she dropped her briefcase onto the kitchen table. Jess opened the refrigerator and took out a bottle of water, twisting the cap off and taking a long drink. She leaned against the counter and opened a second bottle for Harriett. "Jess ran into Lorri today," Harriett said.

"Where?" Irene asked.

"At the high school while we were there checking out the crime scene," Jess answered.

"How was she?"

"I didn't see her." Harriett said as she took a drink and swallowed hard. "But it was probably a good thing. I can't imagine she's changed her opinion of me, even after all these years. It would only have caused another problem and I'm not here to cause problems."

"That's something the two of you will need to work out yourselves," Irene shrugged.

"I'm aware of that, Mother, but homosexuality is not a communicable disease. I hope Lorri doesn't act inappropriately when Lacey visits. She wants to, and should, know her whole family, even the bigoted ones."

Irene placed the spoon she was using in a holder next to the stove and turned to face Harriett. "Everyone has a right to their opinion, Harriett, even if you don't like it."

"Was I an embarrassment to you and Dad?" Harriett asked solemnly.

Irene paused a moment before answering, as if gathering her thoughts. "When you told us you preferred the company of other women, your father and I didn't know what we were supposed to say. It was a...surprise." Irene smiled to herself. "I don't know if Lorri will ever accept your lifestyle. She's spent her whole life trying to live up to the standards you and Jerry set. Superman and Wonder Woman," she said with a chuckle, shaking her head.

Harriett smiled back at her mother. "And Wonder Woman had a flaw," she said.

"You were always the Golden Girl in high school."

"Lorri is much prettier than I am. I was always a little jealous of that," Harriett said with a shrug. "But I got over it."

"When you revealed that you were gay it made Lorri feel superior to you for the first time in her life. Then when Jerry named you as Lacey's guardian, it was like a slap in the face."

"I didn't ask for that. I was as shocked as anyone else."

"Whatever the reason he chose you, it was his final wish."

"I've never had the nerve to ask before, but did you or Dad encourage Lorri to sue me for custody of Lacey?"

Jess took Harriett's hand and squeezed it gently.

Irene took a deep breath. "She didn't ask for our opinion. It was her choice, but I was hurt by the stress and animosity it caused between you."

Harriett felt her throat start to close up. "I was hurt too, Mom," she muttered before pushing away from the counter. "I'm going to change into something more comfortable. Do you mind if I use Dad's study for a while before dinner?"

"Of course not."

Harriett nodded and stopped to throw her bottle into the recycle bin under the sink before picking up her briefcase and leaving the kitchen. It was going to be a bittersweet trip home. Suddenly she knew she wasn't in the town that had embraced her and made her feel safe in her youth. She patted Jess's arm and looked into her eyes. The intensity in Jess's eyes hid her passion and tenderness from most people, but never from Harriett. "We should get changed," she said. "Nick will probably be here in a couple of hours."

Upstairs Harriett stripped out of her suit and changed into a well-worn pair of faded jeans and an old Texas sweatshirt. Jess entered the room quietly and stepped behind her, slipping her hands along Harriett's waist and beneath the sweatshirt.

Harriett leaned back into the warmth of Jess's solid body. "I love the feel of your hands on me," Harriett said.

"What's wrong, Harriett?" Jess asked, moving her hands farther up Harriett's sides.

"Nothing."

"I thought we promised never to lie to each other," Jess murmured as she inhaled her lover's scent and kissed the tender area below her ear.

"It's really nothing, hon," Harriett hummed. "I just never thought I'd have to slink back into the closet, even temporarily. I don't care for it much."

"I thought you were out to your family."

"I am, but all of them won't be thrilled I'm back."

"If you're uncomfortable maybe you should find a local attorney and hand the case off before you get in too deep."

"I don't know if that would help my *lesbian* client much."

"Is that an issue in the case?"

"Potentially."

"Sticky wicket there."

"Ya think?" Harriett said with a laugh.

"Damn. I want you so much, baby," Jess breathed. "I hate not being able to touch you whenever I want to."

"I love you," Harriett said, turning in Jess's arms. "You make me feel safe and I need that."

Harriett lifted her chin to meet Jess's mouth with her own. The welcoming warmth of Jess's lips, combined with the desire Harriett saw in her eyes, took control of her senses, possessing her completely.

"HAVE ANY TROUBLE with the Durango on the way up?" Jess asked Nick over dinner that evening.

"Not a bit, Jess. Made me feel really butch," Nick smiled as he loaded his fork with another bite of apple pie.

"Well, don't let it go to your head," Jess laughed.

"So, Harriett, have you come to any conclusions about your client yet?" Nick asked.

"We've only been here two days, Nick," Harriett answered. "So far my crystal ball isn't sending me any revelations."

"If y'all will excuse me," Irene said as she got up from the table, "I'll start cleaning up this mess and let you talk."

"I'll give you a hand, Irene," Jess said as she swallowed her last bite and picked up her plate.

"No, you stay, dear. I just have to load these in the dishwasher and let it do all the real work," Irene said. "Why don't you get some coffee though and then you can relax in the living room."

"I can do that," Jess smiled.

Jess followed Irene into the kitchen while Harriett and Nick made their way into the cozy living room. Harriett opened the fireplace screen and poked at the logs, resetting them over the embers and waited until flames began to lick at newly exposed strips of wood. As she was sitting on the couch, Jess brought in a tray with three steaming cups and set it on the coffee table. She handed a cup to Nick and then one to Harriett before picking up her own cup. Harriett slipped her shoes off and swung her feet onto Jess's lap.

"Did the police report give you anything you didn't already know?" Nick asked as he reclined in a chair and sipped coffee.

"Not really," Harriett said. "It was pretty much a rehash of what KC and Carl Ray told us. No real witnesses to the crime itself. Just statements from the girls who said they overheard an argument but couldn't make out what the argument was about."

"So, most of the evidence is really circumstantial?"

"Except for the partial print on the murder weapon and a gym towel with KC's hair and blood on it," Jess answered as she set her cup down and began rubbing Harriett's feet.

"Jesus," Nick laughed. "You two look like an old married couple. You can feel free to rub my feet when you're finished there, Jess."

"Pass," Jess grinned.

"I assume you'll be interviewing people while we're gone," Nick said.

"Looks like I don't have much choice," Jess said, looking at Harriett.

"The principal of the high school, Preston Warner, called just before you arrived and said the superintendent has approved Jess as a substitute coach for KC," Harriett said. "Jess isn't exactly thrilled with that part, but it will allow her relatively free run of the school. There was a rumor that DeVore was having an affair with one of the teachers."

"Ah," Nick nodded. "Back to ferreting out who's shacking up with whom, huh?"

"My bread and butter, Nick," Jess chuckled. "Shouldn't take too long. There's only about thirty teachers on the faculty and less than half are women. Of that number, we already know some that can be eliminated because of age. So, that only leaves about seven female faculty members who can claim the grand prize."

"You think it might have been an upset lover?"

"Could have been little green men from Mars for all I care," Harriett said. "I just have to show it's possible it was someone besides KC."

"It wouldn't have taken a mental giant to wait around until after KC left and go into the office and do the deed," Jess shrugged. "It wasn't exactly a secret that KC and the victim didn't like one another. Anyone else with an axe to grind with DeVore could have also heard their argument and used it to frame KC."

"I'm surprised the county grand jury would hand down an indictment based on the evidence they have anyway," Harriett said over her cup. "As far as I know the prosecution will be relying on the partial print and the towel."

"Anything they found in that office could have been deposited there any time," Jess explained. "KC had been in DeVore's office on more than one occasion. Hair and fingerprints could have been left weeks or months before, depending on how often his office was cleaned. And from what we could tell when we saw it this afternoon, I'd hazard a guess that dusting wasn't a priority for the janitorial staff."

"The towel isn't much evidence either," Harriett added. "They don't mark gym towels his and hers, so, for all we know, it could have come from the boys' locker room."

"Okay, so they can't prove beyond a reasonable doubt that your client, this KC, killed anyone. What's the problem?" Nick asked.

"Well, you know how anal Harriett is about this stuff," Jess smiled. "We can explain away almost all of their evidence, but there was the argument thing. We have to be able to show it was possible for someone else to commit the crime. Jilted lover, pissed off wife, jealous assistant. And I have to locate that someone and find enough circumstantial evidence to point to them. Then it's case closed and hello Austin."

"Sounds like a cakewalk to me," Nick said. "How much are you billing your friend, if I dare ask?"

Harriett looked at him and smiled. "She's a school teacher in a small school."

"Then I should assume this case is pro bono or close to it."

"No, KC would never go for that, but it will be something within her reach."

"Damn," Nick laughed. "Guess I can't look forward to that early retirement then."

"We already make more than enough money, Nick," Harriett said.

"No argument here," he said.


A LITTLE BEFORE eight the next morning, Jess kissed

Harriett good-bye and watched as she and Nick pulled away before getting into her Durango and backing out of Irene's driveway. She wouldn't meet with the girls' basketball team until nearly noon, but decided to use the extra time to acquaint herself with the school and perhaps a few female faculty members. As a student, many years before, she had always wondered what went on in that forbidden inner sanctum known as the teacher's lounge.

Stopping at the main office, Jess picked up a temporary staff identification badge and clipped it to the waistband of her Dockers. The secretary directed her to the lounge and she left the office and found herself suddenly immersed in a small sea of talking, laughing teenagers. Jess shook her head as she wondered whether she had ever looked as young and fresh-faced as those students.

As she turned toward the lounge, she was tapped on the shoulder. Turning around, she saw Jamie Gaither smiling at her. A taller, young girl in jeans and a school sweatshirt stood next to her. Jess was struck by the prominent swath of freckles across the girl's cheeks and nose. Her hair was short on the back and sides and an interesting mix of auburn and dark blonde. But her bangs were long enough to fall over her forehead and into her hazel eyes.

There was something oddly familiar about the girl, but Jess couldn't quite put a finger on what it was. She felt as if she should have known the young woman although she was certain they had never met.

"Why are you here?" Jamie asked.

"Covering for Coach Carnes. Just found out last night. How are you today, Jamie?" Jess asked.

"You any good?" Jamie asked.

"I can hold my own," Jess answered with a smile as she glanced again at the girl standing next to Jamie.

"This is my friend, Ali O'Neill," Jamie said.

Jess shook hands with the girl. "I hear you're a pretty good player."

Ali blushed and looked at Jamie, "I guess so," she mumbled quietly.

"Well, y'all better get going before you're late for class," Jess said.

Halfway down the hall, Jess saw a door marked "Lounge" and gently pushed it open. The room was empty and she stepped in and looked around. At the far side of the room was a coffeemaker and Styrofoam cups along with several ceramic coffee mugs. She poured herself a cup and was stirring in creamer when the door burst open. Startled, she turned around and was confronted with an older, balding man, who walked purposefully toward the coffeemaker.

"Damn hall duty," he muttered as he poured coffee into a chipped, brown stained mug. Looking at Jess, he flashed what passed as a smile. "Who are you?" he asked.

"Jessie Raines," she answered.

"Subbing?"

"Coaching. For Coach Carnes."

"Tom Stafford, mathematics," the man said. "I heard KC got her ass in a sling. Guess that'll teach her to curb her temper and her mouth in the future."

"I don't know anything about that, Mr. Stafford," Jess said. "I'm just coaching the basketball team as a favor."

Looking Jess up and down, Stafford said, "Well, looks like you're tall enough to do that."

Stafford took his cup and retreated to a table near the door where he opened a briefcase and pulled out a stack of papers and a red soft cover book. Jess sat down on a couch, crossing her right ankle over her left knee and sipped her coffee.

Twenty minutes later the lounge door opened and two female teachers entered the room and deposited their belongings on a second table before making their way to the coffeemaker. One of the women, tall, with light brown hair, was one of the two she'd assisted with her books the previous day. After pouring two cups of coffee, the taller woman rinsed out the carafe and began a second pot of coffee. She smiled as she glanced at Jess.

"Morning," the woman smiled.

"Good morning," Jess smiled back.

"She's takin' over for KC in basketball," Stafford said from across the room.

"Really?" the woman said. "My daughter is on Coach Carnes's team." Extending a slender hand toward Jess, she said, "Didn't we meet yesterday? I'm Lorraine Gaither. Lorri"

"Jessie Raines," Jess said. "I think I talked to your daughter for a moment when I got here this morning," she added with a smile. "Had to ask for directions to the coffee pot. Seemed like a nice kid."

"Thanks," Lorri said.

"And what do you teach?" Jess inquired.

"English. Are you covering Coach Carnes's science classes, too?"

"No, just basketball," Jess said as she took a sip of her coffee.

"I'm surprised they would hire two subs for her," Lorri said.

"I'm sort of doin' it gratis for Coach Carnes. I have some basketball experience and offered to fill in until she is available again. She didn't want the team to suffer because of her absence."

"Have you met with the team already?"

"Just watched them practicing free throws for a little while yesterday," Jess smiled.

"Well, I'm sure Jamie and the other girls will be relieved to do something besides that," Lorri laughed.

Her laugh reminded Jess of Harriett and now that she knew who the woman was, she pondered whether or not to tell Lorri Gaither that she really worked for Harriett, but decided against it for the moment. From what she had gathered from Harriett, she and her sister weren't on very good terms, and Jess didn't want to jeopardize her investigation by contributing to a family conflict.

When the bell rang for the second period to begin, Jess made her way to the gym and found a custodian to open the locker room. Grabbing an armful of towels and a rolling bin of basketballs, she took everything to the basketball court. She hadn't really decided what she was going to do. It had been years since she had even picked up a basketball, but she hoped it would be like that old adage about riding a bicycle. As she looked down the court, her mind was flooded with memories of high school and college. Sitting on the bleachers, she removed her shoes and slipped into a pair of tennis shoes. She would be stuck with her Dockers and polo shirt for a couple of days until Harriett returned with her sweats.

Picking up a basketball, she ran the pads of her fingers over the bumpy grain of the ball and flipped it over in her hands as she walked onto the court. Beginning slowly, she dribbled the ball around the court. Finally, in a burst of energy she ran the length of the court and finished with a perfect lay-up into the basket. She practiced shooting baskets from the free throw line and at various points around the lane leading to the basket. First from two-point range and then progressing to the three-point area. She had to smile at how well she was doing. Maybe it was like riding a bicycle after all.

"Not bad," a voice interrupted.

Jess turned toward the back of the gym. KC was standing in the doorway with her hands on her hips. She was wearing a gray sweatsuit and tennis shoes. The outline of a knee brace on her left leg was obvious under her sweatpants.

"What the hell are you doing?" Jess demanded. "You can't be here."

"Yeah, I know. But no one saw me," KC answered as she sauntered toward Jess. "I tried to catch you at Irene's this mornin', but who knew you'd be one of those eager beaver types. There were a couple of things I need to have you do with the team. I came in Diane's car."

"Well, make it quick, KC, and then get the hell out of here before someone does see you."

"Yeah, yeah, I know," KC said as she scooped a ball from the bin. "They're a little weak on their pass coverage and Ali has a problem gettin' rid of the ball when she's being double teamed. Turns it over more often than I'd like. Sometimes she's just not aggressive enough." KC pulled a piece of paper from her sweatpants pocket and handed it to Jess. "I came up with this idea to get her around her double team problem. Might want to work on that sometime before the next game."

Shoving the paper into her pocket, Jess said, "Yeah, I will. That it?"

"Pretty much," KC smiled. "Wanna try a little one-on-one?"

"This isn't a great time, KC"

Looking at the clock on the gym wall, KC said, "We got about twenty minutes before anyone will be in here. As I remember, you used to be pretty good. I saw you play in college. How about it? Just so you'll know what you missed since we never had a chance to play against each other."

"I don't need to prove anything," Jess said.

Stepping closer, KC said, "Look, I know I'm probably not your favorite person on the planet. I also know that I'm frequently obnoxious, but I'm not a total bitch."

Jess had to smile. The truth was that when she was a cocky high school player, she always wished she could play against the great Kerrie Carnes. Shrugging, Jess tossed her basketball to KC. "Go for it," she said.

KC rolled her basketball off the court and dribbled to center court. "Of course, I am four or five years older than you and have a bum knee, so you might have to cut an older woman a break."

"Not likely," Jess grinned.

KC laughed and leaned slightly forward, dribbling the basketball with her left hand. Jess watched KC's eyes intently, waiting for her to make her move, arms outspread. KC moved forward, slowly, testing Jess before she began her break. Jess kept pace with KC as they neared the basket. Her peripheral vision told her that KC was easily within shooting range. Never taking her eyes off KC, Jess smiled to herself. She had seen hundreds of scouting videos of KC and was fairly certain what her next move would be. KC took two quick steps toward Jess, followed by two quick steps away from her, and planted her foot to shoot. As the ball rose into the air toward the basket, Jess leaped into the air and hit it with her fingertips, deflecting it away from its target.

KC laughed as Jess retrieved the ball. "Wish I could get the kids to do that. They can't stop starin' at the fuckin' ball long enough to watch their opponent's eyes."

Jess glanced at the clock as she bounced the ball back to center court. Now she wondered whether she could elude KC, who had once been known as the best defensive player anywhere. Jess decided to try her favorite play, hoping she could still manage the moves to pull it off.

Jess leaned forward, dribbled the ball, stopped and looked to her left. KC was in her usual defensive stance, almost daring Jess to try to get through her. Jess began to her left three or four fast steps, planted her left foot and switched directions to her right. Running full speed, knowing that KC was close to her, Jess made it into the lane. KC was waiting to block her shot to the right, allowing Jess to change to ball to her left hand and shoot behind KC's raised hands. The ball bounced twice on the rim before it finally fell through the basket.

Breathing hard, KC said, "That was a fuckin' great move, Jess."

"Thanks. You better get out of here now."

"We'll have to try that again sometime."

"You'd never have fallen for that if you'd watched any old scouting films," Jess admitted with a smile. "Haven't done that in about twenty years."

"You shoulda stayed in the game, kid," KC said, taking a deep breath.

"I'm happy doing what I'm doing, KC. Now scram!" Jess ordered.

KC nodded and strolled toward the back door of the gym. "I'll give you a call this evenin' to see how practice is goin', if that's okay."

"I'll keep you up with how they're doing," Jess said.

"Bring over the tape of last week's game and we can go over it," KC said, "if you want. Friday's game should be a walkover, but the girls have a tendency to get lazy if the other team isn't very challengin'."

"I'll get with you tomorrow evening," Jess said. "We can look at the scouting tape for Friday's game."

"Good deal. See you later, Jess," KC smiled.

# Chapter Seven

FROM THE FIRST day of practice, Jessie found that she enjoyed working with the basketball team. At first most of the girls, except for Jamie, were a little shy around her. There were two or three who simply regarded her as they would any other substitute teacher, deciding they only had to go through the motions and kill time. Jess divided them into two teams for a practice scrimmage.

"That's not the way Coach Carnes divides us up," one of the girls complained.

"Do I look like Coach Carnes to you?" Jess retorted.

"We always put all the starters on one team and the rest play the opposing team."

"Well, not today. Today you do what I tell you or you can find your way to the showers. I don't know who's a starter and who's not, so move on," Jess instructed.

There was some minor mumbling and grumbling as the players organized into their assigned teams. It was obvious to Jess that Ali O'Neil was a very good player, but she didn't seem to have any form of killer instinct in her play. Half way through the scrimmage, Jess stopped them and took Ali aside.

"What are you doing Ali?"

"What do you mean?" the girl answered.

"I mean my grandmother can play with more intensity than you're showing me," Jess said.

"Well, I..."

"You what? You think this is just a scrimmage? You think you're so good that you don't have to give it one hundred percent every minute? What?" Jess demanded.

"No, ma'am. I just thought that until Coach Carnes came back..."

"Until Coach Carnes does come back, *I* am your coach. And I want to see you mow down anyone out there who gets in your way. Understand?"

"Yes, ma'am," Ali answered as she turned to rejoin her squad.

Before they began, Jess walked onto the court and pointed at a player, "What's your name again, number four?" she asked.

"Sara," the girl answered.

"Okay, Sara, you sit this one out. I'll play your position for a few minutes," Jess said.

The girl shrugged and plopped down on a folding chair. Jess had the remaining four girls join her. "Jamie, you and I are going to double team Ali this play. Trap her in the corner. Coach Carnes told me she has a problem getting rid of the ball when she's trapped. Okay?"

"Sure," Jamie said.

As the play unfolded, Jamie and Jess pressed Ali near the out-of-bounds line and waved their hands in her face as she desperately tried to pass the ball. Ali tried to bounce pass the ball to another player, but had it intercepted by Jamie, who ran it under the basket for an easy lay-up.

"Okay," Jess said. "Everyone take a break. Ali with me."

Ali brought a water bottle with her as she trotted over to Jess.

"Coach Carnes told me you had a problem with being trapped and turning the ball over," Jess said.

"Sometimes," Ali said as she squirted water into her mouth.

"You can bet that will show up on any scouting reports for your opponents. We have to find a way to either prevent you from being trapped or a way for you to unload the ball more successfully or both. Got any suggestions?"

Ali shrugged. "You're the coach."

"Do you have a problem with that?"

"Nope." Ali seemed distracted.

Jess snapped her fingers in Ali's face. "Look at me."

"Okay...coach," Ali said with a lop-sided grin. The twinge of familiarity struck Jess again.

"Coach Carnes gave me a couple of plays that might work for you and I have a couple of ideas myself, so after this break we'll try them to see what happens. Okay?"

"Okay," Ali said with a hint of a smile.

"Double teaming always happens to good players, Ali, but you can't let it rattle you. Consider it a compliment from the other team because it's a sign that you worry them. It also means that they're leaving one of your teammates uncovered to deal with you. You have to be willing to give the ball up. And maybe sooner than you want to. Just remember, only the final score counts," Jess smiled. "If the team looks good, so will you."

Ali nodded and loped back to where the rest of the team was sitting, plopping down into a chair next to Jamie.

The team ran a series of plays, some successful and some not. Jess fiddled with the starting roster of players to get a feel for who could do what. As she watched the girls run through their scrimmage, she noticed that Jamie was open more often than not and she had proven herself to be a decent shooter from a medium range. Jess made a mental note to take some game tapes to Irene's that evening and watch them.

ON THE WAY back to Austin, Harriett made a sudden decision. She interrupted whatever Nick was talking about and punched the button to connect her cell phone with the Bluetooth in her truck. "Call Karen Linders," she instructed. A few seconds later, her call was picked up.

"Capitol Realty," Harriett heard a familiar voice greet her.

"Hi, Karen," Harriett responded. "How's the real estate market doing these days?"

"Hey, Harriett! Not bad. It's a seller's market at the moment. You buying or selling?"

"Selling actually."

"A couple of very large companies have moved to Austin recently and there's a rumor that a national investment firm is considering moving their headquarters here after the first of the year and bringing nearly a thousand employees with them from the frozen north."

"I want to put my townhouse on the market as soon as possible, Karen."

"Not a problem. I think I can get it on the next listing coming out early next week. I'll need a key to get our photographer in for a few pictures."

"I'm on my way back to Austin now and will drop one off for you when I get there in about an hour or so. Will that work for you?"

"Perfect, girlfriend. I thought you were going to hang onto that place until you croaked."

Harriett laughed. "I suddenly realized I was being stubborn about letting it go. It was kind of a security blanket, but I don't need one anymore."

"Damn! Don't need a place to hide, huh?" Karen laughed.

"I'm through hiding," Harriett said, glancing at Nick.

"I'm happy for you, hon, and will have the paperwork ready for your signature by the time you get here."

"I'll need a while to get my personal things out though before we close."

"Not a problem. I'll take care of it," Karen said before

hanging up.

"It's about time," Nick said. "I wondered what you were waiting for. You practically live at Jess's now anyway."

"Well, the market hasn't been too good recently. I didn't want to lose too much when I decided to sell it."

"Did you think maybe things with Jess wouldn't work out?"

"Maybe," Harriett admitted. "I *am* living in another woman's house, you know. And Jess isn't ready to break her connection with it yet. Maybe one day she will and we can find a place of our own."

THAT EVENING HARRIETT curled up on the couch in Jess's living room and dialed a familiar number on her cell phone. While the number rang, she glanced around the comfortable room, her eyes pausing on the picture of Jess and Renee on the mantle over the fireplace. Harriett wanted to make this house her own, but wasn't quite sure how to evict Renee yet. In the end, that would have to be Jess's idea, as it should be.

"Hello," a voice finally answered.

"Helen?" Harriett said. "I apologize for calling so late. Am I disturbing your dinner?"

"Not unless you consider reheated Chinese take-out dinner," Helen Mortensen, Harriett's therapist quipped. "How are you?"

"I'm good, at the moment, but there's a potential problem in the near future that I'm not sure how the handle," Harriett said. "I'm out of town for a case but had to come back to Austin for two or three days. I was wondering if you might be able to work me in, tomorrow if possible."

"I'm sure I can, dear. Why don't you come by about twelve-thirty and we can share soup and a sandwich?"

"I appreciate it, Helen. I'll see you tomorrow."

A LITTLE BEFORE twelve-thirty the following day, Harriett rang the doorbell of the graceful two-story home of Drs. Erik and Helen Mortensen, not far from the UT main campus. She loved the large, covered porch which supported a wide second floor balcony. The grounds were enclosed by an ornate wrought-iron fence embedded in brick columns. The trees had been recently pruned back in anticipation of winter. A tall, distinguished-looking man in his mid-sixties, holding a book in his left hand, opened the front door and smiled when he saw Harriett. Erik

Mortensen was a professor of agricultural economics at the university and a quiet man. Harriett stepped inside and embraced him fondly. "It's good to see you again, Erik," she said.

"Helen's in the kitchen," he said in a slightly accented Scandinavian voice. "You know the way, yes."

"I can follow my nose," Harriett said with a smile. "Are you joining us?"

"No, no. Helen told me you would be discussing women's business today," Erik said with a grin.

Harriett made her way down a richly paneled hall. Her eyes were drawn to family pictures interwoven with art Helen and Erik had collected while on their numerous trips. Helen was fond of indigenous art she'd found on virtually every continent. She walked into the large, well-stocked kitchen and inhaled the fragrant odors. Helen stirred a huge pot, stopping occasionally to flip a sandwich that sizzled on a small copper skillet.

"You look like my mother," Harriett chuckled. "She's a multi-tasking cook, too."

"Then perhaps we will meet one day," Helen said as she removed a sandwich from the skillet and slid it onto a small china plate. After putting a second sandwich on another plate, she turned off the eyes on her stove and scooped ladles of soup into matching bowls. "Your timing is perfect. Please have a seat." Once Harriett was seated, Helen used a hand to sprinkle cheese and chopped bacon over the soup. She leaned down and kissed Harriett on the temple. "How are you today? It's so good to see you again. How long has it been?"

"Three or four months, I think," Harriett answered. "This smells delicious."

"The soup is my favorite...potato and will last us for several meals. I sliced Gouda for the sandwiches. It goes well with the soup. How is Jess?"

Harriett smiled around her soup spoon. "She's fine...we're fine. Jess has been wonderfully patient with me."

"I'm glad to hear that. For both of you." Helen dabbed at her mouth with a napkin. "Then why did you need to see me?"

"I've taken a new case involving an old friend in my home town. It's not a particularly difficult case, but...how much have I told you about my family?"

"I don't know that they've ever come up in our previous meetings," Helen said. "Although you may have mentioned a brother the first time we met years ago."

"Yes, Jerry. He is...was Lacey's father. He named me as her

guardian if anything happened to him and his wife," Harriett explained as she took a small bite of her sandwich. "They were killed when Lacey was about five."

"How is Lacey?"

"In college now and doing well."

"Then apparently whatever is bothering you isn't Lacey," Helen said.

"Only peripherally," Harriett said. "As I said, the case I'm working on is in my hometown. I have a younger sister who also lives there. Lorraine. We don't get along very well. Haven't for years, really. I'm sure I'll run into her while I'm in Anson and need help in order to deal with her."

"Why don't you get along? What caused the rift between you?"

"The only thing I can think of is when she sued me for custody of Lacey, but Lorri was distant and stand-offish toward me even when we were in high school. I never knew why. My sexual orientation became an issue in the custody case and Lorri was quite...rabid about it. It was difficult for Lacey. But I've never tried to prevent Lacey from seeing her aunt. It wouldn't feel right keeping her away from her father's family. She should know her family, even the less tolerant ones."

"What about her mother's family?"

"Bonnie was an only child and her parents passed away not long after she and Jerry were married."

"Do you love your sister?"

"Of course, I do!" Harriett insisted. "She's my sister. I'm supposed to, aren't I?"

"Yet you don't really want to see her, do you?"

"No, I don't and I know I shouldn't feel that way. I don't want to hurt my mother either."

"Isn't she aware of the strained relationship between you and your sister?"

"I'm sure she is, but I don't want to aggravate it. When Lorri finds out Jess is there with me, staying under Mom's roof, I'm not sure what she'll do. And before you say it, we offered to stay somewhere else, but Mom wouldn't hear of it. I don't want to cause a problem between Lorri and my mother."

"Well, it sounds to me like you're not the one causing a problem. Your sister is. Maybe your mother and sister need to hash it out."

"Then what am I supposed to do?"

"Nothing. You can't solve everyone's problem, Harriett, no

matter how much you wish you could. Just do what you can."

Harriett shrugged. "I'm probably worrying about nothing anyway," she said. "Jess says I have a tendency to overthink things."

"She might be right, but considering how you make your living, that's not necessarily a bad thing. Remember, you can always call if you run into a problem," Helen said, patting Harriett's hand. "Just try not to let the problem with your sister create problems with others who are close to you," she warned. "How are you and Jess doing working together?"

"We're fine so far. Why? Is there something I need to know?"

"You know, since Jess was once my client, I'm not at liberty to talk about anything we discussed other than generally," Helen said.

Harriett sat back in her chair and looked at Helen. "I know you helped her deal with her grief after Renee died," she said.

"Yes," Helen nodded. "How are you dealing with Renee's death?"

"Me? I never met her," Harriett said, a surprised look on her face.

"But what do you *know* about her?"

"Well...I know Jess loved her."

"Does she miss her?"

"Of course, she does!"

"How do you feel about that?"

"I don't know," Harriett said. "It's hard to be angry with a woman who's dead."

"Are you angry?"

"Occasionally," Harriett admitted. "But I don't really know why."

"Of course you do," Helen said with a soft smile. "Perhaps you don't want to admit it and have to deal with those feelings yet. Until you do, they will always be an invisible barrier between you and Jess."

Harriett could feel her anger growing but didn't want to lose control of her temper.

"Have you told Jess how you feel about living in another woman's house yet?"

"No," Harriett answered through clenched teeth.

"Don't you think you should?"

Harriett shook her head. "The risk is too high," she muttered so softly that Helen was forced to lean closer to hear what Harriett said.

"What risk?"

Finally, Harriett snapped. "I could lose Jess, okay? Every time we make love, I feel like Renee is in the room, watching us. Her picture with Jess is on the mantle for Christ's sake, for me to see every fucking time I walk into or leave *her* house. I hate feeling that way. I hate knowing Jess loved her. Does she still love Renee more than she claims to love me? I'm jealous of a fucking ghost! Is that what you wanted to hear?"

"Have you ever lost your temper with Jess?" Helen asked calmly.

"Not since the...th...thing with...Wilkes. Then look what happened. Jess disappeared for weeks before I saw her. I don't want that to happen again. I don't think I could stand that, Helen."

"I think that might have been Jess wrestling with her own guilt over what happened to you rather than her feelings for Renee," Helen said. "I always had the feeling that she was hiding something from me when I counseled her, but I wasn't able to convince her to trust me enough to deal with it back then. She loves you more than you think, so perhaps one day she'll open up and let you in."

"I need to go, Helen. I have some things I have to get done before returning to Anson," Harriett said. She knew her feelings about Renee were irrational, but it felt good to verbalize them.

# Chapter Eight

KC DIALED A number from memory for the third time that morning. Pick up, she thought. Please pick up! She waited until the familiar voice on the other end told her to leave a message and then hung up. She never left a message, but even hearing the soft recorded voice was better than nothing and aroused her. It had been two weeks since they had spoken. Once it had been a daily conversation and now she craved those conversations as if they were an addiction. She laughed out loud as she made her way back to her bedroom to change. No one would ever believe that Kerrie Carnes, the great KC, had been driven to the precipice of begging.

Diane had driven off to work two hours earlier, promising to be home before five. There was no track practice scheduled that afternoon. They could fix dinner together and watch one of the new DVDs they bought before this whole mess began. Forced to remain home day after day was beginning to wear thin. Very thin. KC pulled a clean white T-shirt over her head and slipped into her favorite pair of workout sweats. Resting a foot on the edge of the dresser, she tied the first tennis shoe and had lifted her leg to tie the second when the cell in her pocket vibrated.

Quickly pulling the cell from her pocket she flipped it open and recognized the number. "Hi, baby."

"Kerrie?"

Backing up to sit on the edge of the bed, KC rubbed her forehead. "How are you, sweetie? I've been trying to reach you all morning."

"It's only ten," the woman on the other end of the line said in a soft, Southern drawl.

"I need to see you."

"I'm not sure that's a good idea right now, Kerrie. I'm frightened."

"Please meet me. Just to talk."

"I have to be home before school is out to pick Brett up."

"You will be. I promise."

"An hour?"

"I'll be waiting."

KC flopped back on the bed and stared at the slowly turning ceiling fan. What had she been thinking? She knew better. She had done some pretty stupid things in her life, but nothing as bad as this. She hadn't planned to fall in love. And certainly not with a married woman. Even knowing they could never be together, the pull of her desire had proven stronger than her common sense.

Rolling off the bed she pulled her T-shirt and warm-ups off and slipped into something better, her best navy-blue Dockers and a blue-and-yellow plaid Chaps shirt. Finishing off her outfit with a pair of cordovan loafers, she grabbed her keys and left the house within minutes.

KC PACED THE carpeted floor of the room at the Holiday Inn Express on the main highway from Abilene to Dallas. It was always the same room, on the first floor in the rear of the motel where their vehicles wouldn't be seen. She checked in twenty minutes early, stopping to get ice and soft drinks before going to the room. Her mouth was dry and she wasn't sure where their conversation would lead them. This could be the last time they met and the thought filled her with sorrow.

The sound of a car engine being turned off in the parking area outside the room made her heart race. She went quickly to the window and looked through a crack in the room's drapes. Reaching over to the door, she turned the knob and watched the raven-haired woman step into the room. As soon as the door closed, KC took the woman into her arms and held her.

"I'm so sorry, Peg," she whispered. "Are you all right? I know this has been a nightmare for you and the kids, but I swear to God I didn't kill him."

"I know you didn't, darling. I should be devastated because Allen is dead, but I can't remember the last time I felt this free." Peggy DeVore said as she buried her face against KC's shoulder.

"When this is over I won't be able to remain in Anson even if the jury finds me innocent. But I know I won't be able to stay away from you either."

Peg turned and walked to the window of the room and crossed her arms over her chest. "I never dreamed I would fall in love with you. But I did and the thought of not being with you is unthinkable. What are we going to do, Kerrie?"

"I'll find a place for us somewhere, honey. Then I'll send for you after Brett is grown."

"Eight years? I can't ask you to wait that long. You should forget me and find someone who can make you happy without compromising who you are. To be with me you've already been forced to sneak around, hide, and lie. That's not who you are."

"I'll do whatever I have to to be with you."

"What about Diane?"

"Our relationship was over long before I met you, baby." KC walked up behind Peg. "I'm goin' to tell her I'm leavin' Anson after the trial."

"I need you so much, Kerrie," Peg said as tears ran down her cheeks.

Taking Peggy's face in her hands, KC brushed the tears away with her thumbs. "I'll find a way. I love you so much, baby," she said, her lips trembling as she drew Peg closer until they met in a desperate kiss.

CARRYING A STYROFOAM cup of convenience store coffee, Jess stepped out of the Durango in the parking lot of the Anson field house around eleven the next morning. The building looked deserted. Pulling open the main door, Jess could hear the distinctive clanking sounds of weights. Following the sounds, she unzipped her jacket as she saw open double doors at the end of a hallway. She leaned against the door casing to watch three or four men lifting weights and working out on various pieces of equipment. It was a few minutes before anyone noticed Jess's presence. Setting his weights down, one of the men wiped perspiration from his face with a white hand towel and looked at her.

"Help you, ma'am?"

Pushing away from the door frame, Jess smiled, "Maybe. Is this weight room available for any high school athletes?"

"Pretty much."

"I'm subbing for Coach Carnes. Do any members of the girls' basketball team ever come down here for a little weight training?"

"Sure. A couple do, but mostly on Saturday mornings when the guys aren't here." He smiled as he stood up, showing off well-developed chest and arm muscles.

"I didn't catch your name," Jess said.

"Sorry. Glenn Freeman. So how's KC doin'?"

"Okay, I guess." Jess smiled as she looked around. "Would you mind if I asked a few questions about Coach DeVore's death? I'm really curious."

Freeman wrapped his towel around his neck and seemed to

think before answering. "I don't know anything about that."

"Wasn't he a friend of yours?"

"He was my boss," Freeman answered with a shrug. "Between you and me, he was probably on his way out anyway."

"Why's that?"

"You can't have two or three losing seasons and expect to stay anywhere very long."

"You think Coach Carnes killed him?"

"DeVore was trying to get her fired for violating the morals clause of her contract. Told me he saw her with another woman at some bar in Abilene over the summer and was gonna fix her wagon but good."

"Anyone else with him when he claimed he saw her?"

"Naw. I think he was lyin' anyway," Freeman chuckled. "A jock like DeVore wouldn't be caught dead in a gay bar. Like who's gonna believe he was there just lookin' for KC? Coulda sunk his own boat with that one. Know what I mean?"

"Yeah," Jess said as she took a drink from her Styrofoam cup.

"Ah, hell, everyone knows KC's a dyke, but she's a damn good coach. She takes some ribbin' but is pretty good natured about it. She don't bother nobody and does her job. Had a lot better record than DeVore. Probably doing better in the lady department, too."

"Wasn't he married?"

"More or less. Wife's a nice lady and deserved to be treated better than he treated her."

"I've heard a rumor he might have been involved with a teacher on your faculty. Any truth to the rumor?"

"Hang on a minute," Freeman said as he stepped into the hallway. "Hey Jackson! Come're a minute, will ya?"

A minute or so later a large, muscular man with deep ebony skin and wearing only shorts sauntered into the training room. "What's up, Freeman?"

"This is Marcus Jackson, our defensive coach." Pointing at Jess, he said, "This lady's subbin' for KC. Tell her what you saw in the coaches' office back in September."

"I don't think that's something I should be repeating, man," the man mumbled.

"Well, it ain't gonna hurt his reputation now," Freeman said.

"I don't want to get anyone in trouble," Jackson said.

"Come on, man. You didn't like the guy any more than the rest of us," Freeman snorted.

Looking around sheepishly, Jackson exhaled loudly. "A

couple of months ago, I needed some paperwork from the coaches' office. We all use it, but not all the time or anything. The main door was unlocked so I went in and opened the file cabinet to grab the form I needed. Then I heard a noise coming from the inner office."

"It's like a break room type thing," Freeman offered. "Got a coffeemaker, microwave, and a fridge." A slow grin crossed his lips. "And a pretty comfy couch."

Frowning at Freeman, Jackson continued. "Anyway, I figured it was just a couple of the other coaches and stuck my head in to say hello." A blush rose up the big man's neck as he recalled the incident.

"And it wasn't who you thought it was?" Jess asked.

"Well, it *was* Coach Devore. Had his pants down around his ankles and there was a woman under him on that damn couch with her legs all wrapped around him." Jackson frowned and shook his head as if trying to dislodge the memory.

"Did they see you?"

"I don't think so. DeVore never said anything to me about it. I just pulled the door closed and beat it out of there. I only caught a glimpse before I split. I couldn't see much and didn't want to, but I'm pretty sure the woman was a blonde. That shit just shouldn't be happening here, know what I mean? What if I had been some kid and walked in on that?"

"Well, I better get goin'," Jess said. "Thanks for helpin' me sign the team up."

"No problem," Freeman said. "Tell KC good luck if you see her."

BY THE TIME Jess was ready to leave to set up everything for Friday night's game, Harriett had called on her cell phone to wish her luck in her first game as a coach. An unexpected problem with a motion she filed with the Travis County court would probably delay her return to Anson until Saturday afternoon. She would rewrite the motion and have Nick file it for her the following Monday. Jess didn't know whether she was disappointed or relieved that Harriett wouldn't make the game. She felt stressed enough as it was without looking like a failure in front of the person she cared most about in the world.

Jess was surprised when Irene walked into the living room carrying her purse and wearing a bright red Lady Tiger sweatshirt.

"You're going to the game?" Jess asked, suddenly feeling slightly on edge.

"I try to go to as many of Jamie's games as I can. Moral support," Irene answered. "Lorri and JD will pick me up in a little while."

"Well, I might be the one who needs moral support tonight," Jess chuckled. "I've played in hundreds of games but never had to call the shots and decide who does what."

"You'll do fine, dear," Irene smiled.

Jess had forgotten that in small town Texas, everyone turned out for local games, boys or girls, mostly for lack of anything else to do. The stands in the Anson High gym filled quickly as proud parents watched the junior varsity game, awaiting the big show. Jess wondered how many were there to check out how good a job she'd done as a temporary coach. Well, she had a few surprises for them tonight and, probably, there would be more than one or two upset parents by the end of the evening. She could deal with KC ranting and raving after she saw the films of the game, but that would be later. During the game was a different matter.

After watching a scouting tape, Jess thought Anson's opponent was, at best, an average team without much height but had apparently been well drilled on the basics of the game. The game should be a walkover for Anson. She was glad she wouldn't be coaching against a more challenging team for her first game.

The JV girls handled their opponent without difficulty and Jess worried that the varsity players who came early to watch the game would begin to think lightly of the other team once their game started. As the two teams ran through their pre-game warm-ups, Jess fiddled with her starting line-up. What she planned to do was risky, but, if it worked, would be worthwhile. Strolling to the scorekeeper's table, she handed them a copy of her line-up. Shaking hands with the opposing coach, she returned to the home team seats.

Jess squatted down in front of her players, glancing into the stands. She spotted Irene immediately and smiled. Irene was seated next to Lorri and a pleasant-looking man Jess assumed was her husband. He was busy adjusting the focus on his camcorder without actually paying attention to what was happening on the floor.

"Okay, ladies," Jess said. "Remember what I've been telling you. Pass the ball off to the player with the best chance of making the shot, never take your eyes off your opponent, and press them as close as you can."

The girls all nodded dully like this was the millionth time they had heard the same thing.

"The starters will be Lucero, Costa, Gaither, Patterson, and Jenkins."

"Uh, Coach...," Lucero started.

"Do you have a problem with my line-up?" Jess asked with a frown.

"Well, no, Coach," said Jamie, "but usually Ali starts."

"I know that, Jamie. What's your point?" Jess smiled.

"Well, nothing, I guess," Jamie shrugged.

"Coach Carnes told me that every player plays every game."

"Yeah," Costa smirked. "After she knows we're so far ahead that no one can screw it up."

"Then tonight, don't screw it up from the beginning. Ready?"

As the girls trotted onto the court, Jess could hear a different sounding buzz ripple through the stands but chose to ignore it and stay with her game plan.

By halfway through the first half, Anson was down by twelve points and had made too many mistakes and given up too many turnovers. Jess called for a time out and the girls returned to their chairs.

"What's the matter, ladies?" Jess asked. "Competition too tough for you?"

"They're killing us, Coach," Jamie said between gulps of water.

"You're letting them. Why is that, Gaither?"

"We're taking too many chances and doing stupid things."

"Patience is a virtue, ladies. Okay, Jamie, the girl who's guarding you is staying pretty close to you."

"No kiddin'!" Jamie said. "If she got any closer we'd be sharing a uniform."

"I think it's time we took her out of the game," Jess said. "Here's what I want you to do, Jamie. When the ball comes to you, I want you to haul ass down the court, running like your butt's on fire. Okay?"

"Yeah," Jamie said with a questioning look on her face.

"Then, and this is the really hard part, Jamie," Jess said, "when you can feel her as close as you think she's going to get to you, I want you to stop."

"Stop?"

"Just slam on the brakes."

"She'll run over me, Coach," Jamie protested.

"Can you take a hit or two?"

"Well, yeah, I guess so, but what's the point?"

"Y'all need to foul her out. Without her, they don't have much left in the way of fire power. Get it?"

Jamie laughed. "Is that even legal?"

"Worked for me all the time," Jess said with a grin. "And if they switch her off Jamie, whoever she guards next, needs to do the same thing. Understand? Either she'll foul out or become so paranoid about committing another foul that you'll neutralize her anyway."

The opposing player guarding Jamie had committed three personal fouls before her coach tumbled to what was happening. Without the pressure on her, Jamie brought her team to within six points by the half and Jess was beginning to feel like her plan might work after all.

When the teams returned to the floor, Jess took Patterson and Jenkins out of the game and, finally, put Ali O'Neill into the line-up

"Remember, move quickly, pass like you mean it and get the ball to the player with the best chance of shooting the basket — no matter who it is. Lucero, they haven't been guarding you very closely, so look for the ball and get to a place where they can get it to you."

As the team broke to resume the game, Jess sat down on a folding chair and leaned her elbows on her knees.

The second half of the game was a blowout for Anson. Even though Ali only played a half game, she had one of her best evenings shooting. Remarkably, Ali, Lucero and Jamie remembered what to do if Ali was double-teamed. The result was that Lucero and Jamie had their best game of the season, scoring-wise.

While the two teams shook hands at the end of the game, Jess started picking up equipment and folding chairs. Unlike larger schools and colleges, there was no floor crew to take care of those minor details. When the girls rejoined Jess, she said, "Y'all did a great job tonight. I'm proud of you because I know it's not the way you're used to playing, but it worked. Anyone have any questions or comments?"

The girls looked at each other, but no one said anything.

"Well, think about it over the weekend and if you noticed anything you think we should work on let me know at Monday's practice. Hit the showers and congratulations!"

As the girls jogged off to the locker room, Jess returned to her cleanup.

"Nice work, Coach," Irene said with a smile.

"Thanks," Jess said. "KC will have a coronary when she sees the tape of the game though."

"You won. And as far as I know, that's all that counts in the end."

Moments later Jess and Irene were joined by Lorri, the man with the camcorder, and a younger girl.

"Interesting game, Coach," he said as he extended his hand. "JD Gaither."

"Mr. Gaither," Jess said as she took his hand.

"Jamie says you used to play college ball," he said.

"A very long time ago," Jess laughed.

"Well, I'm not really sure what you were doing tonight, but I know Jamie appreciated it," Lorri said with a smile. "She doesn't usually play for a whole game."

"She's got enough stamina and she's a reliable point guard," Jess said.

"Do you think she'll have many bruises?" Irene asked. "That big old girl from the other team ran right over her a few times."

"That was the idea," Jess laughed. "We needed to get rid of that player."

"Will that be a continuing play then?" JD asked.

"Hopefully other teams will catch wind of it and not stay as close to Jamie, which will, in turn, allow her to be open for more shots."

"Oh, well," JD shrugged with a chuckle, "my insurance is paid up."

# Chapter Nine

"WANNA GRAB A pizza or something?" Jamie asked as she stuffed her uniform into a duffle bag.

"Sure, but I'll have to ask my dad first," Ali answered, running a brush through her short, still damp hair.

"Tell him it's my treat. I'll drive you home."

"Good game tonight," Ali said. "Maybe we can tell coach we need to work on our long passes a little more," she suggested. "I was open down the court a few times tonight."

"Remember to ask her about it next week. You about ready?" Jamie said, slinging her duffle bag over her shoulder.

Fifteen minutes later, Jamie slid into the driver's seat of her truck and turned the key in the ignition, waiting for Ali to join her. She smiled when the passenger door opened and Ali hopped in. "Everything okay?" she asked, resting her hand on Ali's thigh.

"Yeah. Have to be home by midnight," Ali said with a smile as she covered Jamie's hand with her own.

"That works for me, babe," Jamie said as she shifted into drive and pulled out of the school parking lot. "I was thinkin' we might pick up the pizza and sneak it into the Town and Country over in Abilene," she said with a grin.

Jamie turned into the entrance of the drive-in after dark and joined the line of cars waiting to get into the outdoor theater. She worked a hand into her jean pocket and pulled out a ten-dollar bill. When they reached the window on the side of the brightly lit concession stand, she lowered her truck window and handed the bill to the ticket taker, waiting for her two dollars in change. Then she raised the window and drove slowly over the humps which separated the rows of cars. The first feature had already started when she located a place away from other vehicles and pulled in. Lowering her window again, she took the speaker from the pole next to her and hooked it over her window and adjusted the volume.

"Wanna get something to drink to go with our pizza?" she asked.

"Sure," Ali answered, licking her lips.

"You look really nervous. Why?" Jamie asked. Then she smiled. "Afraid I'll bite ya or somethin'?"

"No, but –" Ali started.

"But what?"

"Doesn't it bother you to lie to your parents?"

"I didn't lie, Ali. I told my mom you and I were going to a movie at this drive-in. I didn't volunteer that we might miss significant portions of the movie, but she didn't ask either." Jamie slid her hand across the bench seat and took Ali's hand, running her thumb over Ali's knuckles. "Now, why don't we get our drinks before it gets any darker and our pizza gets cold. Please try not to look so damn guilty. No one here will know who we are, okay?"

Ten minutes later, the two girls opened the doors of the truck, each carrying a large plastic soda cup. Ali reached into the storage area behind the front seat and pulled out a heat-retaining bag which held their large pizza. She stuck her hand into the bag and hummed happily. "Still warm," she said. "It was genius when you bought this bag."

She pulled the pizza box from the insulated bag and flipped it open before placing it on the seat between them. Jamie grabbed a slice and began devouring the pepperoni and mushroom hungrily. "I'm starving," she mumbled around a mouthful of pizza. "God, this tastes so good!"

Ali sucked in a gulp of soda to wash down her first slice before picking up a second one. "We make pizza at home sometimes, but it never tastes as good as this," she said. "Must be a secret recipe or something."

The girls settled into their seats and proceeded to make their way through the remaining pizza. When they finished, Ali dumped the empty box into the back as Jamie scooted from beneath the steering wheel to snuggle against Ali's side. Jamie rested her hand on Ali's thigh and sighed contentedly.

"I've been waiting for this all week," Jamie said.

"Sure you're not too sore?" Ali asked as she dropped her arm around Jamie's shoulder and hugged her lightly. "You took quite a beating during the game tonight."

Jamie set her drink into a cup holder and slid her hand over Ali's waist, pinching her. "Yeah, I'm fine. At least I won't have to explain any bruises if you get carried away," she laughed.

"I'll be careful," Ali said. "I'd never want to hurt you, but sometimes you —," she started before the warmth of Jamie's lips on her throat stopped her. Ali brought her hand up to press it against Jamie head. "Jeez, I love that, Jamers."

"I know you do," Jamie breathed. "Sometimes I what?" Jamie asked as she worked her hand under Ali's T-shirt and inched it up to knead Ali's small, firm breast. "Huh?" she teased.

"Y…you drive me…crazy," Ali gasped, arching her back and pushing into Jamie's hand. She ran her fingers into Jamie's hair and, ignoring the feel of Jamie's hand, forced herself to lean down far enough to reach Jamie's mouth. She took it firmly, yet possessively, waiting for Jamie's lips to part slightly to allow her entrance. The moment her tongue entered Jamie's mouth, Ali slipped her hand into the heat between Jamie's thighs. "Please, Jamers," Ali begged as her lips moved to Jamie's neck.

"I…I…oh, God…Ali…I love it when you touch me so much," Jamie panted, moving against the hand pressing into her crotch. "Pleease, sweetie!"

"I love touching you," Ali said.

"You always do me first," Jamie groaned. "It's not fair."

"Do you really…want to…argue about this now?" Ali grunted. "Why does it matter?"

"Because…I like making you feel this way, too," Jamie said. "Oh, that feels…so good, baby."

"I like watching you when you get excited. I like knowing that I can make you feel that way."

Jamie reclined on the truck seat and pulled Ali on top of her. Ali pushed Jamie's T-shirt and sports bra up, and encircled Jamie's nipple, sucking it into her mouth.

"Jesus!" Jamie jumped.

"Did I hurt you?" Ali asked with a worried look on her face.

"Hell, no," Jamie answered with a smile. She stroked Ali's cheek. "It only startled me, but in a really good way."

Jamie pressed against Ali's hand again until she found the spot that excited her the most. Within a few strokes, she tightened her fingers and buried her face in Ali's neck. Every nerve in her body seemed to coil tightly before her head flew back against the seat and her body exploded. Warmth flowed onto her underwear and jeans. "Oh, God, Ali," she moaned.

Ali kissed her softly, taking Jamie's head in her hands. "I love you, Jamers," she whispered.


HARRIETT SMILED AS she pulled into the drive of Irene's house well after midnight. Jess was probably sound asleep. Harriett lifted her suitcase from behind the truck seat and lugged it quietly into her mother's home. She removed her parka and hung it on the hall tree before tip-toeing across the entry and up the staircase to her second-floor bedroom.

Jess snored softly as Harriett stripped out of her clothes and moved to the far side of the bed. She lifted the bedcovers and slid beneath them, sighing at the softness of the mattress. She couldn't wait to feel her body engulfed by Jess's strong arms again. She had only been gone three days, but it seemed like an eternity.

She rolled onto her left side and ran her hand over Jess's waist, reveling in the familiar feel of her lover's skin. Jess rolled over, burying her face against Harriett's neck as she ran a hand up her back.

"If this is a dream, please don't wake me up. God, you smell so good," Jess murmured as she pressed her body closer to Harriett's. "I need you," she added, meeting Harriett's lips in a tender kiss.

Harriett pressed a hand against the back of Jess's head and drew her into a deeper, more demanding kiss as she worked Jess's thigh between her legs. "Show me how much, baby," Harriett whispered while she began nipping at Jess's neck and running her hands over her body.

Jess's breathing hitched. Her hands slid over Harriett's hips and traveled over the smoothness of Harriett's skin to cup her firm buttocks. "Mine," Jess whispered as she squeezed the skin beneath her fingers.

Harriett groaned, burying her fingers in Jess's hair. "I've been dreaming about the feel of your hands on me all the way here."

Jess kissed Harriett again, slowly deepening the kiss. "Welcome home," she said, her voice rough with desire when they ended the kiss to breathe. "I've missed you," Jess growled before taking Harriett's breast into her mouth and humming her satisfaction. She sucked and licked and teased the sensitive nipple while she captured Harriett's other nipple between her fingers and flicked it with her thumb.

Harriett's hips began rising and undulating against Jess's thigh. "Please, Jess," she breathed, pressing her crotch harder against her. Jess moaned and moved her mouth to cover Harriett's as their bodies moved in unison. Jess had never known Harriett to be quite so assertive, but she wasn't prepared to question it at that moment. She was too busy trying not to lose her mind from the sensuous assault of Harriett's mouth and hands, which seemed to be everywhere, finding every erogenous area of her body. Harriett raked her fingernails along Jess's sides before dipping them between Jess's legs and into the wetness pooling between Jess's legs. Harriett rubbed the pads of her fingers over Jess's clit causing Jess to groan and buck at the sensation. "God," she managed. "You're killin' me, woman."

"You'll live," Harriett said as her mouth joined her hand between Jess's legs.


LATER HARRIETT AND Jess lay entwined in one another's arms, thoroughly sated.

"I'm glad it wasn't a dream. I needed you," Jess rasped out.

"I'll never get enough of you," Harriett sighed contentedly. She squeezed Jess lightly and raised her head to drop a kiss on her abdomen.

"I can live with that," Jess said with a smile, combing her fingers through Harriett's hair.

"Mmm, me too." Harriett couldn't remember a time when she'd been so happy. She looked up at Jess. "Did you win tonight? Or was it last night?" she asked, biting Jess's chin lightly.

"We did," Jess said.

"I knew you would, so, I brought you a present," she said.

"I have everything I want right here," Jess said as she stroked a hand along Harriett's cheek, pausing to trace her thumb over her lover's swollen lips.

"I'm glad, but I wanted this for you," Harriett said, kissing Jess's thumb. She pushed herself up and took an envelope from the nightstand. She handed it to Jess and folded her arms to rest her head on Jess's chest.

Jess opened the envelope and unfolded the papers inside, reading them. "You're selling the townhouse?" she asked. "When did you decide to do this, honey?"

"On my way home Wednesday. I don't need it anymore. Wherever you are *is* my home," Harriett said, kissing Jess's collarbone.

"Thank you," Jess said as she stroked her fingers up and down Harriett's arm.

She tipped Harriett's chin up and covered her lips with her own. Harriett wrapped her arm around Jess's neck and deepened the kiss, pulling Jess onto her body again. "I love you so much it scares me," she said when she reluctantly ended the kiss and drifted off to sleep snuggled against Jess's side.


HARRIETT READJUSTED HER body under the bed covers. Even though she was still half asleep, her body still tingled warmly from the earlier passion she had shared with Jess. She felt around for Jess, but where Jess should have been, the bed was cool to her touch. Pushing hair away from her face she propped herself up on her elbows and blinked at the clock on the nightstand next to her. Three-thirty. A few minutes later, she slipped out of bed and pulled her bathrobe around her, shivering in the coolness of the room. After checking the bathroom, she peered over the banister and saw a dim light coming from beneath the den door.

When she opened the door, Jess was seated in front of Irene's computer, headphones covering her ears. Walking up behind her, Harriett lightly touched her shoulder. Jess was obviously engrossed in what she was doing and jumped slightly. Pulling the headphones down around her neck, she turned toward Harriett.

"I didn't mean to scare you, sweetheart," Harriett said softly as she stroked Jess's hair.

"What are you doing up?" Jess smiled. "I thought I wore you out."

"You did, my love. But when I reached for you again, you were gone. Are you all right?"

"Oh, yeah. I just woke up a little while ago and couldn't get back to sleep. Figured I might as well check out a few things."

Harriett ran her hands down Jess's arms and rested her chin on Jess's shoulder.

"What are you looking up?"

"I accessed a coaching site to see if there was any mention of DeVore. There isn't much. Then I checked the Anson website. A bunch of their teachers have web pages. I thought I'd see if there was anyone who would catch my eye."

"Should I be jealous?" Harriett growled into Jess's ear.

Jess brought a hand up to caress the side of Harriett's face. "Not in a million years. But I wanted to see if there was anyone DeVore might have been interested in. Pretty dull bunch. Mostly about how great their kids are and a few with what looks like assignment pages for students to access from home," Jess shrugged. "It was worth a shot."

"Well then," Harriett said as she kissed Jess's cheek, "why don't you come back to bed. Maybe I can show you my gratitude for the homecoming you gave me."

"It's pretty late, baby," Jess smiled.

"Tomorrow's Saturday and we can sleep in," Harriett purred. "Besides, Mom told me when I called yesterday that she was going to Lorri's this morning to make Thanksgiving plans."

"Then you're on, counselor," Jess said as she flipped off the stereo remote and removed the headphones.

# Chapter Ten

ELLEN O'NEILL SMILED as she looked at her family gathered around the dining room table in their small home. She worked hard during the week and occasionally worked through the weekend, but Sunday dinners with her family were her favorite times. It was something she never had as a child. There were many things she'd never had and although she and her husband were far from wealthy, they maintained a modest but fulfilling life for their three children.

Ali, her oldest daughter, carried a plate heaped with hot fried chicken to the table. "Tracy," Ellen called to their younger daughter, "please get the potato salad from the refrigerator." Stepping into the nearby living room, she saw her husband Roy playing a board game with their ten-year-old son Clayton. "Dinner's ready," she announced. Years earlier she and Roy had decided there would be no television on Sundays. It would be their family day. Roy smiled at his wife and stood, lifting Clay and throwing the boy over his shoulder as he laughed and semi-struggled to escape the clutches of his muscular six-two father.

They all dressed in their best clothes and went to church that morning. When they returned home, Ellen and her girls prepared their dinner. Now as they sat at the table, Roy said a short simple prayer over the meal before the grab-fest for food began. Ellen knew she was a fortunate woman when she met Roy O'Neill. She was young and scared, virtually homeless when they met. Her father threw her out of their house when he discovered she was pregnant with Ali. With no place else to turn, she called her brother Levi, a minister at a small Dallas church. He left Dallas that evening and drove to Stamford where he picked up his youngest sister and a small bag containing nothing more than a few changes of clothing. Like all the Raines children, she owned little in the way of personal belongings.

After Ali was born, with Levi's help, Ellen found a job and began taking evening courses at a local community college, eventually completing her LVN training. She met Roy while she was working at a nursing home when he came by to visit his grandmother. Suddenly Roy's visits to the cantankerous old woman became more frequent. Although it took him almost three months to work up the courage, he eventually asked Ellen if she would have dinner with him on her next evening off. She liked the young man, but she felt she should be as up front with him as possible. She told him about Ali and confessed she hadn't been married to her daughter's father. Roy's reaction had been to change his plans so Ali could accompany them. Dinner at Chuck E. Cheese's wasn't in the least romantic with Roy spending the bulk of the evening playing games with the rambunctious two-year-old, but Ellen had no doubt by the time he drove them back to Levi's home, she could enjoy spending much more time with Roy O'Neill.

Roy was a man who believed in leading a simple life. He saved for over a year before he finally asked Ellen to marry him, promising that while he would never be a rich man and would probably never be able to give her everything she deserved, he would take care of her and her daughter. A year after their marriage, Roy legally adopted Ali and gave her his name. Not long afterward he was offered a job in Anson as the service manager for the local Ford dealership. Ellen easily found a job at Anson Memorial Hospital and they saved enough money to buy the small house where they were now enjoying Sunday dinner, surrounded by their three children. Ellen couldn't have wished for a better life.

"That was an interesting game last week," Roy said as he passed a bowl of mashed potatoes to Clayton. "Don't take all the potatoes," he admonished his son who was particularly fond of his mother's mashed potatoes.

"Did you play well, sweetie?" Ellen asked her quiet daughter.

"I guess so," Ali answered with a shrug as she took the potatoes from her brother.

"She only played the second half," Roy said. "Coach Carnes is out and they have a temporary coach for now."

"Why only the second half?" Ellen asked.

"Coach wanted to try a different line-up," Ali said.

"But our daughter was still the star of the evening," Roy beamed. "Scored almost thirty points."

"That's good, isn't it, Ali?" Ellen continued. Getting information from her seventeen-year-old daughter was often like pulling teeth.

"My best game so far this season. Clay did really good in his game Thursday, too."

Clayton grinned at his sister's mention of his game. "Yeah, we slaughtered them! You gotta help me with my hook shot, Ali.

It sucks."

"Maybe after dinner," Ali said. With an impish grin she added, "And after you help wash dishes. Tracey has some homework to finish up so you can help tonight."

"Do you have a game Tuesday?" Ellen asked, looking at Ali.

"Yeah, but it's an away game. Next Friday we have a bye, but the Friday after that is senior parent's night. Can you get off?"

"I've already asked and should be able to get it."

"You and Dad will have to be there a little early. Right after the JV game all the seniors and their parents will be introduced."

"What about us?" Tracey asked.

"You can be there too. Maybe we can have a family picture made."

"Cool beans!" Clayton said.

"Coach Raines said since KC can't be there..." Ali began.

Ellen stopped chewing and swallowed hard. "Who?"

"Coach Raines. She's the coach replacing KC."

Ellen looked across the table at her husband, but neither said anything. Roy could see the questions in his wife's eyes as he resumed the table discussion by changing the topic to Tracey's science project. It involved collecting deer teeth and examining them to determine their age in order to see the average age of deer killed during the hunting season in Jones County. Roy promised to take her to visit some hunters he knew in the area the following weekend.

As Ali goaded Clay into clearing the table while she got the dishwater ready and Tracey wandered off to her bedroom to finish homework, Ellen stepped onto the front porch of their small home and looked aimlessly up and down the older, middle income neighborhood. The street was tree-lined and shady during the spring and summer months. Now the trees moved only slightly in the breeze cutting down the street. They had shed their outer layer of bark, leaving white trunks and branches, reminding Ellen of skeletons. She shivered at the thought. Roy came onto the porch and wrapped his arms around her to keep her warm.

"What's wrong, honey?" he asked.

"Nothing. Quite a coincidence that Ali's new coach's last name is the same as my maiden name."

"Yeah. Maybe it's spelled a different way."

"What does she look like?" Ellen asked, holding her breath.

"Older than you, but kinda cute. Tall, slender, wears glasses.

Her hair's darker than yours," he said running his fingers through Ellen's shoulder length reddish hair. "I didn't pay much attention. Sorry."

"Auburn?"

"Yeah, I guess so. You can decide for yourself on parent night."

Turning, Ellen hugged her husband tightly as she buried her face against his chest and took a deep breath. She loved the way Roy smelled. She had never discussed the events leading up to her brother's death other than to say Clayton died in an accident at a young age. Roy had met her older brother Levi, but no one had seen or heard from her sister in at least twenty years. Ellen was only fourteen when Jess left home for the last time. When she didn't return, Ellen was left feeling abandoned and became more than a little wild, forced to fend for herself. Now, secure in the arms of her husband, she was afraid in two weeks she might see a part of her past and wasn't sure how she would react to it. Perhaps it was only a coincidence, she told herself as they walked back into their home.

HARRIETT PUSHED OPEN the front door of the Jones County Office Building Monday afternoon and paused to take a deep breath before making her way to her truck. After a long day interviewing potential witnesses, she was looking forward to returning to her mother's home and changing into more comfortable clothing, not to mention losing her high heels. Usually, in her Austin office, she shed her heels any time she was alone to rest her feet. It was a frequent sight to see her padding around the offices shoeless, wearing only her stockings.

Harriett's thoughts were interrupted by the buzzing of her cell phone. She glanced at the number before answering and she smiled when she saw the name on the display.

"If you'd called a few minutes later, I'd have been ready to get in the shower," Harriett answered in a low, husky voice.

When there was no response, she said, "Jess?"

"Sorry. Just taking a minute to visualize you with water streaming down your beautiful naked body," Jess sighed. "A little distracting since I'm sort of stuck at school."

Harriett laughed. "I'm on my way to Mom's. When are you leaving school?"

"In about an hour. I promised to run a few plays with Jamie before I leave."

"Okay. I love you, baby," Harriett said softly as they disconnected.


JESS PRESSED THE button on the side of her phone to turn it off and slipped it into the pocket of her sweats. She picked up a couple of basketballs and carried them onto the court. She bounced one of the balls and tried a few lay-ups to warm up before her meeting with Jamie.

Several minutes passed before she heard the metallic sound of a door slamming in the hallway leading to the girls' locker room. School had let out nearly half an hour earlier and the door should have been locked, preventing anyone from entering. Curious, Jess walked to the back of the gym and glanced down the hallway. She caught a quick glimpse of Ali leaning down and kissing Jamie lightly. As Jamie came out of the locker room, she adjusted the top to her work-out clothes. Ali walked beside her, holding her hand. Ali blushed when she saw Jess and released Jamie's hand.

"Hey, Coach," Jamie said. "Sorry I'm a little late. I asked Ali to join us. Hope you don't mind, but I thought we might need her to help us run the plays."

"It's fine," Jess said. "How did you two get in without me seeing you?"

Jamie jerked her thumb down the hall. "Through the back door."

"Wasn't it locked?" Jess asked.

"Not if there's something stopping it," Jamie said. "Just pull a corner of the rubber mat into the frame and it can't lock. The janitor usually pulls it out when he mops the hall and vacuums the mat. It keeps us from having to go all the way around the gym to get in," Jamie explained.

"Good to know," Jess said. "You ready?"

"You bet," Jamie grinned.

"Grab a couple more balls and let's get going then. Ali can practice shooting from around the court while we work. How close to the floor can you get and still control your dribble?" Jess asked.

"I don't know."

"Can you dribble with both hands equally well?"

"I think so. Coach made us work on that during pre-season a lot."

"Good," Jess said. "We're going to work on something that

works really well when you're being closely guarded. You can throw a defender off with a fake move in one direction or the other and it makes them move, if only for a split second. Then you move the ball to the opposite hand, lower the shoulder you're not dribbling with while you spin the other direction. Since you're a shorter player, it's easy to get under whoever's guarding you."

Jamie laughed, "Got a diagram for that one?"

"I'll show you in slow motion as I explain what I'm doing. Okay?" Jess said, dribbling a ball. "Ali! Come down here and guard me!"

Ali loped down the court and spread her arms in a defensive stance. Jess picked the ball up and slapped it with her hand. "The ball has come to you, Jamie," Jess explained as she turned with her back to Ali. "She's bigger than I am, but I need to get past her to reach the basket. So, I fake a turn to my left." As Jess faked the motion, Ali leaned to Jess's left to stop her progress.

"Once you have your opponent leaning that direction, spin to your right with the ball in your left hand, lower your right shoulder and dribble past her before she can recover."

In a slowed play, Jess demonstrated the maneuver two or three times before tossing the ball to Jamie. "Now you try it."

"But you already know what I'm going to do," Jamie said as Jess bounced the ball to her.

"But I don't know which direction you're going to go and sometimes it's not the right thing to do. Just give it a shot."

Jess guarded Jamie closely.

"Just take it slow to begin with and concentrate on the move, not the basket."

Jamie dribbled the ball with her right hand several times. She faked a turn to her right and then to her left before deciding which direction to move before the shot. She lowered her left shoulder as if she was going to turn to her right and Jess moved to defend the play. Quickly catching the ball with her left hand, Jamie lowered her right shoulder and drove under Jess's arm toward the basket. Completing the lay-up, Jamie caught the ball and walked back to where Jess was standing.

"It works," Jamie grinned.

"Not every time, but often enough. That was a good move you made to both sides, too. Very difficult to anticipate and if the shot isn't there, you can still pass it off to a teammate who's in a better position to take the shot. As a point guard, it's your responsibility to know where all of your players are at all times.

They have to watch you to get into position in case you have to pass the ball. You're their leader, calling the plays on court based on the other team's defensive setup."

"I'll work on looking at the other players," Jamie promised.

"Well, if you don't, then I'll have to resort to what my old coach did to me," Jess smiled. "She made me guard her all the time in practice and when I didn't look at her eyes, she would reach out and pop me on the face every time."

"No wonder you left Stamford," Jamie laughed.

Jess picked up a towel and wiped the perspiration from her face so she wouldn't reveal the look on her face. "I need a drink now and think that's probably enough practice for today."

"Maybe we can do this again sometime, Coach," Jamie said hopefully.

"Any time, kid."

"Ali and I think we need to work on our long passing game."

"Probably a good idea. Ali's been open a few times, leaving her available for a long pass. Maybe we can work on it after Tuesday's game," Jess said with a smile.


ELLEN SAT IN her car in the gym parking lot Monday afternoon and drummed her fingers on the steering wheel. Her curiosity about her daughter's substitute coach had been building since the day before. What possible reason would Jess have to be in Anson? Ellen wasn't sure how she would react if the woman turned out to be her older sister. She had been so angry at Jess. Even though she hadn't been there, she was at least indirectly responsible for Clayton's death. But Jess loved Clayton. Ellen knew she would never have done anything to deliberately cause him any harm.

Resting her head on her hands as they tightly gripped the steering wheel, she felt the burn of tears beginning to form in her eyes. God! It had all been so ugly, so senseless. If her father had kept his mouth shut no one would have known about Jess and Clayton would still be alive, raising a family of his own. She glanced at the clock on the console and waited. School had ended nearly half an hour ago, but she hadn't seen Ali leave the building. She didn't want Ali involved. Not yet. If she was wrong, her worrying would have been for nothing. But if she was right she hadn't decided what she could say to Jessie. Or how she could tell her daughter that her coach was really her aunt.

Fifteen minutes later she watched Ali push through the gym

doors and trot down the cement steps into the parking lot with her friend Jamie Gaither and walk quickly toward Jamie's truck, pulling their coats around them against the persistent West Texas wind, laughing and hip-bumping one another as they walked.

Waiting until the truck disappeared from the parking lot, Ellen took a deep breath and stepped from her car before she could change her mind. If she thought about it much longer she knew she would simply drive away. But she needed to know. She opened the glass door and caught it before it could slam shut. She walked quietly across the tile floor to the gym doors, stopping when she heard the sound of a basketball pounding on the gym's new hardwood floor. She moved close to the display cases lining the gym lobby and inched her way to the double doors of the gym. The sounds coming from within were familiar and brought back memories of watching Jess and Clayton play. She squeezed her eyes tightly shut, but the picture of Clayton and Jess playing one-on-one refused to leave her.

A loud school bell startled her and her eyes flew open. She watched a janitor push a wheeled mop bucket down the hall. Finally, she went to the gym door and looked through the long glass inset into the gym. What she saw took her breath away. In long, fluid strides Jessie ran the length of the court and executed a perfect lay-up. She caught the ball and dribbled back down the court, weaving in and out of a series of bright orange cones before stopping and launching the ball easily toward the basket.

Jessie had changed in ways that only someone who knew her when she was younger would notice. She was no longer the tall gangly girl she was in high school and college. Her body had filled out and Ellen could easily see the muscles along her calves and shoulders. Her hair remained the deep auburn it always was, but it was cut much shorter than Ellen remembered. The style was casual and low maintenance. The steel-rimmed glasses were the only sign that her sister had aged. She wondered if Jessie's voice sounded the same, soft with a gentleness one wouldn't believe based on how aggressively she played.

As Jess stopped and caught her breath, she rested the ball between her right forearm and her hip. For the first time Ellen clearly saw her face as Jess rolled her head and closed her eyes. There had once been mischievousness and laughter in her hazel eyes. Ellen wondered what Jessie's life now was like, whether the same lightness would be there or if it had been replaced by pain and hurt, by regret and loneliness.

She'd promised to be at Ali's game on Parent's Night, but

now she longed for a way to avoid it. She wasn't sure she would be ready to confront her sister by that Friday, or any other day. She leaned against the wall and saw the clock in the gym lobby. If she didn't leave now she would be late for work. Pushing away from the wall she zipped up the new ski jacket the kids gave her for her last birthday and walked resolutely toward the doors leading to the parking lot. As she reached the door she looked up and saw a woman with shoulder-length light brown hair smiling at her through the glass. Returning the smile, Ellen opened the door and held it as the woman, dressed in a dark blue business suit, entered. With no more than a passing nod Ellen went down the steps toward her car.

HARRIETT SLIPPED OFF off her heels and carried them as she walked toward Jess. She couldn't suppress a smile as she saw the hungry look on Jess's face as she watched her lover walking toward her.

Stroking her hand along Jess's arm, she said, "You do know you look all kinds of sexy in that sleeveless shirt and gym shorts, don't you?"

"I know I'm all kinds of sweaty and smell like a mountain goat," Jess said with a laugh. "I don't think I'd call that sexy."

"I like it when you're sweaty," Harriett said in a low suggestive voice. "Especially if I caused it."

Leaning forward into a light kiss, Jess said, "Come to think of it, you're pretty hot when you're all sweaty too. Not that I'm not thrilled to see you, but what brings you here?"

"When I called earlier you told me you'd be here a while, so I decided to stop by."

Taking Harriett's hand, Jess said, "I was just getting ready to leave. Let me grab my stuff and I'll follow you."

"Did you have a meeting with a parent?"

"No, why?"

"I passed a woman on my way in. When I was coming up the steps I saw her standing outside the gym."

"Might have been here to see another teacher," Jess shrugged.

# Chapter Eleven

ONCE UPON A time a road trip on a big yellow dog had been exciting. It was a chance to get away from her parents for a few hours and be herself. Now as Jess stepped onto the Anson Independent School District bus, she found it less exciting and adventurous. One of the longest trips of the year, it would take them nearly two hours to travel the one hundred miles to Colorado City. She nodded a greeting at the middle-aged woman driving their bus and tossed her duffel bag onto a seat near the front.

"Everybody got everything!" she called out. "Last toilet break for the next hundred or so miles." Most of the fifteen varsity and junior varsity girls had staked out a full seat and were reclining against pillows propped against windows, headphones hanging around their necks. Turning to the driver, Jess said, "We leave in ten minutes."

The bus was already idling and the smell from the exhaust seemed to seep into the passenger compartment. "No sweat, Coach," the woman said. Sticking her hand out she added, "Clemmie Patterson. My daughter's number ten."

"Are you always the driver?"

"Yep. Never miss a game."

"A pleasure, Clemmie," Jess said as she took the firm grasp. "Jess Raines."

"CeCe says you're different from KC, but thinks you know what you're doing. Reckon we'll see in a while."

"I appreciate your confidence, Clemmie."

"No sweat." Looking out the windshield Clemmie grinned. "Last of the chaperones on the radar." They watched as a Chevy Suburban swung into the parking spot near the gymnasium. "That's Lollie Bolton. Number eleven is hers."

As soon as Lollie Bolton, a petite woman with silver hair, settled into a green vinyl seat, Clemmie put the bus into gear and pulled away from the building, honking at the students and teachers still straggling out of the building. She flipped open the side window and yelled, "Clear a path! Tigers on the prowl tonight!"

Jess couldn't help laughing at the enthusiasm of their driver. She spent the next half hour chatting with Clemmie and Lollie, discovering that a different parent from the booster club was designated for each away game. Both women had nothing but good things to say about Coach Carnes. There was a vague reference to her possible sexuality although neither woman seemed to take it too seriously. Clemmie Patterson drove short-haul deliveries for an Abilene trucking company. Jess had no trouble envisioning the stout woman as a force to be reckoned with if anyone pissed her off. She was rough talking and rough looking enough to make KC look like a debutante.

Jess excused herself and wandered through the bus, spending a few minutes talking with each player. It was important that the girls be ready, but relaxed. None of them seemed concerned about the upcoming game. Jamie and Ali were stretched out on seats across from one another near the back of the bus.

"Mind if I join you for a few minutes?" Jess asked, noticing Jamie's hand resting comfortably on Ali's long leg.

"Take a load off, Coach," Jamie said, looking up from her bright yellow Walkman.

Jess swung down onto the seat in front of Jamie. "I didn't get a chance to speak to Coach Carnes about tonight's opponent," she said. "Tell me what you know."

"They're pretty well coached and have a couple of really big girls, but they're not as quick as we are," Ali offered.

"They're all taller than we are," Jamie snorted. "Except for Ali. The center is a big old girl, but she doesn't move very fast."

Ali laughed. "How many times did you steal the ball from her last time, Jamie?"

Jamie shrugged and seemed embarrassed. "Well, she was just standing there practically handing it to me."

"Did we beat them in the last game?" Jess asked.

"Yeah. No problem," Ali grinned.

Jess had trouble not staring at Ali. It had taken her a while, but Jess had finally figured out what was so familiar about her. She looked amazingly like Clayton. In some ways that realization had made her happy while filling her with a sense of sadness. She wished, for the millionth time, she could have watched him grow into manhood. She blinked the memory away quickly.

"Jamie, can I speak to you alone for a few minutes?" Jess said.

"Sure, Coach," Jamie said, turning off her Walkman. She patted Ali's leg as she climbed out of her seat. "Be right back."

Jamie followed Jess to the front and sat beside her. "What's up?"

"Tell me what you know about Ali."

Leaning back Jamie asked, "Like what?"

"KC said she and Coach DeVore were arguing about Ali the night he was killed. He thought Ali should be removed from the team. Do you know anything about that?"

"Is this about what Heather's been telling everyone?"

"I don't know. What's Heather been saying?"

"She didn't say it to me because she knows I'd kick her ass, but Lucero said Heather said Ali wanted to jump her bones."

"That's a lot of she said she said. What does Ali say about it?"

"Nothing. I was pretty pissed at Heather, but Ali told me to drop it. Heather took what she said the wrong way. Twisted it around or something. Trust me, Ali isn't interested in gettin' it on with Heather DeVore."

Jess nodded and searched for a good way to ask the next question. She didn't want to upset Jamie, but it was an issue that might be brought up at KC's trial. Jamie saved her the trouble of phrasing her question correctly.

"Look, Coach," Jamie started, lowering her voice. "Ali and I spend most of our time together playing ball or working out. We both want to play in college and right now that's our only goal. I know some kids think we're a couple, but Ali has a real chance to get out of Anson. I can go even if I don't get a scholarship because my dad earns enough to pay the tab. Ali isn't as lucky. She has a great father, but they're not exactly rolling in the green stuff, know what I mean?"

Jess smiled. "I wasn't trying to pry into your private life, Jamie."

"I know, but in a small town and a small school like ours, rumors have a way of spreading quickly. I haven't told Mom that everyone thinks Ali and I have a thing going on. It would totally freak her out."

"Are you and Ali involved?" Jess hated asking the question, but the rumor could find its way out of a witness's mouth and Harriett would have to be prepared to rebut it.

"I'm busy planning my future right now, Coach," Jamie said, not actually answering Jess's question.

"That's a wise decision, Jamie. When you find someone you care about it won't matter to you whether they're a man or a woman. Just try to be true to yourself."

ALMOST TWO WEEKS later, Jess stood outside the girls' locker room. She wasn't looking forward to the game that night. It was one of those special nights when the parents of the senior players would be introduced along with their daughters and bask in the limelight for a few minutes. She didn't feel right congratulating the parents. Her own parents hadn't bothered to attend her senior night and she faced it alone. She hoped none of the girls sitting in front of her would have to go through that. She didn't know any of them except Jamie Gaither's parents and the animosity between Lorri Gaither and Harriett didn't make it any easier. Grin and bear it had been Irene's advice. It was unlikely anyone would make an ass out of themselves in front of a large portion of the town's population.

At the end of a short pep talk, filled with reminders about the opponent's best players, Jess sent the girls out of the locker room. As they ran through their pre-game floor drills she made her way to the home side of the gym. She checked the water containers to make sure they were full and glanced at the people filling the stands behind her. She found Harriett and Irene and smiled. Harriett was wearing light blue jeans that showed off her figure and a bright red sweatshirt announcing she was an Anson Lady Tiger fan. It was probably as close as Harriett would ever get to any type of competitive sport.

At the far end of the gym Jess saw a large group of people gathered under the basket, clapping every time the players came close. When the buzzer to end the pre-game practice sounded, the players ran to join Jess at the home team seats. She greeted them all with high fives. She told everyone except the seniors to remove their warm-up suits. Preston Warner walked onto the floor with a cordless microphone and Jess took a deep breath as he explained he would be calling each senior forward. The player would be joined by her family and welcomed by their interim head coach. Time seemed to move too quickly and before Jess was ready Warner started the introductions.

"Number Three, Point Guard Jamie Gaither!" Warner began.

Jess smiled as Jamie jumped up and ran toward center court while Warner continued his announcement. "Jamie is the daughter of JD and Lorraine Gaither. Also celebrating with her this evening is her sister, Erin."

Jess shook Lorri and JD's hands, telling them how proud they should be of their hard-working daughter.

"Number seven, Guard Heather DeVore!" As Heather trotted to center court and was greeted by the other players and parents the applause seemed to be less raucous than for previous players. Jess wasn't sure how the fans would react, considering her loss.

"Heather is the daughter of Peggy DeVore and the late Allen DeVore. Mrs. DeVore is accompanied by her son Brett."

Jess shook Peggy's hand and told her how brave Heather had been despite her loss.

"Number Twelve, Center Alison O'Neill!"

The fans in the stands cheered wildly as Ali stood and trotted forward. The girl was as tall and gangly as Jess had been at her age and the way she loped onto the court reminded Jess of her brother again. As she had with the others, Jess high-fived the teenager's hand.

"Ali is the daughter of Roy and Ellen O'Neill," Warner began. Jess glanced at the group of parents and watched as Ali's parents made their way to the front. Ali's father was holding his wife's hand and they were followed by two younger children. "Also here to cheer Ali on are her sister, Tracey, and her brother, Clayton."

The breath stopped in Jess's throat as she watched the family approach. Ellen's light auburn hair reflected the bright lights above her. As they each hugged Ali, Jess turned to them and forced herself to speak. "You should be very proud of your daughter, Mr. and Mrs. O'Neill. She's a wonderful player and a pleasure to coach." No matter how much Jess wanted to avoid looking at her sister, she couldn't. Ellen's eyes were brimming with tears as they glanced in Jess's direction. Jess couldn't seem to tear her eyes away from the woman, trying to read what lay behind the tears. Fear? Hate?

Jess was thankful when the whole ceremony finally ended. After the last set of parents was announced, Jess joined the other team members at the home bench. Jess looked up into the stands and found Harriett. She would need to draw on her lover's strength. Her greatest fear was coming true. Everything she wanted to avoid was in that gym and she would have given anything to run away.

"What's the line-up, Coach?" a voice asked, breaking into her thoughts.

Jess looked up and into the freckled face of the teenager she now knew was her niece. Shaking off her feelings, she handed her clipboard to Ali. "Set 'em up," she ordered. The players gathered in a circle around Jess, raising their hands to meet hers. "On three! One, two, three, go Tigers!"

Jess struggled all evening attempting to concentrate on the

game and what was happening on the court. While she had been animated in the previous games, she was subdued for most of the first half. The girls were all playing well and seemed to be showing off slightly for their parents' benefit. She called a time-out to calm them down halfway through the first half. She could understand their excitement, but overzealousness wouldn't win the game. She squatted in front of her chair and made a few notes on their opponent's plays so they could make adjustments at halftime.

When the buzzer sounded for halftime, Jess ran off the court behind her players. She saw Ellen in the stands on her way out of the gym. In the locker room, she told the team to just rest for a few minutes. She left the locker room and walked down the hallway toward the water fountain. She ran cold water over her face and leaned back against the wall with her eyes closed. Unbidden tears flowed down her cheeks and she wiped them away with the back of her hand.

"Jess?" she heard Harriett's voice say. "Are you all right?"

She couldn't speak and could only shake her head. Harriett walked quickly to her side and ran a hand down her arm. "What's wrong, sweetheart?"

"My...my sister is here," Jess managed.

"Your *sister*?"

"Ali O'Neill is my niece. Her mother, Ellen, is my sister. I saw the look in her eyes when she saw me, Harriett."

"It'll be okay, honey. I'll wait for you after the game and we'll leave together. Okay?"

'Yeah," Jess said as she took a deep shaky breath. "I'm sorry, baby. I'm supposed to be an adult. I ran away once. I want to now, but I can't do it again."


ELLEN HAD SEEN the shocked look in Jessie's eyes when they came onto the floor during the introductions, but she couldn't read what she saw there. Confusion? Disbelief? Fear? Regret? She had to talk to Jessie, but she wasn't sure that night was the right time. They needed to talk without anyone else around. There would be too many explanations that had to be made. Maybe Jessie wasn't interested in having Ellen and her family in her life. She didn't know why Jessie would be in Anson, but Ellen doubted it was because she had hoped to be reunited with her younger sister. No, she would wait until another day to reacquaint herself with her sister. Together they would decide whether anyone else needed to know they were related.

She watched the same woman who passed her in the gym lobby the week before go into the hallway near the locker room. And now she watched her return to the stands a few minutes later. She was obviously a friend of Jessie's and perhaps the reason Jessie was in town.

When she closed her eyes, she could still see Jessie's face the last time they had seen one another. The ugly bruise forming on the left side of her face as she took the beating with tears streaming down her cheeks. Nearly uncontrollable sorrow and anger causing her entire body to tremble as she fought to control the muscles yearning to strike back. She withstood the physical and emotional pain, perhaps perceiving it as the punishment she thought she deserved. It took two men to pull Cordell Raines away from his oldest daughter, cringing on the ground at his feet. Ellen could still hear the vicious words he screamed at her until Jessie found the strength to finally get up, her face bloodied.

Jessie brought her fingers to her bloody lips, kissed them, and then touched them to the simple bronze casket and stumbled away. No one, not their mother, not her brother or sister, took a step forward to help her. Ellen could still see Jessie's hunched, defeated shoulders moving farther away until she got into a car and left the cemetery.

"Are you all right?" Roy asked as his arm encircled her shoulders.

She knew there were tears in her eyes and wiped them away quickly before resting against him. "Just remembering when Ali was a baby," Ellen sniffed.

"Hard to believe she's almost a woman already," he said, kissing her reddish hair.


THE SECOND HALF of the game went smoothly and blessedly quickly for Jess. She glued her eyes to what was happening on the floor and didn't dare look into the stands. By the time the game ended she was emotionally exhausted. As she began collecting the equipment and putting everything away, she knew she would have to speak to Ellen. Within half an hour of the end of the game the stands had cleared and there had been no sign of her sister. Harriett helped her roll the coolers and ball rack into the storage closet.

As she locked the door, she gave Harriett her best smile. "Looks like we can finally go home."

Harriett wrapped an arm through Jess's while she walked through the locker room and hallway to make sure no one would be locked in, turning off the lights as they went. She flipped the last switch in the hallway, plunging them into darkness except from the lights seeping under the doorway into the gym. Stopping Harriett, Jess pressed her against the wall and took her mouth roughly as her hand covered Harriett's breast, squeezing it. She had never felt such a need to touch anyone before and it was overpowering. She needed to feel Harriett's body and to feel her respond to drive away the memories. Finally pulling away, she rested her hands against the wall on either side of her lover.

"I'm sorry, Harriett." Laughing mirthlessly, she said, "God, it seems like all I ever do anymore is say I'm sorry."

"I hope that doesn't mean you don't want me," Harriett said.

"Of course not. You know I want you, but you deserve more than a jock grope," Jess said, shaking her head.

"Is *that* what that was?" Chuckling slightly, she added, "It was still better than the jock grope I got from the captain of the football team."

"I'm sor–"

"Stop saying that, Jess! You don't have anything to be sorry for." She paused for a moment. "I think you need to buy me a cup of coffee and I know just the place."


DISTEFANO'S ON THE Square was a small diner squeezed between two larger buildings. As Jess looked for a place to park, Harriett explained that the diner had been in the same location since she was in elementary school. The owners were Italian immigrants who landed in the United States and ran out of money by the time they reached Anson. It seemed like an unlikely story to Jess, but many citizens of West Texas had come there for stranger reasons, many following oil companies that were drilling for black gold in the desolate area.

The diner was the only establishment other than fast food chains open past nine any evening of the week. It was a little past ten when Jess opened the door and followed Harriett inside. She was surprised by the number of people as she and Harriett waited to be seated. Only a few minutes passed before they were led to a small table for two next to a rear window and ordered coffee.

By the time they finished their second cup Jess was feeling better. "You do realize I might be up all night now, right?" she asked as she took another drink.

"That's the idea, sweetie. Surely you don't think I'd let you go to sleep after that little grope at the gym, do you?"

Jess laughed. "You liked that?"

"I found it...um...strangely arousing, which shocked even me a little."

"I didn't mean to be so...aggressive. I'm..."

Harriett held up a finger and wagged it at her. "Don't say it. I may have to start punishing you to break that nasty habit."

"Promise?"

Harriett laughed loudly, drawing the attention of the patrons seated near them. Jess stood and helped Harriett up. "Now that I'm over-caffeinated, I think it's time for bed," Jess said softly.

# Chapter Twelve

JESS SLEPT IN later than usual Saturday morning. It was rare for Harriett to be up first, but the scent of coffee began to filter into Jess's nose and she fluttered her eyes open and focused on a tall mug not far from her face.

"It's about time you woke up, Sleeping Beauty."

Pushing herself onto her elbows, Jess shook her head. "I feel more like Grumpy right now. Why didn't you wake me up?"

"You needed the sleep. The last couple of days have been an emotional roller-coaster for you."

"You're right about that," Jess said as she took the cup and blew on the contents.

"Today might not be much of an improvement," Harriett said, her voice subdued.

"What's wrong?"

"Nothing yet. Lorri called early this morning. She asked if she could drop by later."

"Do you want me to make myself scarce? I don't want to cause a conflict between you and your sister."

"There's been a conflict between me and my *sister* since we were teenagers. It won't matter who's here. I think Mom's gone to her room to change into her official referee uniform."

Caressing the side of Harriett's face, Jess said, "I guess we both have some family issues to deal with."

"Looks like. This is all KC's fault," Harriett fumed. "If she could have kept her damn mouth under control, neither of us would be here."

"Maybe it's a good thing we are, baby. Sooner or later we'd have to deal with it."

Hugging Jess fiercely, Harriett said, "You're right, of course. I'll act like an adult and hope Lorri does the same."

Half an hour later Jess carried her coffee mug downstairs for a refill. She felt better after a quick shower and the coolness of the hardwood floors felt good beneath her bare feet. She was at the bottom of the stairs heading for the kitchen when the doorbell chimed. "I'll get it!" she called out.

She was smiling as she pulled open the front door, but her smile faded quickly when she saw the woman standing there.

"Ellen," she finally breathed as she took a step back from the door. Her hand remained on the doorknob and she felt the urge to close the door in her sister's face run through the muscles in her arm.

Ellen stepped closer and anger flashed across her face as she quickly raised her hand, slapping Jess's face with every ounce of pent-up anger she could muster. The mug fell from Jess's hand and shattered as she watched Ellen pivot and run down the front steps toward her car. Jess ran after her, ignoring the sound of Harriett's voice behind her. She caught up with her sister before she could open the car door. Jess tried to turn Ellen toward her, but the younger woman spun around and raised her fist once again, tears running down her face. Deflecting a second blow, Jess wrapped her arms around Ellen and held her tightly while she struggled to get away.

"Calm down, Ellen," Jess begged. "Please."

Her head buried against Jess's chest, Ellen sobbed, "Let me go!"

"Not until you calm down." Jess pressed her lips against her sister's hair. "I deserved it, Ellen. Please forgive me."

Ellen jerked her head up, hazel eyes flickering with tears and anger. "You left me there! How could you do that? You knew what he was like!"

Loosening her grip slightly, Jess met her eyes. "Because I was a coward." Jess's eyes shifted to the porch, seeing Harriett standing at the top of the steps. "Can we go inside?" she asked. "My feet are wet and freezing out here. You can hit me again just as easily where it's warmer. Okay?" Jess dipped her head and again saw the hurt in Ellen's eyes.

Ellen glanced at the house. "Who's that?"

"The woman I plan to marry," Jess said with affection.

Ellen nodded sullenly and Jess slid an arm around her shoulders to lead her back toward the house. Harriett smiled when they reached her.

"Honey, this is my sister, Ellen Raines O'Neill," Jess said.

Harriett moved forward and offered her hand. "I'm so glad to meet you, Ellen. Let's go inside."

 Ellen entered the cozy home and unzipped her jacket. "I...I can't stay. I...I have to get to work," Ellen stammered.

"You have time for a cup of coffee?" Jess asked. When Ellen nodded, Jess turned to Harriett. "Can you get me a pair of socks, honey. My feet feel like ice cubes."

Ellen followed Jess down the short hallway into the kitchen as Harriett disappeared up the stairs. The smell of fresh-baked cinnamon rolls filled the room. Irene looked up.

"Oh, hello," she said cheerfully. "I thought you were my daughter, Lorraine."

Jess took a mug from the cabinet to the right of the sink and poured coffee into it. Turning to Irene she said, "This is my sister, Ellen O'Neill." Jess handed Ellen the cup and leaned against the counter top to pull on the thick white socks Harriett handed her. "Ellen, this is Irene Markham, Harriett's mother." Taking Harriett's hand in hers, she added, "Harriett is Coach Carnes's attorney."

Ellen set her mug on the kitchen table and took a step forward to shake hands with Irene. "It's a pleasure to meet you. I hope you'll forgive my manners for not calling before I came. I haven't seen Jessie in...a long time and I'm a little nervous."

"You're Ali's mother, aren't you?" Irene asked. "She's been here many times with my granddaughter, Jamie. Sweet girl. Please, make yourself comfortable and let's have these cinnamon rolls before they get cold," Irene said.

"I've already had breakfast," Ellen said. "But y'all go ahead."

"Nonsense, my dear," Irene smiled as she set four small dessert plates on the table. "There's always room for a cinnamon roll."

"How long have you lived in Anson?" Harriett asked. Jess was glad someone had made the first move and reached under the table to give her lover's thigh a gentle squeeze.

"We moved here about ten years ago, when Ali was about seven. Roy, my husband, is the service manager at West Texas Motors."

"How long have you been married? I mean, you look so young," Harriett said.

"Thank you. Some days, after a long shift, I feel as old as Methuselah." Looking at Jess she said, "Roy and I have been married fifteen years. He isn't Ali's father, but adopted her after we were married."

"When...when did you leave home?" Jess asked.

"When I was sixteen. Actually, Cordell kicked me out when he found out I was pregnant with Ali. I refused to get an abortion and went to live with Levi and his wife in Dallas."

Jess saw the unasked question in Harriett's eyes. "My older brother," she said.

"After Ali was born he helped me go back to school and train to be a nurse. When Ali was two I met Roy and that's about all there is to know about my life. Where are you living now, Jessie?"

"Harriett and I live in Austin. I was an investigator for the State."

Ellen nodded and took a drink of her coffee. Setting the mug down, her eyes narrowed as she stood and blurted out, "Where were you, Jessie? You left us there with Cordell and Clayton died because of it!"

Ellen's words stung Jess and she stood so quickly in response to her sister's accusation that she knocked her chair over. She glared at her sister. "You know why I couldn't go back, Ellen. I sent you and Clayton money every damn month."

"And Cordell found it and drank his way through it every damn month!"

"I didn't know that!"

"Because you never bothered to come back. Even after Clayton was dead, you turned your back on me!"

"I'm not going to discuss that now!"

"Then when? After he died I was alone. Without you or Levi or Clayton there for him to beat on who did you think would be next in line? Or did you think about me at all?"

Jess didn't know what to say. Ellen was right. She should have returned home and taken Ellen with her. "I—I'm sorry, Ellen. I didn't mean for you to get hurt. I was still a kid back then and could barely feed myself, let alone a teenager."

Ellen stepped around the table and stopped in front of Jess. Looking up at her she said, "Do you know how long I hated you for abandoning me in that hell hole we called a home?"

"It sounds like you still do, but I can't undo the past. If I could, I would."

"You sound just like Levi. He's a minister now. Did you know that?"

"No."

"He's a good man. He has a nice wife and two nice kids who are grown now. I was mad at him for a long time too. He's the oldest. He should have done something to protect you and me and Clayton. But he didn't. We finally made our peace. Now I need to make my peace with you, Jessie. I can't live my life filled with this anger. I won't have my kids brought up that way, blaming everyone else for what happens to them. I should have run away or called Levi sooner, but I didn't. I'm still mad, but I don't hate you anymore, Jessie. I survived Cordell just like you and Levi did. He left us all with scars. Clayton wasn't as lucky as we were."

Jess backed up to lean against the kitchen counter and

covered her eyes with her hands, wiping her tears away. She cried as Harriett rubbed her back and stroked her hair. After a few moments Jess managed a deep breath and looked into her sister's eyes. "Every time I look at Ali I see Clayton. The same hair, same freckles across her nose and cheeks, same gangly lope. It's all there, in her."

"I know," Ellen said, her voice a soft tremor. Reaching out she placed her hand on Jess's shoulder and squeezed it gently. Jess wrapped her arms around her sister's waist and pulled her closer.

When Jess released Ellen, she said, "Ali shouldn't know who I am right now, Ellen. We're going to be here for a while and can tell her later. I'd like to meet my other niece and nephew, too."

"I'd like that very much, Jessie."

Looking at Harriett, Jess said, "We have a daughter too. Lacey. She's away at college."

"Mom!" Lorri's voice rang out down the hallway.

"Good Lord!" Irene said. "I hope my nerves can survive the rest of the day." Looking at Harriett she said, "It's nearly cocktail hour somewhere, isn't it, dear?"

Ellen stepped quickly away from Jess. Everyone was smiling as Lorri walked into the kitchen, followed by Jamie. They both looked shocked to see Jess there.

"Hey, Coach," Jamie spoke first, shifting her eyes briefly to Harriett's arm encircling Jess's waist.

"Jamie. Good game last night," Jess said.

Lorrie glared at Harriett with a tight smile. "Ellen, what are you doing here?" Lorri asked as she shifted her eyes to Ellen and tucked her sunglasses into her purse.

Jess saw the panicked look in her sister's eyes. "Mrs. O'Neill had a few questions about scholarship possibilities for Ali," Jess said before Ellen could reply. She looked at Ellen and smiled. "I think we've gone over everything that would give Ali a chance to win a scholarship, Mrs. O'Neill, but if you think of anything else you want to know, just let me know. I'll check with Coach Carnes later and make sure what I told you is accurate."

Ellen extended her hand toward Jess. "I appreciate your help, Coach Raines, and I'm sure Ali does as well." Glancing at the clock she added, "I'd better get going. My shift starts in less than an hour and I have to take reports."

Jamie smiled at Ellen. "Hey, Mrs. O'Neill. Is Ali with you?"

"No, she was helping Clayton with his hook shot when I left home." Looking at Jess, she said, "I needed to speak to Coach

Raines and dropped by on my way to work."

"Can Ali go to the movies this evening?" Jamie asked. "We can take Tracey and Clayton, too."

"It's fine with me, sweetie. Why don't you call her later?"

WHILE JESS WALKED Ellen to the front door, Harriett took a deep breath and cast a fleeting glance at her sister.

"What is *she* doing here, in our home?" Lorri hissed.

"It's still *my* home, too. Can I get you a cup of coffee?" Harriett offered, rubbing her eyes to alleviate the headache building behind them.

"But it's *not* that woman's home. How dare you bring her here!" Lorri said forcefully. She looked at Irene. "I can't believe you allowed her here," she spat.

"I invited Jess to stay here," Irene said. "Why are you here, Lorri?"

Lorri pulled a chair away from the table and sat down, pulling her down jacket off her shoulders. "Jamie thought since Harriett was in town, I should do the *sisterly* thing and come over," Lorri said.

"Jeez, Mom," Jamie breathed as she found the pan of cinnamon rolls and scarfed one up. "Could you possibly make it sound like *less* of a chore?"

As Harriett set a steaming mug of coffee and a plate holding a warm cinnamon roll in front of her sister, Jess re-entered the kitchen. Leaning against the counter she took a drink of cool coffee. She was surprised when Harriett joined her and slipped an arm around her waist. She also saw Lorri's eyes narrow at what must have looked like a blatant display of affection.

"Do you *have* to be so obvious in front of my daughter?" Lorri sniped.

"Jamie, does it bother, or upset, you that your aunt is a lesbian?" Harriett asked, smiling at her niece.

Lorri's face turned bright red as she glared at her sister. "Harriett!"

"Nope," Jamie said, her voice muffled by a mouthful of cinnamon roll. She held a finger up until she finished chewing and finally swallowed. "Coach, do you think I'd have a prayer of playing basketball in college, maybe at a small school?"

"Of course. You're a good leader and others pay attention to you. Ali has a lot of talent, but I think you could easily be picked up by a smaller college and probably see more playing time faster than she would."

"Really?"

"It's true the big schools are after Ali, but they're after every blue-chipper in the state. In all likelihood, she'll be red-shirted her freshman year. You could be a starter the first year if you put in the effort."

Jamie's eyes brightened. "I've been thinking about putting together a tape. You know," she said, sweeping her arm in a wide arc, "Jamie Gaither's Greatest Moments type of thing. Dad said we could send it off to see if there's any interest."

"That's a good idea," Jess said.

"He has videos of every game I've played since junior high at the house. Can you look at them and pick out what you think are the best clips?"

"I'd be glad to, Jamie. But you should do it soon. There's always a chance someone will see it and send a recruiter to check you out before the season ends. Bring the tapes to school and I'll go through them here. I'm sure KC'll be glad to help too."

"Cool! Maybe we can put together a tape for Ali too."

"Ali doesn't need much help."

"Well, I can tell you a secret about Ali, Coach," Jamie said.

"Why don't you just call me Jess here. Leave the coach stuff for school. Okay? Now what about Ali?"

"She doesn't want to go to a big school either. Neither one of us want to be stuck in huge classes where nobody knows we're alive."

"There are some good smaller schools, but a lot depends on what she's planning to study."

"Ali wants to be a forest ranger," Jamie announced.

Jess couldn't stop her laughter. "A girl from the flat plains of West Texas wants to study trees. Now that's ironic. What about you?"

"I don't know. I'm thinking about studying geology, like Dad, or maybe archaeology. I haven't decided for sure yet."

"How long do you think KC's trial will last?" Lorri asked.

"You mean how long will *I* be in town," Harriett smirked.

"Harriett," Jess said, a cautionary tone in her voice.

"That's not what I meant at all, Harriett. You've always chosen to do everything your own way and from what I've seen so far," she said, staring at Harriett's arm gripping Jess's waist, "you haven't changed in the least."

"Mom!" Jamie hissed. "That's rude."

"I have changed," Harriett said. "More than you know. Are

you just as unwilling to accept who I am as you've always been?"

"Pretty much," Lorri said as she cut through the cinnamon roll with her fork. "I only came this morning as a favor to my daughter. Apparently, she's as enamored of your...friend as you are."

Jess almost choked on her coffee. Irene opened her mouth to speak but shut it just as quickly as she looked from one daughter to the other. Jess felt Harriett's body grow tense beside her. Harriett brought her hand up and rubbed her forehead with a frown. Her face was flushed and she trembled as she attempted to collect herself.

"Are you all right?" Jess asked.

"No, I'm not all right," Harriett snapped. "I can't let this bullshit go on any longer. I'll explode if I don't get it out." She looked at Irene sadly. "I'm sorry, Mom. I've tried. I really have." She shifted her eyes to her niece. "You may want to go into another room, Jamie, before you hear something you shouldn't."

"Not when it's just starting to get good," Jamie said.

Harriett stood up straighter and shifted her focus back to Lorri. "You changed my life," she ground out. "When you tried to take Lacey away from me, you hurt me so deeply that I didn't think I would ever recover and I didn't for years. But I never tried to keep Lacey away from you because she loves her father's family, even the bigoted ones. She chose, with no interference from me, to honor her father's last wish. You made her afraid and confused. I have been forced to walk on eggshells the last thirteen years, always looking over my shoulder, afraid to live my life. Afraid to do anything that *might* give you a reason to haul my ass back into court because of who you thought I was. I am a lesbian, but am also your sister, dammit. I have struggled to love you as my sister. I hope I can find a way to forgive you one day, but if I can't, I'll just have to live with that. I refuse to let you make me ashamed of who I am or who I choose to love one—fucking—minute—longer."

"You've been living the way you wanted since high school," Lorri retorted. "Since the night I saw you with KC! It was disgusting!"

"What the *hell* are you talking about?" Harriett challenged.

"I saw you and KC that night she brought you home." Lorrie shivered involuntarily. "I saw you groping each other like bitches in heat!"

"No shit," Jamie muttered, her eyes widening as she grabbed another cinnamon roll.

"KC? For real?" Jess said, grinning over the rim of her mug.

"Shut up, Jess," Harriett said before turning her attention back to her sister. "You spied on me? I was seventeen-years-old for God's sake!"

"And I was only thirteen!" Lorri said, her voice rising noticeably.

"And you didn't tell Mom or Dad?" Harriett asked as she tried to calm down.

"I didn't think they'd believe me, especially Dad," Lorri admitted. Her face twisted into a look of contempt. "*You* were always the *perfect* one to him, the one who never did *anything* wrong!"

"Calm down, Mom. It was only a little necking. Everyone does it," Jamie said.

"Weren't you told to go into the other room?" Lorri snapped. "You can't possibly understand any of this. We'll discuss it later."

"How stupid do you think I am?"

"What the hell are you talking about?" Lorri asked, exasperated.

"What if I—I told you I was gay?"

"*What?* You're lying. My daughter can't be...gay," Lorri said, her face visibly paling.

"Mine is," Irene muttered, stating the obvious.

"That can't be. We brought you up to know that homosexuality is wrong. It's a sin."

"You taught me to think for myself. I can't help how I feel," Jamie said.

Lorri whirled around and pointed a shaking finger at Harriett. "This is *your* fault! Now you and this...this woman have *perverted* my daughter!"

"No one has perverted me," Jamie broke in.

"This is the first time I've even seen Jamie in years!" Harriett replied heatedly, taking a step closer to Lorri.

Jess reached out and took Harriett's arm in an attempt to restrain her. Harriett spun around, shoving Jess away. "No! You don't have any idea what I've gone through because of her small-mindedness. No one does." Spinning back toward her sister, Harriett sneered, "How much did you have to pay that private investigator to follow me around, waiting for me to do something *you* didn't approve of?"

"What private investigator?" Irene asked, staring at Lorri in disbelief. "What did you do, Lorri?"

"What I had to for Lacey's sake!" Lorri shouted.

"I've never done anything to hurt Lacey. I would give my life for her!" Harriett shouted back, clenching her hands into tight fists. "For years I was afraid to accept even an innocent invitation to share a drink or a cup of coffee with another woman. I was afraid to even glance at another woman. But Lacey was worth it and has become a wonderful, tolerant young woman who accepts people for who they are, not who she wants them to be."

"We're leaving," Lorri huffed suddenly. "I can't deal with this leftist *bullshit* right now."

"She'll get over it," Jamie said before walking down the hallway to join her mother.

"I think I need a drink," Irene said, opening the pantry behind her.

"Would you make it two, please," Harriett said, rubbing her forehead. "I'm sorry, Mom. I have a headache and arguing with Lorri only made it worse. I wish I'd never taken this damn case." She took the drink Irene handed her and drank it in one swallow. Then she looked behind her to where Jess had been standing. "Where's Jess?" she asked.

"She sneaked out of here a minute ago," Irene said as she sipped her drink.

"Oh, God," Harriett groaned as she rushed out of the kitchen to search for the woman she so desperately needed in her life. After assuring herself that Jess was still in the house, she rushed upstairs and burst into the bedroom they shared. Jess stood in front of the bedroom window, gazing down into the back yard.

"I'm sorry, Jess," Harriett said.

Jess turned slowly and smiled. "That's my line, you know."

"You didn't deserve –"

"Do you know how sexy you are when you're totally pissed off?" Jess asked, wagging her eyebrows. "I kinda like it, in moderation."

In two steps Harriett was in Jess's arms and kissing her neck. "I love you, Jess. Please forgive me."

"Nothing to forgive, baby," Jess said, stroking Harriett's hair. "Take a ride with me. Give yourself some time to calm down. Maybe you'll feel better afterward."

"Let me tell Mom we're going out," Harriett said as she hugged Jess.

"Do you have any idea how beautiful you are?" Jess whispered. "Or how much I love you?"

"Your eyes tell me everything I want to know every time you look at me," Harriett said. Her skin tingled as Jess slowly slipped her hands around her waist and drew her tightly against her. She heard Jess's breathing quicken as she held her and let her hands memorize every contour of Harriett's body.

"My life would be nothing without you, baby. I couldn't stand it if I lost you," Jess said.

"There's nothing you could do or say that would make you lose me. I love you so much, sweetie. I know I've said it before it's the tr-" Harriett blubbered.

Jess kissed Harriett's forehead. "I hope that will still be true after you know who I really am."

"Not unless you want to. I trust you, sweetie."

"I need to. It's something I thought would go away if I refused to let it into my mind. But it's always there, buried under too many years of guilt."

# Chapter Thirteen

HARRIETT TOOK A deep breath and stared out the passenger window as Jess turned north onto State Highway 277. The sun shone brightly on the fields of golden, dying grass waiting to be cut and bailed for winter feed. Flocks of birds swooped down onto freshly mown fields to gather grass seeds or insects exposed under the grass before descending on the next field.

Jess remembered the fields between Anson and Stamford well, but knew the stark beauty of the area was like the grass, covering up what lay hidden underneath. Coming back to West Texas, the area where she had grown up was a mistake, but what excuse could she have given Harriett for not coming?

The silence inside the Durango only gave her more time to let her memories grow in her mind. More than twenty years had passed since Clayton had died so senselessly. And it had been her fault. She was so absorbed in her thoughts that she was shocked when she saw the sign announcing she was two miles from Stamford, Texas. She couldn't remember anything over the fifteen miles between Anson and her home town. Slowing, she found the two-lane Farm-to-Market road leading to the city cemetery, the last place she had been on her last trip to Stamford twenty years ago.

When Jess left Irene's house she hadn't bothered grabbing a jacket. Now, despite the sun shining down on her, a brisk West Texas wind cut through her as she parked near the bottom of a small rise and walked around her vehicle to open the passenger door and help Harriett out. Without saying anything, she took Harriett's hand and began making her way up the rise until she stood staring down at a small headstone. Clayton C. Raines 1968 – 1985. It was a simple inscription without even the simplest sentiment inscribed beneath the name and dates. That would have been just like Cordell. Engraving extra words probably cost too much for him to bother with. The headstone was a small, polished gray granite stone, without additional ornamentation. Nothing more than a cold gray slab marking the final resting place of the seventeen-year-old. To its left sat the larger, but equally simple, double headstone of Charlotte and Cordell Raines. Jess was surprised when she felt warm tears fall down her cheeks and wiped them away, angry she was still allowing

Cordell Raines to control her emotions. He was a worthless piece of shit, not worth anyone's tears. Yet he had indirectly been involved in Renee's death and now could cause her to lose Harriett as well.

Jess always felt sorry for her mother. Lottie Levi was a simple woman, largely uneducated when she met the gruff and domineering, but charming, oil worker, Cordell Raines. Their union produced four healthy children. Jess couldn't remember much about her early childhood. The family moved numerous times due to Cordell's inability to hold a job for more than a year at a time due to his temper and drinking. By the time she was in high school, Jess began defying her father's demands. When she discovered basketball as a way to escape his abusive treatment, she worked harder than any player in the region to improve. The result was a scholarship to Oklahoma and she found herself a free woman at last.

Although her older brother, Levi, had left home two years earlier, Jess felt some remorse at leaving a younger brother and sister to fend for themselves against their father's drunken rages, blaming them and their mother for his failure to find success. As a result, she only returned home twice a year, at Christmas and during the summer break. Saving her money from a part-time job, she secretly gave it to her siblings for things they wanted or needed. It was only after Clayton's death that she discovered her father had found the money and taken it.

Her next to last visit home was when she announced her departure from the Oklahoma basketball team. Cordell's reaction was less than pleasant. Four months later she made her final trip home to attend her brother's funeral.

Jess took a deep breath as she kissed the top of Harriett's head and ran her hand down the familiar and comforting lines of her lover's back. No matter how much it hurt she wasn't willing to risk losing what she had with Harriett over something that happened so long ago. Jess put her arm around Harriett and drew her closer. Harriett rested her head against Jess's shoulder, giving Jess all the time she needed to organize her thoughts.

"These were my parents, Cordell and Charlotte Raines. Everyone called my mom Lottie. Cordell wasn't a nice man and Mom was too weak to leave him. He blamed his failures in life, which were numerous, on having a wife and four brats who held him back. So, when he was feeling really sorry for himself, at least one of us paid the price for his unhappiness."

Harriett wrapped her arms around Jess's waist possessively

and gave her a gentle hug as Jess continued her trip down a tortured memory lane.

"I have an older brother, Levi, who left home as soon as he could after high school and joined the service. For some reason Cordell never beat on Levi as much as the rest of us. Maybe because he was bigger than Cordell or maybe because he avoided the old man better than the rest of us. I'm a couple of years younger and we were never very close. Four years after I was born my brother, Clayton, came along. Growing up he was so much like me and we did everything together. Then four years later Mom had Ellen.

"By the time I made it to high school Cordell had pretty much singled me out as his favorite punching bag. He would wake me up in the middle of the night just to beat on me. He really enjoyed using his fists. Then I began to rebel against the beatings. After Levi left I guess I thought it was my responsibility to protect Clayton and Ellen from the old man and take the blame for the dumb stuff they did. They were still young and I knew I could take it. Basketball was my way out of that hell hole and I learned to ignore my injuries and hid my bruises. I grabbed that brass ring of hope with both hands and held on for dear life. I couldn't wait to get the hell out of Stamford and go somewhere, anywhere, where people were normal.

"My life finally began to calm down once I left home, but I felt guilty about leaving Clayton and Ellen with Cordell. I knew Mama couldn't protect them and I tried to keep in touch, forcing myself to return home on holidays. When I lost my scholarship and left Oklahoma, I wasn't sure how to tell Cordell or anyone else what had happened. Any way I went it wasn't going to be pretty. I started drinking more than I ever had before. By the time I worked up the courage to tell my mother, someone, probably the university, had already told them I'd been kicked out for violating a morals rule.

"I took my lumps from Cordell and left again. I worked my way through the final couple of years of college. About four months after I left home, I received a call from a friend I trusted telling me Clayton was dead. Turned out he got into a fight with a bunch of other boys who were riding him about his sister being queer. I never found out how they knew. Anyway, someone hit him. When he fell he hit his head on the curb and died the next day. I made it home for his funeral.

"At the cemetery, Cordell lost it. He screamed at me and called me horrible names, blaming me for Clayton's death. If I hadn't been a pervert he never would have been in the fight that killed him. He died trying to defend my honor."

Jess took a ragged breath. "I was numb. I couldn't believe my brother was dead because of me. Cordell was right. It was my fault. I couldn't even defend myself when he beat me again in front of everyone. I deserved it. I remember wishing he would finally just kill me. The look in everyone's eyes, I'll never forget how they looked at me. Like I was some kind of alien and not the kid who had grown up around them and played with their kids. When some men finally managed to drag Cordell off me, I left and never went back again."

"It wasn't your fault, Jess," Harriett whispered.

"Yeah, well, when I left I walked away from Ellen too. I left her there to be the new punching bag for Cordell. I didn't want to think about it. I just wanted to survive. But the son of a bitch wasn't through with me yet. Renee was close to the rest of her family and thought everyone else should be as well. We had a terrible argument the day she died. Somehow, she found out Cordell had died and behind my back she sent flowers to his funeral in my name. I was furious and went to work angry and upset. She died a few hours later before I could tell her I was sorry and how much I loved her."

Harriett looked up at Jess and wiped the tears from her cheeks. "Renee knew you loved her, sweetie. Just because you were angry didn't mean you loved her less."

Jess blinked hard in an attempt to clear her eyes. "I've...I've never told anyone about my family, Harriett. Not Renee, not Helen, not anyone because I was so ashamed. I'm scared I might lose you now that you know how fucked up I am. I don't want to lose you, baby. I couldn't stand to lose anyone else I loved. I don't want to hurt you. I need you so much."

"You'll never lose me, baby," Harriett said, wrapping her arms tightly around Jess. "I'm sorry you had to go through that. Don't ever be afraid to talk to me. As long as we can talk, we'll be fine. Thank you for telling me about your family. Despite everything you've been through, you're a wonderful, loving woman. You're worth fighting for and while I can't promise you'll never be hurt, I'll try not to be the cause."

"What should I do about Ellen? What can I possibly say to her? She has to hate me for leaving her here alone."

"Talk to her. That's all you can do, sweetie."

AFTER DINNER, JESS watched Harriett pull her sweatshirt over her head and toss it on a stuffed chair in the corner of the bedroom. As she ruffled her fingers through her hair, Harriett looked at Jess through the reflection in the mirror hanging over the dresser. Her lips curled slowly into a smile when Jess moved closer and leaned down to place a kiss on her shoulder. It had been an emotionally draining day for everyone and they all decided to go to bed early to recuperate.

Jess felt completely relaxed for the first time in months when she stretched out on the bed and waited for Harriett to join her. The burden she'd been silently carrying around for so many years was no longer crushing her and she felt free. She shivered when Harriett slipped under the bedcovers. A hand floated over Jess's abdomen as Harriett gazed down at her. When Jess caressed the side of Harriett's face and brushed her thumb over her full lips, Harriett leaned into the touch.

"I'm in love with you, Jess," Harriett said before lowering her head and covering Jess's lips softly. "Never doubt my love." Meeting Jess's lips again, she lingered a little longer before she broke the contact. "Trust me with your heart."

When their lips met a third time, a throaty moan rumbled up from Jess's chest as Harriett sank even more deeply into the kiss, her shoulder-length hair falling forward. Jess was breathless when their lips parted but still lightly touched. She was losing herself in the depths of those impossibly blue eyes, being slowly devoured by the softness of Harriett's mouth, drowning in her rising desire with no wish to be saved.

Harriett touched Jess's body gently, sending exquisitely painful shocks along each nerve. She felt as if she was floating outside her own body as she entrusted herself completely to her lover, feeling open and free for the first time. Her body was no longer hers. She surrendered it to Harriett, willingly, lovingly. Harriett accepted it just as willingly and with heartbreakingly tender love. When her orgasm began building deep inside she felt as if her body no longer belonged to her. She was outside of it, watching as Harriett drove her over the edge and held her gently as she floated to the bottom of the precipice.

SUNDAY AFTER LUNCH, Jamie pulled her truck to a stop in front of the O'Neill house. She rubbed her hands up and down her jean-covered thighs nervously, still trying to decide how to tell Ali that she'd told her mother she was gay. Jamie hadn't slept that well the night before. She had heard her parents' voices, occasionally loud, coming from inside the downstairs den. Although maybe the voices had only seemed louder in her imagination. As she lay under her covers, reliving the argument between her mother and her aunt, she was certain Ali's name hadn't come up. But then again, she and Ali were always together. Of course, they had been best friends since elementary school, so it wasn't unusual they spent a lot of time together. Plus, she only said she was gay, not that she had ever acted on those feelings. She smiled in the dark, remembering the first time either one of them admitted she had "special" feelings for the other one.

Jamie would never be able to go to another carnival without recalling the feel of Ali's lips pressing against hers when she was fifteen. The ride was similar to a tunnel of love, but was called Secrets of Pirate's Cove. Their small car bobbed along on a manmade black water stream as they both looked around at the walls which looked like the inside of a cave. It wasn't scary at all. In fact, it was rather peaceful and quiet. The only sound was that of the water sloshing against their car. Periodically, a light on the bottom would come on and illuminate objects resting on the river bottom.

Jamie looked over her shoulder and saw Ali's face. It appeared to glow red from the light in the water.

"You look like a devil or something," Jamie said with a grin. "But a pretty cute one."

"So do you," Ali whispered, placing her hand on the back of Jamie's neck. She felt Jamie shivered slightly. "Cold?" she asked.

"No," Jamie said. "I...uh...like the feel of your fingers on my neck. Feels good in a way."

"A good way or a bad way?" Ali asked hoarsely.

"A good way," Jamie said to Ali. They had been friends since they were little, but only recently Jamie had begun to see Ali as more than a friend, even though nothing between them had changed. "In case you don't know, I like you, a lot, Ali. More than as just my friend," she said.

"I...I'd like to be more than a friend," Ali murmured. "I really like you, too."

"Since when?"

"Sixth grade, I think. At least that's when I first noticed how cute you were."

"Why haven't you said anything about it before?"

"Because I figured I was just weird and didn't want to risk losing our friendship because of how I felt."

"This ride's almost over," Jamie said with a smile as she trailed her fingertips along Ali's jaw.

"We could go through again," Ali said as she leaned forward and quickly pressed her lips to Jamie's. Her lips were as warm and soft as she'd always dreamed they would be. Ali's hand reached under Jamie's T-shirt and up her side. Ali's breath caught when Jamie's tongue slid over hers and sucked slightly.

They flew apart when lights from outside suddenly flooded into the darkness as the exit doors opened and the car in front of them floated out. "I'll buy the next tickets," Jamie said, breathlessly, licking her lips as she blushed furiously. That night they rode through the dark cave until they ran out of money.

Jamie took a deep breath and jumped out of her truck, striding purposely up the sidewalk toward Ali's house. She should have called to let Ali know she was coming over but didn't. She needed to talk to Ali. She was pretty sure Ali would be upset, but Jamie couldn't put off telling her what she'd done the day before. She stuck her hands in her jeans pockets and hopped around on the small porch to keep warm after ringing the doorbell, waiting for someone to open the front door.

"Hey, Trace," Jamie said when Ali's sister finally opened the door. "Ali home?"

"Where else would she be?" Tracey shrugged. "Come on in. She's in the kitchen."

Clayton rushed out of the living room and threw his arms around Jamie. "Wanna play a little one-on-one?" he asked excitedly.

"Doncha think it's a little chilly, Clay?" Jamie asked as she ruffled his cap of reddish hair.

"What are you, a wuss?"

"Yeah. The sun's supposed to be out later. Can I kick your butt then?"

"No way. I've been practicin' a lot. Good game Friday, by the way. But you missed a couple of easy shots you shoulda made," Clayton said with a frown.

"We all did, but it happens." Jamie leaned down and placed her hands on his shoulders. "Listen, I need to talk to Ali for a few minutes, okay."

Leaning closer, he said in a low voice, "She's not happy."

"Uh…why?"

He flashed a brilliant smile. "Because I beat her at rock, paper, scissors again and she got stuck washin' dishes. Two days in a row!"

"Well, maybe she'll feel better if I help her out," Jamie said.

Clay ran back into the living room and Jamie turned toward the kitchen. Ali was standing in front of the sink, one foot crossed in front of the other, washing dishes and slipping them into a pan of steaming hot water to rinse them.

"You look very domestic," Jamie laughed as she entered the kitchen.

Ali looked over her shoulder and smiled. "It's the only time I can be alone to think. Grab a towel and dry some of these dishes so I can change the water. What brings you by today?"

"I need to talk to you about something. So, what are you thinking about?" Jamie asked as she pulled a dish out of the hot water with a pair of kitchen tongs.

"Just stuff. Like where we'll be next year and what we'll be doin'. Stuff like that," Ali answered with a shrug.

"Well, you'll be playing basketball somewhere and I might be...somewhere else," Jamie said. "We need to talk about that, but there's something else we have to talk about first. I'm pretty sure I seriously screwed up yesterday."

"Let's finish up these dishes. Then maybe we can go for a drive," Ali suggested.

Twenty minutes later, after promising Clayton they would shoot a few baskets with him later, Jamie drove silently to a grove of pecan trees growing near a creek bed not far from town. They had discovered the isolated area the previous spring and it had provided a place where they could be alone. Earlier that fall when the first freeze hit the area, Jamie and Ali hauled their brother and sisters with them and spent the day picking up pecans that had dropped after the first frost. Then they divided the pecans up for their parents as a surprise. It had been a fun day and Clayton, who bored quickly, wandered into the dry creek bed and found a couple of fossils and an arrowhead.

Jamie turned off the ignition and reached beneath her to scoot the seat back to stretch out her legs. Staring out the windshield, she said, "You know I love you, right."

"Yeah. Is that what you drove all the way out here to talk about?" Ali asked, sliding her arm along the seat back to play with Jamie's hair. "I love you, too, Jamers," she added. "What's wrong?"

"Yesterday my mom and I were at my grandmother's. Mom

and Aunt Harriett got into an argument because Coach is staying there and Mom didn't like it."

"Why is Coach staying at your grandmother's?"

"Because she's Aunt Harriett's girlfriend. You know how my mom is sometimes. Anyway, she said she'd seen Aunt Harriett making out with Coach Carnes back when they were in high school and thought it was disgusting. That really pissed me off. Before I knew it, I...uh...I told her I was gay. She totally blamed Aunt Harriett and said she didn't believe me. After I went to bed, I heard my parents arguing. This morning Mom wasn't talking at all."

Ali frowned. "I...need some air," she said, opening the passenger door.

Jamie slid out of the truck and walked around to Ali's side. Ali was leaning against the truck, staring up at the sky.

"Did you tell your mom that we...about me?"

Jamie grabbed Ali's arms and forced Ali to look at her. "I didn't. I swear, Ali. Please say you believe me!"

"I believe you, but she probably already knew, you know."

"You mean because we spend so much time together?"

"Maybe we shouldn't."

"Is that what you want?"

"You know it isn't, Jamers, but I wish we could have talked before you...uh –" Ali started.

"Blurted it out?" Jamie said. "I didn't plan it. It just happened."

"People can tell, you know," Ali muttered softly. "Coach Carnes told me that a while back. We're only fooling ourselves by thinking no one knows."

"When did you talk to Coach Carnes about us and why didn't you tell me?"

"Last year sometime. I wasn't really talking about *us*. It was more about how I felt. But I think she knew about you though. Didn't really seem to give a shit." Ali shrugged.

"My mom works at the same school," Jamie said, rubbing her forehead.

"Maybe she thinks it's only a phase and if she ignores it, it will go away."

"Will it...go away, Ali?" Jamie asked with tears in her eyes.

Ali pulled Jamie closer and wrapped her arms around her. "I hope not," Ali said, kissing the top of Jamie's head.

# Chapter Fourteen

LATER THAT AFTERNOON, Harriett, dressed in sweatpants and a T-shirt, opened the front door as she dried her hands on a kitchen towel.

"Jamie! Does your mother know you're here?" she asked. Ali O'Neill stood behind her, shuffling her feet nervously and holding a medium-sized file box in her arms.

"Nope, but I told Dad where I'd be. Can we come in?" Jamie asked. "We brought the videos Coach promised to go through, if she has time."

"I'll ask her. Come in. How are you, Ali?" Harriett asked.

"Okay," Ali mumbled as she followed Jamie inside.

"Will you *please* relax? Sheesh!" Jamie said testily, taking the box from Ali and carrying it into the living room.

"There's sweet tea in the kitchen if you'd like some, girls," Harriett offered over her shoulder as she walked away.

"What did Granny make for lunch?" Jamie called out.

"Chicken and dumplings," Harriett answered. "Plenty left if you're hungry."

Jamie grabbed Ali's hand and pulled her toward the kitchen. When they entered the room, Jess and Harriett were rinsing dishes and loading the dishwasher. Irene was seated at the kitchen table, drinking a glass of tea. Jamie released Ali's hand and kissed her grandmother's cheek before lifting the lid off a large pot on the stove. She inhaled the aroma of the contents deeply and groaned. "My favorite," she sighed. "You want some, Ali?"

"No, thank you. I already ate lunch," Ali answered softly, her eyes glued to the floor.

"You ate a grilled cheese sandwich and a handful of grapes. I was there, remember? I know you're still hungry, so sit down and shut up. Please."

Ali pulled out a chair and sat down as if she was afraid the chair might break while Jamie took two bowls from the cabinet next to the refrigerator. Jess handed her a ladle. "I just rinsed it, so it should be okay," she said. "Your aunt said you brought over some videos."

"Just the ones from the last couple of years," Jamie replied while she ladled chicken and dumplings into the bowls. "I figured no one would want to see anything from when I was eleven or twelve. Besides, I pretty much sucked back then anyway." She carried a bowl and a napkin to the table and set it in front of Ali along with a soup spoon. "You want tea?" she asked with her hand resting on Ali's shoulder.

"Please," Ali said quietly, gazing up at Jamie. "Thank you."

"This smells great, Granny," Jamie enthused when she joined Ali and Irene at the table. "Is Lacey coming here for Thanksgiving since you're kinda stuck here because of Coach Carnes's trial?" she asked Harriett.

"Uh, yes. She's flying into Abilene Monday," Harriett answered.

"They're predicting a little snow around then. Hope it doesn't mess up her flight," Irene said.

"We get snow once a decade in Austin, so I'm sure she'd love it," Harriett said with a smile.

"Are we having Thanksgiving here or our place this year?" Jamie asked innocently.

"We haven't discussed it, dear," Irene answered. "I'll need to talk to your mother first."

"Don't we have a game the day after Thanksgiving, Coach?"

"Yeah, so don't overeat," Jess laughed. "If you do, you'll have to run it off."

"Guess that means only one piece of pumpkin pie then, Granny. Save me some for the weekend," Jamie said with a grin as she scraped the last bite from her bowl. "You want some more?" she asked Ali.

"No, but thanks." Ali looked at Irene and said, "It was delicious, Mrs. Markham. Thank you."

"You're very welcome, my dear," Irene said, patting Ali's hand. "You're always welcome here anytime."

Jamie picked up the bowls from the table and carried them to the sink where she rinsed them and put them into the dishwasher. "Well, movie time!" she announced as she closed the door to the appliance.

Everyone trouped into the living room and Jess squatted down to sort through the stack of videos Jamie brought. Jamie dragged a couple of throw pillows onto the floor for Ali and herself and propped her head on her hand.

"I think we should start with the most recent and work backward," Jess said. "Recruiters will be more interested in seeing the most recent stuff."

"Works for me, Coach," Jamie said. "That work for you, Ali?"

"Sure."

"Jamie, grab some paper and a pen or pencil so you can write down the game and place on each video we want to copy," Jess instructed as she shoved the most recent video in the video player.

"I think there's paper in the drawer of the coffee table," Irene said.

Over the next hour, Jess fast-forwarded and rewound DVDs, asking Jamie to write down game dates, Anson's opponents, and frame numbers for future reference. When Jess ejected a DVD and prepared to slide the next one into the player, Irene got up.

"Anyone need a drink? I can make a bowl of popcorn," she offered.

"I'll help, Granny." Jamie said. "About time for a stretch anyway." She nudged Ali with her foot. "Get up, Ali. We'll need an extra hand."

Jamie slung an arm over Irene's shoulder and asked, "Can we melt some butter over the popcorn, Gran?"

"Of course, we can, sweetheart," Irene answered, wrapping an arm around Jamie's waist as they walked to the kitchen, Ali trailing behind.

Jess scooted back slightly and leaned against the large overstuffed early American chair where Harriett was sitting. She tilted her head back and asked, "Still awake?"

"Uh-huh. Kind of enjoying spending a peaceful afternoon with Mom and my niece. How about you?" Harriett asked, letting her fingers run through Jess's hair. "Does it bother you knowing your niece is apparently my niece's girlfriend?"

Jess thought for a minute before speaking. "It doesn't really bother me, but it's hard to believe Lorri hasn't figured it out yet. Jamie couldn't make it any more obvious."

"Maybe Lorri knows, but doesn't want to admit it. Ali doesn't seem quite as comfortable with the idea as Jamie does though."

"Yeah. I noticed that, too," Jess said as Irene and the girls came back into the living room.

"This will have to be the last video for today, Coach," Jamie announced as they all resumed their places. "I promised Ali's dad I would have her home around four to help him fix dinner before Mrs. O'Neill gets home from work."

"No problem," Jess said as she pushed the play button and grabbed a handful of popcorn. "Okay, this is the scrimmage on October the thirtieth."

She had Jamie add a few possible clips to their list until they reached half time. Then she paused the video. "Who is this?" she asked, pointing at the screen.

Jamie inched forward and squinted at the paused picture. "Has to be Coach DeVore," she said. "His office is in the hall behind the gym."

"And who is that?" Jess asked. "The same woman is on every game video you brought. Always near the back doors between the gym and the locker rooms before disappearing with Coach DeVore around half time."

"Looks kinda like Miss Traeger, doesn't it Ali?" Jamie said, leaning closer and squinting at the television screen. "She'd be at every game. Probably waiting for her girls to return after their break."

"Beats me," Ali said with a shrug, concentrating on the game she was playing on Jamie's Gameboy.

"Don't you have Miss Traeger for math?" Jamie asked as she back-handed Ali on the arm. "Pay attention, girl, and pause that stupid game."

"Ow. You didn't have to smack me," Ali protested, rubbing her arm. Then she looked at the screen and nodded. "Could be her, I guess. It sure ain't Miss Vahrenkamp," she snorted.

"Who?" Jess asked.

"The cheerleaders' co-sponsor, Miss Vahrenkamp. She and Miss Traeger switch off and October wasn't Vahrenkamp's month."

"Are either Miss Traeger or Miss Vahrenkamp blonde?"

Jamie laughed. "Miss Vahrenkamp is a very sweet old maid who's been teaching here for probably over forty years. Pretty sure she taught my mom. She's got to be way over sixty. May have been a blonde back in the day, but I don't think so."

As Jess ejected the video and turned off the power, she said, "I appreciate your help, Jamie. You too, Ali."

"Why all this interest in our cheerleaders, Coach?"

Jess shrugged. "Just trying to get familiar with anyone who takes an interest in the team."

"I think I may have found DeVore's secret girlfriend," Jess told Harriett after Jamie and Ali left. "I'll check it out tomorrow."

"Who?"

"Linda Traeger. A math teacher and the cheerleaders' sponsor. Should be right up your alley," Jess laughed.

JESS GLANCED AT her watch as she leaned against the wall near Linda Traeger's room Monday afternoon. She had over an hour before she had to be in the gym for the afternoon practice. With the room numbers for Traeger and Vahrenkamp on a slip of paper, she made her way into the science and math hallway, the smell of chemicals assaulting her nose. When she reached Miss Vahrenkamp's room, she glanced through the window and smiled. She felt certain she could eliminate the tall, skinny woman as a possible liaison for DeVore. When the woman turned her head, Jess couldn't help but notice the rather large dark mole on her right cheek close to her nose and would have sworn she saw a number of long black hairs protruding from it. Nope, definitely not Allen DeVore's type.

Two doors farther down the hall she found Linda Traeger's room. Peeking surreptitiously into the window she saw the blonde writing a series of numbers on a dry erase board that covered most of the wall at the front of the classroom. Judging by her hair color, Jess believed Linda Traeger was a natural blonde. She had a striking face and with her petite body, she probably was a cheerleader in her own high school years.

A few minutes later, the bell to change classes sounded and Jess stood away from the door to avoid the stampede of students. Waiting until the last student left the room, Jess stepped inside. "Ms. Traeger?"

"Yes," she said, smiling.

Walking toward her, Jess held out her hand, "Sorry to disturb you. I'm Jessie Raines the interim girls' basketball coach while Coach Carnes is away. I wanted to introduce myself. You might have some of my players and I want to make sure they're keeping up."

"It's a pleasure to meet you, Mrs. Raines," Linda said as she shook Jess's hand.

"It's Ms. I'm not married."

"Well, it's always nice to meet another single member of the faculty, even a temporary one."

"I've been told you're the cheerleading sponsor."

"Yes. My girls and I will try to make as many of the girls' games as we can."

"We appreciate any support we get." Jess continued chatting with the woman until she felt they had established a comfortable level of rapport. "I was visiting friends here when they asked me to stand in for Coach Carnes. Did you know her very well?"

"Not socially, but the students seem to like her well enough,"

Linda said as she returned to writing on the dry erase board.

"I heard she has a pretty bad temper."

"Yes, she does."

"Was she having trouble with any faculty members?"

Turning to face Jess, Linda said with a bite in her voice, "Since she's been accused of murdering one of them, I'd guess that could be called having trouble."

"Did you know the person she killed?"

"I knew Coach DeVore," she answered. Clearing her throat she added, "From what I knew of him he seemed to be a decent man."

As Linda began writing on the board once again, Jess said, "I've heard a rumor he was...involved with another teacher."

Linda's hand paused momentarily before resuming. "I doubt it. Coach DeVore was a married man."

"Well, I'll let you get back to whatever you're doing," Jess said. "I hope the team can still depend on your support."


JESS STOOD AT the floor-to-ceiling windows in the small food court on the second-floor of Abilene Regional Airport, holding Harriett's hand. She bent over slightly and pointed to a small commuter airplane lining up for its approach to a runway. "Think that's her flight?" Jess asked with a smile.

Harriett brought their joined hands up and pushed the sleeve of her coat up to check her wristwatch. "It should be." Harriett bounced lightly on the balls of her feet nervously.

They watched as the plane taxied to the gate near where they waited, A jetway made its way toward the doorway of the aircraft. A frequent flyer on business flights, Harriett was certain it would be several more minutes before Lacey joined them. Of course, she usually flew on much larger airplanes, not the twenty-four-seat commuter Lacey had taken from Dallas. Despite the cold temperature outside, the sun was shining brightly. Jess glanced at Harriett and could see nervous excitement in her eyes. Although Harriett accepted Lacey's departure, Jess knew she missed her niece terribly. They had rarely been separated since Harriett became her guardian. Jess hugged Harriett and kissed her temple, murmuring softly, "Almost, baby."

"What if she missed her flight?" Harriett asked.

"She'd have called you, honey. She'll be here. Stop worrying," Jess said.

Passengers slowly began drifting up the jetway in small

groups. Grandmothers, harried-looking businessmen, families with crying toddlers and grumpy teenagers. Finally, walking just in front of the small flight crew, Lacey appeared, chatting amiably with an attractive young man wearing a Stetson and a Western-cut shirt tucked into light blue jeans. Lacey laughed at something he said. Then she saw Harriett and Jess and waved excitedly at them, pointing down.

"She'll meet us downstairs," Jess said. "Passengers leave through a separate door. It's a security thing."

"To intercept the horde of terrorists descending on Abilene, I suppose," Harriett said grumpily.

"It's a different world now, sweetie," Jess said, taking Harriett's hand and escorting her toward the escalators.

By the time they reached the first-floor, Lacey was pushing her way through the glass door into the main lobby. Grinning happily, she ran toward Harriett and Jess. Jess stepped away from Harriett slightly, giving her room to scoop the nineteen-year-old into her arms and spin her around. Lacey turned to Jess as soon as Harriett set her down. "How's it goin', *Coach*?" Lacey laughed as she hugged Jess warmly.

"I'm never gonna live that down, am I?" Jess asked. "You had to tell her, right?" she asked, looking at Harriett.

"We have to have something to kid you about, darling," Harriett answered. "You're perfect in just about everything else."

"I'll get to watch a couple of games while I'm here," Lacey enthused. "Can't wait!" Leaning closer, she added, "At least *I* know that when they score, it's not a field goal."

"I'm not *that* bad!" Harriett protested. "Let's get out of here. Any other luggage?"

"Nope. Traveling light this trip. I can borrow a few things from you or Jamie if I need to." Jess took Lacey's carry-on bag and Lacey and Harriett wrapped an arm around each other's waist, chatting all the way to Jess's Durango. Jess opened the back door and Lacey jumped in. "Why don't you ride back here, too, baby," Jess said. "It'll be easier for y'all to talk."

Harriett stepped closer to Jess and ran her hands under her jacket and around her waist. "Thank you," she mouthed before kissing Jess lightly. "You know me too well," she said.

"Hey! Not in front of the kid," Lacey said loudly.

"She knows *us* too well," Jess laughed, kissing Harriett quickly. "Later, baby."

"Can't wait," Harriett said as she stepped into the back next to Lacey.

# Chapter Fifteen

"I'M STARVING, GRAN!" Lacey announced loudly as she walked into Irene's home. Irene came out of the kitchen and hugged her oldest granddaughter tightly.

"All your favorites are waiting in the kitchen," Irene said.

"That's why I didn't bring more clothes, Aunt Harriett," Lacey laughed. "I expect to gain at least ten pounds while I'm here."

"You can always go jogging with Jess every morning before dawn," Harriett smirked.

"That's why she jogs," Lacey said. "She'll be eatin' Granny's goodies until she leaves."

"And that's such a chore, I'm sure," Harriett said, shoving Jess playfully.

"It's good," Jess said with a shrug. "And I have a weakness for sweets."

"Among other things," Harriett teased with a hip-bump.

Jess blushed one of the few times Harriett had ever noticed. "Uh…where should I put Lacey's bag," Jess asked.

"Upstairs to the right," Irene said. "End of the hall." Looking at Lacey, she said, "Now let's get you fed. What are you eating? You could stand to gain ten pounds, girl."

For the next two-and-a half hours, the four women talked and laughed, the time broken only by periods of snacking. A little before four that afternoon the front door popped open suddenly and Jamie burst into the house, followed by Ali. Lacey jumped up and rushed to greet her cousin.

"Jamers!"

"Lace!" the two shouted simultaneously as they hugged and jumped up and down in one another's arms. When they finally stopped, Lacey flung her arms around Ali, swaying side-to-side. "It's so good to see you again, Ali," Lacey said. "Still takin' good care of my cuz?"

Ali nodded and stared at the adults in the living room, unsure what to say.

"There's food and drinks in the kitchen," Irene said. "Help yourselves."

Jamie grabbed Ali's hand and dragged her to the kitchen.

When Lacey resumed her seat and picked up her drink,

Harriett cleared her throat and asked, "How long have you known?"

"Known what?" Lacey asked.

"Don't try that with me, Lacey," Harriett fumed. "You know damn well what."

"About a year-and-a-half," Lacey mumbled. "I thought she'd already told you, too."

"Two damn days ago! Your Aunt Lorri isn't happy and blames me. You girls have put me in a very bad situation."

"I'm sorry, Aunt Harriett. You and Aunt Lorri must be the last ones to know. Even Erin knows."

"Erin knows!" Harriett covered her eyes with her hand. "She's only twelve! Please, please don't tell your Aunt Lorri or I'll get blamed for that, too," she groaned. She sat up and took a deep breath. She glanced at Irene. "Did you know before Jamie's little revelation Saturday?"

"I...I may have suspected, but until Jamie said something, I didn't think it was my place to bring it up," Irene admitted.

"Fabulous," Harriett muttered.

Jamie and Ali finally wandered into the living room carrying two plates of food. Jamie set hers on the coffee table and pulled two large pillows onto the floor. She picked up her plate, crossed her legs, and lowered her body onto the pillow.

"Did you leave anything for the rest of us?" Lacey asked as she examined the food piled on Jamie's plate.

"A little," Jamie nodded with a grin. "You coming to our game tomorrow?" she asked Lacey.

"Planning to, but I'll need to borrow one of your sweatshirts," Lacey answered.

"No problem. I'll give one to Coach tomorrow. You'll need it again for Friday's game anyway," Jamie said. "It's an away game, but it's close."

"Where?" Lacey asked.

"Stamford. Ugh," Jamie answered.

"My mom's from Stamford," Ali piped in.

"Really?" Lacey said, looking at Jess. "So is Jess."

"For real, Coach?" Jamie asked. "You used to play for the enemy?"

"Back in the day," Jess answered. When she noticed Ali staring at her curiously, Jess stood and picked up her glass. "Did you two leave any tea? I need a refill. How about you, Harriett?"

"Thank you," Harriett answered, handing her glass to Jess with a smile.

"Where are we having Thanksgiving this year, Granny?" Jamie asked.

"I...uh...don't know that we've decided quite yet, sweetheart," Irene said.

"Since it's only three days away, doncha think you should? I thought you and Mom had already hashed it all out."

"We discussed it, but never came to a decision. Your mother might want to stay at home with just her family this year," Irene explained.

"I was thinkin' we should all come here. This would be the first Thanksgiving the *whole* family has been together since Uncle Jerry, Aunt Bonnie, and Grandpa passed away. I'll come over to help you chop stuff up and clean the house. I'll even wash the dishes afterward," Jamie said. "Please."

Lacey placed her hand on her cousin's shoulder and squeezed it, tears sparkling in her eyes.

"I...I can't promise anything, Jamie, but I'll speak to your parents about it."

Ali leaned closer to Jamie and whispered in her ear.

"I have to take Ali home to help get dinner ready before her mom leaves for work," Jamie said. She stood and took their plates into the kitchen.

Ali got up and said, "Thank you for the snack, Mrs. Markham. It was great."

"You're welcome, dear. I'm glad you enjoyed it," Irene said with a smile.

Jamie returned and hugged Lacey before taking Ali's hand as they moved to the front door and left. A moment later, Harriett and Jess came back into the living room and sat down. Harriett took a drink of her tea and looked at Irene. "You know Jamie's idea for Thanksgiving will never work," she said.

"I wasn't here when you and Aunt Lorrie got into it, but I thought Jamie's suggestion was sweet," Lacey said.

"It was," Harriett acknowledged.

"At least she's trying to bring the whole family together again, despite all the animosity that's been going on for so long," Irene sighed. "Families can do terrible things to one another. I hope, one day, you and Lorri will work out your differences. Or at least learn to live with them."


TUESDAY EVENING AT dusk, Harriett, Lacey, and Irene climbed into Harriett's truck and drove to the Anson High School gymnasium. Jess had left a couple of hours earlier to get everything ready for the game. When the three walked into the gym, the varsity team was already on the floor beginning their warm-up. They were assembled on the floor in a circle with Jess seated in the middle, going through stretching exercises to loosen up. Harriett couldn't take her eyes off Jess. All she could picture was Jess hovering over her, gazing down before slowly lowering her body onto hers. She shivered involuntarily at her thoughts and felt her face flush.

"Is this good?" Lacey asked, stopping about halfway up the bleacher section and roughly in the middle of a row.

Irene unfolded a stadium seat and sat, looking around. "This is fine," she said.

Harriett climbed up a row and then stepped back down to let Lacey sit between herself and Irene.

"Is the team we're playing any good, Gran?" Lacey asked. The far side bleachers were filling up fast. "They have a pretty good following with them."

"Jamie said Hawley is in second place behind Anson right now. They're well-coached and play very aggressively."

The visitors' side cheered wildly when their team jogged onto the floor to begin their warm-up. Lacey looked at each girl as they circled the court. "They're pretty big," she commented.

"But I think we're faster," Irene commented, watching the Anson team practicing lay-ups. Jamie missed her lay-up and quickly jumped back up to catch her rebound and pass it to the next girl. While Jamie was still in the air, a Hawley player lowered her shoulder and slammed into Jamie's body. Anson supporters jumped up, yelling their outrage. Jamie fell heavily to the floor on her back and lay there for a moment, stunned. Jess ran onto the floor, shoving a couple of Hawley players out of her way. Ali grabbed the girl who'd hit Jamie and was now laughing.

The Hawley player was shorter, but shoved Ali away and said something. Ali stepped closer, crowding the other girl's space and looking down at her menacingly as her hands clenched into tight, white-knuckled fists. Jess jumped up from Jamie's side and quickly placed herself between the two players, talking to Ali as she guided her toward the home bench. Once Ali was seated and calmed down, Jess rejoined the school trainer to make sure Jamie wasn't seriously injured.

When she hit the floor, her breath had whooshed from her lungs, leaving her gasping in an attempt to breathe and her head bounced off the hardwood. Jess encouraged Jamie to calm down and take a breath before she and the trainer helped her to her feet. A couple of steps later, she made her way to the bench unassisted and plopped down next to Ali and drew in a deep gulp of air. Ali handed Jamie a bottle of water and leaned closer to tell her something that made Jamie nod and smile.

Lacey looked around and pointed to seats a few rows below them. "There's Aunt Lorri and Uncle JD," she said before standing and going down on the seats in front of her until she reached her aunt and uncle. They hugged and talked for a minute, then Lacey climbed back up to her seat. "Uncle JD caught that crap with his camera," Lacey said. "They'll be up here after Erin gets back with her popcorn and drink. Is that okay?"

"Of course," Harriett said.

A few minutes later, JD and Erin climbed up the wide metal steps to where Harriett, Lacey, and Irene sat. JD waited as Erin paused to hug Harriett and Lacey. "Can I sit between Lacey and Granny?" Erin asked.

"If they can squeeze you in," JD said. Before he followed Erin down the row, he stopped and smiled warmly at Harriett before embracing her. "It's good to see you again, Harriett," he said. "It's been too long," Patting Lacey on the arm he added, "I can't believe how much our girl has grown since just last summer. Must be all that California sunshine or something," he said.

"Where's Aunt Lorri?" Lacey asked.

"Oh, she went to check on Jamie. You know how fidgety mamas get when one of their cubs is hurt," JD laughed. "Probably embarrassing Jamie to death, but she'll be up once she's satisfied Jamie's okay." He made his way along the row, stopping to hug Irene before sitting next to her and securing a stadium seat for his wife.

Harriett watched the Anson players run through the remainder of their warm-ups and pass the ball around the court. Ali held a cold pack against the back of Jamie's head while the athletic trainer squatted in front of her, holding up his fingers and talking to her. Lorri stood behind her daughter with a hand resting on Jamie's shoulder. Finally, the trainer stood up and motioned to Jess to join him.

After a minute or two, Jess nodded and pointed at another player. Jamie started to jump up, but Ali took her arm and held her in place. Then Lorri patted Jamie's shoulder and turned to leave.

Lorri looked up into the bleachers and walked to the steps closest to where JD was sitting. She was stopped a few times by other parents asking how Jamie was before edging her way to her seat beside her husband.

"How is she?" Irene asked.

"Mad," Lorri said. "She has a knot on the back of her head, but the trainer doesn't think she has a concussion." She leaned forward slightly and glanced down the row at Harriett. "She's mad because her coach is benching her as a precaution. Doesn't want to take a chance."

"The coach is right, honey. I'll take her in to see our doctor tomorrow. I'm sure she'll be fine," JD said, taking Lorri's hand.

"I know," Lorri said. "Jamie still wants you to record the game though so Ali's mother can see it later. No school tomorrow. I'll go with you to the doctor."

"No problem. Roy and the kids are sitting right down there," JD said, pointing down a few rows.

Harriett looked around the bleachers and recognized a few people she knew from her files for the case. Although none of them were sitting together, she saw the Costas, the Luceros, and Mrs. DeVore. Dr. Costa looked excited while his wife looked bored as she killed time texting on her cell phone. The Luceros tried to keep their four younger children occupied with small bags of popcorn. Mrs. DeVore sat with her son. They seemed to be having an animated conversation, during which she hugged him frequently or pushed his hair off his forehead, perhaps to take his mind off the recent loss of his father.

Jess walked to the officials' table and handed them her amended starting line-up, then turned to shake hands with the Hawley coach before returning to her team. Harriett also noticed that the girl who'd caused Jamie's fall was sitting sullenly, glaring at her coach when Hawley's starters gathered with the young woman for last minute instructions.

JESS KNELT IN front of her players. "Okay, Jamie's out for this game. Lucero, you're point tonight. You know what to do. You all know what to do. Block them out when you can, rebound, and don't be afraid to pass to whichever player has the best chance to score. They're well coached and know what they have to do, too. Tonight, we'll either remain alone in first place or we'll be tied for first place. That depends on you, so play the best you're capable of." She caught Ali's eye and added, "I want a clean game and won't hesitate to take anyone out who can't control their emotions. You owe it to your teammates, your parents, and yourself." Jess stood and extended a hand. All the players, including Jamie, stood and placed their hands over Jess's. "On three!" Jess said loudly. "One, two, three! Go Tigers!" As soon as they broke, the five starters trotted onto the court to the cheers of the home spectators. Jess glanced into the stands and spotted Harriett and Lacey. She smiled as they waved their encouragement.

Jess sat next to Jamie and handed her a clipboard. "Mark down who scores. Think you can do that?"

"Yeah," Jamie grunted.

"You'll be ready for Friday's game, so get over it," Jess said, bumping Jamie's shoulder with her own.

Jamie shrugged. "Could've been worse. Could've been Ali. Then there would have been a fight when I kicked that girl's ass," she smirked with a grin.

The game started a little rocky as Hawley surged to a quick lead. Then the Anson players met at center court and had a little discussion, amazingly led by Erica Lucero. Jess didn't know what she said, but when they took their places again, they were a different team. Lucero took the ball out of bounds and two Hawley defenders were in her face immediately. Lucero looked like she wasn't sure what to do to get the ball inbounds. Jess grinned as she saw Ali break away from the girl guarding her and run down the court. Suddenly, Lucero threw the ball over the outstretched hands of the Hawley defenders. It hit the floor in front of Ali, who caught it in full stride and made a perfect lay-up before running back down the court, pointing to Jamie as she ran. From that play on, Ali played like a machine, rebounding, blocking shots, and stealing balls by intercepting them as they were passed. Jess took her out a couple of times to let her catch her breath and cool off.

Once, surprising even to Jess and Jamie, Heather DeVore reached in and stole the ball from a Hawley player who wasn't protecting it. She shot it to Ali, who quickly passed it to Lucero cutting along the back line under the basket. However, Lucero couldn't catch the ball cleanly enough for a shot, but managed to get it back to Ali. Ali drove through the paint and slammed the ball into the basket, drawing a foul in the process and setting up a three-point play. By halftime, Anson was ahead by five points. They were all sweating and breathing heavily as they made their way toward the locker room. Jess stood in front of them as they gulped down water and caught their breath.

"I don't know what to say," Jess said. "I've never seen you

play like that."

"It was for Jamie, Coach," one of the girls said. "She took a cheap shot and we couldn't let them get away with it. Erica only reminded us of that."

"Nobody wants to be second," Erica said. "Besides, you're always telling us to execute, execute, execute," she added with a grin. "So, we're executin'." Everyone laughed, even Jess.

"Yeah, that was a great steal, Heather," Ali said.

"Bet you thought I couldn't do it, but she was just standing there. Practically handed it to me," Heather said with a shrug.

"Still a good pass," Ali said.

"Okay, now that we've all congratulated each other, just remember the other team is getting ready to knock us down in the second half. I'm sure they don't think you'll be able to keep up this pace and intensity. They'll be watching for those passes and will probably try to block you out to prevent you from rebounding. Five points is nothing. It's only a couple of shots. So, do what, Lucero?"

"Execute, execute, execute!" Lucero yelled.


AS HALFTIME BEGAN JD asked everyone if they wanted anything from the concession stand. Then he recruited Lacey to help him carry back popcorn and a few drinks. Lacey stepped over Harriett and met her uncle on the apron in front of the bleachers. Harriett was glad that the two got along so well. Lacey needed a man like JD in her life and he loved her as much as he did his own girls. Glancing down the row, Harriett saw her sister lean closer to Irene to hear what they were saying.

"Jamie told me while we were driving home from school today that apparently we're having Thanksgiving at your house," Lorri said softly without looking at her mother. "I wish you had consulted me first."

"Would you have agreed to come?" Irene asked.

"I'm not sure," Lorri answered. "Maybe under different circumstances."

"If Harriett and Jess weren't there you mean?"

"Yes. I'm sorry, Mom, but they're a terrible influence on the girls."

"Really? Your sister is a lovely, intelligent, well-educated woman who owns a successful law firm in Austin. Her partner is also intelligent and has established a successful career in law enforcement for the last twenty years. I can see what a terrible influence they might be on impressionable young women like Jamie and Erin," Irene snorted. "We didn't raise you to think like that."

"You didn't bring us up to love other women either," Lorri snapped.

"Did you tell JD about Jamie's little confession?"

"Yes. He's not very concerned about it as long as she does what's best for her and doesn't hurt anyone in the process," Lorri said.

"Sounds wise to me," Irene said.

Lorri turned her head to look at her mother. "I'm not as stupid as you might think I am, Mom. I've heard the rumors at school and I know how much time Jamie and Ali spend together, but I still hope it's nothing more than a phase or something. I might ignore it, refuse to encourage it. I have to. It's either that or reject everything I've believed since I was a kid." Lorri took a deep breath and forced a strained smile. "Now, what do you want us to bring for Thanksgiving?" she asked.

# Chapter Sixteen

EARLY WEDNESDAY MORNING Jess walked into the roomy kitchen and made her way to the coffee maker. She opened a cabinet to take down a large mug and filled it. Then she turned and leaned against the counter to take her first sip. "Morning," she said, acknowledging Irene who was seated at the kitchen table.

"Good morning. You're up early," Irene responded, bringing her cup to her lips.

Jess shrugged. "Figured you might need some help getting things ready for tomorrow. Harriett will be down in a little bit."

"Harriett doesn't cook much, you know," Irene said with a smile.

"Moral support," Jess grinned. "Besides, I'm fixing breakfast today and tomorrow. I know she enjoys eating and I don't mind cooking. We stopped at the store last night and picked up a few things. I hope you don't mind."

"Not at all. I can start getting a few things ready so we won't be rushed later," Irene said.

"I smell coffee," Lacey said cheerfully as she came into the room. She stopped to give her grandmother a hug and a kiss before filling a mug and stirring in sugar and creamer. "Jamie texted me a while ago," she said as she sipped her coffee.

"How's she feeling this morning?" Jess asked.

"Aunt Lorri and Uncle JD were getting ready to take her to the doctor, but she says she feels fine. That place on her head is a little tender, but the knot is gone. Said she'd probably be over around lunch for chopping duty after she helps Aunt Lorri."

"Lorri is making dessert for tomorrow," Irene said.

"Enough talking about food," Harriett said as she strolled into the kitchen. "I'm starving now." She paused to hug Irene, then kissed Lacey on the cheek and squeezed Jess's arm affectionately while Jess poured her a cup of coffee. Harriett took the cup and softly said, "Thank you, darling," as she took it and blew on the steaming liquid.

"Lacey, why don't you make another pot of coffee while I start breakfast," Jess said, squatting down to find a skillet. She set it on the eye of the stove and took a jar from the cupboard. Popping it open, she removed the contents and tore it into smallish pieces. She found the remaining ingredients and placed them on the counter. "Harriett, you can toast eight pieces of bread, two on each plate, while I make this, okay?"

"What can I do?" Irene asked, preparing to stand.

"Uh...nothing," Jess said. "Drink your coffee and relax." Jess spooned a couple of tablespoons of bacon grease into the skillet. After it was heated, she stirred in a tablespoon and a half of flour, followed by salt and pepper and a generous amount of milk. Once everything had heated together and began to thicken, she dumped the shredded dried beef from the jar into the skillet and stirred everything together, turning the eye down to simmer.

"Well, I'm done," Jess announced. "How's the toast coming along?"

"Last two are in," Harriett said with a smile.

"Everyone sit down and we can eat," Jess said. She placed two pieces of toasted bread on each plate and ladled the gravy mixture over the bread before setting plates in front of Irene, Harriett, and Lacey. She refilled all of their cups with fresh coffee before joining them at the table. "It's not a gourmet meal," she said after swallowing her first bite. "But it's filling."

"You've got to teach me how to make this," Lacey said. "My roommate will love it! Can we make it when we go camping?"

"As long as you put everything in a container, you should be able to," Jess nodded.

"It's so simple and very good," Irene said.

"Thank you. Glad you like it," Jess said.

"It's wonderful, sweetheart," Harriett said.

"What are you fixing tomorrow?" Irene asked. "You said you were making breakfast today and tomorrow."

"A breakfast casserole. It takes a little longer, but it's good when it's chilly outside," Jess said. She glanced at Harriett. "Renee used to make it sometimes." She shrugged. "Old family recipe or something. Do you mind?"

"Of course not, Jess. I wouldn't expect you to forget Renee. She was an important part of your life," Harriett answered softly, running her hand across Jess's shoulder and into the hair at the nape of her neck, massaging gently. "I know that, honey."

"Well, then I'll clean this up and we can start chopping anything we'll need for tomorrow," Jess said.

THE NEXT AFTERNOON Jess was checking the turkey when the back door opened. Lorri walked in, holding a pie in each hand. "Where do you want these, Mom?" she asked.

"On the credenza in the dining room," Irene said.

Jess approached Lorri. "I can take those for you."

"I've got them, thank you," Lorri said. "But JD might need some help, if you don't mind."

"No problem," Jess said with a smile. "I'll be right back, Irene, and take the turkey out of the oven for you."

"Thank you, dear," Irene said over her shoulder as Jess opened the back door and stepped outside.

"Happy Turkey Day, Coach," JD said cheerfully when Jess joined him.

"It's just Jess, Mr. Gaither," Jess said with a smile. "I thought Mrs. Gaither was only bringing dessert."

"It's JD and I reckon you don't know yet that Lorri and her mama both cook when they're frustrated. And I mean they cook a *lot*. They claim it relieves stress," he laughed.

"Then they must be really stressed because that turkey must weigh at least thirty pounds," Jess said as JD stacked a couple of large containers in her arms. "Where's Jamie?"

"I forgot the damn ice and sent her to get a bag," he said, grabbing a couple of bags. "Should be here soon. She wouldn't miss a chance to eat all this food."

Harriett stepped out the back door and wrapped her arms around her body for warmth and made her way carefully down the steps. Jess smiled watching her. Harriett was wearing a form-fitting forest green sweater over a rust colored wool skirt and knee-high brown boots. Harriett stopped close to Jess, using her to block the chilly breeze that occasionally kicked up. "Y'all need help?" she asked. Jess could hear Harriett's teeth chattering slightly.

"Can you take these inside for me?" Jess asked, handing Harriett the containers in her arms. "I'll get the cooler. Hope your mom has room for all of this."

Leaning closer to take the containers, Harriett said under her breath, "Don't leave me alone in there with Lorri."

"I won't be long, honey," Jess said, rubbing her hands up and down Harriett's arms. "You look...amazing."

Harriett blushed. "You, too, sweetie."

Jamie pulled her truck behind her father's Tahoe and jumped out, dragging a ten-pound bag of ice behind her. "Jeez! It's freezing out here!" she exclaimed loudly. "Where do you want this?"

"In the cooler," JD said as Jess lifted the cooler from the

Tahoe. "Thought we'd set it outside the kitchen door so it'll stay frozen."

Jamie dropped the bag on the driveway a couple of times to break the ice up, ripped it open, and dumped the ice into the cooler. Then she and Jess grabbed the handles and followed JD up the back steps.

"How's your head today?" Jess asked.

"Fine," Jamie said. "Just don't smack me on the back of the head. Still tender."

When they entered the kitchen, JD pulled his gloves off and rubbed his hands together briskly. Lorri and Harriett were carrying various containers of food into the dining room while Irene poured gravy into two gravy boats.

"I turned the oven off, Jess, and you can take the turkey out now," Irene said.

"Need a forklift?" JD asked with a laugh.

"Keep it on standby," Jess said, smiling as she pulled down the oven door and grabbed a couple of pot holders. Slowly, she slid the turkey pan out and lifted it onto the stove top. She pierced it with a fork, testing the joints to make sure they were done. Lastly, she picked up a pair of heavy-duty forks and drove them into the large bird to lift it onto a ceramic turkey platter.

"Harriett, will you take the pans out of the second oven for me, please? I'll round everyone up," Irene said.

Harriett opened the oven door below the one Jess had emptied and pulled out mashed potatoes, green bean casserole, cornbread dressing, and dinner rolls. As she set them on the counter next to the stove, Lorri and Lacey took them into the dining room and set them on hot pads. Finally, JD followed them with the turkey and set it in a space left open for it as everyone assembled around the large dining table.

As they all sat, Irene asked quietly, "Lacey, would you please give the blessing?" She held her hands out, one to Lorri, the other to Harriett. They each took their mother's hand and extended the other to the person next to them until they encircled the table with their heads bowed.

Lacey took a deep breath. "Father, thank you for the bounty before us today and every day. Thank you for bringing our family together as one again and watching over each of us, keeping us safe in the circle of your love. Protect the loved ones we've lost and keep them always in our hearts and memories. In your son's name, amen."

After a soft round of "amens", JD stood and began cutting the turkey. "Who wants what?" he asked as he made the first cut. Jamie and Erin claimed the legs while assorted bowls were passed around the table. Soft, bluesy jazz filtered from the living room and everyone quickly began filling their mouths with minimal conversation. Once the initial eating frenzy began to slow, JD started an easy conversation with Jess.

"I know you're not a full-time coach, Jess, but I don't know that Irene or Harriett have ever mentioned what you do for a living," JD asked as he sliced into his meat.

Jess cleared her throat and swallowed before answering. "I was an investigator for the Texas Attorney-General's Office, working in sex crimes for the last ten years. Interesting work. But I've been working in the private sector for the last six months or so."

"Jess is working for Aunt Harriett's firm now," Lacey added.

"How *handy* for you both," Lorri muttered.

Jess could feel Harriett's temper flare at the comment and placed her hand on Harriett's leg under the table to stop her from snapping back.

"Is that how you and Harriett met then?" JD carried on pleasantly.

"Yes. Harriett had a problem with a former client who was a sex offender. When he was released from prison, he threatened Harriett, as well as Lacey, and my office became involved at that point," Jess explained calmly. "Jamie tells me you're a geologist," she added, steering their conversation to something less personal.

"And he's an amateur archaeologist," Jamie threw in. "You should come over sometime and see all the stuff he's found while drilling for water. It's really cool."

"I have some real dinosaur footprints!" Erin piped in.

"Where did you find those?" Jess asked.

"New Mexico," JD answered with a smile. "We were looking for a good spot to drill out in the boonies somewhere. We dropped a pipe in for a core sample and went through what turned out to be an ancient mud flat. Since the whole area had once been covered with water, we dug down to the level of the mud flat. It peeled up in the smoothest layers I'd ever seen and sandwiched in the layers we located thousands of foot casts. None were very big, but they were unmistakable. We had the age of the soil tested and it caused quite a controversy in geology circles," JD explained before taking another bite.

"Why?" Jess asked.

"Because some of the foot casts we found had *five* toes and no one believed the little critters had more than *four* toes until much later in their evolutionary development," he said. "That's why I keep so many around. When I give a guest presentation for some college or university geology department, I can drag out the casts to use as an example of questionable geologic timing. You just can't take what you've always been told as the truth. Invalid assumptions should always be questioned and not taken as irrefutable facts."

"That's really fascinating, isn't it, honey?" Jess asked, looking at Harriett.

"Yes, it certainly is," Harriett agreed, staring at her sister.

For the remainder of the meal, Harriett and Lorrie took turns occasionally sniping at one another. The animosity between them had gone on for so long that their semi-biting comments seemed to slip out without much effort or planning.


BY THE END of the meal, Irene stood up and glared at Harriett and Lorri. "I think we're long overdue for a talk. I've kept my mouth shut for years hoping you two would eventually work out your differences, but it is grossly apparent that biding my time obviously isn't working."

"I'm sorry, Mom," Harriett said quietly.

Irene shifted her eyes toward Lorri and waited.

"I'm sorry too, Mom," Lorri finally said.

"I've heard you're sorry before, but it hasn't changed a damn thing. I'm going into the living room where I can put my feet up and be comfortable. I'd appreciate it very much if you all joined me." Picking up her tea, Irene turned on her heel and marched toward the front room.

Jess looked at Harriett, waiting for her to get up. After a moment, she glanced across the dining room table at JD and shrugged. "How about a cup of coffee, JD, before we join Irene?"

"Sounds like a winner to me. But then again, my mama ain't mad at me." A smile crossed his lips as he stood and helped Lorri up.

"Lacey, will you, Jamie, and Erin help me in the kitchen for a minute?" Jess asked as she stood and walked toward the kitchen. "Get some cups from the cabinet for everyone. Erin, get the sugar and creamer, please."

By the time Jess and the girls returned everyone had found a place to sit in the living room. Jess, Jamie, and Lacey handed cups and spoons to everyone while Erin set cream and sugar on the coffee table. Irene was sitting in her rocker near the fireplace, seemingly lost in her thoughts as she stared into the embers. Jess sat next to Harriett on the loveseat and draped her arm over her shoulders. The girls pulled pillows onto the floor close to the fireplace while JD settled beside Lorri on the couch and rested a hand on his wife's thigh.

Irene kept her gaze on the small flames that occasionally flared up around the remaining wood. The room was so quiet that everyone seemed startled when Irene spoke.

"The happiest days of my life were when my three children were born. Each one was special in his, or her, own way. Jerry because he was our first-born. Harriett because she was the little girl I'd always wanted." Looking toward Lorri she continued, "And Lorraine because she was our miracle baby. After Harriett was born I lost two other babies and Farley and I thought we'd never have another child. But then Lorraine came along. We knew she'd be our last and we wanted another baby so much. So, you were our gift, the answer to our prayers."

Jess glanced across the space to the couch and saw tears beginning to glisten in Lorri's eyes.

"We raised you all the same way and even though you were each special in your own way to us, we tried never to allow any favoritism. You all grew up healthy and happy and loved for the little individuals you were." She smiled as she looked from one daughter to the other. "And naturally, considering who your parents were, you all grew up to be beautiful adults. A part of us died when Jerry and Bonnie were killed, but they left us Lacey to remind us of them." A tear made its way slowly down Irene's cheek at the painful memory. "Some of what I'm going to say may not sound like me, but I want to clear the air about a few things."

Turning her head toward Harriett, Irene took a deep breath and appeared to be searching for the right words. "Harriett, when you came home from college and told your father and me that you were a lesbian, I would be lying if I didn't admit it was a blow to both of us. We loved you. That was never an issue. We just didn't know what we were supposed to do or say. It hurt us both deeply. As a woman, I knew you would never experience the joy of having children of your own and feeling about them the way I did as you watched them grow every day before your very eyes, hoping you were doing right by them. As a man, your father knew you were putting yourself into a position that could jeopardize your future. Other than that, neither of us knew anything about gays or lesbians. We struggled with the idea we'd done something wrong, we hadn't raised you the right way. There was so much we didn't know but were afraid to ask for fear we would drive you away.

"When Jerry and Bonnie were killed and you were given custody of Lacey I felt enormous sadness for the loss of my son and his wife as well as great happiness that you would be able to feel what I had felt as a mother. I knew you would love her as much as her own mother had. Since then I've learned what a remarkable woman you are."

Pausing to re-gather her thoughts, Irene looked at Lorri. Smiling, she began, "My miracle baby. Now you're a woman with two beautiful daughters of your own. We worried all the time you were growing up that something would happen to you. You were such a small and fragile-looking child, but you turned out tougher than anyone would have guessed. You married a fine man. The day your father escorted you down the aisle and gave you to JD he only gave part of you away because you would always be ours. You made good choices for your life and we were always proud of you. However, the day you told me you were going to sue Harriett to take Lacey away from her was the saddest day of my life. I knew you were making a mistake and no matter how hard she tried, Harriett would never be able to completely forgive you. Now it's been nearly thirteen years and you still have not been able to overcome your feelings about Harriett.

"What do you plan to do, Lorri, now that Jamie has announced she, too, is a lesbian? You gave birth to her, you nurtured her, loved her, and hoped for nothing but the best for her. And yet she came to you and changed your whole life in an instant. Will your love as a mother simply evaporate as if it had never been? Can you turn your back on your own child because in one part of her being she is different? I would like to think you won't. Is that what you expected me to do? Turn my back on one child that I loved to agree with another child I loved just as much? Harriett placed me in a difficult situation and you compounded my problem by your actions. But there was such relief in Harriett's demeanor after she told us. It was as if she had been carrying a huge weight around. I'm sure she felt like she had been walking on eggshells for years. No one should have to live with that fear, the fear that her family, or anyone, might reject her because of who she was."

Irene leaned back in her rocker and closed her eyes for a moment. Jess took Harriett's hand and felt the cool clammy feeling of her skin. She slid her eyes to JD as he tightened his grip around Lorri's shoulders. She seemed shaken but was unable to speak.

"Your father and I used to talk about what we wanted for our children," Irene's voice said, breaking the silence. "We wanted you each to be happy, to find the kind of happiness we had. I've never discussed my feelings for your father with you before. I guess I assumed you knew we loved one another. We were so much more than lovers; we were soul-mates. I could tell many things about your father by just looking into his eyes. They couldn't hide anything from me. Sometimes he was worried, sometimes sad, but underneath that there was always something more. I know you're all going to laugh when I say this, but underneath every other emotion in those beautiful blue eyes was desire. Desire...for me. Until the day he died, I never stopped seeing that when he looked at me. No child wants to contemplate the idea of their parents together, romantically or sexually. The idea of my own parents ever having a sexual relationship seemed totally out of the question and I couldn't imagine such a thing. I didn't want to imagine it. I thought they had never felt what I felt for your father, but I was wrong. When your grandfather passed away my mother had this same little talk with me. Of course, I thought she was just a grief-stricken old woman. It was only later I knew what she had been talking about. Love is a powerful emotion and when you find it, really find it, you have to grab hold of it for all you're worth and hang on. When I see JD look at you, Lorri, I see the desire in his eyes and I know you two will be all right. Now when I see the way Jess looks at Harriett it takes my breath away. It's the same look I used to see in your father's eyes. You all have that. Someday, I hope Jamie, Erin, and Lacey will find someone who looks at them the same way. Someone who makes them feel weak with nothing more than a glance or a touch. It is the most indescribably wonderful feeling of total love at every level. I found it and all of my children found it. Not everyone is that lucky. I can't stand by any longer and watch you two snipe at one another. And I won't allow Jess and JD to suffer because of it. Jess, all I can promise you is my acceptance of your love for my daughter and welcome you as a member of our family, which now includes a sister and brother-in-law and two beautiful nieces.

"JD, I've loved you like the son I lost. You've made Lorri happier than I could have wished for. Now, as far as this family is concerned, you have a new sister-in-law and Jamie, Erin, and

Lacey have a new aunt. I expect you all to respect my wishes. If you can't then I expect you to leave my home and not return until you can." Looking at Lorri, Irene said, "You and Harriett will always be sisters. It doesn't really matter, sweetheart, who you love. It only matters *that* you love. Harriett and Jess have no more desire to imagine you and JD together than you have of imaging them together."

Jamie blinked and looked at Erin. Together they screwed their faces up and exclaimed, "Eewwww!"

Laughter from everyone in the room broke the tension that had been as tangible as an uninvited intruder all afternoon. JD leaned forward and picked up his coffee cup, taking a sip of his now tepid liquid. Looking at Jess over the rim he said, "Well, how 'bout them Cowboys, Jess?"

"Now that I've said my piece, I'll get the kitchen cleaned up," Irene said.

"I'll get it, Mom, and maybe Harriett will help me," Lorri volunteered.

Harriett stood and said, "I might not cook, but I do know how to clean." She leaned down and patted Jess's knee. "In the meantime, why don't y'all find a football game to watch?" she asked.

"Great idea!" JD said. "Hey, honey! Any chance of getting some popcorn," he called out.

"This isn't a restaurant, JD!" Lorri called back.

"I'll get it, Dad," Jamie offered as she stood up. "More coffee, too."

"Yep. Thanks, baby," JD answered with a smile as he located the remote for the television. "You too, Jess?"


LORRI WALKED INTO the kitchen as Harriett began clearing the dining room table and credenza. She carried bowls in and set them on the round kitchen table. "Well, at least Mom won't have to cook again for a few days," Harriett chuckled.

"She loves to cook," Lorri noted as she began rinsing pots and pans.

"I know. She and Jess have been swapping recipes all week," Harriett said as she looked through cabinets for smaller storage containers. "Where does Mom keep her other containers?"

"There's a cabinet in the mud room and there might be some in the credenza, too," Lorri answered.

Jamie bounced into the kitchen and located a large plastic

mixing bowl. Then she popped a bag of popcorn into the microwave.

"Has your father found a game yet?" Lorri asked her.

"You know he has. Now he and Aunt Jess are ogling the Dallas Cowboy Cheerleaders as they bounce around shamelessly," Jamie smirked.

"What is everyone else doing?" Harriett asked.

"Well, Gran wandered off to take a nap and digest. Erin and Lacey went outside to play a little one-on-one soccer. You know, European football. Yuck!" Jamie grimaced.

"It's Erin's sport," Lorri said.

"Not when it's below freezing outside!" Jamie exclaimed.

"Maybe all that running around will keep them warm," Harriett said.

"I give them thirty minutes, maybe less, and they'll be back inside," Jamie smirked as the timer on the microwave dinged. She removed the popcorn and carefully opened the bag, dumping the contents into the mixing bowl. Then she scooped out butter into a smaller bowl and slid it into the microwave. A minute later she removed the melted butter and drizzled it over the popcorn, tossing a piece into her mouth. She tossed the popcorn to mix the butter in and grabbed the carafe from the coffeemaker. Finally, she backed out of the kitchen, clutching the popcorn and coffee with a soda can tucked under each arm.

Harriett walked back into the dining room and began scraping leftovers onto one plate as she stacked the plates and placed the silverware on top before carrying them into the kitchen and setting them on the counter next to the sink. "You want me to rinse for a while?" she asked.

"No thanks," Lorri answered. "I don't mind and it gives me some time to think."

Harriett took a bowl that has been rinsed and put it into the dishwasher. "I'm glad you all came over today," she said.

"I bet," Lorri snorted, handing Harriett a plate.

"We have a wonderful family," Harriett said, biting back a snide remark. "I miss Dad, Jerry, and Bonnie. Hell, I've even missed you," she said, bumping her shoulder against Lorri's. "You may not like how I live my life, but this is it. I'm sorry if I traumatized you way back when, but I think it's time you got over it. I miss my sister and I refuse to continue hurting Mom. So, give it your best shot now and let us get on with our lives."

"What am I supposed to do about Jamie then?"

"Don't be afraid to talk to her and try not to judge her. She loves you and doesn't want to hurt you or feel like you're ashamed of her. She doesn't act like it, but she's just as confused as you are. As I was at seventeen. I didn't understand what I was feeling and there wasn't anyone I could talk to. Jamie is incredibly level-headed and should know she can talk to me or Jess. She doesn't have to go through this alone."

"But what about her future?" Lorri cried.

"That's up to her just like it would be if she wasn't gay," Harriett said and tentatively reached out to squeeze her sister's shoulder. "She'll be leaving Anson in a few months and will find a place where she feels safe, doing something she wants to do. Trust her, Lorri. You and JD have given her the basics to make good decisions. It all starts with baby steps."

"What if I can't accept that she's…gay?"

"That's up to you. I can't help you with that, but you might try talking to Mom."

"Will you come back to Anson sometime?"

"As long as Mom is alive, I'll always come back occasionally, I suppose," Harriett said with a shrug.

By halftime, Dallas was winning handily and JD was struggling to keep his eyes open. The dining room and kitchen were cleaned and the dishwasher was running. Harriett was snuggling in the curl of Jess's arm.

Lorri patted JD's abdomen. "We should think about getting home before you start snoring," she said.

"You're right," he said, sitting up and stretching. "We'll have to feed the horses soon anyway."

"Can Lacey spend the night?" Erin asked, looking back and forth between Lorri and Harriett. "She can help us feed the horses and we have a cool new game where you have to drive really fast."

"That's up to Lacey and your mom, honey," Harriett said.

Erin crawled toward her mother on her knees with her hands clasped together. "Please, please, please, Mommy," she pleaded.

"It's okay with us, Squirt," Lorri said with a smile as she ran her hand over Erin's hair.

"Can we take the pumpkin pie?" Lacey asked.

"Of course," Harriett said. "But not the pecan. It's my favorite."

"What time do you want me home tomorrow?" Lacey asked.

"Well, we'll all be at the game tomorrow, so if you want to spend the day, we can bring you back here afterward," Harriett said. "Maybe your Uncle JD will take you all out for a ride."

"Just let me pack a few things," Lacey said before she and her cousins ran upstairs.

Harriett looked at Lorri and smiled. "Baby steps," she said.

# Chapter Seventeen

FOLLOWING A ROUND of hugs and handshakes, Jess helped JD pack everything into the back of the Tahoe. The girls piled into Jamie's truck and backed out of the driveway, followed by JD and Lorrie. Jess and Harriett waved and started back to the house. The back door opened and Irene stepped out, pulling her gloves on.

"Where are you going?" Harriett asked.

"Before your father passed away, a group of us discovered the one thing we had in common was our husbands falling asleep after dinner. Since none of us were fans of football or snoring, we decided to get together and play pinochle Thanksgiving evening," Irene explained. "I hope you don't mind. There's plenty to eat if you get hungry." Her eyes twinkled when she looked at them. "I'm sure you'll find something to do, dear," she said with a smile. "Don't wait up for me. It may be a late night."

"Be careful, Irene," Jess said as she pressed her hand into the small of Harriett's back, escorting her toward the back door. "The roads might get slick later."

"I've been driving in this weather since I was fourteen," Irene said over her shoulder as she opened the garage door.

Jess grabbed Harriett's hand after shutting and locking the back door and pulled her closer. "I think we've been set up," she murmured as her lips met Harriett's. "But I can live with it." When they separated, Jess asked, "Are you and Lorri all right?"

"I think so, but—" Harriett started before being interrupted by a second, more insistent kiss.

"I don't really care," Jess whispered as her lips traveled down Harriett's throat, kissing and sucking the soft skin. Her hand twisted in Harriett's hair as she licked the hollow at the base of Harriett's throat. "I want you so much, baby," she said.

Harriett wrapped her arms around Jess's neck and stroked the short hair at the nape of her neck. "Touch me, Jess. I want to feel your hands on my body," Harriett groaned.

"Oh, you will, baby, but not here. I want your undivided attention while I touch you," Jess promised softly, taking Harriett's hand to lead her upstairs. "Everywhere."

Harriett caught her bottom lip between her teeth and grinned at Jess as she followed her up the stairs. The moment they entered the bedroom and closed the door, Jess pushed Harriett against it and kissed her hungrily as her hands slipped under Harriett's sweater to caress her breasts.

"Take me now, baby," Harriett gasped as Jess fondled her aching nipples.

"Soon," Jess groaned. She pulled Harriett's sweater over her head and unfastened her black lace bra, drawing it down Harriett's body and dropping it on the floor with her sweater. Jess lowered her head to suck Harriett's full breast into her mouth, teasing the erect nipple with her tongue while she unzipped Harriett's skirt and pushed it down. When she released it, Harriett's breast left Jess's mouth with a small, wet popping sound. "You're so fuckin' beautiful," Jess said hoarsely as her eyes took in Harriett's slender nude body.

Harriett licked her lips and stepped closer, reaching up to unbutton Jess's shirt and tug it from her slacks. "I need to see you, too," she said as she pushed the shirt over Jess's shoulders and let it fall to the floor. Harriett dropped her hand to Jess's crotch, pressing lightly. She smiled up at Jess. "You're wet. I like that," she said.

"It's your fault, you know," Jess managed as she felt her clitoris twitch.

"How? I haven't done anything...yet," Harriett whispered. Pressing closer, she added, "But I plan to." She pushed Jess's slacks and underwear down, kneeling in front of her. She took a deep breath and stood, running her hands up Jess's sides. "You smell...delicious," Harriett sighed as she kissed Jess deeply and possessively.

Jess ran her arms under Harriett's knees and lifted her against her chest without breaking their kiss. She lowered Harriett onto the bed and balanced her body over Harriett's. Jess brought a leg up to settle it between Harriett's thighs. Harriett began a slow, undulating glide up and down Jess's leg while Jess buried her head on Harriett's shoulder, feeling the pulse in Harriett's neck increase against her lips. Jess moved down Harriett's body.

"Noooo," Harriett ground out.

Jess felt the engorged bundle quivering beneath her lips and drew it into her mouth, circling it with her tongue. Harriett found the back of Jess's head and pressed it against her clit. Her hips began to move against Jess's mouth. "Right...there, baby. Please. I need to come so much...it feels so...good," Harriett groaned and moved on the bed as if trying to escape the intensity of what she was feeling. Jess lessened the pressure of her mouth and slid her hand down to enter her smoothly, filling Harriett. Jess alternately sucked Harriett's clit and drove her fingers into Harriett, more deeply with each stroke. Harriett's head fell over the side of the bed, her mouth open, her hands fisting the covers, trying to hold back the orgasm that was building within her body.

"Let it go, baby," Jess said. "Come for me. You're so beautiful when you come."

"Too…goodtoo…good…don'twant…to…end…moremoremore…Oh God…more," Harriett pleaded as her hips drove against Jess's fingers. Finally, a scream of release burst from Harriett, her body stiffening as a wave of warmth flowed over Jess's hand. Jess quickly shifted her mouth to catch the second wave and savor the taste of Harriett's release. Harriett continued to shudder and Jess crawled over her to fold Harriett into her arms, holding her until she stopped gasping for breath.

"You taste so good, baby, so sweet," Jess murmured as she kissed Harriett's throat while her fingers played down Harriett's body. "I love you so much," she said when she found the moist heat pulsing at Harriett's center. Jess brushed hair back from Harriett's face with her other hand. She felt Harriett's hips rise, inviting Jess to fill her again.

"God, you take my breath away," Jess whispered as Harriett's body succumbed once more to Jess's deep penetrations.

"I…I don't think I can move," Harriett gasped. "I love how you make me feel."

"Marry me," Jess said, wrapping her arms around Harriett.

"Any time, any place," Harriett said, catching her breath.

"The Hill Country is beautiful in the spring when the wildflowers are blooming," Jess said.

"You're serious?" Harriett asked as she stared up at Jess.

Jess reached over Harriett's body and pulled the nightstand drawer open. She took out a small box and settled it in the valley between Harriett's breasts.

"What's this?" Harriett smiled.

"My promise," Jess said softly. "That I'll belong to you and never another until the day I die." Jess slowly opened the box, revealing a garnet solitaire ring surrounded by diamonds. "Anyone can have a diamond engagement ring." Jess smiled as she removed the ring and slipped onto Harriett's left ring finger. "Happy Thanksgiving, baby."

"My birthstone. It's perfect," Harriett said as she slid her arms around Jess's neck and kissed her.

"Is that a yes?" Jess asked.

"Did you ever doubt it, my love?" Harriett answered with a smile as she pushed Jess onto her back, her hands skimming down Jess's well-muscled body, eliciting a throaty groan.


LATE FRIDAY MORNING, Harriett was helping Irene prepare brunch in the kitchen. Harriett wasn't sure when her mother had returned home the night before.

"Did you win last night?" Harriett asked.

"A game or two," Irene answered. "But we had fun and that's the real reason we get together. Hand me the ladle, please?"

Harriett picked the utensil up with her left hand and held it out to Irene. "That's a lovely ring. I don't recall seeing it before. Is it new?" Irene asked.

"Uh...yes," Harriett answered with a wide smile. "Jess asked me to marry her last night," she added, her voice trembling slightly.

Irene dropped the ladle and wrapped her arms around her daughter. Then she stared at Harriett. "Please tell me you said yes."

"Of course I did," Harriett grinned, hugging her mother. "I'm so happy, Mom. I love her so very much."

"Anyone with eyes can tell how much Jess loves you, too, sweetheart. I'm thrilled for both of you," Irene said with tears in her eyes. She took Harriett's face in her hands. "You deserve to be happy. I'm sorry you've had to wait so long though."

"If I hadn't waited, I might not have found her. She was worth waiting for," Harriett said.

Jess popped into the kitchen. "Food almost ready?" she asked, grinning at Harriett. "I'm starving for some reason."

Irene grabbed Jess by the arm and pulled her closer. "Welcome to my family, Jess," she said. "I couldn't ask for a better daughter-in-law."

"I see your daughter couldn't keep it a secret until tonight," Jess said as she returned the hug.

"We haven't told anyone else, Mom," Harriett said. "We'd like to tell Lacey ourselves."

"I understand, honey. I won't tell anyone else until it's okay with you two." Irene said before returning to preparing their plates.

Jess stepped next to Harriett, wrapped an arm around her

waist, and kissed her on the temple. "I love you," she whispered.

EARLY SUNDAY AFTERNOON, Jess, holding Lacey's carry-on duffle bag, followed Lacey and Harriett into the Abilene airport. Jess smiled watching the two women walking with an arm draped loosely around one another's waist, chatting happily as they approached the ticket counter to get Lacey's boarding pass. Then they all walked to a small food court near the entrance to the gate area to spend the time left before Lacey went through security.

Jess set the carry-on down as Harriett and Lacey sat at a small table to wait for Jess, who was ordering drinks from a nearly counter. When she returned, Lacey said, "Promise you won't do anything for the wedding until I come back for Christmas. Don't make me drop out of school to be here for the planning."

"We might have to do a few things," Jess said.

"Like what?" Lacey said sharply.

"Well, since it's only four months away, we will have to reserve a venue, find a florist, find a new house, and—" Jess began.

"I can do that from my cell phone in California!" Lacey insisted.

"We know what we want," Harriett said softly, patting her niece's hand. "But don't worry, there will be more than enough for you to do."

Jess shrugged. "It doesn't matter to me where or how we get married as long as we get married."

"Wait!" Harriett said, her eyes widening as she stared at Jess. "We already have a house."

Jess grinned and took Harriett's hand, entwining their fingers. "No, I already have a house. Now, *we* need our own house where *we* can build a new life together, doncha think." She brought Harriett's hand to her lips and kissed it.

Lacey bounced up and down in her chair excitedly. "Don't do anything until Christmas. I'll be back in less than a month and I have to be here for that!"

Harriett leaned forward and hugged Jess. "Thank you, baby," she whispered. "I love you."

THE FOLLOWING MORNING, Harriett entered the Jones County Courthouse and stepped into an elevator which would take her to the third floor. She smiled at others who joined her in the elevator and tried to focus on her job that day. But, if pressed, she would have to admit to being somewhat distracted. Events in her own life made it difficult to organize her thoughts. It was, quite possibly, the happiest time in her life, but the needs of her client, an old friend, forced Harriett to shove that happiness further back in her mind. KC expected, and deserved, the best Harriett could provide. Even though she felt confident she could successfully defend her client, Harriett had participated in more than one case that had suddenly and unexpectedly taken a left at Albuquerque, jeopardizing her client. One of her law professors often reminded his students to "expect the unexpected" and Harriett always took that advice seriously.

When the elevator doors slid open, Harriett, who was dressed comfortably in a light gray woven silk suit pinstriped by a darker gray over a bright red long-sleeved turtle neck, walked down the corridor toward the assigned courtroom. She took a deep breath before pushing the courtroom doors open to settle any lingering nerves and stepped inside. It didn't matter how large or ornate a courtroom was. She was always awed by the thought of what they represented.

She smiled at a middle-aged man who wore a uniform identifying him as the court's bailiff as he prepared the room for the day's proceedings as she swung the wooden gate between the spectators and the business areas open. She opened her briefcase and laid out her legal pad, her fountain pen, and her eyeglasses. A pitcher of water and two glasses sat in the center of the defense table. After she sat, she poured a half glass of water and drank it.

The bailiff placed a list of potential jurors who had been called to hear KC's trial on the defense and prosecution tables. Harriett leaned back in her chair and glanced over the list. She mentally acknowledged that there probably wasn't anyone on the list who didn't know KC. Despite that, Harriett marked a few she might challenge, depending on their possible opinion regarding homosexuality, assuming it might become an issue during the trial.

When court was adjourned for lunch, Harriett was satisfied with the jurors who had been selected. KC had no objection to any of the panel members called and had little to offer. She was unusually quiet, spending most of the morning doodling on the legal pad Harriett had given her.

"Is something wrong, KC?" Harriett asked as she stuffed everything back into her briefcase.

"Nope," KC answered, tearing off a sheet of paper from the pad. "Give this to Jess, will ya?" she said as she slid the paper to Harriett.

"Sure. What is it?"

KC shrugged. "Just a play I've been thinkin' about."

"Okay. Buy you a burger?" Harriett offered.

KC smiled. "Sounds good. I never turn down free food and I'm gettin' a little tired of turkey."

"Maybe while we eat you can tell me a few things about a couple of witnesses," Harriett said, patting KC's back.


AFTER LUNCH, DAVIS Barnett rose to give his opening statement. Harriett leaned back in her chair and picked up her eyeglasses, sticking the end of an earpiece between her teeth.

"My friends, everything Ms. Markham will tell you about the defendant is true," Barnett began. "There is no debate that Kerrie Carnes is a well-regarded citizen of Anson. One of her former players was my own daughter. Most of you know who the defendant is, so I won't waste your time telling you things you already know." He looked at KC and smiled. "I respect Kerrie Carnes," he said before his smile dropped to a frown. "But I am also aware of her occasionally volatile temper. The People will show that on the night of October thirtieth, Kerrie Carnes lost control of that temper during an argument with the deceased. At some point, unable to control her anger, she struck him with an object and killed him. We are not asserting that she went to the school that night *planning* to kill Allen DeVore, but during a heated argument, her anger exploded, leading to the death of Allen DeVore." He rested his hands on the rail of the jury box and made eye contact with each juror. "Someone must be held accountable for that death," he said in a low voice that forced the jurors to lean slightly forward in order to hear what he said. "I am just as confident as my opponent that after you see all of our evidence and hear the testimony of our witnesses, you will have no choice but to declare Kerrie Carnes guilty of causing the death of Allen DeVore. Thank you," Barnett concluded.

Harriett smiled to herself, appreciating Barnett's flair for the dramatic during his amazingly short remarks to the jury. She, too, knew ways to make a jury trust her. She stood and partially closed the earpieces of her glasses and let them dangle from her fingers as she approached the jury.

Harriett smiled slightly and gazed at KC a moment before

beginning her opening statement. "Ladies and gentlemen of the jury. My client and I appreciate the time you are willingly giving up to listen thoughtfully to the facts and evidence being presented by the People and the defense.

"In order for you to find my client guilty of the charge against her, the evidence must show, beyond any reasonable doubt, that she, and she alone, committed this crime. It must show, not that she *may* have committed the crime, or *probably* committed the crime, but that she *did*, in fact, commit the crime. We will show, however, that the evidence in this case cannot prove that. In order to prove that my client, Kerrie Carnes, intentionally and willfully murdered Allen DeVore, the People must show that she had not only the means and the opportunity to commit the crime, but also a motive, a reason, to commit the crime."

Harriett turned to look at KC a moment before continuing. "Kerrie Carnes is a life-long resident of Jones County. She is currently a member of the Anson High School faculty. In that capacity, she has been named Teacher of the Year and coaches the girls' basketball team, leading them to numerous state championships since assuming responsibility for her team. Many of her former players, like Mr. Barnett's daughter, have gone on to play collegiately at the finest colleges and universities in our state, as well as other states. Kerrie gave up a lucrative career coaching at the collegiate level to return to Anson ten years ago to care for her mother, who now resides in a long-term nursing facility in Abilene.

"Some of you may know Kerrie either through her youth activities in our community or perhaps because she either taught or coached your child. Kerrie and I expect each of you to consider the evidence carefully and listen to the testimony of the witnesses before rendering your verdict. We are confident you will find her innocent of the charge against her. Thank you."

As soon as Harriett resumed her seat, the prosecutor stood. "Your Honor, the People call Alejandro Cavazos," Barnett said.

"I'm sure you would, Mr. Barnett, but I have an appointment this afternoon that I've already had to reschedule three times. In order to avoid another cancellation, and more aggravation, I'm adjourning court today. We will reconvene tomorrow morning at nine a.m.," Judge Clemons ordered, slamming her gavel down firmly.

# Chapter Eighteen

THE DOOR OF the courtroom opened a few minutes after nine Tuesday morning and a skinny man in his mid-thirties with black hair and dark eyes entered. He was neatly dressed in plain clothing. He was dark complexioned and a thin mustache separated his nose and full mouth. Harriett noticed that his hair was neatly cut, but had probably been cut by his wife. According to her notes, Cavazos and his wife were the parents of a five-year-old daughter. He had a juvenile record of minor offenses, but there was nothing as an adult. He appeared slightly nervous as he smiled and nodded at KC when he took the stand.

"Please tell the court your occupation, Mr. Cavazos," Mr. Barnett said.

"Um...I am a custodian at Anson High School," Cavazos said.

"How long have you been employed at the high school?"

"Three...no, four years at the new year."

"And does part of your job include cleaning the gymnasium and locker rooms?"

"I...um...volunteer to clean that area on the weekends to earn a little extra money."

"Did you clean that area on October thirty-first?"

"Yes. I came in early because there was a practice game the night before." He glanced toward the defense table. "Coach Carnes gave me a schedule the week before. The girls they don't make such a big mess and the coach, she always puts everything away before she leaves."

"Why did you decide then to clean Coach DeVore's office on Saturday morning?"

Alejandro blushed slightly before answering. "I didn't clean it before I left Friday," he said. "I usually do, but my wife and I were taking our daughter to an early Halloween party and I knew I would be there Saturday morning, so I didn't clean it then so I could be home early."

"When you clean Coach DeVore's office, what does that entail?"

"What is entail?"

"What do you do to clean the room?"

"I dust his secretary's room in front of the Coach's office first, empty the trash, and vacuum the carpeting."

"Was the door between the reception area and the coach's office open or closed when you walked into the area?"

"It was closed. I hurried to clean the secretary's room because I thought the coach might be there."

"How did you determine that Coach DeVore wasn't in his office?"

"I put my ear against the door and tapped it. I didn't hear nothing so I opened the door. Then I saw him on the floor. There was blood on the floor around his head. He didn't answer me when I ask him if he was okay." Alejandro made the sign of the cross and kissed his thumb as he finished his answer. "Then I call the police and left to wait in the hall."

"No further questions, Your Honor," Barnett said.

"Ms. Markham, do you wish to cross-examine this witness?" Judge Clemons asked.

"Yes, thank you, Your Honor," Harriett answered as she stood and glanced at her legal pad.

"Mr. Cavazos, you testified that you primarily clean the gym after Friday night home games. Is that correct?"

"Si."

"Who cleans it during the week?"

"Whoever is available."

"Do you always clean the coach's offices?"

"Usually."

"Do you *usually* dust, empty the trash, and vacuum the offices every day?"

"No. I only empty the trash every day. I dust and vacuum once a week unless I can see the offices need it sooner."

"That makes sense," Harriett said. "How often do you deep-clean them?"

Alejandro looked confused.

"When do you use furniture polish or a carpet cleaning product?"

"Ah. We do that every two weeks."

"When was the last time you deep-cleaned the coach's office?"

"I did that the week before I found the coach."

"So the week you found his body, you primarily emptied the trash. Is that correct?"

"Si."

"Besides Coach DeVore's body, what else did you notice in his office? Anything seem out of place?"

"There was a towel on the file cabinet and a trophy on the floor. I would have removed them when I cleaned."

"Thank you, Mr. Cavazos. I don't have any other questions at this time."

"The witness is excused with the reminder that you can be recalled. If you are, you will still be under oath," Judge Clemons intoned.

Barnett stood. "The people call Officer Terrance McElroy." McElroy was a tall, well-built young man in his late twenties. According to the information sheet Jess had compiled, McElroy had joined the Anson Police Department after he separated from the military and had attended numerous law enforcement seminars and classes. He was single and enjoyed the small-town atmosphere in Anson.

After Officer McElroy was sworn in and seated, Barnett asked, "How long have you been a member of the Anson Police Department, Officer McElroy?"

"Five years, sir."

"Did you have any previous experience in law enforcement before joining the department?"

"Yes, sir. I served in the military police for six years before separating from the Army."

"Can you tell the court why you left the military?"

"I was injured in the line of duty. However, my injury does not interfere with my current duties, sir."

"On behalf of us all, we thank you for your service, Officer McElroy," Barnett said.

"Thank you, sir."

"Do you remember the events on October thirty-first of this year?"

"Yes, sir. I was on patrol and received a request involving the discovery of a deceased individual at Anson High School. Because it was Halloween, I thought it possibly was a prank, but went to the school to check it out. I was met by a custodian, Mr. Cavazos, outside the school gymnasium. He explained that he found the body while cleaning the athletic office and identified the victim as Allen DeVore, the head football coach and athletic director."

"Had Mr. Cavazos disturbed any part of the office?"

"According to his statement, he only touched the door knob into the room and the phone, to call 9-1-1."

"Did you touch anything after you entered the office, Officer McElroy?"

"I checked the victim's carotid and determined that he was deceased. Then I called for back-up and the justice of the peace to formally make the official declaration. I secured the area and took Mr. Cavazos's statement."

"No further questions, Your Honor," Barnett said.

"Ms. Markham?" Judge Clemons asked.

Harriett stood and said, "The defense has no questions for this witness at this time, Your Honor."

"You're excused, Officer. You may call your next witness, Mr. Barnett," Judge Clemons said as Officer McElroy stepped down.

"The people call Samuel Durden," Barnett intoned. Durden made his way down the main aisle of the courtroom. He was a man of average height, but appeared mildly overweight. He had thinning brown hair and wore metallic glasses. He cleared his throat and adjusted his glasses more than once while being sworn in, a sign of nervousness. As soon as Durden was seated, Barnett asks his first question. "Where are you employed, Mr. Durden?"

"I'm...um...employed by the Abilene Police Department as a forensic technician."

"Please tell the court what that position involves."

"Basically, I go to crime scenes in Abilene and surrounding counties to gather evidence. Usually fingerprints, blood samples, and ballistic evidence," Durden answered, seemingly comfortable with discussing his job.

"I assume you are not the only investigator employed by the Abilene PD," Barnett asked with a friendly smile.

"No, sir. We have six investigators on our staff."

"When did you arrive at Anson High School on October thirty-first?"

"After we received the call to sweep the area where the body was found, it took me about forty minutes to arrive. It was a little before noon, I believe."

"What did you find at the scene?"

"I dusted the office and reception area for fingerprints. Inside the office itself there was a white hand towel on top of a file cabinet with what appeared to be blood on it. I bagged and labeled it, along with a trophy that was laying on the floor next to the decedent. I took prints, hair fibers and a blood sample from the victim after he was declared dead by the JP. I vacuumed the office carpeting to examine for any additional evidence that may have been left behind and photographed the scene from various angles. Finally, I released the body and had it transported to the

Dallas County Medical Examiner for autopsy."

"Have you since tested the fingerprints, the towel, and trophy?"

"There were probably over a hundred fingerprints in the reception area and the office. All have not been identified yet. Those are high traffic areas and most likely belong to students."

"Did you find any fingerprints that belonged to the defendant, Kerrie Carnes?"

"Her fingerprints were on the doorknob of the reception area, inside and out, and on the desk in the coach's office. There was a partial print that belonged to the defendant on the trophy as well."

Barnett picked up a trophy from the prosecutor's table and carried it to the judge. "The People wish to have this trophy marked as People's Exhibit One for purposes of identification, Your Honor."

"So marked. Does the defense have any objection?"

"No, Your Honor," Harriett said.

Barnett carried the trophy to the witness stand and set it on the wooden railing in front of Durden. "Is this the trophy you found in Coach DeVore's office, Mr. Durden?"

"It is. I marked it with my initials when I bagged it."

"Where was the fingerprint located?"

"Under the figure on top."

"Were you able to determine which finger it belonged to?"

"The middle finger of the right hand, probably the defendant's."

"Objection," Harriett said. "There is no proof that my client assaulted anyone."

"Sustained. Strike the last answer from the record and the jury will disregard it," Clemons instructed.

"That seems to be an unusual way to pick up a trophy," Barnett said.

"If I may," Durden said, reaching for the trophy. He picked it up, wrapping his fingers around the figure atop the trophy. "I believe the assailant grabbed the trophy in this manner and used it as a club to strike the victim on the head, killing him. The weight of the trophy is primarily in the marble base and the deceased's blood and hair were found on the base."

"Was the blood on the towel also the victim's?"

"No. It was determined to belong to the defendant, Kerrie Carnes."

"How did you determine that?"

"After she was arrested, the Anson Police collected fingerprints, hair, and a blood sample for comparison. The blood and hair matched those on the towel and her fingerprint matched the partial print on the trophy."

"Thank you, Mr. Durden. The prosecution has no further questions, Your Honor."

"Do you wish to cross this witness, Ms. Markham?" Judge Clemons asked.

"I do Your Honor," Harriett said. "But, if it pleases the court, since I'm certain the jury might need a break, I am willing to begin my cross-examination of this witness after the lunch break."

"Court will be in recess for ninety minutes. We will reconvene at one-thirty. Jurors are reminded not to discuss this case with anyone, not even one another. You will be provided with a box lunch and escorted to a conference room to eat," Judge Clemons instructed.

Harriett gathered her legal pad and pen, stuffing everything into her briefcase. "Where do you want to have lunch?" she asked KC.

"There's a pretty good diner a couple of blocks from here that has a buffet lunch," KC suggested.

"Sounds good to me," Harriett said.

"Is Jess meetin' us?"

"No. She's running down a few things I'll need later. Everything so far has been preliminary testimony. No real surprises. I don't expect anything too substantial until tomorrow, probably," Harriett said with a smile.

"I don't know how you can stand this borin' crap," KC said. "I nearly fell asleep once or twice."

"If you feel drowsy again, pinch yourself. It wouldn't look good if the defendant snored during their own trial. I need you to pay attention. I don't know some of the witnesses very well, but you do. One of them might say something I don't know about."

Harriett and KC walked down the courthouse steps and turned down the sidewalk toward the diner. Several pedestrians acknowledged KC along the way. She opened the door to the diner and waited as Harriett entered. Once they were seated, Harriett leaned against the cushioned back in their booth and took a deep breath. A chuffy, middle-aged waitress hurried to their table, dropping off glasses of water. "How're y'all doin' today?" she asked as she pulled a small pad from the pocket of her uniform.

"No complaints, Anita. How 'bout yourself?" KC answered with a smile.

"Busier than the dickens, girl," the waitress chuckled. "Y'all gonna need a menu?"

KC glanced at Harriett. "I think we'll both try the buffet today. Smells pretty good," KC said with a smile.

"Good choice, KC. Drinks?"

"Two sweet teas should do it. That okay with you, Harriett?"

"It's fine," Harriett said.

"Then help yourselves and I'll get your drinks," Anita instructed.

A few minutes later, KC sat down and placed two plates on the table. One was piled with salad and the second with chicken and dumplings, accompanied by pieces of cornbread. A small bowl of banana pudding completed her meal. Harriett joined her with a large plate of what she had put together as a chef salad, with chunks of ham, turkey, and cheese cubes, covered with ranch dressing.

"Still eatin' that damn rabbit food, I see," KC said as she stabbed her fork into the lettuce and tomatoes on the plate in front of her.

"I don't want to overeat before court resumes," Harriett said. "I didn't see Diane this morning. Will she be there this afternoon?"

"I doubt it. I told her not to use a vacation day. Besides, I know it would be uncomfortable for her to be there."

"She doesn't think you're guilty, does she?"

"Of course not, but she doesn't want to...um...cause any questions, ya know."

Harriett chewed a bite of her salad and swallowed it, thinking back to the young woman she remembered. "You know, KC, I know you've never hidden who you are and I've always respected that about you, but I can't believe you'd ever have a partner so deeply closeted."

"What can I say. Shit happens," KC said with a shrug. "Diane wasn't always this way."

"When did she change?"

"A couple of years ago. I never knew why, but she just became...distant."

"I'm sorry, KC," Harriett said softly.

"I've been thinkin' about leavin' anyway. There are a few opportunities available overseas if I beat this rap."

Harriett was opening a package of crackers when KC reached

out and grabbed her hand. "Nice ring," she said. "Don't remember seein' it before."

Harriett blushed. "Jess gave it to me over Thanksgiving...as an engagement ring."

"No fuckin' shit!" KC exclaimed as Harriett shushed her and wished the floor would open and swallow her.

"Happy for you, honey," KC said. "You let me know if that gal ever mistreats you. I'm startin' to like her, but I will kick her ass for you if she needs it, okay?"

Harriett laughed. "I think I can take care of her ass myself, but thanks, KC."

"She's doin' a good job with the team, so far."

"She's enjoying it for the most part, I think."

Following the lunch recess, Samuel Durden retook the stand and settled into his chair while Harriett thumbed through her notes from his previous testimony. "Mr. Durden, earlier you testified that my client's hair was found on the towel you tested, along with her blood. Is that correct?" she asked.

"Yes," the witness answered.

"Did you perform a test for DNA on the towel as well?"

"I did."

"And what did that test reveal?"

"The blood on the towel was a mixture of the defendant's blood and that of the victim."

"Is it possible my client could have struck Mr. DeVore and cut her hand as a result? If she then wiped her bleeding hand on the towel, she could have deposited Mr. DeVore's blood along with her own, couldn't she?"

"It's possible, I suppose," Durden admitted.

"Was there enough of Mr. DeVore's blood on the towel to lead you to believe that loss of blood killed him?"

"No. It was a very small amount."

"Are the towels at Anson High School marked for use by men or women?"

"Not the one I tested. It was a generic towel. I'm not acquainted with how they separate their laundry," Durden said with a grin, drawing a ripple of laughter from the observers.

"So, there's no way to determine how long that particular towel was in Mr. DeVore's office or who deposited it there, is there?"

"The custodian told me it wasn't there the last time he cleaned that office," Durden deflected.

"Then it could have been left any time the previous week,

couldn't it?"

Durden paused before answering. "I suppose."

"And there isn't any way to determine when the blood or hair was left on the towel, is there?"

"The hair, no, but the blood was relatively fresh, probably not more than twenty-four hours old when I tested it."

"May I approach the witness, Your Honor?" Harriett asked.

Judge Clemons nodded and Harriett walked to the witness stand, picking up the trophy on her way. "Mr. Durden, you have identified this trophy as the one you collected from Mr. DeVore's office the day his body was found. Can you show me where the partial fingerprint was located?"

Durden leaned forward and pointed to a place just beneath the figure at the top of the trophy.

"Can you tell the court when the fingerprint was left on the trophy?" Harriett asked.

"No."

"Then it could have been there a week or a month?"

"I'm not familiar with a test for the age of a fingerprint, Ms. Markham. However, the blood, skin, and hair on the trophy was deposited recently, within twenty-four hours."

"But the fingerprint does not prove that my client used this trophy as a weapon to kill Mr. DeVore, does it?"

"Not the fingerprint alone, no."

"What event was this trophy presented for?"

"The engraved faceplate says it was presented to the girls' basketball team for their second place finish last season."

"Then it wouldn't be unusual to find their coach's fingerprint on the trophy, would it?"

"Probably not."

"Thank you, Mr. Durden. I have no further questions for this witness, Your Honor," Harriett said, walking back to the defense table after returning the trophy to the evidence table.

"The People call Dr. Thomas Gilford," Barnett said. A tall, slightly rumpled-looking older man with salt-and-pepper hair entered the courtroom with a file folder tucked under his arm. Dressed in a well-cut three-piece suit, he walked confidently to the witness stand and nodded at the judge. After being sworn in, he unbuttoned the jacket of his suit and sat down.

"What is your current position, Dr. Gilford?" Barnett asked.

"I am a medical examiner for Dallas County," Gilford answered.

"Where did you receive your training, Doctor?"

"I received my medical degree from Texas A&M University Medical School before receiving advanced training at Johns Hopkins in Baltimore, Maryland."

"How long have you been certified as a medical examiner?"

"Twenty-five years, the last five years in Dallas County."

"Can you briefly describe what your position entails?"

"Our primary job is to perform autopsies and determine the cause of death for individuals who expired while either not in a hospital or under the care of a licensed physician at the time of their death."

"And approximately how many autopsies does your office perform annually?"

"Over three thousand."

"I request that this witness be declared an expert in his field, Your Honor," Barnett stated.

"No objection, Your Honor," Harriett said.

"The witness is declared an expert," Judge Clemons said flatly.

"Dr. Gilford, when did you receive the body of Allen DeVore for autopsy?"

"May I consult my notes on this case?"

"Of course. I'm sure it would be difficult to remember the specifics of over three thousand cases a year," Barnett said with a smile.

"No objection," Harriett said.

Gilford opened the folder he had carried into the courtroom and turned a few pages before answering Barnett's question. "My office received the body at nine the evening of October thirty-first, along with the Jones County Justice of the Peace report."

"Was your autopsy done that same night?"

"No. The receiving clerk logged the body in and transferred it to storage in our morgue. I was called in the following morning to perform the autopsy."

"Was the deceased's body temperature determined after the body was discovered?"

Glancing at a page, Gilford answered, "A rectal reading was taken at approximately two p.m. and the body's temperature was recorded as eighty point six."

"What time would that indicate the victim died, Doctor?"

"Objection," Harriett said. "There is insufficient evidence to make that determination, Your Honor."

"Sustained."

"What else had the justice of the peace determined after

examining the body?"

"That the body had already passed through rigor mortis and based on livor mortis had not been moved." Dr. Gilford shifted his eyes toward the jury. "In laymen's terms, the muscles of the body had relaxed and the blood in his system pooled beneath him because it had ceased to circulate."

"Was a body temperature taken when it was received at the Medical Examiner's Office?"

"It was. The body's temperature was recorded as sixty-two point six degrees, but there were a number of variables that undoubtedly effected the later reading. The body was transported in an air-conditioned vehicle for a little more than three hours and the ambient temperature of the body's original location was not recorded. Other factors could have also compromised an accurate reading as well. However, based on the original temperature taken by the justice of the peace, it's probable that the victim died somewhere between eight p.m. and midnight on October thirtieth."

"What was the condition of the body when you performed your autopsy, Doctor?"

"The body was that of a well-nourished male in his early forties. His musculature showed signs of athletic development and his internal organs revealed no signs of disease. There was an abrasion on his face and a deep contusion on the side of his head, which I determined was the cause of death. The deceased apparently suffered a blow to the right temporal region of the skull above the right ear. The blow caused a fracture of the bone and penetrated the skull cavity."

"Was that blow enough to cause his death?"

"Yes, but probably not immediately. The blow itself caused bleeding in the temporal area. The pressure of the accumulating blood eventually caused the brain to shut down, resulting in death."

"How long would it have taken for him to die from this injury?"

"An hour, maybe two."

"Would he have been conscious during that time?"

"Depending on the force of the blow, it's unlikely he regained consciousness."

"If he had been taken to a hospital immediately, could he have survived?"

"Absolutely."

"If Mr. DeVore was attacked by an *angry* individual, how

could that effect the force of such a blow?"

"Objection," Harriett said as she rose from her chair quickly. "There is no evidence of the assailant's emotional state and this witness is not a psychologist, Your Honor. He is only qualified to give such an opinion or how that may have skewed the estimated time of death and Mr. Barnett knows that."

"I know he is a licensed physician in this state and as such should know the effect of adrenaline on the human body," Barnett retorted.

"Overruled," Judge Clemons said. "You may answer the question, Dr. Gilford."

"Exception," Harriett said.

"Noted," the judge said.

"Individuals involved in an argument, depending on the severity of the argument, usually produce elevated amounts of adrenaline as a bodily response. Elevated adrenaline has been known to produce above average strength. The stories we've all heard about mothers lifting a car to save their child who was pinned underneath are primarily based on highly elevated adrenaline, the result of fear for the child's life." Gilford glanced at the defense table and smiled slightly. "While the same can be said for an individual involved in a heated argument, I cannot say whether anger was involved in this case. The assailant may simply have been stronger."

"Thank you, Dr. Gilford. No further questions, Your Honor," Barnett finally said. "Your witness, counselor."

"So, you were unable to determine the time of death, is that correct?" Harriett asked.

"Not with any degree of certainty. That's correct," Gilford answered.

"Even after he was struck on the head, he could have lived for at least an hour or two, is that correct?"

"Yes."

"Could he have survived longer?"

"Possibly, depending on the ambient temperature of the room and his heart rate."

"Isn't it true that the heart rate slows when we're asleep or unconscious?"

"It does."

"Therefore, bleeding into the brain could have taken considerably longer than an hour or two?"

"Regardless of how long it took the deceased to die, the blow to his head was still the cause of death."

"But his body temperature, taken by the justice of the peace, would have been affected, would it not?"

"Possibly."

"Is a rectal temperature the most accurate way to determine time of death?"

"It's the most common method, but the liver temperature is more accurate since it registers the body's core temperature."

"Why wasn't the liver temperature test performed then?"

"A liver temperature requires additional training and because most justices of the peace are elected, they don't have the required medical training and it's easier to take a rectal reading."

"No further questions, Your Honor."

Before Barnett could call his next witness, Judge Clemons announced the court would recess until the following morning. Harriett had no objection. So far, the case against KC appeared to be circumstantial at best and the next scheduled witnesses shouldn't be able to testify to anything substantial. The additional time would give her time to prepare for her own witnesses and get ready to provide another possible suspect, one with as good a reason to kill Allen DeVore as KC.

# Chapter Nineteen

THE NEXT MORNING, armed with the information Jess had compiled and a list of questions, Harriett, wearing a teal suit over a white silk blouse, made her way up the steps of the Jones County courthouse, accompanied by Jess. She wanted to appear as non-threatening as possible if her motion was denied and she was forced to cross-examine each witness scheduled to testify that day. The previous week and holiday left her exhausted and she hadn't slept well, even in Jess's arms. The situation between her and Lorri still wasn't fully resolved, and Harriett doubted it ever would be. Irene would remain hurt and the best thing would be to finish this damn case and return to the relative safety of Austin.

She was beginning to wish she'd never received KC's phone call and peeled back the lid on the whole can of worms. No one would come away untarnished. Not her, not Jess, not Lorri or her family. And most regrettably, not Irene. But when she walked away from this case, she thought with a smile, she and Jess would have time to plan their wedding. She felt like a giddy teenager again at the thought of it.

The parents of the students expected to testify were gathered outside the third-floor courtrooms with their daughters and talking quietly when Harriett and Jess stepped off the elevator and made their way to Judge Clemons's courtroom. Harriett nodded to them briefly before pulling the courtroom door open and walking to the defense table to wait for KC. Jess took a seat near the back of the room. At nine o'clock, Harriett turned and smiled at Jess as the parents entered and found seats behind the prosecution table. Barnett stood and leaned over the railing which separated him from those observing the trial and spoke briefly to the concerned-looking parents. While waiting for KC, Harriett looked through the folders she had on each family.

Gabriel Costa was a handsome Hispanic man with black hair and intense-looking brown eyes. Behind his slight smile, he seemed mildly uncomfortable. Mrs. Costa was similarly attractive and Caucasian with long dark brown hair and blue eyes. She also looked nervous and uncomfortable, glancing at her wristwatch as if she was going to be late for another appointment.

Harriett's notes indicated that he was a physician at Anson

Memorial Hospital and his wife was a realtor in Abilene. Dr. Costa was also recently-elected to the city council. Mrs. Costa sat up straighter in her seat and brushed her long dark hair away from her face with French-tipped fingernails. Harriett noticed that belying their professions, both parents were well-dressed.

Abel and Graciela Lucero were seated behind the Costas and looked solemnly around the room. Jess had listed Abel Lucero's occupation as a driller with a local oil company. Graciela was listed as a homemaker. They were the parents of five children. The Luceros were dressed in clean, but well-worn clothing. Abel was darkly tanned from the days he spent working in the oil fields. A slightly droopy, but neatly trimmed, mustache adorned his upper lip. Harriett felt certain that the Luceros did not socialize with either the Costas or DeVores in any meaningful way.

Peggy DeVore, a striking looking woman with inky black hair and piercing light gray eyes, sat several feet away from the Costas. To Harriett, she didn't look like a part of the parents' group and seemed uncomfortable in her surroundings. She was casually dressed in slacks and a lightweight sweater over an Oxford button-down shirt. She was obviously only there to lend support to her daughter.

Harriett stood to greet her client when the side door of the courtroom opened. KC looked almost roguish and at ease. The wind outside had blown her short hair and a lock fell onto her forehead. Her pressed, button-down shirt was tucked neatly into her belted, navy blue slacks. Her matching jacket was open and well-fitted to her body. She extended a hand to greet Harriett as her eyes swept over the rapidly filling gallery. They paused for a moment before she pulled out a chair to sit.

Harriett glanced over her shoulder. Had KC paused to look at Peggy DeVore? Perhaps it had only been a glance of sympathy for the woman's loss. Harriett shrugged it off and organized the papers in front of her.

The door behind the bench opened and the bailiff called out, "All rise," as Judge Clemons entered.

"Be seated," she directed. Adjusting her glasses, she asked, "Are the People prepared to call their next witness, Mr. Barnett?"

"Yes, Your Honor. The People call Jennifer Costa to the stand," DB said. Apparently, Judge Clemons was planning to dismiss Harriett's motion.

Standing, Harriett said, "Your Honor, the defense renews its objection to this witness, as well as to the testimony of Erica

Lucero and Heather DeVore. Any testimony given by these witnesses would be based on nothing more than supposition and hearsay."

"They were present and heard the argument," Barnett retorted.

"None of them saw either participant in the *alleged* argument or heard the specifics of such *alleged* argument," Harriett persisted.

"Your objection is overruled, Ms. Markham," Judge Clemons said. "If I'm wrong, you have grounds for an appeal, but the jury has a right to hear the testimony."

"Exception," Harriett sighed before sitting.

"Noted," Judge Clemons said. "Please call in the witness, Fred," she instructed her bailiff.

The bailiff went to the door at the back of the courtroom and held it as Jennifer Costa came in. Her eyes widened slightly as she took in the interior of the room while walking to the witness stand. She appeared to be nervous, and Harriett thought it was probably the first time the girl had been in a courtroom. The teenaged girl seemed to have an affinity for blue eye shadow, which did little to make her look either older or more sophisticated. Harriett recalled a thankfully short period when Lacey had also experimented with cheap make-up to enhance her looks. Perhaps it was simply a phase all young women went through in an attempt to make themselves more appealing to the opposite sex.

After Jennifer was sworn in, she slouched slightly in her chair and intertwined her fingers across her chest. She had long dark hair like her mother's, but the similarity ended there. She was dressed more for school than court in tight, form-fitting pants and a white T-shirt tied in a knot at her waist, displaying a hint of mocha skin.

"Good morning, Jennifer. How are you today?" Barnett asked with a friendly smile.

"Peachy keen," Jennifer answered. "How are you?"

"I'm fine, thank you. How old are you, Jennifer?" Barnett asked.

"Seventeen," the girl answered. "I'm a junior at Anson High this year."

"Just a moment, Mr. Barnett," Judge Clemons interrupted, turning her attention to the witness. "Please untie that knot on your shirt, Miss Costa. It's inappropriate in this, or any, courtroom."

Jennifer frowned but released the knot and stood slightly to readjust her shirt. Harriett stared at the tablet in front of her, hiding the smile on her face at the judge's rebuke.

"Did you know the decedent, Allen DeVore?" Barnett continued after Jennifer resumed her seat.

"His daughter, Heather, and I are friends," she said.

"How long have you been friends with Heather DeVore?"

"Since we started high school," Jennifer answered. The coat of blue eye shadow and a line of black eyeliner, gave her eyes a semi-sultry, drowsy appearance. Harriett felt sure the boys at Anson High School found the look alluring, in a strange way.

Barnett thumbed through a few pages of notes on the table in front of him. "Coach DeVore and his family came to Anson three years ago, so you and Heather have been friends since you both began high school."

"That's what I just said," Jennifer smirked.

"How long have you *lived* in Anson, Jennifer?"

"Five *glorious* years," the girl sighed.

"After the scrimmage on October thirtieth, did you overhear an argument coming from Coach DeVore's office?"

"Yeah. Him and Coach Carnes were going at it again, but I couldn't make out what they were arguing about."

"About what time was that?"

"No clue."

"How did you know the persons arguing were Coaches DeVore and Carnes?"

"Lucky guess," Jennifer answered with a shrug. "When we left the gym for the locker room there weren't any other adults around. Guess I just figured it had to be them. Heather said it was and she ought to know her own father's voice."

"What time did you arrive home that night?"

"No clue, but probably after nine. My mother wanted me to come straight home after the game because I had a paper to finish for the next week."

"Were you alone when you heard the argument?"

"No. Erica and Heather were there."

"Did either of them stay?"

"Nope. Heather had a date and Erica's father was waiting to drive her home."

"Did you notice whether or not Coach Carnes's vehicle was still in the parking lot when you left?"

Jennifer shrugged. "Kinda hard to miss that big white tank she drives. It was parked in the first parking spot next to the gym, same as always."

"Were there many other vehicles parked near the gym or in the parking lot?"

Jennifer closed her eyes and thought. "I don't know how many for sure, but most of them belonged to other girls on the team."

"How many girls were still in the locker room when you left?"

Jennifer shrugged again. "A few. Maybe five or six."

"Did any of them later mention hearing the argument when they left?"

"Not to me."

Barnett studied his notes for a moment. Jennifer shifted around on her chair trying to find a more comfortable position.

Finally, Barnett said with a smile, "When your parents decided to leave Dallas for a town as small as Anson it must have been quite an adjustment for you."

"Total understatement," Jennifer muttered.

"Aside from your friendship with Heather, did your parents socialize with Coach DeVore or his family?"

"Nope."

"Did you actually see either Coach DeVore or Coach Carnes go into Coach DeVore's office?"

"There weren't any other adults there after the game," Jennifer answered, her tone bored.

"Did you ever have a problem with Coach Carnes? Think she treated you unfairly?"

"Coach has chewed out lots of players, including me when she thought I was slackin'. But that was only her opinion. She had favorites and we all knew it. She never reamed out Ali."

"Who?"

"Ali O'Neill, our center. She's a dyke like Coach," Jennifer said, glaring at KC.

"Objection," Harriett said quickly. "Defense objects to this unwarranted characterization of my client and Ms. O'Neill."

"Sustained," Judge Clemons said. "The jury will disregard the witness's last statement."

"Heather told me Ali hit on her a few weeks ago," Jennifer volunteered. "As if," she added.

"Objection. Hearsay," Harriett said, jumping up. "This witness's unsolicited statement should be stricken from the record as nothing more than teenage gossip."

"Sustained! Strike the witness's last foray into teenaged angst from the record. The jury will disregard."

KC leaned closer to Harriett. "How can they disregard what they've already heard?" she whispered.

"They can't and Barnett knows it," Harriett whispered back.

"No further questions, Your Honor," Barnett said smugly.

Harriett glanced down at the paperwork in front of her and pretended to scan the material. She took a deep breath and smiled at Jennifer.

"I gather Anson isn't your kind of town, is that correct, Jennifer?"

"We moved here from Dallas. You guess," Jennifer smirked.

"I lived in Dallas myself for several years and agree that it has a lot to offer," Harriett admitted.

"I didn't hear a question, Your Honor. Is Ms. Markham now working for the Dallas Tourist Bureau?" Barnett said with a smile.

"And I didn't hear an objection, Mr. Barnett," Judge Clemons responded. "Unless you just enjoy the sound of your own voice, allow the defense to continue."

"You said you, along with Erica Lucero and Heather DeVore, heard an argument in Coach DeVore's office, is that correct?"

"Yes."

"Could you tell what was being said?"

"I already said I couldn't."

"Did you actually see Coach Carnes either enter or leave Coach DeVore's office?"

"Well, no, but there wasn't anyone else in the gym," Jennifer tried. "Heather said –" she started.

"And didn't you just assume who was arguing because Heather DeVore told you who *she* thought it was?" Harriett pressed. "Yes or no, please."

"Yeah, I guess," Jennifer pouted.

"It doesn't matter what Heather said, Miss Costa. Anything she told you is not evidence. It's hearsay."

"I didn't realize we were already at the summation portion of this trial, Your Honor," Barnett sighed. "The People will be calling Heather DeVore to the stand. She can verify what she told Miss Costa."

"Move on, Counselor. We get the idea," the judge directed.

"How long have you been friends with Erica Lucero?" Harriett asked, taking a different tack.

"Just since last year. Heather was friends with her first."

"I see that Erica was born and raised in Anson," Harriett

noted, looking at her notes.

"Lucky her," Jennifer said, rolling her eyes.

"The three of you are on the girls' basketball team, is that right?"

"Yep."

"And none of you actually saw Coach Carnes entering or leaving Coach DeVore's office, did you?"

"Nope...*again.*"

"In fact, none of you saw Coach DeVore enter his office accompanied or unaccompanied, did you?"

"Nope."

"Why didn't you stick around until the argument ended to see who was in the office?"

"I had better things to do besides listen to a couple of adults argue. I can hear that at h...uh...anywhere."

"The defense has no further questions, at this time, for this witness, but reserves the right to recall her, Your Honor," Harriett said.

Jennifer said, "Can I go back to school then?"

"You may," Judge Clemons answered, "but you may not discuss this case with anyone."

Jennifer stepped down and tromped out of the courtroom, followed quickly by her parents.

"The People call Erica Lucero to the stand, Your Honor," Barnett said.

"Does Mr. Barnett propose to call the entire girls' basketball team, Your Honor?" Harriett asked.

"Only if necessary, Your Honor," Barnett said with a grin.

"The defense renews its objection," Harriett said.

"So noted," Judge Clemons said.

The bailiff escorted Erica Lucero into the courtroom. She was an average-looking young girl who seemed nervous and uncomfortable as all eyes followed her to the witness stand. She was plainly dressed and wore no make-up. Her long, dark brown hair was tightly braided and fell down her back. Her rich brown eyes were cast down as she made her way down the center aisle and she looked frightened as she took a seat next to the judge's dais. Barnett smiled at Erica and the girl smiled back, slightly hesitantly. Her eyes searched the spectators until she located her parents

"Good morning, Erica. How are you feeling?" Barnett asked.

"A little nervous, sir. I've never done this before and am not sure what to expect," Erica answered, fidgeting in her seat.

"I'm just going to ask you to tell me, in your own words, what you saw or heard on October thirtieth after your basketball scrimmage. Be as accurate as you can. Okay? Just tell the truth," Barnett instructed.

"Is that the night Heather's father was killed?"

"Yes. Can you tell the court what happened when you left the locker room that night?" Barnett asked.

"Heather and Jennifer were ahead of me and when I came out they were standing at Coach DeVore's office door."

"Did you hear arguing inside the office?"

"Not at first. Heather and Jennifer had their ears pressed against the door and were giggling. I asked them what was happening and Heather said her father was chewing Coach's...um...butt off."

"Did *you* hear Coach DeVore say that or was that what Heather told you?" Barnett clarified.

"I didn't hear what they said, but then Jennifer pulled me closer to the door and I heard loud voices. But I still couldn't hear what they were saying."

"How long were the three of you at the door listening?"

Erica shrugged. "A few minutes. Five maybe. I was afraid the adults inside would come out and catch us eavesdropping. Besides, I had to leave because my father was waiting outside for me," Erica concluded.

"But you knew it was Coach DeVore and Coach Carnes who were arguing?"

"Heather said it was her father."

"Did you see Coach Carnes in the gym or her office?"

"No."

"Then isn't it possible that Coach Carnes was the second person involved in the argument you heard?"

"Objection. Calls for a conclusion the witness isn't qualified to give, Your Honor," Harriett said.

"Withdrawn," Barnett said. "No further questions, Your Honor."

Harriett looked at her notes. Erica Lucero wasn't the strongest witness for the prosecution, but she had been believable.

"Erica, do you know what time you left the locker room the night of October thirtieth?" Harriett asked.

"I think it was between eight and nine. I glanced at the clock in the locker room while I was combing my hair and it was around eight-thirty then. I left a few minutes later."

"And Jennifer and Heather left before you, is that correct?"

"Yes. A minute or two," Erica confirmed.

"Was Coach Carnes in the gym when you entered the locker room after the scrimmage that night?"

"Yes. She was picking up towels and equipment like she always does."

"You didn't see Coach Carnes enter Coach DeVore's office, did you?"

"No, I didn't," Erica said with a frown.

"Thank you, Erica," Harriett concluded. "No further questions, Your Honor."

"The People call Heather DeVore, Your Honor," Barnett said as he stood.

Heather DeVore entered the courtroom and seemed calm as everyone watched her make her way toward the witness stand. She exemplified what most observers would classify as a member of the high school elite. The only hint of nervousness came after she was sworn in when she began picking at the polish on her fingernails as she waited for the first question. When Barnett finally spoke, the girl jumped as if startled momentarily.

"Heather," Barnett said, "I know this has been a very difficult time for you and your family. I'll try not to make this any more stressful."

"Thank you," Heather said in a voice soft.

Barnett began by asking Heather's age, grade level, and extracurricular activities at Anson High School before finally getting to the most pertinent information.

"Do you remember what time you last saw your father on October thirtieth, Heather?" Barnett asked.

"Right after the scrimmage that night, but I'm not sure what time it was."

"Was your mother at the game as well?"

"No. My brother, Brett, had a middle school game the same night. She went to his game while my father attended mine."

"Was it a common practice for your parents to divide up their children's activities?"

"Yes. It was."

"Did you see your father before or during the game?" Barnett asked.

"I spoke to him for a few minutes right after I got to the gym," Heather said with a shrug. "He said he had some work to catch up on in his office before the game started."

"What time was that?"

Heather shrugged again. "Coach Carnes makes us sit through the JV games as a show of support, so it was pretty early. Probably around five or five-thirty."

"And did you see him during the game?"

"When we went in for the half time break, I saw him leaning against his office door."

"Do you know if he was in his office during the entire halftime?"

"I have no idea," Heather said, beginning to look bored.

"Did you play in the first half?"

Heather laughed derisively, "Coach never plays me in the first half. She usually puts me in the second half."

"Had you ever heard Coach Carnes and your father argue?"

"Well, I never really heard it, but I've seen them talking from a distance and their body language didn't look very friendly."

"Did your father complain about the way Coach Carnes handled the team?"

"He thought I didn't get enough playing time."

"Did you think you deserved more time?"

"Sometimes."

"On the night in question did you overhear an argument between your father and Coach Carnes?"

"Yes."

"Were you alone when you overheard the argument?"

"I was with Erica and Jennifer. But none of us heard what they were actually saying. Just loud voices. There's a reception office before you get to Dad's office. The inside door was probably closed."

"Then how did you know it was your father and Coach Carnes?"

"I've heard Coach yell at me enough times to recognize her voice and, obviously I know my own father's voice."

"Were you just passing by or did you hear the loud voices and go to investigate?"

"We weren't eavesdropping, if that's what you mean."

"In her testimony, Erica Lucero said you told her your father was quote 'chewing Coach's butt out' unquote. Is that an accurate statement?"

Heather paused and frowned before answering. "I may have said something like that. I don't really remember."

"Do you know Alison O'Neill?"

"Of course. She's the *star* of our basketball team," Heather said, crossing her arms in front of her chest.

"Did you tell your father Miss O'Neill made an unwanted sexual advance toward you?"

"Who told you that?" Heather snapped. She looked at the judge. "Do I have to answer that? It's personal."

"Please answer the question, Miss DeVore," Judge Clemons ordered.

Heather blushed as she nodded.

"You'll have to give a verbal response for the record," Barnett said.

Exhaling loudly, Heather said, "Yes. I told my father Ali made a pass at me."

"What did Miss O'Neill say to you?"

"She asked if I wanted to get together with her sometime. It was disgusting."

"And what did you take that to mean?"

"She's been staring at me kinda weird and stuff in the locker room when I got suited out. It creeped me out. Everyone knows Ali likes girls," Heather said, staring at Harriett. Then she added, "Maybe you should ask Jamie Gaither. They're...*real* tight."

"Objection, Your Honor. Irrelevant," Harriett said. "None of this testimony has anything to do with my client's case and only slanders other students who are not present to defend themselves."

"It's relevant if the defendant killed Coach DeVore to protect a homosexual student," Barnett argued.

"By involving other students, the witness is attempting to lead this court on an unnecessary and irrelevant snipe hunt as well as slander a student not involved in this case in any way," Harriett said.

"Move along, Mr. Barnett," Judge Clemons said.

"I'd like a ruling on my objection, Your Honor," Harriett said. "For the record."

"Overruled, but be very careful, Mr. Barnett. You're opening the door to a civil suit for slander if you continue this line of questioning," Judge Clemons warned.

"Did you tell others that Miss O'Neill was a homosexual?" Barnett asked.

"I may have told friends that Ali made a pass at me. So what?"

"Did you tell your father?"

"Yes."

"What was your father's reaction when you told him?"

"He was pis...furious and said he was gonna make Coach

take Ali off the team."

"Did he?"

"He was going to tell Coach the night he...he...was killed," Heather answered as tears began to fill her eyes. "Maybe that was what they were arguing about. Everyone knows Coach is a dyke and protects Ali."

"Why do you remain on the team if you're uncomfortable with either Ms. O'Neill or Coach Carnes?"

"My f-f-father wanted me to play," Heather sniffed.

"Your witness, Counselor," Barnett said.

Harriett jotted down a few quick notes and flipped back a few pages in her legal pad. Making a witness wait before launching into questions was her way of both calming the witness and making them nervous. She glanced over her shoulder at Peggy DeVore and placed her pen on the table in front of her.

"I'm sorry for your loss, Heather," Harriett said.

"Thank you," Heather sniffed.

"Do you know Seth Sullivan?"

"Yes."

"Isn't he your boyfriend?"

"So what?"

"What did your father think about you dating Seth?"

"He doesn't have anything to do with this," Heather said angrily.

"Isn't it true that Seth and your father argued about it on more than one occasion?"

"That's a lie, you bitch!" Heather screamed, jumping out of her chair. "Coach Carnes murdered my father!"

"Isn't that nothing more than your opinion?" Harriett asked calmly.

"No! I heard her arguing with my father in his office," Heather insisted.

"Two previous witnesses, your friends, have testified that they heard 'loud voices'," Harriett said calmly, raising her hands to form quote marks, "but were unable to identify the persons arguing positively. And neither saw my client entering your father's office. Both also said that *you* told them one of the voices belonged to your father. Is that true or were they lying to the court?"

"I know my father's voice. I told them," Heather seethed.

"Couldn't the other voice have been that of an adolescent boy, such as Seth Sullivan?"

"No, it...it wasn't Seth's voice. Why are you dragging him

into this?" Heather asked as tears fell onto her cheeks.

"It's no different than your claim against Miss O'Neill. Neither opinion is proof of a fact."

"Are you calling me a liar?" Heather asked, narrowing her eyes.

"No one else heard this *alleged* sexual advance, did they?"

"No, we were alone in the locker room after a practice."

"Did you bother to tell your mother about it?"

"No."

"Why didn't you tell both of your parents?"

"My mother is a...housewife. My father was in a position to actually do something," Heather said, glancing in her mother's direction.

"You didn't see your father after the scrimmage, did you?"

"No. He told me he was going to talk to Coach Carnes after the game about Ali."

"You didn't see Coach Carnes enter his office after the scrimmage, did you?"

"No, but I know it was *her* in his office," Heather persisted, pointing at KC.

"And...you didn't see *who* came out of that office, did you?"

"Badgering the witness, Your Honor," Barnett said as he stood.

"Overruled," Judge Clemons barked. "Answer the question, Miss DeVore."

"No! I didn't see her kill my father, but I know it was Coach Carnes!"

"No further questions, Your Honor," Harriett stated, but her hands were shaking slightly as she sat down. There was possibly nothing she hated more than attacking a grieving young girl in court.

Heather stomped away from the stand and threw open the courtroom door with all her strength on her way out, allowing it to slam against the wall.

"The People rest, Your Honor," Barnett said as he rose to his feet.

"Very well," Judge Clemons said before slamming her gavel down. "Court will adjourn until nine o'clock tomorrow morning at which time the defense may call their first witness."

Harriett and KC stood as Judge Clemons left the bench. Harriett began packing her briefcase and leaned closer to KC. "Go home and try to get a good night's sleep before we come up to bat tomorrow. Eat a good breakfast in the morning, too."

"Okay, Mom," KC said with a grin.

Jess worked her way to the defense table to wait for Harriett. KC extended her hand to Jess. "I understand congratulations are in order," KC said. "Take good care of our girl. Otherwise, I'll have to kick your ass and I'm just beginning to like you."

"No problem," Jess nodded, shaking KC's hand firmly.

# Chapter Twenty

HARRIETT WATCHED INTENTLY as assistant football coach Glenn Freeman made his way to the witness chair and swore to tell the truth. From the evidence gathered by Jess, she had prepared a number of questions she hoped would cast doubt on KC as Allen DeVore's killer. As Freeman settled his large frame into the witness chair Harriett felt a tap on her shoulder. She glanced over and saw Chief Thomas handing her a folded sheet of paper. She quietly thanked him and tried to divide her attention between glancing at her opening questions to Freeman and the note. She looked quickly at KC who seemed relaxed, leaning back in her chair.

Rising, Harriett said, "Your Honor, may I approach the bench?"

Judge Clemons looked mildly annoyed at the interruption, but motioned her forward. Harriett waited until Davis Barnett joined her before speaking.

"Your Honor, I've just received this message concerning the defendant's mother," she said, handing the note to Clemons.

Clemons glanced over the note. "Has your client been apprised of this?" she asked.

"No, Your Honor. Therefore, I would like to request a recess to allow her to take care of this situation."

"Do you wish to object to a recess, Mr. Barnett?"

"Not under these circumstances, Your Honor," Barnett answered. Looking at Harriett he said, "I'll have an officer drive her to the hospital."

"Step back," Clemons ordered. When Barnett and Harriett had returned to their seats the judge said, "The defense has requested and I am granting a recess in this case. Court will resume at nine o'clock the morning of December eighth. The witness will make himself available once again at that time. Court is adjourned." Clemons slammed her gavel down and departed as everyone in the courtroom rose.

"What's going on?" KC asked as Chief Thomas and another police officer approached her.

Harriett cleared her throat. Gripping KC's forearm she said, "It's Ruth, KC. She's been taken to the hospital and the doctor has put her on life support."

"What? They can't do that! I signed a DNR order last year." Looking around she said, "I have to get there as soon as possible."

"We'll get you there as fast as we can, KC," Carl Ray said.

"I'll meet you there," Harriett said as she tossed everything into her briefcase.

KC nodded and followed Carl Ray from the courthouse. As soon as she was in the back seat the vehicle pulled away from the curb using lights and siren. Harriett made it to her truck as quickly as she could, dialing Jess's cell as she watched for traffic passing by on Commercial Street. When Jess's phone went to voice mail, Harriett briefly told her what had happened.

Harriett arrived at the hospital in Abilene thirty minutes later. She pulled into an empty slot in the Emergency Room parking lot. Carl Ray was waiting and escorted her down the hallway. Harriett swallowed as the smells around her reminded her of her own trip to the emergency room in Austin less than a year before. Carl Ray stopped outside an open treatment room. Harriett looked in and saw KC standing next to a gurney holding Ruth's hand and whispering to her.

A few minutes later KC came out of the room and for the first time Harriett could remember, she looked visibly shaken. A doctor followed her into the hallway. "I want that ventilator removed immediately," KC said. "I signed a damn DNR order last year. She wouldn't want this."

"The DNR you signed was when she was admitted for a potential bleed into the brain. Once that situation no longer existed, you should have signed a permanent DNR order."

"Well, where the hell do I have to go to do that?" KC demanded.

"Calm down, KC," Harriett said. Turning to the doctor, she said, "I'm Ms. Carnes's attorney. Give us the appropriate paperwork and she will sign it."

"Go to the nurses' station. They should have the forms there. There should be someone in administration who can notarize it for you. I'll check back later."

"Fuckin' asshole," KC muttered under her breath.

"Wait here and I'll get whatever forms you need," Harriett said.

"I don't fuckin' believe this shit," KC said, shaking her head.

Harriett handed KC her cell. "Call Diane. She should be here for you."

"I don't need Diane to comfort me, Harriett. Just get the paperwork."

Half an hour later KC held her mother's hand as the doctor removed the breathing tube. KC stayed with her mother while the doctor went into the hallway and spoke to Harriett.

"I've advised Ms. Carnes that, in all likelihood, her mother won't last through the night. We'll transfer her to a private room and make her as comfortable as possible. You may want to contact her minister or priest. She made the right decision to sign the DNR, but we had no choice when Mrs. Carnes was brought in."

"I understand. Thank you, Doctor."

Four hours later Ruth Carnes passed away peacefully. KC had insisted on staying alone with her. When she left the room, she gave the nurse on duty the name of the funeral home that would be handling the arrangements. It seemed to Harriett that KC was incredibly calm. The thought of having to go through what KC was when Irene died wasn't something she wanted to think about.

"Are you all right, KC?" she asked as she hugged her friend.

"I'm fine. The woman in that room wasn't anyone I knew. She was only a body. My mother died years ago and I've already grieved for her."


THE SUN SHONE down brightly even though the wind was a piercing cold. Harriett, Jess, and Irene waited nearby as the rose-tinted casket was taken from the rear of the hearse and carried toward its final resting place beside KC's father. KC and Diane followed the casket as the others gathered to say their final farewell fell in behind them. KC hadn't spoken much at the church and even though Diane walked beside and slightly behind her, they hadn't touched. KC's mind didn't seem to be on what was happening around her. Dark sunglasses hid her eyes and it was hard to see what she was feeling.

Harriett held Jess's hand as they stood to the side of the gravesite. The headstone bearing KC's father's name glistened in the sunlight. Harriett wrapped an arm around Irene to protect her from the wind as they waited for everyone to settle into place. She was glad to see most of the members of the Anson varsity and JV girls' basketball teams make an appearance to support KC. Lorraine accompanied Jamie to the service, but chose to stand on the opposite side of the burial site. Harriett was surprised to see Judge Clemons standing at the edge of the mourners, wiping her eyes occasionally.

KC sat stiffly, not really hearing what the minister intoned. She seemed lost in her own thoughts...and very much alone. While her mother's death was a relief when it finally came, Harriett wasn't sure anyone was ever truly prepared for the final loss. She remembered her brother and sister-in-law's funerals and everything had passed by in a blur. Lacey had been so young and had clung to Harriett. She blinked the memory away and looked at Jess, moving closer against her. Jess smiled down at her, but her eyes weren't smiling. She, too, seemed to be lost in a memory.

When the minister spoke his last words of comfort and offered the final prayer, KC stood and shook his hand. As the line of well-wishers filed past she spoke to each one briefly as she shook their hands. Even though Diane had been sitting next to KC, she mysteriously faded away, leaving KC standing alone to greet the well-wishers. It wasn't until Jamie and Ali reached her that she hugged anyone. Harriett suspected they had become more a part of her life than even she realized. By the time Harriett, Irene, and Jess approached, KC seemed exhausted. She hugged Harriett and Irene tightly and whispered to both of them how grateful she was to have them as her friends. She thanked Irene for spending some time with Ruth after she entered the nursing home and told Harriett to take good care of her mother.

As Jess and Harriett made their way back toward Jess's Durango, Harriett saw someone standing a little way away from the funeral party, partially hidden in the shadow of a large maple tree. It was a woman and she looked familiar, but she wasn't close enough to be seen clearly. As they moved closer, Harriett finally caught a glimpse of the woman's face. To Jess she said, "That's Peggy DeVore."

"Where?" Jess asked.

"Over by that large maple."

"Are you sure?"

"I saw her in court not that long ago. I wonder what she's doing here."

"Maybe she just wanted to pay her respects."

"To the woman accused of murdering her husband?"

"Do you want me to ask her?"

"Not now, but I think I should pay her a visit later."


WHILE JESS RETURNED to school, Harriett changed her clothes and drove to Peggy Devore's home a few miles outside of Anson. It was a well-kept home with freshly turned flower beds, ready for fall planting.

Peggy didn't seem surprised when she opened the front door a little after two-thirty that afternoon.

"Ms. Markham. I was expecting you," Peggy said in a soft drawl.

"I saw you at Ruth Carnes's funeral this morning. May I come in?"

"Please. Would you like a cup of coffee?" Peggy asked as she stepped back to allow Harriett into her house.

"I should advise you," Harriett said as she stepped inside. "You are not required to speak to me without an attorney present."

"Why would I need an attorney? There really isn't much I can tell anyone," Peggy said as she led Harriett into a comfortable-looking living room.

"Why were you at the funeral this morning?" Harriett asked as she sat on the edge of the couch.

"I was simply paying my respects. As I'm sure you already know, because my daughter is on Coach Carnes's team we worked together on occasion on fund-raisers and other booster events."

"Does that mean you don't believe she murdered your husband?"

Peggy looked uncomfortable and shifted her position in the wing-back chair she was sitting in. "I don't have an opinion about that one way or another. It's not for me to pass judgment on Kerrie. I'm sure the jury will make the right decision."

"Do you like Coach Carnes?"

"She's always been very nice to me, despite the disagreements she might have had with Allen."

Harriett chuckled. "When I saw you in court, I didn't get any sense of animosity from you toward KC and I don't now. I suppose I find that a little unusual."

"That's because I know Kerrie didn't kill Allen, Ms. Markham."

"How can you be so certain? She has absolutely no alibi."

"Because she was with *me* when Allen was killed."

Harriett expelled a loud breath. "Well, I wasn't quite ready for that one."

Peggy DeVore seemed amazingly calm as she again offered Harriett a cup of coffee. Accompanying the demure-looking woman into her kitchen, dozens of questions tumbled in Harriett's mind as she waited for Peggy to join her at a table in the breakfast nook.

"You'll have to forgive me, Mrs. DeVore, if I seem a little surprised. As KC's attorney she should have told me everything and apparently hasn't," Harriett said as she accepted a steaming mug from Peggy.

"And I'm sure I'm the last person you would ever expect Kerrie to be interested in," Peg said quietly.

"I really wouldn't know about that."

"Kerrie would never have told you. I was certain you saw me at the cemetery earlier and was actually hoping you'd contact me. I told her I should come forward, but she asked me not to in order to protect my children."

"Quite truthfully, Mrs. DeVore..."

"Would you please call me Peggy? It sounds much less formal. Kerrie trusts you and that's good enough for me."

"Peggy, by coming forward with an admission that you've had an affair with KC, you do realize you make yourself a suspect in your husband's death."

"But I was with Kerrie. At a motel in Abilene. Therefore, neither of us could have killed him."

"Did she tell you about her argument with your husband?"

"I knew something was wrong when she arrived, but I didn't ask any questions." Peg's face seemed to redden slightly. "When Kerrie and I were together, neither of us wanted to talk about our problems. We only wanted to enjoy one another's company."

"I don't want to intrude on your privacy, but had you discussed your future at all?"

"Truthfully, neither of us believed we had a future together."

"So it was nothing more than a sexual liaison?"

Peggy's eyes flashed as she looked at Harriett. "It wasn't a casual relationship for either of us. Potentially we could have hurt many people. Not only Allen and Diane, but my children, my parents as well. It wasn't something we undertook lightly. No matter how hard we tried to think of a viable solution, there wasn't one. So, either Kerrie and I could be hurt or we could hurt a great number of others."

"Were you thinking about separating?"

"Possibly."

"Did your husband or KC's partner know about your affair?"

"I'm certain Allen had no idea and couldn't have cared less. Like everyone else, I'm sure he thought no one could possibly be interested in me. I don't know about Diane but doubt Kerrie told her anything either."

"Do you think your husband might have been having an affair?"

"I'm certain he was. Allen and I had a marriage in name only, Ms. Markham. I slept with him at a frat party in college and became pregnant. We married because it was the right thing to do for the child, not because we were in love. Our relationship didn't improve over the next seventeen years, despite having Brett several years later. However, until I met Kerrie I was never unfaithful."

"Had you been attracted to women before?"

"Yes, but I am from an extremely religious family. It wasn't something we ever discussed. I just thought I was strange and it would go away."

"I think a lot of us have thought the same way."

"I had never been with anyone who made me feel as special or as loved as Kerrie has. She has been so patient and caring and I was terrified of what I was feeling."

"But you didn't think it was a permanent feeling."

"How could it be? We could never be together without hurting others."

"And your children have no idea that you were having an affair?"

"No. Brett is too young yet to understand. He didn't get along well with his father. Heather worshipped Allen and I'm sure she knew he was having an affair, but she didn't blame him. We're not close."

"You know all of this could come out at the trial, don't you?"

"Then I'll just have to deal with it, won't I?"

# Chapter Twenty-one

AFTER RUTH CARNES'S funeral, Diane drove KC home. It was a silent trip with KC staring out the passenger window. Diane had taken the day off, claiming she had a medical appointment. She had never met Ruth Carnes, but now she was one less problem Diane needed to worry about and she was relieved. She swung into the side drive of the home she shared with KC and pressed the automatic garage door opener clipped to the visor of her Explorer to pull into the double car garage next to KC's Suburban. She wished KC would trade her vehicle in for something smaller. It was a tight fit and Diane always had to be careful not to get too close to the wall on her driver's side. While KC got out, Diane reached back inside, retrieving a tote bag full of papers to be graded and her soft side briefcase. She followed KC through the back garage door into the kitchen and pressed the button on the wall to close the large garage door.

As she usually did, she dropped everything onto their dining room table and began pulling off her driving gloves, stuffing them into the pocket of her jacket as KC began stripping off the jacket to her suit while she continued through the house. Diane hung their jackets on the hall tree and ruffled her hands through her hair.

"Kerrie?" she called out. "Where did you go?"

"Back here," her partner's voice answered.

Walking across the living room, she gazed at its furnishings and smiled. It was exactly the way she had always envisioned it would be. Everything was in its proper place and guests always commented about how well-decorated it was. She turned down the short hallway leading to Kerrie's office and leaned against the doorframe.

"Hey," she said. "What are you doing?"

Except for the banker's light that illuminated her desktop, the room was dark. KC looked up from her desk and removed her glasses, rubbing her eyes. "Just tryin' to put together some things for Harriett, but my mind's not on it. I'm tired."

"Will you be okay?" Diane asked as she pushed away from the wall. When she reached Kerrie's desk she bent down and kissed her lightly and ran a hand across her broad shoulders.

"As good as anyone accused of murder and not allowed to do

their job." KC sounded bitter and Diane wished there was something she could do to make things better for her lover.

"You have a good attorney. I'm sure you'll be found innocent."

"So what if I am? Do you seriously believe I'll ever be able to return to my job? Who the hell wants their kid coached or taught by an accused murderer, even if they are innocent? Small towns never forget shit like that."

"You'll find something, honey," Diane soothed.

"I've emailed a couple of inquiries. When this is all over I need to have somethin' lined up. Probably have to sell the house."

"Why would we do that? You could get on at a high school here in Abilene."

KC stood and looked at Diane. "You know the only reason I'm here was because of my mother, Diane. Now that she's gone there's nothin' keepin' me here."

"What about me? I'm here."

"I might be able to work a deal where if they take me, they'll have to take you as well," KC shrugged.

Diane's eyes narrowed slightly as she looked at KC. "Where are you thinking about going?"

"I should be able to get a position with a European team, probably in Moscow or Belarus. Maybe the Ukraine. They're finally beginnin' to take women's basketball seriously for international competition. A lot of American players go there for seasonin' and to pick up extra cash durin' the off-season."

"That's ridiculous, Kerrie! I can't believe you'd consider moving to a foreign country just to coach *basketball*," Diane laughed.

"It's all I know how to do for Christ's sake! No one else in their right mind would touch me with a ten-foot pole right now."

"I don't want to move someplace where I don't speak the language and live in God-knows-what housing," Diane said.

"Then don't go. It's up to you, but if they make me an offer and I beat this rap, I'm leavin'."

Diane was in shock. KC walked past her and turned down the hallway toward the master bedroom. Stepping into the bathroom, she turned on the faucet and splashed cold water on her face. Grabbing a hand towel, she scrubbed the water from her skin and took a deep breath. Diane put a hand on her back.

"I'm sorry, Kerrie," Diane said. "It's still a shock to me and I guess I wasn't expecting that."

Spinning around, KC said, "Yeah, well, this whole fucked up mess is a shock to me too. It's too much all at once. Mom, DeVore, bein' arrested, having to defend myself with no idea how to do that. It's too goddamn much."

Diane stepped closer and wrapped her arms around KC, pulling her into a hug. KC hesitated a moment before returning the hug. "I hate to admit it, Diane, but I'm a little rattled. I guess maybe even scared. I know I didn't kill DeVore, but there's still a doubt in my mind that no one will believe me."

"I believe you," Diane said.

"I'm so tired," KC sighed. "And my life is so out of control."

Diane stepped back and took KC's hand, pulling her into the bedroom. "Lay down for a while. You'll feel better after one of your famous power naps."

KC sat on the edge of the bed and pulled her shoes off, tossing them next to a stuffed chair near the closet. Diane gazed down at her partner. Their relationship had been going through a rough time the last year or two, but she wasn't ready to give up on it. She knelt in front of KC and pulled her shirt over her head. She would make Kerrie forget her problems, at least for a while. Rising up on her knees she took Kerrie's face in her hands and kissed her, waiting for her lips to part as they always did. She worked her hands slowly up Kerrie's sides. Her skin was hot.

As her mouth slipped to Kerrie's neck and upper chest, KC asked, "What are you doin', Diane?"

"If you have to ask, then it's been too long," Diane laughed. Her hands kneaded Kerrie's breasts as she brought her mouth back to meet her partner's, her tongue seeking entrance.

KC's hands gripped Diane's shoulder and forced her away. She stared at Diane. "Do you think this will make me feel better?"

"It can't hurt," Diane said, a crooked grin crossing her lips.

"A *pity fuck* won't make me feel better," KC snapped.

"It's not a pity fuck."

"Then why now? You haven't touched me or let me touch you in longer than I remember. You suddenly discover your missin' libido?"

"I love you, Kerrie. Is that so hard to believe?"

"Not if I really believed it. Look, Diane, admit it. We've basically been nothin' more than roommates the last two years. We share a house and that's it. I don't know why or how it happened, but it has."

"Are you telling me you don't love me?"

"I could say it all damn day, but what does it really mean? I tell people I love them all the time. Those are the easiest three words in any language to say. Women expect to hear them, especially if I'm takin' them to bed to fuck 'em."

Diane stood up and bent over to grab her shirt. "In other words, you never loved me and just said you did to get me in your bed."

"I probably did at first, but it was more than that. I believed I was fallin' in love with you. I really wanted to, but you've changed. Once we moved in together you became settled and the sexual part of our lives didn't mean a damn to you. You always have a reason why you can't or won't."

"You said it didn't matter, that sex wasn't the most important part of our relationship."

"It isn't, but once we stopped it seemed like all the intimacy disappeared. Hell, until today you wouldn't let me touch you in any way that could be thought of as sexual. I like to touch you, feel your skin against mine. That doesn't mean we have to fuck like rabbits. It's a connection between two people who are supposed to care for one another and it's gone! I'm sorry."

"Is there someone else?"

"No."

"I don't believe you." Pulling her hair from under her shirt collar Diane said, "Do you want me to leave?"

"Of course not. This house is yours as much as mine. Probably more. Hell, I need to get out of here for a while."

"Will you be back?"

"Of course."

"Don't forget your cell. Let me know when you're on your way home and I'll fix dinner."


KC STARED AT Diane's back as she left the bedroom. Diane had changed since they first met. The loss of an active sex life was only one of their problems and she wasn't sure their relationship could be salvaged, even if she wanted it to be. She knew it wasn't fair to ask Diane to leave everything she was comfortable with and start over in a strange, foreign place. The conversation with Diane hadn't gone the way she'd anticipated. KC knew she'd hurt her and hated that she had. She needed to talk to Harriett.


AFTER KC PUSHED the doorbell at Irene Markham's house, she looked around the old neighborhood. It seemed like only recently that she and Harriett made out in front of the well-cared-for home. She had fallen hard for the beautiful, tawny-haired young woman, but Harriett made no secret of her desire to leave Anson and spread her wings and KC wanted that for Harriett. No longer in love with Harriett, she was happy Harriett had found someone.

The front door opened and Irene Markham, still wearing the dress she'd worn to Ruth's funeral, blinked up at her.

"KC? You should be at home resting, dear," Irene said.

"I...uh...need to talk to Harriett, Irene. She here?" KC asked.

"Of course. We were just having a snack. Come on in," Irene said as she stepped back. "Can I get you anything?"

"I wouldn't turn down a cup of coffee," KC said with a smile, stepping into the warm home. "Chilly out here."

"Harriett's in the kitchen. I'll get your coffee then leave you two alone while I go change," Irene said as she took KC's coat and hung it on the hall tree.

"Who was it, Mom?" Harriett asked around a mouthful of a turkey sandwich when Irene returned to the kitchen.

"It was me," KC answered, walking in behind Irene. Irene poured a mug of coffee for KC.

"I'm going to change. I'll be back later," Irene said as Harriett chewed and swallowed.

"Thanks, Mom," Harriett said before turning her attention to KC. "I was going to call you later, KC. We need to talk. Apparently, you haven't told me a few things."

"I told you everything you needed to know," KC said, sipping her coffee.

"You didn't tell me about Peggy DeVore or that you were having an affair with her," Harriett said in a low voice.

"Because it didn't matter," KC said with a shrug.

"So, you were just fucking her then?" Harriett asked.

"No, it was more than that," KC admitted.

"Well, I spoke to her after the funeral, and, fortunately for you, she is willing to give you an alibi for her husband's murder," Harriett said.

"She was at my mother's funeral?" KC asked. "Why?"

"To pay her respects and support you during a hard time, I suppose," Harriett said. "I'll add her to my witness list when the trial resumes Friday."

"No! You can't do that, Harriett!"

"She can prove you didn't kill Coach DeVore."

"I don't care! If you call her as a witness, I'll change my plea to guilty. I swear to God! You can't do that to her or her family!" KC said excitedly. "I won't let you!"

"Calm down, KC," Harriett said. "She wants to testify."

"No! How many fuckin' times do I have to say it?" KC argued.

"Why are you being so obstinate?"

"Because...I fell in love with her," KC muttered. "I didn't mean to, but I did. I can't hurt her kids like that and I'll take my chances with what we've got now."


"MAIL'S HERE," BARNETT'S secretary chirped as she placed a stack of envelopes on her boss's desk.

"Thank you, Eunice. Anything interestin'?" Davis Barnett asked as he set down his mug of coffee.

"Only that large manila envelope on the bottom. It's marked personal. What's YEO mean?" Eunice asked. "You order somethin' naughty to surprise your wife?"

"Nope," Barnett answered as he glimpsed through the stack of regular envelopes. "Next year's an election year, so it might be campaign crap from some eager beaver tryin' to get a jump on the competition," he chuckled.

Once Eunice left his office, he began opening the envelopes, tossing most into the metal garbage can beside his desk and shoving a couple into his in box for later. He finally picked up the manila envelope and examined it. No return address. Local postmark. Addressed to him personally, not to the District Attorney or District Attorney's Office. Apparently, the contents intended for his eyes only. Barnett flipped the envelope over to examine the back. It was closed with a small brass clip and glued down. He felt around the edges of the envelope but found nothing unusual. He slid his letter opener along the edge of the flap and reached inside. He carefully slid out what felt like thick paper. Although he didn't need it, he opened a desk drawer and took out a magnifying glass and laid it next to the two pictures from the envelope. Both had been taken at night, probably with a telephoto lens. The faces were slightly granulated, but the first one clearly showed two women stepping out of a room. The number on the door indicated it was probably a motel room somewhere. One of the women was clearly Kerrie Carnes. The second woman was turned slightly, looking back at Kerrie. She looked familiar, but Barnett wasn't sure of her identity. But she appeared to have medium-length black hair. Nothing was written on the back of the eight-by-ten photograph and it wasn't time-stamped or dated.

Barnett picked up the second photo, apparently taken a few seconds or minutes later. It showed the same two women, in the same clothing they wore in the first picture, standing in front of an open car door. Light from the inside of the vehicle illuminated them as they kissed passionately, pressed tightly together. Barnett picked up his magnifying glass and held it a few inches away from the picture. He concentrated on the left hand of the black-haired woman as she caressed the back of Kerrie Carnes's head. Barnett could clearly see a ring on her left ring finger. It was a simple band, but obviously she was a married woman. When he flipped the photo over, there was a label on the back and typed in the middle was: *Can you spell M-O-T-I-V-E?*

"Fuckin' right I can," Barnett said to himself with a grin. Then he grabbed the magnifying glass and studied the first photo once more. "I know you," he laughed, slamming his fist on the desk. He hated to lose, but until that minute his case was pretty much in the toilet with Harriett Markham's hand on the lever preparing to flush. He pulled a legal pad over and began writing a list of things he needed to do before Friday. He had rested his case, but a surprise witness was always fun and he was positive Judge Clemons would allow him to call a new and important witness. Nothing could go wrong.

# Chapter Twenty-two

FRIDAY MORNING, HARRIETT sat patiently at the defense table, prepared to recall her first witness, Glenn Freeman, when Davis Barnett and his assistant Krista Bernie entered carrying two large covered poster-sized items along with an easel. Harriett looked back over her shoulder and smiled at Jamie, who had taken the day away from school to observe the trial. Ali sat next to Jamie and they chatted quietly while they waited for the trial to begin. Five minutes before nine, the side door into the courtroom opened and KC walked in, joining Harriett at the defense table.

Despite not being able to convince KC to allow her to call Peggy DeVore as a witness, Harriett was confidant she would still be able to direct attention away from KC and toward another person with a motive for the crime. Reasonable doubt was on her side. At precisely nine o'clock, the door behind the judge's bench opened and Judge Clemons swept in.

"All rise," the bailiff announced.

"Be seated," the judge said with a wave of her hand. "Fred, please escort the jury in."

When the jury was seated, Harriett stood to recall Glenn Freeman to the stand. Barnett jumped to his feet immediately and said, "If it pleases the court, the People would like to call an additional witness, Your Honor." The left at Albuquerque began.

"The people have already rested their case, Your Honor," Harriett said.

"This witness and accompanying evidence has just come into the People's hands, Your Honor," Barnett stated.

"Approach," Judge Clemons said.

"When did you locate this new evidence and witness, Mr. Barnett?" Judge Clemons asked after covering the microphone on the bench with her hand.

"We received it in the mail Wednesday afternoon, Judge Clemons," Barnett explained.

"Then why is the defense learning about it *two* days later?" Harriett hissed. "To allow the entering of new evidence now is trial by ambush. The defense hasn't had an opportunity to examine this new evidence or prepare to question a new witness. If the People are granted permission to drag in a new witness and show new evidence after closing their case, then I demand a mistrial."

"Denied," Judge Clemons snapped. "Once the evidence and witness have been seen and heard, the defense will be given additional time to prepare their rebuttal. Is that understood, Mr. Barnett? I won't allow games in my courtroom...ever! Step back."

Judge Clemons turned to the jury. "After a spirited discussion, I will allow the People to call one additional witness. If I decide, after hearing the witness's testimony, that it adds nothing to the People's case, I will have it stricken." Turning back to Barnett, she said, "Call your witness, Mr. Barnett."

Barnett stood and said boldly, "The People call Margaret DeVore, Your Honor." Harriett immediately stood up, but before she could say anything, Barnett added, "Mrs. DeVore is a reluctant witness, Your Honor. Therefore, the People ask permission to treat her as a hostile witness."

As the doors at the back of the courtroom opened and Peggy DeVore stepped inside, KC sprang to her feet. "Judge Clemons, I demand to change my plea from not guilty to guilty."

"Your Honor, I need a moment to speak with my client," Harriett said, remaining as calm as possible.

"No!" KC said loudly. Then she looked at Harriett sadly and mouthed, "I'm sorry," before saying clearly, "You're fired!"

With everyone at the defense and prosecution tables standing and chatter running up and down the rows of observers, Judge Clemons was hovering on the verge of losing control of her courtroom. She slammed her gavel down three times and demanded order. Then she said, "Fred, please remove the jury."

When the door closed behind the last juror, she ordered the courtroom cleared. Left with only the defense and prosecution, she took a deep breath and worked her way from right to left. "Kerrie Carnes, your demand to dismiss your attorney is unfounded and, therefore, denied. Ms. Markham will continue as your attorney of record. This court will not entertain a change of plea at this time but may consider it in the future. In the meantime, you will consult with your attorney about your case. Ms. Markham, as attorney of record, you will have until one p.m. Monday to examine the new People's evidence and prepare to cross-examine Margaret DeVore. Is that sufficient time, Counselor?"

"Yes, Your Honor. The defendant appreciates this consideration," Harriett said.

"The fuck I do," KC said harshly.

Judge Clemons glared at KC. "Perhaps you would rather spend the weekend as a guest of the county for contempt, Ms.

Carnes? I would be more than glad to arrange that."

"No, thank you, ma'am," KC answered. "I lost control of my mouth."

"Out of respect for your late mother, the court accepts your apology," Judge Clemons said. "Mr. Barnett, the People will turn over copies of their new evidence today, as well as any material that may have accompanied it, without delay. Got it, DB?"

"Yes, Your Honor," he said.

"You will include typed or electronically recorded transcripts you obtained from your new witness as well." Looking at Krista Bernie, she said, "Do you have anything pertinent to this case that I have not already addressed, Ms. Bernie? I wouldn't want you to jeopardize your future by making a stupid mistake at the beginning of your career."

"Thank you, ma'am," Krista said. "I have nothing else."

Clemons dropped her gavel firmly. "We're adjourned until Monday then," she said. "I trust there will be no more surprises to disrupt these proceedings." She stood and quickly left the courtroom.

"You can't let Peg testify, Harriett," KC said. "I don't care if I have to throw a hissy every fuckin' day."

"Then Judge Clemons will have you removed to watch on closed-circuit television. The best I might be able to do is file a motion asking that the courtroom be cleared while Peg testifies, but that may not be granted," Harriett said while she packed her briefcase.

"Didn't you *ever* think it might be important to tell your attorney you were having an affair with the victim's wife?" Harriett hissed.

"It's a small town and the jurors will talk after the trial," KC said miserably. "I've ruined Peg's life and her kids will hate her. I'd be better off dead."

"Do you want to sneak out of here with your tail between your legs like a coward then?" Harriett said.

"No," KC snapped. "I'm not ashamed of who I am, only of what I did."

"Peg had a choice, too, KC," Harriett said softly.

When they finally pushed through the doors of the courtroom, no one was there except Jess, Jamie, and Ali.

"Honey, can you take everyone to the car while I go downstairs to the D.A.'s office and pick up whatever they have for us?" Harriett asked.

"Sure," Jess answered as she leaned down to kiss Harriett

lightly. "Interesting day," she added.

"Yes, it was," Harriett said with a smile. Looking at KC, she said, "KC, I'd appreciate it if you would meet us at Mom's house. You might be able to help us get our shit together."

"That was really intense in there, Aunt Harriett," Jamie said.

"Changing your mind about becoming an attorney?" Harriett asked.

"You were so calm. I'm not sure I could do that," Jamie frowned.

"What about our game tonight, Coach?" Ali asked.

"We'll *both* be there," Harriett said, then looked at Jess and shrugged. "Looks like a late night and a long weekend ahead, *Coach*," she added. "Jamie, are you taking Ali home?"

"Yeah, we gotta get goin'," Jamie said, passing out hugs for everyone before clasping Ali's hand and leading her to the elevator.

"I'd bet Lorri isn't real thrilled about that," KC smirked, nodding at the two girls.

"She's...adjusting," Harriett acknowledged. Squeezing Jess's arm, she added, "I'll meet you at the car as soon as I can."

Twenty minutes later, Harriett slid into the passenger seat of the Durango and exhaled loudly.

"Something wrong?" Jess asked.

"Let me count the things that are wrong. One, I have until midnight to submit a motion to clear the courtroom when Peggy testifies. I'm not confident Judge Clemons will grant it. Two, I'm not sure what KC will do if she doesn't. Three, the new evidence is damning and I'm not sure how I can refute it. And four, it absolutely gives KC a very strong motive. Other than that, everything's just dandy," Harriett recited.

"That good, huh?" Jess said with a grin as she turned the key in the ignition.

"Yeah. What time is the game tonight?"

"Six-thirty, but I'd understand if you can't make it. So would Jamie."

Harriett shook her head. "That gives me about six hours and I'm sure I'll need a break by then. Besides, I already promised to take Mom."

HARRIETT SPOKE PRIVATELY with KC in her father's office, trying to calm her down after showing her the pictures Harriett had gotten from the D.A.'s office.

"Do you know where these were taken?" Harriett asked.

"Probably at the Holiday Inn Express in Abilene on the Dallas highway. We met there when we could," KC sulked. "But no one knew."

"Obviously *someone* did," Harriett stated shortly.

"Fuck you, Harriett!" KC responded loudly.

"Go home, KC," Harriett said coldly. "I have work to do if I hope to save your sorry ass!"

A tap on the office door interrupted their argument. "What?" Harriett snapped, glaring at KC.

"Everything okay in here, honey?" Jess asked as she poked her head around the door.

"Everything's fine," Harriett breathed. "KC is just getting ready to go home." She reached out and squeezed KC's arm. "I apologize, KC. I'll call you later, okay? I'm sorry, but please don't attempt to contact Peggy."

KC pulled Harriett into her arms and hugged her tightly, then marched out of the room. Jess stepped in and shoved her hands in the pockets of her slacks. "I made you a sandwich. Come eat and relax for a few minutes, baby, then show me this new evidence. We'll figure out what to do."

"Have I told you how much I love you?" Harriett asked softly with a smile as she joined Jess and rested a hand on her chest.

"Once or twice," Jess said, leaning down to drop a kiss on Harriett's lips.


AFTER LUNCH, HARRIETT gave Jess the pictures to examine and closed herself in the small home office to concentrate and prepare her motion. Jess sat on the living room couch and looked at the two pictures closely. Irene wandered into the room and glanced down at them.

"This the new evidence everyone's so excited about?" Irene asked.

"This is it," Jess answered, raising a picture closer to her eyes.

"Would you like a magnifying glass? I think I have one...somewhere," Irene offered.

"Wouldn't hurt," Jess said with a smile.

"If I can't find it, I'm pretty sure JD has a microscope. I can call and ask him to bring it to tonight's game if you think that might work."

Jess shoved the pictures into a folder and stood. "I need to run an errand, but I should be back in about an hour. While I'm gone, call JD for me. If Harriett comes out of the office, just tell her I'll be back soon. Do you have a camera I can borrow?"

"Only a small digital."

"That should work. Thanks."


THE NEXT MONDAY after lunch, Jess escorted Harriett into the Jones County courtroom once again and waited until she was settled at the defense table. Harriett appeared calm and confident as she flipped through pages of notes on her legal pad. She unbuttoned the jacket of her charcoal gray, pin-striped suit and glanced at her wristwatch. It had been a busy two and a half days. Jess's team won their game on Friday evening and would begin preparing for their next game Monday afternoon. Harriett hoped there would be no further surprises in KC's trial. She had spent quite a bit of time preparing KC for today's session and assuring her she would deflect as much of Peg's testimony as humanly possible. Judge Clemons rejected Harriett's motion to have spectators removed during Peggy DeVore's testimony, primarily because children were not involved, but Harriett still had a few tricks up her sleeve that Barnett might not be expecting.

"I'll be back as quick as I can," Jess whispered, running her hand over Harriett's back.

Harriett nodded. "Have a good practice this afternoon," she said with a smile.

Barnett and Krista Bernie walked into the courtroom and set up an easel, propping what Harriett believed were enlarged copies of the pictures on the easel tray. Barnett also seemed confident and composed as he nodded in Harriett's direction. When the side door opened and KC entered to join her attorney, Harriett stood to greet her. Quickly after that Judge Clemons stepped onto the bench and called for the jury. Once everyone was seated, Barnett stood.

"The People call Margaret DeVore, Your Honor, and request permission to treat her as a hostile witness," he said.

"Is this witness unwilling to testify, Mr. Barnett?" Judge Clemons asked.

"No, Your Honor, but her testimony is potentially embarrassing and—", Barnett started.

"Request denied," Judge Clemons said firmly. "Call the witness, Fred," she instructed.

Peggy DeVore came into the courtroom, her smoky gray eyes

looking straight ahead. Her raven hair shone under the fluorescent lights of the courtroom and bounced slightly as she walked. She wore a light green and rust plaid wool skirt that fell to just above her knees, topped by a rust cable-knit sweater. After being sworn in, Peggy sat, smoothing her skirt. Her eyes shifted to KC for an instant as she took a deep breath to prepare to answer Barnett's first question.

"Mrs. DeVore, do you know the defendant, Kerrie Carnes?"

"Yes, I do," Peggy answered clearly.

"How do you know her?"

"She is the head coach of the girls' basketball team at Anson High School, of which my daughter is a member. I've worked with her on various fund-raisers and chaperoned a few out-of-town games."

"Did Ms. Carnes get along with your husband?"

"Allen said she was obstinate and didn't respect his position at athletic director."

"Objection, hearsay," Harriett said.

"Since Allen DeVore cannot be here to tell his opinion of Kerrie Carnes, the People only have what he may have told his wife during a spousal utterance, Your Honor," Barnett said.

"Overruled," Judge Clemons said.

"What else did he say, Mrs. DeVore?"

"He thought she was difficult."

"And what, if anything, did Kerrie Carnes say about your husband?"

"We never discussed it."

"Did you know that Coach DeVore planned to demand the removal of a player, Alison O'Neill, from the team for making a sexual advance toward your daughter?"

"No. The first time I heard about that was during my daughter's testimony."

"Would Coach DeVore have demanded the removal of Miss O'Neill under those circumstances?"

"Probably. His was extremely protective of Heather."

"Do you consider Kerrie Carnes a friend?"

"Yes."

Barnett stripped the cover from the picture resting on the easel. "Can you identify the two individuals in this picture, Mrs. DeVore?"

Peggy sucked in a deep, calming breath before answering. "Kerrie Carnes and myself."

Flipping to the second picture of the two women kissing, he

asked, "Is this you and Kerrie Carnes as well?"

"Objection!" Harriett said, standing. "Other than embarrassing his own witness, what purpose does this serve, Your Honor?"

"It serves to provide a motive for Allen DeVore's murder by Kerrie Carnes, Your Honor," Barnett argued.

"But Kerrie was with me the night Allen died, she couldn't have killed him!" Peggy insisted miserably, then covered her eyes with her hand.

KC started to stand, but Harriett stopped her.

"Overruled!" Judge Clemons said loudly as she pounded her gavel. "The witness will not volunteer information unless asked a question directly. The jury will disregard the witness's last statement and it will be stricken from the record. Mr. Barnett, you may continue."

"No further questions, Your Honor. The People rest," Barnett said.

"Ms. Markham, do you wish to cross?" Judge Clemons asked.

Harriett stood to address the judge. "Yes, thank you, Your Honor. Mrs. DeVore, I'm sorry you have been forced to testify against your will," Harriett said.

"Thank you," Peggy said softly.

"Would you classify your marriage as a good one, Mrs. DeVore?"

"Unfortunately, no," Peg answered. "And my children have suffered as a result."

"In what way?"

"Allen was extremely opinionated and intolerant. He was homophobic and I considered him a bigot and a racist. Our daughter, Heather, idolized him and began verbalizing the same ideas at an early age. When I attempted to correct her, Allen would be abusive and denigrating, calling me weak. Our son, Brett, is under-sized for his age and uninterested in sports. As a result, Allen belittled him, calling him a sissy and a...uh...little faggot," Peg explained.

"Then, if I may ask, why did you agree to marry Mr. DeVore?"

"When I was in college, I went to a fraternity party with a friend. After too many drinks, I'm ashamed to admit, Allen and I were intimate. A couple of months later, I discovered I was pregnant with Heather. When I told Allen, we decided to get married. Do the right thing, as people used to say, even though *I* knew it was the wrong thing. It wasn't long until I discovered who he really was."

"Did you cheat on your husband?"

"Never! Fundamentally, I believe in marriage as an institution."

"Even when you knew your husband had cheated with other women persistently?"

"Objection," Barnett said. "There's no evidence that Coach DeVore cheated on his wife."

"She's your witness," Harriett said. "You should have asked her."

"Overruled," Judge Clemons said.

"I convinced myself that if Allen was occupied with other women, he would…um…leave me alone."

"Did he? Leave you alone?"

"Not all the time."

"Would your husband have believed you were involved with another man?"

"No. He didn't believe anyone else would be interested in me."

"Yet, you broke your marriage vows with my client, didn't you?"

"Yes," Peg said looking at KC.

"Are you claiming that my client seduced you, Mrs. DeVore?"

"No! Kerrie wouldn't do that! I…I seduced her."

"Do you know where those pictures were taken?"

"Probably at the Holiday Inn Express on the Dallas Highway in Abilene," Peg answered. "Kerrie and I met there several times."

"Were you there with my client the night of October thirtieth?"

"Yes."

"According to the Dallas County Medical Examiner, Mr. DeVore was killed between nine and midnight on October thirtieth. At what time was my client with you that night?"

"She arrived about nine and stayed until eleven forty-five. She couldn't have killed Allen. That picture proves it," Peg said, pointing at the photo on the easel.

"Objection, Your Honor," Barnett said. "There is nothing on that photograph that indicates the date it was taken. It could have been taken a week, a month, even a year before Coach DeVore was killed."

"Sustained," said Judge Clemons.

Harriett reached down and picked up another piece of covered cardboard and a black marker. "If I may, Your Honor," she said, stepping from behind the defense table.

"Go ahead, Ms. Markham."

Harriett walked to the easel and rested the items in her hand against the leg of the easel. She drew a circle around an object in the distance on the photograph of Kerrie and Peg kissing. "This is a sign in front of a drive-in branch of the First State Bank of Abilene on the Dallas Highway, a block behind the Holiday Inn Express," she said.

"You can barely see that, Your Honor, let alone read it," Barnett protested.

Harriett lifted the cardboard and set it carefully on the easel. "I think I can help with that, Your Honor," she said as she flipped over the cover on the cardboard.

"Please do," Judge Clemons said.

"Thank you," Harriett said. "This is a photograph of the bank sign taken by my investigator last Friday. Please note that it displays the time, date, and temperature." She flipped to the second picture. "And this is an extreme enlargement of that section of the People's evidence made by a laboratory in Abilene. It clearly shows the time as eleven forty-four and the date as October thirtieth." Facing the bench, she said, "Since my client and Mrs. DeVore are obviously saying goodbye, this clearly verifies what the witness testified to."

"It doesn't verify what time the defendant arrived," Barnett huffed.

"Your witness told us that already, Mr. Barnett. Are you now accusing your *own* witness of lying under oath?" Harriett asked. She turned the easel to face the jury before returning to the defense table. "Your Honor, the only thing the people's evidence proves is that my client and Mrs. DeVore were having an apparent affair, which while ill-advised, is not illegal in and of itself. Unless Mr. Barnett wishes to fabricate another piece of newly discovered evidence, the defense would like to *finally* recall Glenn Freeman to the stand." Harriett squeezed KC's arm and retook her seat.

"Rebuttal, Mr. Barnett?" Judge Clemons asked.

"No, Your Honor," Barnett said sullenly.

"You may step down, Mrs. DeVore," Judge Clemons ordered. "Fred, call the next witness for the defense, please."

# Chapter Twenty-three

HARRIETT SKIMMED THROUGH her notes concerning the tall, blond assistant football coach and allowed him to adjust his linebacker's frame into the chair in the witness stand again.

"Thank you for your patience, Mr. Freeman," she started.

"No problem," Freeman said with a deep, rumbling voice.

"Did you work under Coach Allen DeVore at Anson High School?"

"Yes, as his offensive line coach."

"Were the two of you friends then?"

"I wouldn't say that, ma'am. His assistant coaches were more like his...underlings," Freeman answered with a smile.

"How long have you been the offensive line coach?"

"This is my third year, ma'am."

"Can you describe Coach DeVore's relationship with his players?"

Freeman shifted in his seat. "It changed from day to day. Sort of depended on his mood."

"Can you give us an example?"

"We had this kid a couple of seasons ago, a pretty decent quarterback with potential. At first Coach DeVore spent quite a bit of time working on his skills and stuff. Then overnight the kid couldn't do anything right. DeVore rode him all the time, demanding more and more out of him. They argued constantly and couldn't agree about the color of the grass. At the end of last season, the kid walked off the field and didn't come back this year. So, we had to break in a new quarterback. He's done that a couple of times."

"Who was that quarterback?"

"Seth Sullivan."

"Did Coach DeVore's attitude toward Seth change after he started dating the coach's daughter, Heather?"

"Yeah, right around then, I think."

"Do you know the defendant, Kerrie Carnes?"

"Sure," Freeman answered with a smile. "Everyone knows KC."

"Does she have a temper that you know of?"

"I wouldn't want to be on the other end of it," Freeman chuckled.

"Do you know anything about her relationship with her players?"

"KC's a good coach. Does she chew her players out? Sure, but when she does, they know they deserved it. Usually the next day, she has whoever screwed up in the gym doing a little one-on-one with her to correct whatever their problem was, but she never harangues them until they leave the team." Freeman shrugged. "Whatever KC does, it must work because they usually have a winning record and a lot of her girls get scholarships to some pretty good colleges. Truth be told, she was a better coach than DeVore and I think he had a tough time dealing with that."

"Then Coach Carnes wouldn't have removed a player from her team for something like an unwanted sexual advance toward another player?"

"Never. She would investigate something like that, then maybe tell the kid to cool it, but not toss them off the team. She told me once that kids did stupid stuff all the time. Her job was just to point them in the right direction, not break them."

"Was there ever a time when Coach DeVore asked you to accompany him to Abilene to look for Coach Carnes?"

"Not me."

"Do you know anyone he might have asked to accompany him?"

"Nope. I don't think he was close to any of his assistant coaches. If he was looking for proof that KC was a dy...uh...homosexual, he could've just asked her. It isn't exactly a secret and as long as she doesn't rub it in anyone's face, no one really cares, you know."

"No further questions, Your Honor," Harriett said. "Pass the witness."

Barnett looked at Freeman and smiled. "You didn't like Coach DeVore, did you, Mr. Freeman?"

"He was my boss. You like your boss?" Freeman answered, causing a ripple of laughs among the court spectators. "He wasn't a warm and fuzzy guy."

"You testified that everyone knew Coach Carnes was a homosexual, correct?"

"Yes."

"Didn't you simply assume that?"

"No. KC told me she was," Freeman said.

"Why would she tell you anything about her private life, Mr. Freeman?"

Freeman shifted around in his chair slightly before

answering. "I...was having a problem in my family. Over the summer, m-my sister brought a friend home and introduced the friend as her g-girlfriend. When I got back to Anson, I needed to talk to someone about it and wound up in KC's office. During our chat, KC admitted she was...a lesbian."

"Since she confessed to violating the morals clause of her contract, did you report your conversation to anyone?"

"No. KC wasn't hurting anyone," Freeman said. "She told me in confidence and I didn't want to betray her trust."

"No further questions, Your Honor," Barnett said.

"Re-direct, Ms. Markham?"

"Just one question, Your Honor," Harriett said. Looking at Freeman, she asked, "How are you getting along with your sister now, Mr. Freeman?"

"Better. I'm working on it," he answered. "Talking to KC helped."

"Thank you. No further questions," Harriett said.

"The defense calls Marcus Jackson, Your Honor," Harriett said as Freeman left the stand. Marcus Jackson, an ebony-skinned man, entered the courtroom and low-fived Freeman as they passed one another. Jackson's head appeared freshly shaven and his short facial hair was neatly trimmed around his mouth and chin.

"Mr. Jackson, where are you currently employed?" Harriett asked.

"At Anson High School, as a defensive line coach," Jackson answered.

"How long have you been the defensive line coach, Mr. Jackson?"

"This is my second year."

"Did you consider Coach DeVore as your friend?"

"Not really. He was my immediate supervisor."

"Did the two of you get along?"

"As long as the guys on the defensive line did their jobs. If they did, me and Coach were cool."

"Did you have an occasion to go into the coach's lounge in early September?"

"Yeah, I needed a form we kept in a file cabinet there."

"What, if anything, did you see when you entered the lounge?"

"Coach was there and he wasn't alone. His pants were down around his shins and there was a woman beneath him, who was moaning and seemed to be urging him on."

"Did either of them see you?"

Jackson shook his head. "No, ma'am and I skedaddled out of there quick as I could."

"Could you identify the woman with Coach DeVore?"

"No, and I really didn't want to. I was more worried about a kid going in there to get something out of the vending machine."

"Why didn't you wait to see who came out of the lounge?"

"Wasn't any of my business," Jackson said with a shrug.

"Was that the first time Coach Devore used the lounge for a personal liaison?"

"I have no idea, but I did hear a little schoolhouse gossip from time to time."

"And you couldn't identify Coach Devore's companion?"

"She was a blonde, but that's all I know."

"Coach DeVore was married, wasn't he?"

"Yes."

"Did you ever meet his wife?"

"Yes."

"Could it have been his wife with him that day?"

"No. The woman with him was definitely a blonde and Mrs. DeVore has black hair," Jackson answered.

"So, would it be a fair assumption that Allen DeVore was cheating on his wife?"

"Yes."

"Thank you, Mr. Jackson," Harriett said. "No further questions, Your Honor."

"No questions," Barnett said.

"The defense calls Linda Traeger," Harriett said as she stood. Jess watched Linda Traeger enter the rear doors of the courtroom, her eyes scanning the spectators watching her as she made her way to the witness stand. She was dressed professionally in a color-coordinated red suit over a black shell that accented her full, but voluptuous figure. Blonde hair curled around her face. After she was sworn in, she sat and tried to relax.

"You're employed by the Anson Independent School District, aren't you, Miss Traeger?" Harriett asked.

"Yes. In the math department at Anson High School," Traeger nodded.

"How long have you worked at Anson High School?"

"Five years this year."

"Are you involved with any extracurricular activities?"

"I sponsor the Math Club and am a co-sponsor of the Varsity and Junior Varsity cheerleading squads."

"Is one of the sports your group attends the girls' basketball games?"

"Yes, but the season is just starting. We have to divide our time between basketball and football in the fall."

"You spend most of your time with the girls' basketball team though, don't you?"

"I volunteered to take some of the cheerleaders to the girls' basketball games once they began. My co-sponsor, Miss Vahrenkamp, prefers football," Traeger smiled.

"Do you know the defendant, Kerrie Carnes?"

"Of course. There are only twenty-four teachers on our faculty."

"What is your opinion of Coach Carnes?"

"We're not friends or anything, but students seem to like her well enough. I've heard she has quite a temper though," Linda volunteered.

"So, can I assume you also knew Allen DeVore?"

"Yes."

"And what was your opinion of Mr. DeVore?"

"I didn't know him very well, but he seemed like a decent enough man. Concerned about his players, how they were performing academically."

"Isn't it true you knew him *very* well? In fact, so well that you were having an affair with him?"

"What! Of course not. He was a married man for God's sake! I resent—" Linda huffed indignantly.

"Your Honor, if I may," Harriett said, pressing a button on a remote. "Please identify the individuals on this tape." The tape clearly showed Linda Traeger and Allen DeVore entering his office. His hand skimmed over her butt as she preceded him into the office.

"Miss Traeger?" Harriett asked.

"It's me and Allen entering his office. I asked to use his phone for a minute."

"Really?" Harriett asked, pressing the fast-forward button. She stopped the video when they left the office. Miss Traeger was straightening her hair while Allen tucked his shirt into his trousers and pulled his zipper up. "You were in Mr. DeVore's office during the entire fifteen-minute halftime break, weren't you?"

"I may have been," Traeger admitted.

"Who did you call from Coach DeVore's office that night, the night of October thirtieth?" Harriett picked up a few sheets of paper. "Let me remind you that any phone calls from that number can be traced."

"I...uh...I didn't call anyone. Allen and I just talked."

"Did that require him to unzip is pants?"

"Objection, argumentative," Barnett said.

"Withdrawn," Harriett replied.

"Where were you after the scrimmage that night?"

"I had to drive a couple of my cheerleaders home after the game and didn't get home myself until ten. So, I didn't kill Allen, if that's what you're trying to insinuate," Traeger protested.

Jess sat behind the defense table and smiled at Harriett as she returned to her seat. "No further questions, Your Honor."

"Cross, Mr. Barnett?" Judge Clemons asked.

"No, Your Honor," Barnett responded.

Once Linda Traeger was dismissed, Judge Clemons dismissed court for the day. "You don't have any other witnesses, do you?" Jess asked as she helped Harriett gather and pack everything.

"Just KC," Harriett muttered.

"She doesn't have to testify, does she?"

"Technically, no, but this is a small town. If she doesn't, the jurors might see her as guilty because she didn't try to defend herself."

"You've presented a strong case, honey. Why chance it?"

"KC will probably be leaving Anson, but she wouldn't want to be remembered as a probable murderer with a slick lawyer." Harriett shrugged as she closed her briefcase with a snap. "And I can't say I blame her. Most of us want people from our youth to see us as we were. Not the adults we grew into."

"Is that how you honestly see yourself? As just another slick lawyer?"

Harriett grinned, holding her briefcase with both hands against the front of her thighs. "Only when I look at you, darling," she said.

JESS COULDN'T SLEEP that night and slipped quietly out of bed without waking Harriett. Something was niggling at the periphery of her mind and it nagged at her, searching for a way to escape. Jess needed something to take her mind off whatever the hell it was. She decided to go through JD's videos to pick out a few clips of Jamie for her highlight reel.

When she got to the October thirtieth video, she saw a

momentary flash of the spectators sitting on the opponent's side. She and Harriett had been through that video a dozen times, but they had only been looking for Linda Traeger and Allen DeVore. Now Jess saw a familiar red baseball cap, its blue bill pulled low on a spectator's head. She rewound the small section of the tape back and played it several times to examine the figure more closely. After a couple of hours, Jess's vision began to blur and she shut everything down. Then she climbed the stairs and crawled into bed next to Harriett again.

"Something wrong," Harriett muttered as she moved closer to Jess and draped an arm over her abdomen.

"No. Go back to sleep, honey," Jess whispered.

"'Kay," Harriett managed before sleep reclaimed her.

Early the next morning, Jess woke Harriett up by slowly running a hand up and down Harriett's back and sides.

"I love that," Harriett mumbled.

"What, baby?" Jess whispered in her ear.

"I love the feel of your hand on my body," Harriett said as she rolled over to look up at Jess. "It drives me crazy," she added huskily. Harriett pushed her fingers through Jess's hair and drew her down until their lips brushed together. "Everything about you drives me crazy," Harriett said softly a moment before she drew Jess into a deeper, slower kiss, sucking her tongue lightly.

When the kiss finally ended, Jess kissed the hollow of Harriett's neck and pillowed her head on Harriett's breast. "I love you so very much," Jess said, bringing a hand up to caress Harriett's other breast.

"I love you, too, baby," Harriett sighed contentedly.

"Think you can get a delay in the trial? A day or two maybe."

"I don't know. The judge will want to know why. What can I tell her?"

"Tell her your investigator needs a couple of days to track down a hunch," Jess said.

"A *hunch*? She might want something more specific."

"It's just something I saw on a video. It might be nothing, but I have to check it out. You should fire my ass for not seeing it sooner anyway. Can you do it?"

"I'll think of something to satisfy Judge Clemons and Barnett," Harriett said. "I mean, he was allowed to bring in an impromptu witness and surprise evidence already. Now it's my turn. I hope."

Jess jumped out of bed and grabbed her cell phone to contact a friend at the state crime lab.

"Hey, Ross. It's Jess and I need a huge favor."

"Hey, Jess. Kinda early to ask for *huge* favors, isn't it, gal?"

"Yeah, I know, but we're out of town for a case and something just popped up. Best I can give you is hopefully two days, but it could be one."

"I ain't a miracle worker, Jess. What are we talking about?"

"I need a couple of frames from a video enlarged and cleaned up as much as possible. Best I can get is a copy from my laptop to email to you."

"In that case, I can't guarantee how good a copy from a copy will be, but I'll do the best I can."

"I need it as soon as possible and will pay for it out of my own pocket."

Ross laughed. "You can't afford me, Raines."

"Then I guess I'll just have to owe you my eternal gratitude, pal...again," Jess chuckled.

"Rather have a double cheeseburger with a Scheiner Bach," he laughed.

"It's a deal," Jess said.

While Jess talked to Ross in Austin, Harriett went into the bathroom and stepped into the shower. Jess smiled and pulled her T-shirt over her head, pausing to plug her cell in to charge it. She flipped it over in her hands and stared at it for a moment, making a mental list of what she needed to do. Then she walked into the bathroom, stripped out of her boxers, and stepped quietly into the shower. Harriett was rubbing shampoo into her thick hair when Jess leaned down and sucked Harriett's nipple into her mouth. Harriett jerked and slipped before Jess wrapped her arms around her lover to stabilize her.

"I'm not really complaining, but a little warning would have been nice," Harriett groused as she leaned her head back to rinse her hair.

"Where's the fun in that?" Jess laughed. "I'm sorry."

With water streaming down her face, Harriett planted a hungry kiss on Jess's mouth that made her knees weak. "I didn't say I didn't enjoy it, sweetie," Harriett said when their lips parted. "I'd love to continue this, but I have to be in court in an hour."

"I can be quick," Jess said roughly.

"I don't want quick, baby," Harriett purred as she ran a finger down the middle of Jess's chest and abdomen. "I want you to take all the time you need. I plan to," she added with a smile as she stepped out of the shower.

"Damn," Jess said, putting a hand out to support her body and turning the hot water off to blast her overheated libido with cold water.

# Chapter Twenty-four

TWO HOURS LATER, Harriett walked out of Judge Clemons's courtroom. She found Jess leaning against a wall in the corridor, talking on her cell phone.

"That thing is going to attach itself to your ear permanently," Harriett said.

"How did it go?" Jess asked.

"You've got twenty-four hours to work your magic," Harriett answered. "But Barnett wasn't happy about it."

"He'll live," Jess huffed. "I'll take you home, but then I'll be running the rest of the day. You have Diane's cell number?"

"In my phone," Harriett nodded.

"You might be calling her as a witness," Jess said with a frown. "If I'm right."

"KC won't like that," Harriett exhaled.

"Would she be happier sitting in a prison cell?" Jess asked.


JESS DROPPED HARRIETT off at Irene's, telling her she had to check out a few things but hoped to be home by dinner. As she drove away, she punched in a number and waited until someone answered.

"Hello," a woman answered.

"KC, it's Jess."

"Missed you in court this morning."

"Are you at home and alone?"

"Just got here. Diane's at work. Why?"

"Would it be okay if I dropped by in about half an hour? I...uh...have a couple of questions before the next game," Jess lied.

"Sure, no problem. I was just gettin' ready to grab a sandwich. Want one?"

"I'm good, but thanks. I'll see you in a while."

Twenty-five minutes later, Jess pulled into the drive of KC's home and strolled to the front door. Jess noticed a stack of mail filling the mailbox near the front door, but before she could glance at it, the door opened. KC stood there chewing a bite of her sandwich. She waved Jess inside and leaned out to grab her mail, carrying it in and dropping it on a table just inside the office door.

"How're you feeling about how the trial is going so far?" Jess asked as she pulled her jacket off.

"Don't look like DB has much of a case to me," KC said with a shrug. "Who're we playin' next game?"

"Alvarado," Jess answered.

KC leaned back in her chair, taking another big bite, and nodded. "Not very well coached. You can probably start our second stringers against them. I'm sure our usual starters would like putting up big numbers, but they should save all that energy for a tougher team."

"What are you planning to do after the trial?" Jess asked.

KC shrugged. "I got a few feelers out but haven't heard anything definite back yet. Diane's not happy about it, but I think I have a pretty good shot at coachin' overseas somewhere. Of course, that only works if I'm acquitted. I can't just sit here on my ass forever thinkin' about the good old days."

"Who's your cell provider?"

"I don't know. Why?"

"I've been having some trouble with my phone and been thinking about trying a new provider."

KC picked her phone off the desk and glanced at it. "Diane gave me this one last Christmas as a present. She's always been into this electronic stuff. When I need something put on the damn thing, I just give it to her to figure out."

"Is your GPS working?"

"I don't think I have GPS, but can ask Diane about it later, if it's important."

"It would say on your bill, if you have one laying around," Jess said casually.

"Diane pays the phone bill, but she hasn't mentioned it."

"You know, I'm not hungry but could sure handle a cup of coffee, if you have one."

"I can make a pot as long as you don't mind waitin' a few minutes."

"I hate to put you out, KC."

"No problem. While I'm gone, look around. I have a tape of Alvarado in here somewhere."

"Thanks. I'll check."

As soon as KC left the room, Jess shuffled through the stack of mail KC had dropped on the table inside the door. Close to the bottom of the stack she saw a bill from AT&T and smiled to herself. Then she glanced around the room. Hanging from a hall tree on the opposite side of the door, she saw a dozen baseball caps. She went through them until she found what she had hoped would be there. She removed the caps covering the red and blue cap and took it off the hall tree. She stuffed it under her jacket and sat down again.

A few minutes later, KC appeared with a fresh cup of coffee for Jess.

"I can't stay in Anson after the trial, KC, and you probably won't be allowed to coach the team again. Who do you think will replace you? I know it will matter to the girls because a couple have a pretty good shot at scholarships."

"My assistant coach, Megan Reynolds, will probably be moved up to head coach when the volleyball season ends. If she makes it through district play, then they'll have a year to recruit a decent head coach. I'll miss my girls, but it's a valuable life lesson."

"What's that?"

"There's nothing for certain in the real world. Adjust or die."

Jess finished her coffee and stood up, shoving her jacket under her arm. "Well, thanks for the chat, KC. I promised to be back at Irene's by dinner and still have a couple of things to do before then."

Jess waved and backed out of the driveway. Three blocks later she pulled over and looked up the number for AT&T. When the clerk answered, Jess said, "Yeah, my GPS tracking isn't working properly and I was hoping you could run a diagnostic on it for me. Right now, I'm paying for nothing."

"What's the number and the name on the account, please?"

Jess recited the number and thought for a second. "The name on the account should be Diane Saunders."

A few minutes later, a voice came on the line again. "My apologies for the wait Miss Saunders. According to our diagnostic check, the GPS seems to be working fine. If it continues to act up, you might need to bring it in to our local store and have it replaced," the technician said.

Jess called a second number and asked, "Is Chief Thomas in this afternoon?"

"He'll be here a couple of more hours. Then he's leaving about four," the front desk officer said. "Would you care to leave a message?"

"No, thanks. I should be there in half an hour," Jess said and disconnected.

THE FOLLOWING MORNING, court reconvened at ten. Harriett was exhausted. She and Jess had been up most of the night pouring over the new information Jess had uncovered. She stifled a yawn as the judge entered the courtroom.

"Now that we've had a day off, are you ready to proceed, Ms. Markham?" Judge Clemons asked grumpily. "You people need to get your...act together," she admonished.

"My apologies, Your Honor," Harriett said. "The defense calls Diane Saunders to the stand."

KC grabbed Harriett's arm, forcing her to lean down. "You can't call her, Harriett," KC hissed. "What the hell are you doing?"

"Trying to save your ass. Now shut up and let me do my job," Harriett said firmly. "Trust me, KC. Please."

"Objection, Your Honor," Barnett said wearily. "The People were not in—" he started.

"If Mr. Barnett will check his records, Miss Saunders was listed as a *possible* character witness before this trial began," Harriett said. "The Defense had hoped her testimony wouldn't be necessary, but the People were notified yesterday afternoon that she would be called. We are willing to give Mr. Barnett time to prepare his cross after Miss Saunders testifies."

"Overruled," Judge Clemons said crisply. "I seem to remember giving you the same latitude, Mr. Barnett."

Diane entered the courtroom, looking nervous. Her eyes met KC's as she was sworn in and took her seat.

"Please tell the court your name and where you are employed," Harriett said.

"Diane Saunders. I am employed by the Abilene Independent School District," Diane answered.

"And how long have you been employed there?"

"About five years."

"In what capacity?"

"As the head track coach and computer science teacher."

"Where are you from originally, Miss Saunders?"

"The Houston area. I grew up there."

"Were you teaching there before moving to Abilene?"

"Yes."

"Where?"

"Um... at Spring Branch High School."

"That's a wealthy district, isn't it?"

"I suppose."

"What made you decide to leave to go to a district where you wouldn't earn nearly as much?"

"I thought there was a better opportunity for me in Abilene. Money isn't everything, you know."

"Do you know the defendant, Kerrie Carnes?"

"Yes. She's my...uh...roommate."

"Your roommate. Isn't that simply a euphemism for your *lover*?"

"No! That's ridiculous," Diane insisted.

"Do you attend the basketball games that my client coaches?"

"No, I don't."

"Where did you attend college, Miss Saunders?"

"I graduated from Southern Methodist in Dallas."

"Ah, they're the Mustangs, aren't they?"

"Yes."

Harriett set a baseball cap onto the table in front of her. "Do you recognize this cap, Miss Saunders?"

"It looks like an SMU baseball cap. I have one similar to it at home."

"Would it surprise you if I told you this is your cap? It was taken from the home you share with Kerrie Carnes yesterday."

"So what? There are a million of those around the state."

"SMU is a pricey university. There probably aren't that many floating around this part of Texas."

"I don't hear a question, Your Honor," Barnett said.

"Move along, Ms. Markham," the judge ordered. "I'm aging by the minute."

Harriett reached into her briefcase and pulled out a folder.

"Approach, Your Honor?" Harriett asked.

Judge Clemons motioned Harriett forward. "The Defense would like to enter these pictures as Defense Exhibits One and Two." Clemons marked them and nodded. "May I show them to the witness, Your Honor?" she asked.

"Go ahead," Clemons said.

Before she approached Diane, Harriett placed copies of the pictures on the prosecution table. "These pictures are enlargements of frames from a video of the Anson scrimmage on October thirtieth by James Gaither, the father of an Anson player," Harriett said. "Those frames were enlarged and enhanced by the Texas Forensics Laboratory in Austin, Texas." Harriett turned and handed the pictures to Diane. "Please tell the court what is shown in these pictures, Miss Saunders."

Diane squinted at the pictures and said, "It appears to be an individual wearing a red sweatshirt and jeans. His or her face is obscured by a baseball cap similar to the one apparently *stolen* from my house yesterday."

"Do you own a cell phone?" Harriett asked, changing the subject.

"Of course. Everyone owns one," Diane admitted.

"But according to the records at AT&T, there are two separate numbers listed on your account. Why is that?"

"I gave my roommate a new phone as a Christmas gift last year. Hers was an antique."

"The records indicate my client's new phone has a GPS tracking application installed on it. Why is that, Miss Saunders?"

"It came on the phone."

"Not according to your provider. Didn't you have it installed?"

"No."

"Who pays your AT&T bill each month?"

"I do."

"And you never noticed the additional fee for that application?"

"No. I don't examine the bill that closely."

Harriett returned to the defense table and took a few sheets of paper from her briefcase. She walked back to the bench and slapped them down in front of the judge. "I would like these marked as Defense Exhibit Three, Your Honor," she said.

"What is it?"

"The local usage details for the witness's phones on October thirtieth, Your Honor. And may I approach the witness again?"

Clemons marked the sheets and nodded again. Harriett handed them to Diane. "Please read the highlighted line to the court, Miss Saunders," she said.

"Outgoing call from 325-555-0169 at eight forty-six to 325-555-0159," Diane read.

"Was that the time my client called you letting you know that she would be home late after the scrimmage?"

"Apparently."

"So, you spoke to her at approximately that time from your home?"

"Yes."

"Thank you. No further questions, Your Honor," Harriett said abruptly and returned to the defense table.

Barnett scanned through his notes and stood. "No questions at this time," he said.

As soon as Diane stepped from the witness stand, Harriett

said, "Defense calls Harlan Tucker, Your Honor."

"Who is this witness?" Barnett asked.

"A telephone technician, Your Honor," Harriett said.

Harlan Tucker, a short, well-fed man in his fifties with a day-old beard growth, shuffled into the courtroom and approached the witness stand. Once he was seated, Harriett asked, "Where are you employed, Mr. Tucker?"

"At Prairie Communications."

"And what do you do for them?"

"Basically, we maintain the cell towers in five counties in this area."

"How long have you been employed by Prairie Communications?"

"About fifteen years. It's steady work and pays the bills, you know."

"Are you familiar with local usage details?"

"Oh, yeah. I'm in the office now and we use them all the time if there's a dispute about a bill. Sometimes the cops request them to track suspects in a case," Tucker said with a smile.

"Approach the witness, Your Honor?" Harriett asked.

Judge Clemons nodded and Harriett went to the evidence table to pick up the sheets of local usage details Sheriff Thomas had obtained for Jess the previous day. She handed the sheets to Tucker and he glanced over them.

"What does this detail report tell us about the highlighted call on October thirtieth?"

"More than most think," Tucker said. "The six-nine number called the five-nine number at eight forty-six, pinging off the tower just outside Anson. On the second page, the five-nine number received a call from the six-nine number, also pinging from the Anson tower."

"But, according to the testimony we've heard, the five-nine number was answered in Abilene," Harriett said.

"Not according to this detail report," Tucker said, shaking his head. "The sending phone and the receiving phone both pinged off only the Anson tower."

"What does that mean, Mr. Tucker?"

"Both phones were in Anson at eight forty-six on October thirtieth."

"Then neither call went through an Abilene tower?"

"Nope...er...no, ma'am."

"Thank you, Mr. Tucker. No further questions, Your Honor," Harriett concluded.

"No questions," Barnett said.

Harriett sat down gratefully and patted KC on the arm.

"I want to testify, Harriett," KC said.

"You don't need to and, as your attorney, I don't recommend it," Harriett said. "We've created enough reasonable doubt that the jury would have a difficult time convicting you now."

"I *need* to testify. Let me walk away with a clean conscience. Please, Harriett. It's all I have left."

Harriett nodded and stood up slowly. "The defense calls Kerrie Carnes, Your Honor," she said.

"You're sure, Ms. Markham?" Judge Clemons asked, looking at KC.

"I've advised my client that she isn't required to testify, Your Honor, but, against my advice, she feels she has to," Harriett responded.

"Very well. Approach and be sworn in, Ms. Carnes," Judge Clemons sighed.

When she was seated, KC looked at the judge. "Can I make a statement first, Judge Clemons?"

"If you wish," Judge Clemons nodded.

"Thank you," KC said, then turned to gaze at the jury. "My name is Kerrie Carnes and I grew up in Anson. I know most of you, but very few of you have ever really known me. Hell, there were times when I didn't even recognize myself. I've hurt people who didn't deserve to be hurt. I didn't mean to hurt anyone, but I know I have. I've hurt Peggy DeVore and her children. I could have walked away when I knew I was attracted to Peg. She was vulnerable because of an unhappy marriage, I knew that, and I took advantage of her unhappiness. I fell in love with her even though I knew her children could be hurt.

"I've hurt my partner, Diane Saunders, because I was angry and upset because she was ashamed of our relationship. When I couldn't convince Diane to be more open, I offered my affection to another woman and forced Diane to do things she believed were necessary to keep us together.

"I know, most regrettably, that I've hurt the people I love most, my players. They trusted me and depended on me. Nothing I say can earn their forgiveness and it would be hypocritical to ask for it. All I can say is that I am sorry for letting them down. They didn't deserve that.

"Of all the things I confess to doing, I swear I didn't kill Allen DeVore. I may be a philanderer and untrustworthy, but I am *not* a murderer."

KC glanced around before saying, "That's all I needed to say, Judge."

"Questions, Ms. Markham?" Judge Clemons asked, clearing her throat.

"No, Your Honor," Harriett answered.

"Mr. Barnett?"

"One or two," Barnett said as he shuffled through his notes. "You were in Coach DeVore's office the night of October thirtieth, weren't you, Ms. Carnes?"

"Objection," Harriett said. "Assumes facts not in evidence."

"Sustained," Judge Clemons said.

Changing his initial tack, Barnett asked, "How many years have you and I known one another, KC?"

"Five or six," KC answered before Harriett could object.

"Great times," Barnett said. "I know you're a tough coach and basically an honest and honorable woman who shares her knowledge freely with her players, always doing what's best for her team."

"Was there a question in there and I missed it, Your Honor?" Harriett asked.

"Mr. Barnett?"

"Sorry, Your Honor," Barnett said. "KC, would you like to tell the court what happened the night of October thirtieth?" he asked.

"Objection!" Harriett said, jumping up.

"I'll answer that," KC said, looking at the judge.

"Overruled. The witness may answer," Judge Clemons said.

"The girls' varsity team played a scrimmage on October thirtieth. After the game, Coach DeVore came over to me while I was picking up some equipment and demanded to see me in his office. He was angry, wanting to know why his daughter, Heather, didn't get more playing time. I told him I made the best decision based on Heather's performance during practice. I didn't think she was ready to play full time. Then he threatened to have me fired on a morals claim. If that didn't work, he would go after Diane.

"I don't know how he found out about me and Diane, but I don't react well to threats. We were talking pretty loudly, but I didn't do anything until he got in my face and shoved me. Then I just reacted. I punched him in the face, and it must have been a pretty good shot because he dropped to his knees, bleeding. My hand began to sting and I saw my knuckles were bleeding. I suppose I cut them on his teeth when I punched him. I grabbed a gym towel from around my neck and wiped the blood from my knuckles, then threw the towel to him and left his office.

"The last time I saw him, he was holding the towel to his nose. I expected to be fired for hitting him on Monday after he reported the incident or even be arrested for assaulting him. If I'd known what would happen after I left, I would have gone on home. But I didn't."

"Why didn't you go home?" Barnett asked.

"My relationship with Diane had been going through a rocky patch for a year or so and I decided to spend the rest of the evening elsewhere."

"With another woman?"

"Yes. I didn't expect Diane to lie for me and didn't want Peg to be forced to acknowledge our relationship. Not exactly the 'honorable' thing to do, but it was the best I could hope for under the circumstances. I don't know what happened after I left DeVore's office."

"No further questions, Your Honor," Barnett said as he sat.

"Redirect, Ms. Markham?"

"No, Your Honor," Harriett said. "The defense rests."

"The witness is excused." Judge Clemons glanced at the clock over the back doors of the courtroom and said, "Considering the hour, the court will adjourn and hear closing arguments at nine tomorrow morning." She hit her gavel soundly on the bench and stepped down as everyone else stood for her departure.

"I'm exhausted," KC said as she joined Harriett behind the defense table. "It's hard to admit the kind of person you really are."

"You're not perfect, KC, but you're not a killer either," Harriett said, reaching out to squeeze KC's bicep.

KC saw Jess approaching them and pulled Harriett into a warm hug. "Thanks for everything you've done for me, Harriett. You've found a good woman who will love you the way you deserve. Cherish that," KC whispered. "It's everything."

"I know, KC," Harriett answered. "I'll see you in the morning."

KC smiled faintly and nodded. "Yeah. Tomorrow," she said as Jess reached them and slid her arm around Harriett's waist.

"That was interesting testimony," Jess said, picking up Harriett's briefcase. "Ready to go to Irene's and relax?"

"Absolutely," Harriett said with a smile.

# Chapter Twenty-five

KC PULLED HER car into the garage next to Diane's and entered the home they shared through the kitchen door. The house was quiet, but she could hear the sound of water running from the back of the house.

"Diane?" she called out.

"Back here," her partner's voice answered.

Walking across the living room KC gazed at its furnishings and frowned. It was exactly the way Diane had envisioned it should be with everything in its proper place. KC turned down the hallway leading to her bedroom and leaned casually against the doorframe.

"Hey," she said when Diane came out of the attached bathroom, drying her face. "How are you doing?"

Except for the soft glow cast from the lamp on the nightstand, the room was dim. "Just thinking," Diane answered. She stopped in front of KC and kissed her lightly on the cheek. "Are you okay?"

"As good as anyone accused of murder, I suppose," KC answered with a shrug.

"You have a good attorney. I'm sure you'll be found innocent," Diane said to calm her partner.

Diane moved closer and wrapped her arms around KC, pulling her into a hug. KC hesitated a moment before returning the hug. "I didn't kill DeVore, but I'm afraid no one will believe me."

"I believe you," Diane said as she slid a hand beneath KC's shirt. When Diane's mouth slipped to her neck, KC stepped back and asked, "What the fuck are you doin', Diane?"

"Letting you know I forgive you," Diane said calmly.

"For what?" KC snapped as her hands gripped Diane's shoulders and forced her away.

"For cheating on me with that bitch, Peggy DeVore. She doesn't deserve you and I couldn't let you get away with that," Diane said, a crooked grin crossing her lips.

"You sent those pictures to Barnett, didn't you?" KC accused.

"You deserved to be punished for hurting me like that," Diane snapped.

"But why kill DeVore?" KC asked.

"I had to! He was going to ruin everything by telling everyone we were lovers. I *love* you, Kerrie, but I couldn't let that happen." Diane cried. "I just couldn't," she muttered, opening a dresser drawer and rummaging around.

"I understand," KC said, rubbing her face with both hands. "In a day or two, I'll be outta here, but I won't call Chief Thomas. I owe you that much, I guess. I'm sorry life didn't turn out the way you wanted, Diane."

"Me, too," Diane said as she turned to face KC again. "Forgive me, baby."

HARRIETT'S CONCENTRATION WAS broken by the front doorbell, followed a few minutes later by a tap on her father's office door.

"Come in," Harriett called out.

When the door opened, Jess frowned and said, "Chief Thomas needs to see you for a moment."

"Sure. I'm about ready for a break anyway. Is there still some coffee in the kitchen?" Harriett asked with a smile.

"I'll get it," Jess said.

"Thank you, sweetie," Harriett said, reaching out to touch Jess affectionately. "We'll be home again soon."

Jess nodded but didn't smile as she stepped around Harriett. Carl Ray stood in Irene's living room staring into the fireplace and twirling his Stetson through his fingers. He wasn't smiling either.

Harriett crossed her arms beneath her breasts and asked, "What's up, Carl Ray?"

He turned and looked at Harriett, his mouth working as if he'd forgotten why he was there. Finally, he found his voice. "Um...I got a...uh...phone call from the Abilene Police...um...about an hour ago." Stalling as long as he could, he sucked in a deep breath. When he released it, the words came out in a rush of breath. "KC's dead."

"What? How?" Harriett asked, unable to fully comprehend what Carl Ray was saying. She fisted her hands to stop them from shaking.

Jess walked in with two mugs of coffee, handing one to Carl Ray before setting Harriett's down and wrapping her arms around Harriett. "Sit down, baby," Jess said softly as she guided Harriett to the couch.

Harriett took a sip of her coffee and leaned back, taking

several deep breaths to settle her mind. "Tell me what you can, Carl Ray," she said dully.

"All I know is that KC and her roommate were both shot. The Abilene cops found a weapon and a note at the scene. Other than that, there's really nothin' definitive until the final forensics and autopsy reports come in," Carl Ray said. "Sure never expected anything like this. Damn shame," he muttered.

"Will you let me know later what the final determination is?" Harriett asked as she stood up.

"Might be a while. If you're already gone, I'll fax what we get to your office, if that's okay," Carl Ray said as he shuffled toward the front door. At the last minute, he pulled Harriett into his arms and hugged her. "Sorry I had to be the one to tell you she was gone, honey."

Harriett ran a hand up and down his back until he gathered himself and left.

"You okay?" Jess asked as Harriett closed the front door.

"Not really, but I will be," Harriett sighed.

"Irene should be home in an hour or so, if you want to wait for her," Jess said.

Harriett smiled slightly as she approached Jess and brought a hand up to rest over Jess's heart. "If you don't mind, sweetheart, I'm feeling a little drained and would love to soak in a nice hot tub. Then go to bed and just...sleep," she said.

"Whatever you want, baby," Jess said softly, kissing Harriett's forehead.


EARLY THE NEXT morning, Jess slipped quietly out of bed and dressed without waking Harriett. She leaned down to kiss Harriett softly on the forehead and tip-toed out of the room. She wasn't looking forward to arriving at the high school and wasn't certain whether any of her players would even show up, but she wanted to be there for them although there wasn't much she could tell them.

She sat in the bleachers, sipping from her cup of convenience store coffee, trying to think of some way to explain an unexplainable tragedy. She felt sure Harriett had cast enough doubt to make Diane a viable suspect in Coach DeVore's death, but it didn't matter much anymore now that no one would be arrested and tried for that offense. And no one would be punished for taking KC's life.

Jess sat in the bleachers watching students come and go most of the morning until the bell announcing the beginning of her basketball class rang. She stood and stretched to loosen her body before walking to the locker room and rolling a cart full of basketballs onto the court. She twirled a ball in her hands before shooting a few baskets. She was interrupted by a few girls wandering into the gymnasium. Rather than chattering noisily as usual and heading to the locker room to change, they silently sat on the first row of the bleachers and stared at Jess. A few had been crying but most simply looked confused and uncertain about what they were supposed to do. Noticeably absent were Ali, Jamie, and Heather DeVore.

"What are we supposed to do, Coach?" Erica Lucero asked.

"What do you want to do?" Jess asked.

"Understand what happened," Erica said.

"Wish I could help you with that, Lucero, but I don't understand it myself," Jess explained.

After the final bell, the gym doors opened again and Ali shuffled in holding Jamie's hand.

"They were with me, Coach," Lorri said, sticking her head in briefly to explain the two girls' tardiness. "Please excuse them."

It was obvious to Jess that both girls had been crying and were still distraught. She waved and nodded at Lorri, then set her basketball on the floor and sat on it. She rested her forearms on her knees and took a deep breath. "Everyone grab a ball and make a circle around me on the court," Jess said.

"Why?" Jennifer Costa asked.

"Because I asked you to and so you can share your memories, good or bad, about Coach Carnes," Jess said. "Costa, do you know where Heather is?"

"It's not my day to watch her," Jennifer answered sullenly.

"I saw her this morning," Erica said. "She told me she was withdrawing and going to live with her grandparents."

"Why would she tell *you* anything?" Jennifer snapped. "I'm her best friend. You're nothing."

Erica shrugged and stared at the floor. Jamie reached out and hugged her lightly, whispering to her. Erica nodded and managed a small smile.

"Coach Carnes was a good coach," Ali mumbled.

"For you," Jennifer sneered.

"For all of us," Ali retorted. "She made us work as a team, not a bunch of individuals doing their own thing. She wanted us to be good as a team and help each other."

"You're so full of it, Ali. You became such a prima donna that she didn't care what happened to the rest of us," Jennifer pressed on.

Ali started to stand, but Jamie gripped her hand to prevent Ali from getting up. "She's not worth it," Jamie said.

Jennifer jumped up and walked out of the gym, pushing the doors so hard they slammed into the corridor walls, the sound echoing through the gym lobby.

"Can you tell us what happened, Coach?" Erica said.

"What's going to happen to the team now?" Clarissa asked. "Are you staying?"

Jess met each girl's eyes briefly before taking a deep breath. "First of all, none of this happened because of you, so it's not your fault. I've spoken to Chief Thomas and Mr. Warner this morning. All I can tell you is that Coach Carnes was shot last night by her roommate. I'm sure more information will come out after the Abilene Police complete their investigation. I know this is a tough time for many of you, but the best thing you can do is continue to play the way Coach Carnes would want you to play."

Jess stopped for a minute and rubbed her forehead. "It's been an honor for me to coach you for the last month. I've learned more than I...I thought I would. Mr. Warner plans to appoint Coach Reynolds as your coach temporarily while he looks for a permanent replacement for Coach Carnes."

"What about you, Coach?" someone asked.

"I will stay until the weekend and help for the next couple of games, but then I'll be returning to Austin and resume my regular job. I'll leave my number in case any of you need to get in touch with me, for any reason. If you're up to it, I think we should have a short practice after school today to shake off any cobwebs and just loosen up a little. If anyone needs to talk between now and the after-school practice, I'll be here all day."

"Can we dedicate tomorrow's game to Coach Carnes?" Jamie asked.

"If that's what you all want, it's not a problem for me," Jess said.

The players chatted, sharing their memories of KC, and laughed through the remainder of the period. Near the end, they stood and placed the basketballs in the basket, then formed a tight circle around Jess and placed their hands over hers, shouting "Tigers!" Jess hugged each girl before they left when the bell rang, saying something she hoped would comfort them. The last two in line were Jamie and Ali. Jess embraced them a little more tightly and struggled to keep her tears at bay, knowing she would miss them the most, for personal reasons.

THE FOLLOWING SATURDAY, Jess was packing the Durango for the journey back to Austin while Harriett and Irene were searching the house for anything Harriett may have forgotten to pack. The case against KC had been dismissed and, in all probability, no one would be held accountable for the death of Allen DeVore. In a few years, the whole episode would fade from the memories of the citizens of Anson as nothing more than an interesting aberration in their otherwise normal small-town lives.

Harriett came out of her mother's house and trouped down the front steps. The cold weather had given the area a break. Although there was snow on the ground and the temperature hovered just above freezing, the skies were bright blue and the semi-constant wind had died down to a tolerable light breeze.

Harriett smiled when she walked to the back of the Durango and saw one of Jess's legs sticking straight out while her body leaned into the cargo area of the SUV arranging a suitcase into a snug position. Harriett ran a hand up the denim-covered leg, then slid both hands over Jess's butt and squeezed.

"Hey!" Jess hollered as she wiggled her butt to dislodge Harriett's hands.

"Sorry, darlin'," Harriett laughed. "You can't really blame me though," she said, leaning between Jess's legs. "It's such a cute butt, and I'm only human."

Harriett patted Jess's butt one more time and stood up before grabbing Jess's hand and pulling her out of the vehicle. "When do you think we'll get home?" she asked.

"After dark if we leave this afternoon. By lunch if we leave after breakfast tomorrow morning," Jess said. "Depends on whether you can keep up with me or not," she grinned.

"No problem," Harriett winked.

Jamie's truck horn honked as she pulled the vehicle to the curb in front of her grandmother's house. She and Ali slid out and quickly joined Jess and Harriett.

"Need help?" Jamie asked.

"You know what? You two showed up just in time," Jess said, delivering a fake punch to Jamie's shoulder. "Now that we're finished. Good timing."

"Sorry," Ali said. "Jamie had to wait for me to fold and put away a load of clothes for my mom. She was called in for an extra shift today."

"It's okay, babe," Jamie said, waggling her eyebrows. "Now I know where you keep your undies."

Ali blushed and stuck her hands into her jean pockets. "Can I talk to you for a minute, Coach?" she asked looking shyly at Jamie and Harriett. "Uh...like alone?"

Harriett wrapped an arm around Jamie's shoulders and suggested a snack while Jess and Ali moved to the front of the Durango.

"When are y'all leavin'?" Ali asked, scratching her nose.

"In the morning probably. We're kinda anxious to get back home," Jess answered.

"I bet," Ali said. "I...we'll miss you, Coach. Just wanted you to know."

"I'm sorry about KC. I know you all depended on her. If it helps, as long as you keep playing the way you have been, someone should offer you a free ride at the end of the season. Whoever it is will be lucky to have you, Ali," Jess said.

"Thanks," Ali said, playing with her sneaker toe in the snow. "Was it hard when you left home, Coach?" she asked.

"Hardest thing I've ever done," Jess admitted after a minute.

"Because of...my mom?"

"Yeah," Jess answered hoarsely. "How long...have you...uh...known?"

Ali shrugged. "A while. Mom started actin' kinda weird after Parent's Night and then I noticed y'all had the same mannerisms sometimes. Just made sense after I learned you were from Stamford and your last name was Mom's name before she married Roy. Didn't take a genius to figure out we were probably related. How come you didn't want to tell me?"

"Your mom and I decided to wait until we thought the time was right. I didn't want it to affect how you played," Jess explained.

"Well, since you're leavin' tomorrow, doncha think now might be the right time?"

"Yeah," Jess said. She straightened up and said, "I'm your aunt, Ali. I hurt your mama when she was about your age and didn't want to repeat that mistake, but I didn't know how to tell you. The minute I saw you though, all I could think about was how much you looked like your Uncle Clayton and I didn't want to face those memories. Too damn painful. I'm sorry, kid."

Jess was shocked when Ali threw her arms around her newly discovered aunt and hugged her. "I hope I never disappoint you, A-aunt Jess," Ali muttered.

"You won't," Jess choked out, returning the hug tightly. "Tell your mom I'll stop by before we leave, okay." When they parted, she took a card from her wallet and handed it to Ali. "Call me anytime and I'll be in touch, too."

"Promise?" Ali asked.

"Promise," Jess said, lightly caressing her niece's cheek.

# Epilogue

## Mid-April

JESS STOOD NERVOUSLY in the shade of the spreading canopy of a huge ancient oak, surrounded by a sea of intermingled bluebonnets and Indian Paintbrush, taking deep breaths of the cool April air to calm her nerves. She hadn't expected to be so nervous. This was their moment, theirs alone, following a tumultuous winter that had been filled with alternating moments of joy and sorrow. The final week had been hectic, but somehow, they all managed to survive. Their honeymoon would be consumed moving into their new home.

Jess fidgeted with the sleeves on the long, light gray morning coat Harriett had chosen for her. Charcoal dress pants fell over her polished black Ropers. She managed a smile as she looked over her shoulder at Ali, dressed in a charcoal morning coat and black dress pants. She was so young with her whole life still ahead of her. Jess could only hope she would make good decisions. Ali had accepted a basketball scholarship from the University of Texas at Austin and Jess was glad she would have the chance to get to know her niece better.

Roy and JD chatted in between escorting guests to their seats. Ellen sat with Tracy and Clayton on the right side of the aisle and Lorri with Erin on the left. Music from a string quartet softly played "Ode to Spring" in the background as guests were being seated. Then, before Jess expected it, Judge Howard Landers of the Austin Criminal Court, an old friend of Harriett's, stepped up and the moment was there.

Jess glanced back and watched Jamie come slowly down the aisle toward her, smiling, her bouquet held at her waist, followed by Lacey. They each paused to kiss Jess lightly on the cheek before taking their places. Then, Judge Landers motioned for everyone to rise and the music changed as the string quartet, now accompanied by a guitar, began an arrangement of "You've Got a Way," the first song she and Harriett had danced to the night they met.

Jess thought she might faint when she saw Irene and Harriett step up to the flower-covered white wrought-iron arch at the entrance to the aisle. Harriett had refused to let Jess see her wedding dress and now Jess's mouth went dry at the sight moving slowly toward her. Harriett had chosen a simple floor-length white gown. The sleeves and high-necked top were embroidered with delicate, light blue flowers woven into the mesh fabric. The remainder of the A-line gown was unadorned and hugged Harriett's body to the waist before flowing softly to the ground, a split in the fabric revealing a hint of thigh. Her large bouquet matched the bluebonnets and Indian Paintbrush that thickly filled the fields encircling the venue.

Jess barely remembered anything after taking Harriett's hand and looking into her calm blue eyes until their lips met tenderly at the end of the ceremony. She had no idea what she'd said. She remembered accepting the congratulations of their family and friends. She remembered posing for a thousand pictures and the feel of Harriett's hand running over her back. She remembered Harriett taking her hand, leading her toward the limousine that would take them to the reception and dance at the Austin Country Club.

Alone at last, Jess turned toward Harriett and forced words from her mouth. "My God, you're so beautiful. I love you."

"And I love you, my darling," Harriett said softly as her hand rested on Jess's thigh. She leaned closer until her lips were inches away. "Now shut up and kiss me," Harriett said with a grin.

# About the Author

Originally from the Appalachian region of Eastern Tennessee, Brenda and her wife, Cheryl, recently moved to Central Michigan to be closer to family. She began writing in junior high school where she wrote an admittedly hokey western serial to entertain her friends, Completing her graduate studies in Eastern European history in 1971, she worked as a graphic artist, a public relations specialist for the military and a display advertising specialist until she finally had to admit her mother might have been right and earned her teaching certification. She retired from teaching world history and political science in 2013 after thirty years. Brenda and Cheryl celebrated their twentieth anniversary by getting legally married in June of 2017. They are the parents of four grown children, Kenneth, Amy, Laura, and Jamie, and the grandparents of eight grandchildren. Rounding out their home is a ten-year-old laid-back cat named Tudie and a seven-year-old Puggle named Peanut, who snores like a freight train. Brenda may be contacted at adcockb10@yahoo.com and welcomes all comments.

# More Brenda Adcock titles:

## *Redress of Grievances*

Harriett Markham is a defense attorney in Austin, Texas, who lost everything eleven years earlier. She had been an associate with a Dallas firm and involved in an affair with a senior partner, Alexis Dunne. Harriett represented a rape/murder client named Jared Wilkes and got the charges dismissed on a technicality. When Wilkes committed a rape and murder after his release, Harriett was devastated. She resigned and moved to Austin, leaving everything behind, including her lover.

Despite lingering feelings for Alexis, Harriett becomes involved with a sex-offense investigator, Jessie Raines, a woman struggling with secrets of her own. Harriett thinks she might finally be happy, but then Alexis re-enters her life. She refers a case of multiple homicide allegedly committed by Sharon Taggart, a woman with no motive for the crimes. Harriett is creeped out by the brutal murders, but reluctantly agrees to handle the defense.

As Harriett's team prepares for trial, disturbing information comes to light. Sharon denies any involvement in the crimes, but the evidence against her seems overwhelming. Harriett is plunged into a case rife with twisty psychological motives, questionable sanity, and a client with a complex and disturbing life. Is she guilty or not? And will Harriett's legal defense bring about justice — or another Wilkes case?

**Recipient of a 2008 award from the Golden Crown Literary Society, the premiere organization for the support and nourishment of quality lesbian literature. *Redress of Grievances* won in the category of Lesbian Mystery.**

ISBN 978-1-932300-86-4

Available in print and eBook formats

# Gift of the Redeemer

Jourdaine Troyce is the commandant of the Guardians, her entire life spent training to kill, literally, anyone that poses the slightest threat to her emperor or the royal family. Killing is as natural as breathing.

Ambreen Prins is a pacifist by nature, killing only as a last resort as she and her young companions fight against the tyranny of the emperor.

Rowan Shayne is the captain of an Intergalactic ship crewed by all the misfits the Fleet can't put anywhere else. They aren't expected to do great things. They're not even expected to function well enough to do their jobs.

Alec Travers is one of the best fighter pilots the Fleet has ever seen, especially when flanked by her two closest friends, creating what they call The Furies. But being posted to Captain Shayne's ship of misfits, out where there are no enemies to fight, is stifling. All she and the other Furies want is to get out there and take down the enemy. Whoever that enemy might be.

Heartbreak, treachery, evil, and the need for justice bring these four together on an adventure to discover the gift of the Redeemer, and the heroines they are destined to become.

ISBN: 978-1-61929-360-1
eISBN: 978-1-61929-361-1

## The Heart of the Mountain

Lucinda "Lu" Calder is an experienced miner, sent to investigate possible irregularities at Brushy #3, a coal mine owned by her step-father, in eastern Kentucky. Acting as a transfer from another mine in the West, she is hired as a general miner and mechanic. As the first, and only, female miner at Brushy #3, she puts up with some distrust and hazing from her male counterparts to test her mettle.

One of the first people she meets is an attractive woman in personnel named Regina Kinlaw. Regina is the single mother of a nine-year-old daughter, who is relentlessly curious. When Regina's van breaks down, Lu stops to assist and is drawn to the young woman. Even though Regina seems stand-offish and secretive, something about her intrigues Lu. But she has a job to do and can't allow herself to be distracted by wishful thinking.

The area surrounding Brushy #3 is a close knit, rural community and Lu finds herself thrown into situations that bring her into more frequent contact with Regina than she planned. They also bring her into contact with a man who believes Regina is his future wife and resents the time Regina spends with Lu. It's a situation that jeopardizes Lu's mission, and eventually her life.

ISBN: 978-1-61929-330-4
eISBN: 978-1-61929-331-1

## Untouchable

Dr. Emma Rothenberg is the most feared professor at Overland University because of her failure rate. Laramie "Ramie" Sunderlund is a senior art major, desperate to earn three lousy English credits to graduate.

Thrown together in a battle of wills, the two women grudgingly establish a measure of respect for one another during one long semester. Emma is a lonely woman of forty-five who occasionally risks her career with dangerous liaisons.

Ramie faces unwanted advances from Rothenberg's graduate assistant, resulting in an assault that threatens her future as a sculptress. Relieved when the semester ends and Ramie leaves to recuperate at home, Emma is suddenly faced with the fact that she misses the woman with curly blonde hair and deep blue eyes who occupied an aisle seat on the third row. She was also a young woman half her age, virtually a child. The notion of anything between them is ridiculous.

When Ramie returns to the university a decade later as the artist-in-residence, Emma is shocked that the younger woman seems interested in actively pursuing her. Against the objections of parents, friends, and colleagues, and despite their own reservations, what are these two very different women willing to sacrifice to find the happiness both are seeking?

ISBN: 978-1-61929-210-9
eISBN: 978-1-61929-209-3

## In the Midnight Hour

What happens when you wake up to find the woman of your dreams in your bed? All-night radio hostess Desdemona, Queen of the Night draws her listening audience with her sultry, seductive voice, the only thing of value she possesses. During the day she becomes an insecure, unattractive woman named Marsha Barrett, living in a world with too many mirrors. She is comfortable with her obscurity until she meets Colleen Walters, a tall, attractive woman hired to expand her listening audience by selling Desdemona to new markets. When she wakes up in bed with Colleen after a night at a club, Marsha is terrified. A woman like Colleen would never go to bed with a woman like Marsha. She might dream about such a thing, but in the harsh reality of daylight, it would never happen. Beauty is only drawn to beauty and Marsha refuses to believe beauty could ever be drawn to anyone who looks like her. Just as she begins to believe happiness may be possible, the past returns determined to destroy them.

ISBN: 978-1-61929-188-1
eISBN: 978-1-61929-187-4

## The Chameleon

Six years ago Detective Christine Shaw left her happy life and a good job in Texas to follow her libido to New York City. She's still a cop, but her stewardess girlfriend has flown the coop and Chris hasn't been able to fill the void. Everything in her life begins to change when she and her partner are assigned to a high profile case.

The murder of Broadway star Elaine Barrie propels Chris into a whole new world. A fan of the murdered actress since she was a teenager, Chris isn't prepared for the secrets she uncovers during their investigation, including her attraction to the daughter of her number one suspect.

Was the victim any of the personalities witnesses describe, or was the real person a chameleon, satisfying the expectations of each person she met?

ISBN 978-1-61929-102-7
eISBN: 978-1-61929-103-4

# The Game of Denial

Joan Carmichael, a successful New York businesswoman, lost the love of her life ten years earlier. Alone, she raised their four children, always cherishing her deep love for her wife. Her memories of their life together come back even stronger as one of their daughters prepares to marry. Joan and her four adult kids fly to Virginia to meet the groom's family and attend the ceremony at the small horse farm owned by the mother of the fiancé.

Evelyn "Evey" Chase, also a widow, has secrets in her past, and her memories of her dead husband aren't pleasant. She's concerned about meeting her future daughter-in-law's family, certain that she and her three kids will have little in common with the wealthy New Yorkers. Besides, the thought of two women in a relationship bringing up a family together makes her uncomfortable, even though her daughter-in-law assures her that lesbianism is not hereditary or catching.

When the two women meet they are drawn to one another in a way neither anticipated, and the game of denial begins. Evey fights her attraction and doesn't realize the effect she has on Joan. Joan tries to shake off her feelings, seeing them as a betrayal to the memory of her wife. Besides, isn't Evey Chase straight? After Evey and Joan share an intimate moment at the wedding reception, they are both emotionally terrified and Joan flees. Will Joan overcome the feeling of betraying her former mate and stop denying her desire to be happy again? Can Evey finally face her past in order to accept the love of another woman and the desire to live the life she had once dreamed of?

ISBN: 978-1-61929-130-0
eISBN: 978-1-61929-131-7

## The Sea Hawk

Dr. Julia Blanchard, a marine archaeologist, and her team of divers have spent almost eighteen months excavating the remains of a ship found a few miles off the coast of Georgia. Although they learn quite a bit about the nineteenth century sailing vessel, they have found nothing that would reveal the identity of the ship they have nicknamed "The Georgia Peach."

Her rescue at sea leads her on an unexpected journey into the true identity of the Peach and the captain and crew who called it their home. Her travels take her to the island of Martinique, the eastern Caribbean islands, the Louisiana German Coast and New Orleans at the close of the War of 1812.

How had the Peach come to rest in the waters off the Georgia coast? What had become of her alluring and enigmatic captain, Simone Moreau? Can love conquer everything, even time?

ISBN 978-1-935053-10-1

Available in print and eBook formats

## Pipeline

What do you do when the mistakes you made in the past come back to slap you in the face with a vengeance? Joanna Carlisle, a fifty-seven year old photojournalist, has only begun to adjust to retirement on her small ranch outside Kerrville, Texas, when she finds herself unwillingly sucked into an investigation of illegal aliens being smuggled into the United States to fill the ranks of cheap labor needed to increase corporate profits.

An unexpected visit by her former lover, Cate Hammond, and the attempted murder of their son, forces Jo to finally face what she had given up. Although she hasn't seen Cate or their son for fifteen years, she finds that the feelings she had for Cate had only been dormant, but had never died. No matter how much she fights her attraction to Cate, Jo cannot help but wonder whether she had made the right decision when she chose career and independence over love.

ISBN 978-1-932300-64-2

Available in print and eBook formats

# Reiko's Garden

Hatred...like love...knows no boundaries.

How much impact can one person have on a life?

When sixty-five-year old Callie Owen returns to her rural childhood home in Eastern Tennessee to attend the funeral of a woman she hasn't seen in twenty years, she's forced to face the fears, heartache, and turbulent events that scarred both her body and her mind. Drawing strength from Jean, her partner of thirty years, and from their two grown children, Callie stays in the valley longer than she had anticipated and relives the years that changed her life forever.

In 1949, Japanese war bride Reiko Sanders came to Frost Valley, Tennessee with her soldier husband and infant son. Callie Owen was an inquisitive ten-year-old whose curiosity about the stranger drove her to disobey her father for just one peek at the woman who had become the subject of so much speculation. Despite Callie's fears, she soon finds that the exotic-looking woman is kind and caring, and the two forge a tentative, but secret friendship.

When Callie and her five brothers and sisters were left orphaned, Reiko provided emotional support to Callie. The bond between them continued to grow stronger until Callie left Frost Valley as a teenager, emotionally and physically scarred, vowing never to return and never to forgive.

It's not until Callie goes "home" that she allows herself to remember how Reiko influenced her life. Once and for all, can she face the terrible events of her past? Or will they come back to destroy all that she loves?

ISBN 978-1-932300-77-2

Available in print and eBook formats

## Tunnel Vision

Royce Brodie, a 50-year-old homicide detective in the quiet town of Cedar Springs, a bedroom community 30 miles from Austin, Texas, has spent the last seven years coming to grips with the incident that took the life of her partner and narrowly missed taking her own. The peace and quiet she had been enjoying is shattered by two seemingly unrelated murders in the same week: the first, a John Doe, and the second, a janitor at the local university.

As Brodie and her partner, Curtis Nicholls, begin their investigation, the assignment of a new trainee disrupts Brodie's life. Not only is Maggie Weston Brodie's former lover, but her father had been Brodie's commander at the Austin Police Department and nearly destroyed her career.

As the three detectives try to piece together the scattered evidence to solve the two murders, they become convinced the two murders are related. The discovery of a similar murder committed five years earlier at a small university in upstate New York creates a sense of urgency as they realize they are chasing a serial killer.

The already difficult case becomes even more so when a third victim is found. But the case becomes personal for Brodie when Maggie becomes the killer's next target. Unless Brodie finds a way to save Maggie, she could face losing everything a second time.

ISBN 978-1-935053-19-4

Available in print and eBook formats

## Soiled Dove

In 1872, sixteen-year-old Loretta Digby fled her home in Indiana to escape an abusive step-father. Rescued from the streets of St. Joseph, Missouri by brothel owner Jack Coulter, she turns to the only work available. By twenty she became a much sought after prostitute catering to St. Jo's most influential men and dreaming of the day she can leave her past behind and start her life anew. Working with teacher, Hettie Tobias, who is traveling west for a teaching position in Trinidad, Colorado, Loretta and Amelia leave their former lives behind.

In the foothills of the Sangre de Cristo Mountains outside Trinidad, Clare McIlhenney has been struggling for years to make her father's dream of owning a cattle ranch in the west come true. Working with a few ranch hands and her foreman, Ino Valdez, Clare has slowly built the ranch over the last twenty years while overcoming everything that should have stopped her.

In the spring of 1876 Loretta and her friends arrive in the dusty Colorado town. Her first meeting with Clare McIlhenney is less than inspiring. When Clare is injured, over her strenuous objections, Ino hires Loretta as a temporary cook and housekeeper for the ranch. Over the next few months, Clare struggles with her unwanted attraction to the much younger woman, unable to forget the events of her past that led to the deaths of everyone she had been close to. Determined to never lose anyone else, Clare closed off her emotions and became a distant and disliked stranger to everyone around her.

Will Loretta be able to keep her past a secret and find a new life? Will Clare open herself up to loss yet again and put her own prejudices behind her? In a story of the struggles in a harsh and unforgiving time will the two women find peace at last?

**Recipient of a 2011 award from the Golden Crown Literary Society, the premiere organization for the support and nourishment of quality lesbian literature. *Soiled Dove* won in the category of Historical Romance.**

ISBN 978-1-935053-35-4

Available in print and eBook formats

# The Other Mrs. Champion

Sarah Champion, 55, of Massachusetts, was leading the perfect life with Kelley, her partner and wife of twenty-five years. That is, until Kelley was struck down by an unexpected stroke away from home. But Sarah discovers she hadn't known her partner and lover as well as she thought.

Accompanied by Kelley's long-time friend and attorney, Sarah and her children rush to Vancouver, British Columbia to say their goodbyes, only to discover another woman, Pauline, keeping a vigil over Kelley in the hospital. Confronted by the fact that her wife also has a Canadian wife, Sarah struggles to find answers to resolve her emotional and personal turmoil.

Alone and lonely, Sarah turns to the only other person who knew Kelley as well as she did — Pauline Champion. Will the two women be able to forge a friendship despite their simmering animosity? Will their growing attraction eventually become Kelley's final gift to the women she loved?

ISBN 978-1-935053-46-0
eISBN: 978-1-61929-032-7

# Picking Up the Pieces

Athon Dailey hasn't had many breaks in her life other than the ones she made for herself by living up to her reputation as a tough girl until she meets Lauren Shelton, a new girl at school in Duvalle, Texas. Tamed by Lauren's affection, Athon begins to believe there could be a brighter future. When Lauren's parents discover the growing relationship they send her away, making sure the two girls never have contact, leaving Athon alone and abandoned.

Twenty years later the two women meet again. Athon has established a successful military career as a helicopter pilot while Lauren has returned to Duvalle to teach. It doesn't take long for them to rekindle their feelings for one another and they finally get the chance to rebuild their teenage dreams. Permanent happiness is within their grasp when Athon's unit is deployed.

Athon comes home in a coma, diagnosed with a traumatic brain injury. She awakens to find Lauren by her side to welcome her home. When Athon chooses to retire and return to Texas, neither realizes the twists and turns the journey home will take. The Athon Dailey who returned to Lauren is not the woman she remembers. In order for their relationship to survive, Lauren begins her search for the woman she loves. Will Athon finally find her way back to Lauren and the dream they both once had? Does Lauren have the courage to live with a woman who is now a stranger?

ISBN 978-1-61929-120-1
eISBN: 978-1-61929-121-8

# OTHER REGAL CREST PUBLICATIONS

Be sure to check out our other imprints,
Mystic Books, Silver Dragon Books, Troubadour Books,
Yellow Rose Books, Young Adult Books, and Blue Beacon Books.

## VISIT US ONLINE AT
www.regalcrest.biz

At the Regal Crest Website You'll Find

- The latest news about forthcoming titles and new releases

- Our complete backlist of romance, mystery, thriller and adventure titles

- Information about your favorite authors

www.ingramcontent.com/pod-product-compliance
Lightning Source LLC
Chambersburg PA
CBHW071833020726
47502CB00004B/1342